Mother Gothel, they call me.

I have become known by the name of this tower. A vine-covered spire stretching into the trees, cobbled together from stone. I have become known for the child I stole, little girl, my pretty. Rapunzel— I named her for her mother's favorite herb. My garden is legendary: row after row of hellebore and hemlock, yarrow and bloodwort. I have read many a speculum on the natural properties of plants and stones, and I know them all by heart. I know what to do with belladonna, with lungwort and cinquefoil.

I learned the healing arts from a wise woman, the spinning of tales from my mother. I learned nothing from my father, a no-name fisherman. My mother was a midwife. I learned that from her too. Women come to me from all over to hear my stories, to make use of my knowledge of plants. Traipsing in their boots and lonely skirts through the wood, they come, one by one, with their secret sorrows, over the river, across the hills, to the wise woman they hope can heal their ails. After I give them what they seek and take my fee, I spin my stories, sifting through my memories, polishing the facts of my life until they shine like stones. Sometimes they bring my stories back to me, changed by retelling. In this book, under lock and key, I will set down the truth.

Praise for
THE BOOK OF GOTHEL

"Smart, swift, sure-footed, and fleet winged, *The Book of Gothel* launches its magic from a most reliable source: the troubled heart. Mary McMyne is a magician. Her take on the Rapunzel tale glows like a cloisonné gem set against a fist of dark soapstone."

—Gregory Maguire, *New York Times*
bestselling author of *Wicked*

"Both gently and fiercely told, *The Book of Gothel* is a sweeping, sharp story of how history twists into fairy tale and back again."

—Hannah Whitten, *New York Times*
bestselling author of *For the Wolf*

"*The Book of Gothel* is wonderfully rich with historical detail, and sparkles with the intermingled magic of gods and goddesses, seers and wisewomen. Haelewise is a memorable heroine, worthy of legend. Readers will see the story of Rapunzel in a new and refreshing light."

—Louisa Morgan, author of
A Secret History of Witches

"McMyne's shimmering debut gives a fresh, exciting backstory to one of the most famous villains in fairy tale lore: the witch who put Rapunzel in her tower.... The result is a sprawling epic, full of magic, love, and heartbreak. Fans of *Circe* and *The Wolf and the Woodsman* will devour this taut, empowering fairy tale."

—*Publishers Weekly* (starred review)

The BOOK *of* GOTHEL

Memoir of a Witch

MARY MCMYNE

REDHOOK

Copyright © 2022 by Mary McMyne
Reading group guide copyright © 2023 by Hachette Book Group, Inc.
Excerpt copyright © 2023 by Mary McMyne

Cover design by Lisa Marie Pompilio
Cover illustrations by Arcangel and Shutterstock
Cover copyright © 2023 by Hachette Book Group, Inc.
Author photograph by David S. Bennett

Redhook Books/Orbit
Hachette Book Group
1290 Avenue of the Americas
New York, NY 10104
hachettebookgroup.com

First Paperback Edition: September 2023
Originally published in hardcover and ebook in Great Britain by Orbit
and in the U.S. by Redhook in July 2022

Redhook is an imprint of Orbit, a division of Hachette Book Group.
The Redhook name and logo are trademarks of Hachette Book Group, Inc.

The Library of Congress has cataloged the hardcover edition as follows:
Names: McMyne, Mary, author.
Title: The book of Gothel / Mary McMyne.
Description: First edition. | New York, NY : Redhook, 2022.
Identifiers: LCCN 2021054656 | ISBN 9780316393119 (hardcover) |
ISBN 9780316393317 (ebook) | ISBN 9780316425506 (ebook other)
Subjects: LCGFT: Novels.
Classification: LCC PS3613.C58557 B66 2022 | DDC 813/.6—dc23
LC record available at https://lccn.loc.gov/2021054656

ISBNs: 9780316393218 (trade paperback), 9780316393317 (ebook)

Printed in the United States of America

LSC-C

Printing 1, 2023

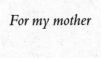
For my mother

PROLOGUE

The cellar was, at least, a cool respite from the murderous heat wave afflicting the Black Forest, though it smelled like a crypt and I nearly broke my trick knee on my way down the crumbling steps. There was no railing, and my knee ached the way it always did when rain was due. Ingrid Vogel took the stairs recklessly, though her long white plait and rheumy eyes betrayed that she was at least four decades older than I am. Apparently, she was one of those lucky octogenarians for whom arthritis was something that happened only to other people.

When she flicked on the light, I followed her through the archway into an ancient stone cellar, startled by how old it seemed. The cellar was faded rock, almost cavernous, built with simple buttresses and curved archways, obviously a remnant of a much older structure than the thatched-roof cottage above. What did this place use to be, I wondered absently, surveying the stacks of parcels and canned goods in the corner. Before I accepted my position at the University of North Carolina, I spent fifteen years in Germany—earning my PhD, doing a postdoc, lecturing—but the nonchalant way Europeans used ancient spaces as basements still felt like sacrilege.

"*Frau Professorin Eisenberg*," she said, addressing me formally despite my repeated requests to call me Gert. She stood beside an uneven stone that had been removed from the cellar floor, holding an ancient lockbox. I knew from our emails that the codex must be inside. "*Hier ist er.*"

Three days earlier, Frau Vogel had emailed to tell me about a medieval codex she found in her late mother's cellar. She said she'd attended a talk I gave in Germany, but I had no memory of meeting her. Her email described what she knew of the manuscript—it was illuminated, written in Middle High German by a woman—and asked if I would be interested in the find. Attached were radiocarbon dating results verifying the manuscript's age, and an image of a single sample page. The handwritten text was a sinister rhyme about Snow White in an obscure Alemannic dialect; beneath it was a painstakingly decorated illustration of a wicked fairy dancing on a rose. She had blood-red lips, deathly pale skin, and a tangle of black hair.

When Frau Vogel's email pinged my inbox, I had been sitting in my office, prepping syllabi for the fall semester, trying to ignore two tenured male colleagues who were prattling on about their latest books in the hall. I couldn't focus. There was a ball of dread in my throat so large, it felt like it was blocking the flow of oxygen. I was scheduled to apply for tenure the following year, and the application process at UNC was brutal. I needed a book under contract, and my study of the treatment of women in medieval German illuminated manuscripts was going nowhere. It was under review at a solid press, but one of my peer reviewers had dismissed its subject matter as "domestic minutiae." The criticism made me livid. Centuries of sexist scribes had left huge gaps in what we know about the lives of medieval women, and I was *trying* to do something about it.

The image of the fairy made me gasp, loudly enough that one of my colleagues peeked into my office with a question on his face. I forced a smile, mouthed the words *I'm fine*, and waited for him to go back to his conversation before I returned my focus to the screen. The colors of the illustration were jewel-toned, bright; the fairy's expression could only be described as malicious. My heart fluttered with a delicious thrill of excitement. Was I looking at some kind of gothic ancestor to the Snow White folktale as we knew it? The prospect of studying something new—and so *different*—made me giddy.

I wrote Frau Vogel back immediately, expressing interest. Her reply was a bizarre request for me to describe my personal religious beliefs. Her prying ruffled me, but I got the distinct impression that she was testing me, so I answered carefully. My religion was complicated. I was raised Catholic, but I hadn't been to church in ages—a fact that, hopefully, Frau Vogel would understand, given my sixty-four hours of graduate credit on the period that brought the Crusades. Whatever her test was, I must have passed, because her next email contained more digital photographs of the manuscript and a request for my assistance reading it. The additional photos were enough to put me on the plane the next day.

Now, crossing the cellar toward Frau Vogel and her lockbox, I felt an eerie shiver of anticipation. My breath caught in my chest, and I thought I sensed a shift in the room's energy, as if I could *feel* the drop in air pressure from the coming storm. The sensation alarmed me, until I recognized the rest of the premonitory symptoms of my too-frequent migraines. The lightbulb hanging from the stone ceiling seemed too bright. My vision was blurry. The dizziness I'd blamed on the twisty drive up the mountain had returned. Of course I would get a migraine *now*, I thought, cursing my luck.

Resolving to take a sumatriptan soon, I peered into the lockbox. Inside was a burnished codex, timeworn. The cover's leather shimmered faintly around the edges, as if it had been painted centuries ago with gold dust. When I saw how ornate it was, a faint gasp escaped my lips: There was an embossed frame decorated with a diamond pattern, and the interior of each shape was decorated with intricate swirls. In the center of it all was a huge design that looked like a sigil. A circle writhing with snakes, large-winged birds, and beasts, at once grotesque and beautiful.

The charged feeling in the air intensified, making me dizzier. I blinked, trying to recover some semblance of professional detachment. The migraine, I thought, it's knocked me off balance.

"*Entschuldigen Sie*," I said, fumbling in my purse for the bottle of sumatriptan.

Swallowing a pill, I glanced at Frau Vogel, silently asking permission to pick up the codex. She nodded. I picked it up by the edges, trying to get as little oil from my skin on the cover as possible. It was heavy for its size. I could smell the faint musty scent of the leather, feel its age beneath my fingers. I glanced up at my host again, irrationally uncertain about opening the codex, as though she hadn't asked me here precisely for the purpose of reading it.

An amused smile spread across Frau Vogel's face, wrinkling the skin around her lips. "*Es ist alles gut.* It will not bite."

I opened the book, embarrassed. On the first page was a declaration of truth signed by someone named Haelewise, daughter-of-Hedda. My fingers twitched with the urge to trace her signature, though I knew better than to touch the ink. The use of a parent's name as a surname would be unusual for a noblewoman, and I had never seen a mother mentioned instead of a father. Who was this peasant woman who could write, who chose to be known only by her maternal lineage?

I took care not to disturb the pigment, touching only the edges of the pages as I turned them. The ink was surprisingly well preserved for the age of the manuscript, as if it *hadn't* spent centuries under a stone in a cellar floor. The parchment was thin but still flexible to the touch. What I had surmised from the photographs was true: The manuscript was illuminated as if it were a holy book, though the text itself seemed to be a narrative, interrupted occasionally with recipes and verse and what, during the time in which the book was written, could only have been considered heretical prayers.

As I paused to read one, the static electric aura became so pronounced that the hairs on my arms stood on end. Intense vertigo overtook me, strong enough that I wondered if it was a migraine symptom at all. I smothered the thought, telling myself to focus. I had taken the sumatriptan. The aura would pass soon.

The manuscript was decorated with colorful marginalia, faded red and gold initial letters in the style of Benedictine scribes, though none of the text was Latin. There were masterful illustrations; the images were every bit as detailed as those monks painted on prayer books. But the imagery was so out of character for what one would expect to find in an illuminated manuscript from this period. Some of the illustrations were mundane, a mother and daughter in a garden, everyday scenes of births and cooking. Others were the stuff of folktales. On one page, a black-haired woman in a bright blue hood extended her hand, as if to offer the reader the gold-dusted apple in her palm. On another, a ghostly woman in blue knelt in a tangled garden, arms outstretched, psychedelic rays of gilded light radiating from her in every direction. I couldn't help but linger over an image of a beautiful raven-haired young woman lying dead on what appeared to be a stone coffin—her eyes open, her body encased in pale-blue swirls of ice.

"You can read it?" Frau Vogel asked softly. Her voice sounded far away. I had forgotten she was there.

I looked up. Her eyes were fixed on me. "*Ja. Das ist Alemannisch.* I need time."

"How long?"

"All day," I said. "At least."

She met my gaze for a moment, then nodded at the rocking chairs in the corner. "I'll be upstairs," she said, smiling encouragingly. "I want to know everything."

DECLARATION

This is a true account of my life.

Mother Gothel, they call me. I have become known by the name of this tower. A vine-covered spire stretching into the trees, cobbled together from stone. I have become known for the child I stole, little girl, my pretty. Rapunzel—I named her for her mother's favorite herb. My garden is legendary: row after row of hellebore and hemlock, yarrow and bloodwort. I have read many a speculum on the natural properties of plants and stones, and I know them all by heart. I know what to do with belladonna, with lungwort and cinquefoil.

I learned the healing arts from a wise woman, the spinning of tales from my mother. I learned nothing from my father, a no-name fisherman. My mother was a midwife. I learned that from her too. Women come to me from all over to hear my stories, to make use of my knowledge of plants. Traipsing in their boots and lonely skirts through the wood, they come, one by one, with their secret sorrows, over the river, across the hills, to the wise woman they hope can heal their ails. After I give them what they seek and take my fee, I spin my stories, sifting through my memories, polishing the facts of my life until they shine like stones. Sometimes they bring my stories back to me, changed by retelling. In this book, under lock and key, I will set down the truth.

In this, the seventy-eighth year of my earthly course, I write my story. A faithful account of my life—heretical though it may be—a chronicle of facts that have since been altered, to correct the lies being repeated as truth. This will be my book of deeds, written from the famous tower of Gothel, where a high wall encloses the florae and herbs.

—Haelewise, daughter-of-Hedda
The Year of Our Lord 1219

CHAPTER ONE

What a boon it is to have a mother who loves you. A mother who comes to life when you walk into the room, who tells stories at bedtime, who teaches you the names of plants that grow wild in the wood. But it is possible for a mother to love too much, for love to take over her heart like a weed does a garden, to spread its roots and proliferate until nothing else grows. My mother was watchful in the extreme. She suffered three stillbirths before I was born, and she didn't want to lose me. She tied a keeping string around my wrist when we went to market, and she never let me roam.

There were dangers for me in the market, no doubt. I was born with eyes the color of ravens—no color, no light in my irises— and by the time I was five, I suffered strange fainting spells that made others fear I was possessed. As if that wasn't enough, when I was old enough to attend births with my mother, rumors spread about my unnatural skill with midwifery. Long before I became her apprentice, I could pinpoint the exact moment when a baby was ready to be born.

To keep me close, my mother told me the *kindefresser* haunted the market: a she-demon who lured children from the city to drink their blood. Mother said she was a shapeshifter who took the forms of people children knew to trick them into going away with her.

This was before the bishop built the city wall, when travelers still passed freely, selling charms to ward off fevers, arguing about the ills of the Church. The market square was bustling then. You could find men and women in strange robes with skin of every color, selling ivory bangles and gowns made of silk. Mother allowed me to admire their wares, holding my hand tightly. "Stay close," she said, her eyes searching the stalls. "Don't let the *kindefresser* snatch you away!"

The bishop built the wall when I was ten to protect the city from the mist that blew off the forest. The priests called it an "unholy fog" that carried evil and disease. After the wall was built, only holy men and peddlers were allowed to pass through the city gate: monks on pilgrimage, traders of linen and silk, merchants with ox-carts full of dried fish. Mother and I had to stop gathering herbs and hunting in the forest. Father cut down the elms behind our house, so we had room to grow a kitchen garden. I helped Mother plant the seeds and weave a wicker coop for chickens. Father purchased stones, and the three of us built a wall around the plot to keep dogs out.

Even though the town was enclosed, Mother still wouldn't let me wander without her, especially around the new moon, when my spells most often plagued me. Whenever I saw children running errands or playing knucklebones behind the minster, an uneasy bitterness filled me. Everyone thought I was younger than I was, because of my small stature and the way my mother coddled me. I suspected the *kindefresser* was one of her many stories, invented to scare me into staying close. I loved my mother deeply, but I longed to wander. She treated me as if I was one of her poppets, a fragile thing of beads and linen to be sat on a shelf.

Not long after the wall was built, the tailor's son Matthäus knocked on our door, dark hair shining in the sun, his eyes flashing with merriment. "I brought arrows," he said. "Can you come out to the grove, teach me to shoot?"

Our mothers had become friends due to my mother's constant need for scraps of cloth. She made poppets to sell during the cold season, and the two women had spent many an afternoon sorting scraps and gossiping in the tailor's shop as we played. The week before, Matthäus and I had found an orange kitten. Father would've drowned him in a sack, but Matthäus wanted to give him milk. As we sneaked the kitten upstairs to his room, I had racked my brain for something to offer him so we could play again. Mother had taught me everything she knew about how to use a bow. Shooting was one of the few things I was good at.

"Please please please," I begged my mother.

She looked at me, tight-lipped, and shook her head.

"Mother," I said. "I need a friend."

She blinked, sympathetic. "What if you have a spell?"

"We'll take the back streets. The moon is almost full."

Mother took a deep breath, emotions warring on her face. "All right," she sighed finally. "Let me tie back your hair."

I yelped with joy, though I hated the way she pulled my curls, which in general refused to be tamed and which I had inherited from her. "Thank you!" I said when she was finished, grabbing my quiver and bow and my favorite poppet.

Ten was an odd age for me. I could shoot as well as a grown man but had yet to give up childish things. I still brought the poppet called Gütel that Mother made for me everywhere. A poppet with black hair just like mine, tied back with ribbons. She wore a dress of linen scraps dyed my favorite color, madder-red. Her eyes were two shining black beads.

I was a quizzical child, a show-me child—a wild thing who had to be dragged to Mass—but I saw a sort of magic in Mother's poppet-making. Nothing unnatural, mind you. The sort of thing everyone does, like set out food for the Fates or choose a wedding date for good luck. The time she took choosing the right scraps, the words she murmured as she sewed, made that doll alive to me.

On our way out, Mother reminded me to watch for the *kinde-fresser*. "Amber eyes, no matter what shape she takes, remember." She lowered her voice. "You'll want to warn that boy about your spells."

I nodded, cheeks flushing with shame, though Matthäus was too polite to ask what my mother had said under her breath. We hurried toward the north gate, past the docks and the other fishermen's huts. I pulled my hood over my head so the sun wouldn't bother my eyes. They were sensitive in addition to being black as night. Bright light made my head ache.

The leaves of the linden trees were turning yellow and beginning to fall to the ground. As we stepped into the grove, ravens scattered. The grove was full of beasts the carpenters had trapped when the wall was built. It was common to see a family of hares hopping beneath the lindens. If you were foolish enough to open your hand, a raven would swoop down and steal a *pfennic* from your palm.

Matthäus showed me the straw-stuffed bird atop a pole that everyone used for archery practice. I sat Gütel at the base of a tree trunk, reaching down to straighten her cloak. My heart soared as I reached for my bow. Here I was, finally outside the hut without Mother. I felt normal, almost. I felt free.

"Did you hear about the queen?" Matthäus asked, pulling his bow back to let the arrow fly. It went wild, missing the trunk to stray into the sunny clearing.

"No," I called, squinting and shading my eyes as I watched him go after it. Even with the shadow of my hand, looking directly at the sunlight hurt.

He reappeared with the arrow. "King Frederick banished her."

"How do you know?"

"A courtier told my father while he was getting fitted."

"Why would the king banish his wife?"

Matthäus shrugged as he handed me the arrow. "The man said she asked too many guests into her garden."

I squinted at him. "How is that grounds for banishment?" I didn't understand, then, what the courtier meant.

He shrugged. "You know how harsh they say King Frederick is."

I nodded. Since his coronation that spring, everyone called him "King Red-Beard" because his chin-hair was supposed to be stained with the blood of his enemies. Even as young as ten, I understood that men make up reasons to get rid of women they find disagreeable. "I bet it's because she hasn't given him a son."

He thought about this. "You're probably right."

I strung my bow, deep in thought. After the coronation, the now-banished queen had visited with the princess, and Mother had taken me to see the parade. I remembered the pale, black-haired girl who sat with her mother on a white horse, still a child, though her brave expression made her seem older. Her eyes were a pretty hazel with golden flecks. "Did the queen take Princess Frederika with her?"

Matthäus shook his head. "King Frederick wouldn't let her."

I imagined how awful it would be to have my mother banished from my home. Where my mother was protective, my father was cold and controlling. A house without Mother would be a house without love.

I forced myself to concentrate on my shot.

When the arrow pierced the trunk, Matthäus sucked in his breath. At first I thought he was reacting to my aim. Then I saw he was looking at the tree where Gütel sat. A giant raven with bright black hackles was bent over her.

I charged at the bird. "Shoo! Get away from her!"

The bird ignored me until I was right beside it, when it looked up at me with amber eyes. *Kraek*, it said, shaking its head, as it dropped Gütel on the ground. It kept something in its beak, something glittering and black, which flashed as it took off.

On the left side of Gütel's face, the thread was loose. The wool had come out. The raven had plucked out her eye.

A cry leapt from my throat. I fled from the grove, clutching Gütel to my chest. The market square blurred as I ran past. The tanner called out: "Haelewise, what's wrong?"

I wanted my mother and no one else.

The crooked door of our hut was open. Mother stood in the entryway, sewing, a needle between her lips. She had been waiting for me to come home.

"Look!" I shouted, rushing toward her, holding my poppet up.

Mother set down the poppet she was sewing. "What happened?"

As I raged about what the bird had done, Father walked up, smelling of the day's catch. He listened for a while without speaking, his face stern, then went inside. We followed him to the table. "Its eyes," I sobbed, sliding onto the bench. "They were amber, like the *kindefresser*—"

My parents' eyes met, and something passed between them I didn't understand.

Overcome by a telltale shiver, I braced myself, knowing what would happen next. Twice a month or so—if I was unlucky, more—I had one of my fainting spells. They always started the same way. Chills bloomed all over my skin, and the air went taut. I felt a pull from the next world—

The room swayed. My heart raced. I grasped the tabletop, afraid I would hit my head when I fell. And then I was gone. Not my body, but my soul, my ability to watch the world.

The next thing I knew, I was lying on the floor. Head aching, hands and feet numb. My mouth tasted of blood. Shame filled me, the awful not-knowing that always plagued me after a swoon.

My parents were arguing. "You haven't been to see her," Father was saying.

"No," Mother hissed. "I gave you my word!"

What were they talking about? "See who?" I asked.

"You're awake," Mother said with a tight smile, a panicked edge to her voice. At the time, I thought she was upset about my swoon. My spells always rattled her.

My father stared me down. "One of her clients is a heretic. I told your mother to stop seeing her."

My gut told me he was lying, but contradicting him never went well. "How long was I out?"

"A minute," Father said. "Maybe two."

"My hands are still numb," I said, unable to keep the fear out of my voice. The feeling usually came back to my extremities by this point.

Mother pulled me close, shushing me. I breathed in her smell, the soothing scent of anise and earth.

"Damn it, Hedda," Father said. "We've done this your way long enough."

Mother stiffened. As far back as I could remember, she had been in charge of finding a cure for my spells. Father had wanted to take me to the abbey for years, but Mother outright refused. Her goddess dwelt in things, in the hidden powers of root and leaf, she told me when Father was out. Mother had brought home a hundred remedies for my spells: bubbling elixirs, occult powders wrapped in bitter leaves, thick brews that burned my throat.

The story went that my grandmother, whom I hardly remembered, suffered the same swoons. Supposedly, hers were so bad that she bit off the tip of her tongue as a child, but she found a cure for them late in life. Unfortunately, Mother had no idea what that cure was, because my grandmother died before I suffered my first swoon. Mother had been searching for that cure ever since. As a midwife she knew all the local herbalists. Before the wall was built, we had seen wise women and wortcunners, sorceresses who spoke in ancient tongues, the alchemist who sought to turn lead into gold. The remedies tasted terrible, but they sometimes kept my spells away for a month. We had never tried holy healers before.

I hated the emptiness I felt in my father's church when he dragged me to Mass, while my mother's secret offerings actually made me *feel* something. But that day, as my parents argued, it occurred to me that the learned men in the abbey might be able to provide relief that Mother's healers couldn't.

My parents fought that night for hours, their white-hot words rising loud enough for me to hear. Father kept going on about the demon he thought possessed me, the threat it meant to our livelihood, the stoning I would face if I got blamed for the wrong thing. Mother said these spells ran in her family, and how could he say I was possessed? She said he'd promised, after everything she gave up, to leave her in charge of this *one* thing.

The next morning, Mother woke me, defeated. We were going to the abbey. My eagerness to try something new felt like a betrayal. I tried to hide it for her sake.

It was barely light out as we walked to the dock behind our hut. As we pushed our boat into the lake, the guard in the bay tower recognized my father and waved us through the pike wall. Our boat rocked on the water, and Father sang a sailing hymn:

> *"Lord God, ruler of all, keep safe*
> *this wreck of wood on the waves."*

He rowed us across the lake, giving a wide berth to the northern shoreline, where the mist the priests called "unholy" cloaked the trees. "God's teeth," Mother said. "How many times do I have to tell you? The mist won't hurt us. I grew up in those woods!"

She never agreed with the priests about anything.

Pulling our boat ashore an hour later, we approached the stone wall that surrounded the abbey. Elderly and thin with a long white beard and mustache, a kind-looking monk unlocked the gate. He stood between us and the monastery, scratching at the neckline of his tunic, as Father explained why we had come. I couldn't help but notice the fleas he kept squelching beneath his fingers as he listened to my father describe my spells. Why didn't he scatter horsemint over the floor, I wondered, or coat his flesh with rue?

Mother must have wondered the same. "Don't you have an herb garden?"

The monk shook his head, explaining that their gardener died last winter, nodding for Father to finish his description of my spells.

"Something unnatural settles over her," he told the monk, his voice rising. "Then she falls into a kind of trance."

The monk watched me closely, his gaze lingering on my eyes. "Do you suspect a demon?"

Father nodded.

"Our abbot could cast it out," the monk offered. "For a fee."

Something fluttered in my heart. How I wanted this to work.

Father offered the monk a handful of *holpfennige*. The monk counted them and let us in, shutting the heavy gate behind us.

Mother frowned as we followed the monk across the grounds. "Don't be afraid," she whispered to me. "There is no demon in you."

Through a huge wooden door, the monk led us into the main chamber of the minster, a long room with an altar on the far end. Along the aisle, candles flickered below murals. Our footsteps echoed. When we reached the baptismal font, the monk told me to take off my clothes.

Father reached for my hand and squeezed it. He met my eyes, his expression kind. My heart almost burst. It'd been so long since he looked at me that way. For years, he'd seemed to blame me for the demon he thought possessed me, as if some weakness, some flaw in my character had invited it in. If this works, I thought, he'll look at me that way all the time. I'll be able to play knucklebones with the other children.

I stripped off my boots and dress. Soon enough I was barefoot in my shift, hopping from foot to foot on the freezing stones. Six feet wide, the basin was huge with graven images of St. Mary and the apostles. I bent over the edge and saw my reflection in the holy water: my pale skin, the vague dark holes of my eyes, the wild black curls that had come loose from my braids as we sailed. The basin was deep enough that the water would rise to my chest, the water perfectly clear.

When the abbot arrived, he laid his hands on me and said something in the language of clergymen. My heart soared with a desperate hope. The abbot wet his hand and smeared the sign of the cross on my forehead. His finger was ice cold. When nothing happened, the abbot repeated the words again, making the sign of the cross in the air. I held my breath, waiting for something to happen, but there was only the chilly air of the minster, the cold stones under my toes.

The holy water glittered, calling me. I couldn't wait any longer. I wriggled out from under the monk's hands and climbed into the basin.

"*Haelewise!*" my father bellowed.

The cold water stung my legs, my belly, my arms. As I plunged underwater, it occurred to me that if there was a demon inside me, it might hurt to cast it out. The silence of the church was replaced by the roar of water on my eardrums. The water was like liquid ice. Holy of holies, I thought, opening my mouth in a soundless scream. How could the spirit of God live in water so cold?

When I burst out, gasping, the abbot was speaking in the language of priests.

"What do you think you're doing?" my father yelled.

Finishing his prayer, the abbot tried to calm him. "The Holy Spirit compelled her—"

I clambered out of the basin, wondering if the abbot was right. Water rolled down my face in an icy sheet. Hair streamed down my back. I stood up, flinging water all over the floor. My teeth chattered. Mother fluttered around me, helping me wring out my hair and shift, trying to dry me with her skirt.

Father watched while I shivered and pulled on my dress. He looked at the abbot, then Mother, his brow furrowed. "How do you feel?"

I made myself still, considering. Wet and cold, I thought, but no different. Either there had been no demon, or I couldn't tell that it had left. The realization stung. I thought of all the remedies we'd tried so far, the foul-tasting potions, the sour meatcakes and bitter herbs. Who knew what they'd try next?

I met their eyes, making my own grow wide. Then I knelt in my puddle on the stones, making the sign of the cross. "Blessed Mother of God," I said. "I am cured."

CHAPTER TWO

After the exorcism, my spells stayed gone for six blessed weeks, the longest respite from them I'd ever had. When they returned, I tried to hide them from Father. I couldn't bear to disappoint him. Eventually he found out, decreeing that we would only seek healing from holy men and women, since the exorcism had lasted longer than anything we had tried before. By the time I was fifteen, we had visited every church and shrine within two days' travel, and I had become deeply skeptical about the permanence of these cures. Some of these pilgrimages were followed immediately by spells, while others stopped them for a month or so. Mother wouldn't let me leave the house without her. I could only see Matthäus when she took me to the tailor shop.

That summer, Father found an anchoress a full three days south of town who was known for performing miracles. After our pilgrimage, I didn't suffer a swoon for many weeks, and my skepticism began to fade. By the beginning of my third month without a spell, I was deliriously hopeful. Even Mother believed. She began to talk about a time when I would marry, have children, and start seeing my own clients. She started sending me on errands to purchase midwifery supplies and letting me go shooting with Matthäus, though she still warned me to beware the *kindefresser*.

That month, Matthäus stopped by nearly every day after he finished work at the tailor shop. Our friendship flourished. As we practiced our shooting, we talked, gossiping and telling each other stories. He told me secrets—how obsessed his father was with the nobles whose clothes he sewed, how he had nightmares about the beasts in the woods—his head lowered in shame. I confided how distant my father had been before my spells stopped, how badly I wanted his approval.

One late summer evening on our way to the grove, I found myself preoccupied by the way Matthäus's hand kept brushing mine. Is he doing it on purpose, I wondered, watching his expression out of the corner of my eye. He whistled cheerfully, oblivious. My desire for him to take my hand was so strong, I couldn't breathe.

Could he tell how I felt? I wondered. I jerked my hand back, mortified, resolving to stop before he caught on. He could tell when something was bothering me.

"Haelewise," he said.

I cursed inwardly, certain he had read my mind. "Aye?"

He nodded in the direction of the public fountain. The tanner's son was hunched before it, wrapped in a tattered animal skin, growling and menacing his sisters. "Albrecht and Ursilda," Matthäus said under his breath. "Remember when we used to play that game?"

I smiled, relieved. "Behind the tailor shop."

"Ursilda is *mine*. Forever!" the older girl yelled, clutching her younger sister.

"Help me, Father!" the little girl screamed. "The witch keeps me locked in a cage!"

Children had been playing that game as long as I could remember. Supposedly, when I was about five, the wise woman who lived in the forest near Prince Albrecht's castle kidnapped the princess. The story went that she locked Ursilda in her tower, which was protected by a mist that made men blind. To get his daughter back, Prince Albrecht put on a magic wolf-skin so the spell wouldn't affect him. As a wolf, he led his men to the tower and rescued his daughter.

When we played, Matthäus always pretended to be Prince

Albrecht, and I always pretended to be the wise woman. The kitten we'd found behind the tailor shop had fulfilled the role of princess. The memory made me smile.

"We were like brother and sister," Matthäus said fondly.

He meant the statement to be kind, no doubt, but it only highlighted the inappropriateness of my feelings. My smile faltered.

"By thunder," he said, still watching the children. "The little girl looks *terrified*."

I followed his gaze. He was right. The little girl seemed to have worked herself into some kind of frenzy of belief. "She probably begged to be Ursilda."

As we passed, the little girl shrieked with glee. Her older brother lifted her to his shoulders. Rescued at last. Matthäus grinned at me, gray eyes laughing, sharing in the girl's joy. God's teeth, I thought. When did he get so handsome?

I sped up my pace so his hand wouldn't be in danger of touching mine. Turning his attention from the children, Matthäus hurried to catch up with me. For once, he didn't seem to notice my stiff posture or the awkwardness of my smile. "I wonder what really happened to Ursilda," he said as he fell into step with me. "Did you ever get your mother to talk about it?"

Mother had seen so many clients over the years, she knew every version of every tale. When I asked her about this one, the subject made her uncomfortable. "She got angry whenever I mentioned it. All she would tell me was the story was a lie."

Matthäus looked thoughtful, falling silent until we reached the grove. "Father's been trying to get Prince Albrecht to wear his clothes for years. He says Albrecht is a good Christian and that story is nonsense, but I wouldn't want to be the one to fit him."

"Neither would I be," I said, with a rush of fear for his safety that was stronger than I'd like to admit.

We had arrived at the grove. I smiled at the familiar straw-stuffed bird atop the pole and shrugged off my quiver, relieved to pursue a pastime that would require my full concentration. During the moment I aimed my bow, my mind went blessedly blank.

The act of shooting would distract me from my feelings.

The harder I tried to ignore my feelings for Matthäus, the worse they got. By the end of that month, the third since I had gone to see the anchoress, he was the first thing I thought about in the morning and the last thing I thought about before I slept. I knew that I could tell him anything, that he treasured our friendship, but there wasn't a single sign that he shared my affection. It felt like my mind was tormenting me. I was a fisherman's daughter. Matthäus was the son of a wealthy merchant. There was no reason for the object of my affection to be so unattainable.

Three months to the day after my father took me to see the anchoress, I woke up thinking of him, cursing every god in the heavens who might be responsible for my infatuation. In a foul mood, I pushed my feet into the slippers Mother had made me from scrap yarn. In the front room, which doubled as her workshop, lace and cloth fluttered from the rafters, alongside the dried parsley, sage, and parsnips she grew in the garden. A string of golden glass beads, which my mother used as eyes for her poppets, refracted light as they hung in the window-slot. I squinted, cursing my sensitive eyes. Bright sunlight dappled the straw floor, that buttery color the priests say should remind us of God's love. Yes yes yes, I thought miserably, shading my eyes. Beauty and beauty and joy. We know.

I closed the shutters. The hut dimmed. What was left of last night's embers glowed in the fire. I stamped them. Poppets stared down at me mindlessly from the crooked shelves on the walls, queer little girls with unstuffed arms and half-finished dresses, blank-faced princesses with yarn for hair, a king and queen in motley robes. On the top shelf were the monstrous poppets Father hated. Wild men and women, Mother called them. This year she'd sewn both Lamia and Pelzmärtel dolls, which sold well in winter. At Christmastime, the demon-goddess was said to eat poorly behaved children, and Pelzmärtel was supposed to appear and beat them with sticks. Beside them was the poppet Mother had made in my image. Gütel. She had been waiting years for the glassmaker's wife to give us a matching bead for her missing eye. Her scrap dress was neatly arrayed, her black hair tied with ribbons, her eye-thread still loose. Some trick of the light made her look as if she was peering at me, one-eyed, sad to be left on the shelf.

"Haelewise," Mother called. "Are you up?"

"Yes. Which of the poppets shall we take to market today?"

"The queens."

King Frederick—whose rule now extended over the whole of the Roman Empire—had remarried, and Mother was fascinated with his choice of bride. Queen Beatrice had been orphaned young, Mother said, and raised by her grandmother, a sorceress in Francia who taught her the old ways. Father scoffed when he overheard such talk. Last week, the royal couple had visited the bishop-prince, and Mother had taken me to watch the parade. As the queen passed in her bright blue carriage, Mother had waved fervently, and the queen had been kind enough to wave back. I had been astonished by her ankle-length golden braids, which had glimmered like her crown in the sun. During the parade, the shoe-maker said he caught a glimpse of her whispering an incantation into a hand-mirror, and his story had spread like fire.

The day after the parade, Mother had made three poppets in the new queen's image with long yellow braids. I put them in a sack and followed her out.

The street was dim. The sky was dark, cloud-filled. My favor-ite weather for market day; the sun wouldn't bother my eyes. The sound of our footsteps disappeared beneath the noise of the crowd. The flower peddler selling her wares, the beggar on the minster steps seeking alms. The only thing wrong with the day was the

unlucky direction of the wind, which carried the stench of the tan-
nery. I cleared my throat, deciding to bring up something that had
been bothering me. "Do you remember the sorceress we visited
when I was ten?"

Mother opened her mouth, then closed it.

"That resin she tried to sell us to speed my progress toward
womanhood. Do you think we could go back for it? I'm still about
as flat as a tart crust, and there's no sign of my monthlies."

My failure to develop had been on my mind, more and more, as
my uncomfortable affection for Matthäus had grown. The prob-
ability of attracting his interest was already so small, I wanted to do
anything I could to improve my chances with him.

Mother shook her head. "We can't go back to her. You know
that. Only holy healers. I gave your father my oath."

The bright blue of her dress was swallowed by the crowd as
she hurried toward the square. I didn't move, disappointed by her
answer, angry at my father for compelling it. What harm would
it do?

A light rain tapped the minster steps. The beggar called, "These
are troubling times. What is a king without an heir?" His eyes
searched the crowd, then rested on me. "Would that I could flee
this land, like you."

I tried to control my expression. Mother had taught me to respect
my elders, and his comment made no sense. Still, something about
him moved me. His kindly face. His ragged cloak. "Blessings to
you," I said, dropping a *holpfennic* in his cup.

"Oh, no." He fished it out. "You'll need this more than I."

As he placed the coin in my palm, I shivered, wondering what
he knew that I didn't.

"Haelewise!" I could barely make my mother out, a small dot
of blue at the end of the street, as she waved. I hurried after her.
One of the prince's physicians, an elderly monk with a perfectly
trimmed beard, stumbled out of the apothecary. He nodded at me

as he clumsily untangled his robe from where it'd caught on an herb bushel.

Next door, the furrier frowned outside his shop, carving the skin off the palest fox I had ever seen. Normally I tried to avoid him—he was foul-tempered—but the fox's fur was fine and white and soft, the color of snow or stars. As I stopped to watch, a huge raven swooped down to the street beside me. It looked up at me, its amber eyes glittering. I shivered, remembering the amber-eyed bird who stole Gütel's eye. A childish fear knotted my stomach, and I felt a chill. The air snapped taut.

The next thing I knew I was lying crumpled on the stones, devastated by the realization that the anchoress's cure hadn't worked. Someone was holding my head. When I finally opened my eyes—cross-eyed, squinting—I was looking right up the tanner's nose. "Where's your mother?" he said. "I thought you were cured!"

I sat up. A crowd had gathered around us. The furrier's two pimple-faced sons were watching me, eyes narrowed. The physician stood behind them all, his robe untangled from the bushel, frozen in the act of leaving the shop. Outrage filled me as I watched him disappear into the crowd. Clearly, the health of a lowborn girl like me was no concern of his. I was so angry—at him, at my spells for returning—that I muttered an oath my mother only used when Father wasn't around. "*Dyēses linekwmy twe,*" I spat, though I didn't know what the words meant.

The tanner pulled back, stricken, as if I had cursed him. A hush fell over the crowd. I sat up, fearing what folks would think: the oath, my swoon.

"Don't meet her eyes," the furrier's elder son hissed. "That's how demons move from one body to the next—"

One of the storekeeps crossed himself. The gesture rippled from one person to the next. The miller's sister made the demon-warding sign, forming a circle with her thumb and forefinger. Those who saw it stepped back, looking at one another, whispering.

My chest tightened. Something dark and mindless settled over the crowd. A voice deep inside urged me to run.

Then I saw Mother, elbowing her way toward me, her face tight with fury. "Leave her alone!" she yelled. The crowd froze. She gave the furrier's elder son a look that would curdle milk. "These spells. St. Mary save us. For generations, they've burdened my kin."

Reaching me, she put her hand on my shoulder. "Thank you," she told the tanner brightly. She met the others' eyes, her voice cold. "We're done here."

Whatever had settled over the crowd seemed to lift. People shook their heads and went back to their business. The tanner blinked and murmured a blessing. The miller's sister hurried into the furrier's shop. The furrier scowled at my mother, following the miller's sister inside. His elder son slammed the door behind them.

Mother's expression was grave as she drew me to her breast. "That was close."

The next morning seemed a day like any other. No raven lit on the windowsill. No bat flew into the house. If there was anything out of the ordinary, it was that the house seemed quieter than usual. The only sounds were those of horses outside, clip-clopping the stones. For a moment, I didn't think of the scene I'd made in the square the day before. And then I did, staring at the dried herbs hanging from the rafters, cursing myself. If my feelings for Matthäus had been difficult before, they were downright impossible now. It was bad enough that I was a fisherman's daughter. His father would never let him marry the girl who cursed the tanner.

I wanted to pull my blanket over my head and pretend the previous day hadn't happened, to go back to sleep and wake up from this horrible dream. But that wasn't going to happen, so I made myself get up. I expected to find Mother—and the comfort she would offer—at the table, putting the finishing touches on a poppet. But the table was empty, the rush lights on the wall beside it unlit. Was

Mother out selling poppets so we could pay the anchoress's fee again?

In the window, a strand of beads she'd obtained from the glassmaker's wife refracted the sun into a gaudy rainbow. God's teeth, I thought, squinting with pain as the light hit my eyes. Sometimes I wished I could sleep all day like an owl.

The sack Mother usually took to market hung by the door.

"Mother?" I brushed by a sack of parsnips in the cupboard, a garlic rope. "Are you home?"

The back shutters were closed, so no sunlight came in from the garden but for the single stripe between them. Mother was asleep, her thick black hair like a thundercloud around her head. Something about the way she lay concerned me. She was like a pile of sticks scattered across the bed. The angles were all wrong. I touched her ankle beneath the wool. She didn't respond. I opened the shutters. Sunlight poured in, yellow and pure, bathing the bed. Mother's limbs moved, as if she was collecting herself, putting herself aright. Out from the covers she peered, blinking. Nothing seemed out of sorts until she smiled. Then I noticed how tired her eyes were, how bloodshot. She looked like she hadn't slept at all.

"Mother," I asked. "What ails you?"

"What do you mean?" Her voice was all wrong. There was little actual sound to it, like wind whispering through the trees.

Some sixth sense, out of proportion with the details before me, filled me with dread. "You never sleep this late. You look half dead."

She cleared her throat nervously, as if she was surprised about her voice. "I couldn't sleep last night. I went for a walk."

"Where did you go?"

"Only a little way into the forest."

A weight settled on my shoulders. But she refused to say more.

Never before had I seen Mother fall asleep on her feet. Not at the table while she worked, her needle in her mouth. First her jaw slackened and her eyes went soft. Then she dropped the poppet whose cloak she was sewing. When she dropped her prized—her only—needle in the straw, I coaxed her back to bed. She had never missed a day of work before. Even if she and Father argued until late, she got up early. In the mornings, she put on her lucky gloves and gardened. In the afternoons, she visited pregnant women who needed her help. At night she sewed poppets. There had never been an idle moment.

The next week, her forehead burned, and she stopped going out. Gone was the woman who popped up as soon as the sun rose. She slept even after I opened the shutters. Her eyelids would flutter when the sun filled the room, but she wouldn't wake until almost noon. Father tried to get the bishop to send a physician, but his petitions were ignored.

As word spread about Mother's illness, her friends began to bring food. The fishwife who lived next door brought flour so I could make bread in the embers. Matthäus's mother brought over a stew, but her son didn't come with her. When I noted I hadn't seen him in over a week, Mechtilde apologized, saying he was very busy sewing clothes for an upcoming wedding. She shared the sad news about our friend, the tanner, who had fallen ill with a fever while trimming the hide of a bull. His wife found him slumped in front of the lime pit, mumbling nonsense, his face flushed.

I couldn't help but fear my mother had also been stricken thus.

That evening, there was a rapping on our door. The miller's wife was in labor. Her nephew was here to fetch Mother for the birth. When I went into the back to tell her, her eyes fluttered open. "The miller's wife?" It took her a moment to understand. Her expression was pained. I could see her thinking, skin stretched tight around her eyes, which had acquired a yellow tint. Her voice cracked as she said, "Tell them I'm sick."

"What?" I breathed. We had never abandoned a client during her pangs. The miller's wife would be fine; she could send for someone else. But her mother, the baker's wife, knew *everyone*. If we didn't show up, everyone would find out that we'd abandoned a client during her time of need. We'd lose half our clients in a day. "Her mother will tell everyone!"

Mother sighed, her thin voice barely audible. "I can't go. I haven't the strength."

I looked at her. It was true. She could barely muster the energy to speak. There had to be something I could do to help. I'd served as her apprentice for five years, and I was good at our work. "Why don't I go alone?"

Mother looked alarmed. "Haelewise, no. They won't want you."

Her words stung. "I've gone with you to visit her many times. I know about her swollen leg, her preferences in birthing oils."

"I know you *could* do it, and you could do it well. But no one wants a childless midwife, and it's a terrible idea after what happened in the square. If something goes wrong, the baker's wife will tell everyone it's your fault. You'd be putting your life in danger."

Her answer maddened me—she was right, I knew—but her words filled me with self-hate. Why had I spoken that oath in the presence of so many people? Everyone already thought me strange. My thoughts raced. Out the front window, I heard the sound of normal people laughing. A resentment filled me that I couldn't even do this simple thing for her. "Fine," I said bitterly, feeling defeated. "We'll let our practice fall to ruins."

"Thank you," she breathed, too ill to remark on my rancor.

After her eyes fluttered closed, I stared at her for a long time, watching the way the moonlight made her face glow, the sickly yellow of her complexion. Her illness terrified me. How could I let her abandon our livelihood? What would we do when she got better if no one wanted us to attend births?

I braided my hair as quickly as I could. When I opened the door, the boy was still waiting. "Hedda is ill," I whispered. "I will come in her place."

As the boy led me toward the miller's stately cottage, I could hear the millwheel groaning, locked against the river's current. I hesitated at the door, worried that Mother was right. All my life, I had loved attending births. Staying up all night with the expectant mother. Helping a new soul into the world. Whenever I entered a woman's chamber, I could sense an otherworldly weight, a possibility that pulled the child's soul from the next world into this.

I could sense that possibility in the air as soon as I walked into the miller's house. The veil thinning between this world and the next, the pull. Suddenly, I was nervous to face it by myself. During a particularly difficult birth the month before, we had lost both mother and child: the wife of a fisherman and a baby that never made it out of her womb. I'd told my mother when I felt a trembling at the threshold, which she had taught me to recognize as a soul. But the fisherman's wife didn't have the strength to push. Nothing my mother did helped. On the third night, the wife became racked with chills. The pull shifted suddenly in the opposite direction, and the wife's soul was sucked from her breast. What if something like that happened to the miller's wife? If she or her baby died, her family would blame me. My mother was right. It was dangerous for me to be here by myself.

The boy went into the next room to announce me. "Hedda is ill," I heard him saying. "Haelewise has come in her stead."

Voices rose and fell in the next room. Moonlight shone through the window, lighting the tapestries on the wall. The air was full of the spicy scent of the caudle brewing over the fire. "Come back," a voice finally said.

I paused for a moment, gathering my courage. Every midwife has her first birth, I told myself. You're ready.

A sheet had been hung over the doorway that separated the rooms. Pushing it aside, my hand met a dozen or more rope charms, intricate knots of garlic and sage, clay amulets chalked with crosses to ward off demons and death.

Inside the dark room, half a dozen women were gathered around the bed drinking caudle. A tapestry had been drawn over the window to keep out spirits. Candles burned on every surface. The light caught the whites of the women's eyes. No one would meet my gaze. In the corner, the miller's sister made the demon-warding sign. The miller's wife looked up from the birthing stool. She held a crucifix in one hand, a St. Margaret's charm in the other. Her breath was ragged. She was retaining even more water than the last time we visited. Her face was pink and shiny, her fingers puffy and plump, but I could see that she had hours of labor left.

"Send her home!" the miller's sister was saying.

The miller's wife sighed. "She's come with Hedda all this time. She's good at her trade."

"She's never had children," her sister-in-law said. "Her skill is *unnatural*."

The rope charms swayed as she stormed out. The miller's wife looked wary. As soon as her sister was gone, I set about showing her that she'd made the right choice. If I was going to work as a midwife one day, I needed to prove myself.

I helped her up and got her walking. I massaged her swollen leg. Between contractions, I rubbed her back with peppermint oil. Her pangs were still several minutes apart. As she paced, I started a fire to keep the water warm.

With the passing hours, the other women curled up on the floor and slept. From time to time, they woke and watched us, eyes wary. I pretended not to notice their mistrust until sometime after midnight when the wife's contractions subsided, and everyone but her gossipy mother, the baker's wife, fell asleep. I was already worried about the cessation of her pangs. Often, when that happened, it was not a good sign. As I waited for the contractions to return, counting the minutes, the hairs on the back of my neck rose. Out of the corner of my eye, I caught the baker's wife watching me from her pallet, as if she wanted to say something.

I imagined her telling everyone what happened tonight, spreading vicious rumors about me if something went wrong. I tried to ignore the feeling that she was watching me, but the feeling of her gaze upon me didn't subside. After a while, I couldn't bear it. "What?" I whispered, whirling on her, resigning myself to a conversation. "Whatever it is, please, out with it. Say it to my face."

The woman balked at my boldness. "Surely it's common for a client's mother to ask questions. Surely you don't mind answering mine."

"Of course not," I muttered, certain whatever she was about to say wasn't so innocent.

She smiled prettily in the candlelight. "How many times have you attended a birth alone?"

I met her eyes, defiant. "This is my first."

She shifted on her pallet so the darkness hid her face. "Can you really sense death before it happens? I heard you could."

This again. I sighed. "Sometimes."

"Is it here now?"

I couldn't tell if she was being earnest or trying to reveal me as a heretic. "It's not death I sense exactly. Only tension in the air, the trembling of souls. All I can sense now is the possibility, the weight that will eventually pull the child's soul into this world."

"So you don't know if my daughter will live?"

"I'm sorry. That's not how it works."

The baker's wife fell silent, but I could sense her unsettlement from her pallet. She lay there for hours, tossing and turning, waiting for her daughter's pangs to resume in full force. When they did, I could feel the possibility of the birth growing stronger, a shimmering weight in the air. The bells for lauds had just sounded at the abbey down the street when the woman's pangs finally began to come one on top of the next. Then I felt a subtle trembling in the air around us. The soul, ready to enter the child's throat. "It's time," I said, leading the new mother toward the birthing stool while her mother held her hand. She was tired, deathly so, from the difficulty of her labor. The transition to motherhood was always more work than women thought.

"You can do this," I said, willing the statement true, still worried that something was going to go wrong with the birth.

"I can't," the miller's wife said weakly.

"We just have to get you to that stool," I said, guiding her toward it, though the weakness of her voice scared me. Like a new mother underestimating the difficulties of labor, I had underestimated the burden of attending a birth alone. I could feel everyone's eyes on me now, watching me, waiting for me to do what I had come here to do.

Another pang came over the woman before her mother and I got her seated. I cursed myself inwardly. The soul was waiting. I was letting the birth go on too long.

"Can you feel it now, Haelewise?" the baker's wife pleaded. "Is everything going to be all right?"

I waved her away. "Let me focus."

As we finally got the new mother to the stool, the child's soul shook with fierce tremors.

I squeezed the woman's shoulder and smiled at her encouragingly. It occurred to me that my mother always mouthed a prayer before she told a client to push. I had no idea what she said, though, because she only ever crossed herself and moved her lips. I crossed myself, following suit. I had no idea to whom she prayed. St. Margaret? Her goddess? St. Mary? *Let this woman's transition into motherhood be easy*, I settled upon finally, sending up the prayer to whoever was listening. *Help me keep this woman and child safe.*

That settled, I put my hand over the woman's belly and waited for the next contraction. When I felt it stir, I spoke. "Now. When you feel the urge, push!"

The sound the woman made as she pushed was like a growl and scream combined. Her sisters jumped up from the floor, wild-eyed, straightening their skirts. They squeezed her hands, murmuring encouragement, reciting prayers for her and the baby's health.

The possibility in the air was so great. I could feel a powerful weight, pulling the child's soul from the next world into this. It was vibrating wildly at the threshold. I crouched beside the miller's wife, watching the space between her legs. After two pangs, I could see the baby's crown, shiny with mucus and blood. A shoulder emerged with the third. With the fourth, the mother emitted a blood-curdling growl, and the child slid out into my arms.

A fat little boy, hale and silent and stout. I slipped my hand inside his mouth as my mother had taught me, to clear the way for his soul to enter his throat. My arms prickled with goose bumps, as I felt it whoosh by, overeager—a silvery mist—on its way into his mouth. As soon as it entered him, he started crying, so loud and wild I forgot everything else.

And just like that, the weight in the air collapsed. The veil between worlds closed. I swaddled the child, looked into his blue eyes, felt his hunger and fear. It was only a moment before his mother reached for him, but that was long enough for me to fall in love with the need in his eyes. The act of holding him, of answering that need, felt *natural*. He was so small, so helpless. When his mother held out her arms, I didn't want to give him up.

A thought occurred to me, unbidden. Who knew if I would ever get the chance to have a child of my own? I could remedy that, right now, steal away with him and raise him as my own.

I only hesitated a moment, but the miller's wife must've read my expression. "Give him to me!" she said, alarmed.

Her mother narrowed her eyes.

"Sorry," I said quickly, giving him up. "Here you go."

As soon as the babe was in his mother's arms, the baker's wife turned to me. "Thank you very much, Haelewise," she said. "That'll do. I can deliver the afterbirth myself."

Before I knew what was happening, she was putting some coins in my hand and ushering me out. As the door shut behind me, I paused, trying to come to terms with how quickly they'd cast me out. I felt indignant that they had become so irate at my simple desire to hold a baby a bit longer. What woman hadn't felt that? He's the first child I ever delivered, I thought petulantly. Of course I got caught up in the moment.

Let she who is without sin cast the first stone.

CHAPTER THREE

O n my way home from the miller's cottage, I decided to take the
road that went past the tailor's shop. Matthäus was opening the
door for a wealthy client as I passed. It looked like he was going to
come over to talk to me, until his father saw what he was doing and
called him inside. Before Matthäus shut the door, he met my eyes—
an apologetic look on his face—and mouthed the word *sorry.*

The encounter was so humiliating, I tried to put it out of my
mind. When I got home, Father was nowhere to be found. I spent
the next few days cooking and cleaning and trying to nurse my
mother back to health. I couldn't stop thinking about the moment
I held the miller's son, the urge I'd felt to steal him away. Before,
I had simply assumed I would become a mother because it was
expected of me. Now, it was something I *longed* to do.

Every morning, I checked the dock behind our hut for my
father's boat, but he didn't come home until four days later. When
he did, his clothes were filthy, and his face was covered with inex-
plicable pockmarks, but he came bearing good news. The bishop
had finally granted his petition to send a physician to heal my
mother's illness.

The physician the bishop sent was the same monk who'd deserted
me in the square. When I opened the door and saw his fine robe,
his cold eyes and perfect beard, my outrage rekindled itself.

"Well, look who the bishop sent." I didn't bother to hide my
resentment. "Thank you for humbling yourself enough to visit us."

He stiffened, squinting in the late morning sun. "I go where I'm
told. Someone wrote the bishop on your mother's behalf."

My father must have found someone to write the bishop, somehow, during the four days he was gone.

It took me a moment to master my anger and lead the physician into the back room. As soon as he saw my mother asleep on the cot, he handed me a phial. "Fill this with water from the public fountain," he said, presuming I would do as told.

"We just filled the jug at the well," I said, hesitant to leave her alone with him. "I'll fill it with that."

The physician shook his head. "The water must be from the fountain."

"God's teeth," I swore. "The well water's clean."

On the bed, my mother opened her eyes. "Haelewise," she whispered. "Mind your manners."

The physician met her eyes, then mine, resigning himself to delivering an explanation. "Everything I do, I must do with God's blessing. The well is stagnant, a dozen feet underground. Only the fountain water is clean enough to bless."

"Fine," I said angrily. I took the phial and stomped off toward the fountain, though I suspected the well water was cleaner. The Lord knew it certainly tasted better.

When I brought it back, the physician was sitting by my mother on her cot, peering down at a small chart of inscrutable symbols. "Moon in Libra," he murmured, retrieving a fleam from his bag. With a flick of his wrist, he slit her forearm.

My mother seemed oddly fine with his action.

The physician peered thoughtfully at the droplets of blood on the blade. "Give me the phial," he demanded, holding out his hand.

I practically threw it at him.

He ignored my anger, saying a quick prayer over the phial in the language of priests, then mixing a few drops of water with the blood on the fleam. "Sluggish," he said after a moment, looking up at my mother. "You're too phlegmatic. You need foods flavored with marjoram. More baths and exercise."

Mother smiled a tight smile. "If you say so."

I could tell she was just being polite.

"Before you took ill, did you notice any foul odors in the house?"

Mother shook her head, her smile false.

The physician wrapped his fingers around her arm, pressing the underside of her wrist. I suppressed an urge to swat his hand away. "Have you sins to shrive?"

Mother shook her head. "This is no spiritual sickness, Brother."

My thoughts swung between two extremes. I mistrusted the physician, but I feared for my mother's health. "Tell him where you went the night before you took ill."

"How many times do I have to tell you I only went for a walk?" she snapped.

Something about the look in her eyes told me to stay quiet. It was the same look she gave me when I was little, when she tied the keeping string around my wrist in the market.

The physician peered at her. "Where did you go?"

"Only a little way into the forest."

He raised a brow. "Beyond the north gate? At night?"

Mother nodded, closing her eyes.

"The forest fills with poison vapors at night," the monk pushed. "The mist carries disease."

"The mist does no such thing," Mother snapped, losing her temper. "It's perfectly benign. The stuff of which souls are made—"

The physician looked stunned. "What are you raving about? The mist derives from the filth on the forest floor. Rot and ordure, crawling things and dead leaves. The tanner went hunting in the forest the night before he took ill. The mist was bad that night. I don't know if you heard, but yesterday, he died."

Sorrow clouded my mother's face. Tears stung my eyes. For a moment, the physician looked pleased to have made his point. Then he remembered to bow his head. "God rest his soul."

He waited just long enough to be respectful, then went back to lecturing us about the mist. He called it miasmata: an evil essence of death and disease that rose from the soil. "It's gotten into your blood," he said. "We'll need to do a bloodletting."

Mother's eyes crossed, like they did when Father said something ridiculous, but she held out her forearm. "Mark my words," she said to me. "I'm doing this because of a promise I made to your father. The mist has nothing to do with my illness."

The physician shook his head, eyebrows raised, then told me to light the rush lights and torch. When I returned, he had taken out his leeches, horrid little flat black worms, which he kept in a pot. It took him two hours to place them on my mother's skin, and one more for her to faint. Then she lay still, sweat on her brow, as the leeches worked. I watched her chest rise and fall, eager to see some sign of improvement, but there was none. Only an increasing pallor to her complexion that brought out the faded pink scar on her cheek. The physician touched the scar. "How did she get that?"

"Hunting in the woods. Before the wall was built. At least that's what she says. She's had it as long as I can remember."

He nodded quietly, thinking. "Your mother is stubborn."

I had to laugh at that. The room fell quiet. "Will she live?"

The physician looked into the leech jar. There was movement at the bottom, a small black mass of worms. "If the Lord wills it."

He frowned as he pulled the leeches from her skin, glistening with jewel-drops of blood. When he finished, he told me some patients slept for a while after a bloodletting, and I would need to see that her throat stayed wet. He showed me how to cup the bottom of her jaw to open her lips. He gave me a phial full of a thick red draught, which he said would calm her. "No more than three swallows a day," he said. "It's strong."

I nodded, warming toward him a little.

From his bag, he pulled a censer covered with tiny filigrees and cross after cross after cross. He handed it to me. Inside were several small, sweet-smelling bricks of incense. "Burn these," he said. "They've been blessed by the bishop."

I took the censer, though I knew my mother would be skeptical.

"Hippocrates thought fainting spells were brought on by the phase of the moon. Do yours happen at any particular time of the month?"

I nodded, confused at the change of subject. "More often around the new moon."

"Look here?" He stretched my eyelids open, then brought a candle close to my face. A ball of light exploded across my vision. "Your pupils don't respond to the light at all. That's why your eyes are so dark."

Pain stabbed my temples.

"Did your father ever bring you to get an exorcism?"

"It didn't take."

The physician cleared his throat and stood. "Let me give you some advice. If your mother survives, keep her out of the wood. And you, stay home as much as you can. They just drowned a girl with fits in the next village. There are many who blame you for the fever."

Mother fell into a deep sleep and wouldn't wake. I set the incense burning and opened the shutters, but it didn't do any good. I watched her with my back to the light, taking in her slack expression, the limpness of her black hair. How still she is, I thought, over and over. I brought her water. She slept and slept. Father came home late. His breath smelled of spirits, and he wouldn't look at me while we ate. Not that this was unusual. He drank often, and we had spoken little since my spell in the square.

When he left the next morning, she still hadn't stirred. Her chest rose and fell beneath the blanket, but she did nothing else. All that day, I stood at the edge of her room and watched her breathe. The signs of her illness seemed similar to those of the deadly fever that was going around. I was afraid that the physician was right, that she'd caught it somehow in the woods.

Father came home late again that night, unsteady on his feet, as if he'd spent the day in the tavern. He said no blessing when we sat down for dinner. He didn't carve a cross in the bread. He even forgot to wash his hands with water from the jug. As we shared the tart I'd made from eggs and perch, he complained that the physician had only made things worse.

"How did you convince the bishop to send him, anyway?"

Father's eyes shifted in my direction.

"The physician said someone sent a letter."

"All I did was put in a request."

I met his eyes. "That was weeks ago. He only agreed to come after you went away for four days. Where did you go?"

The rain beat the roof. He picked a fishbone from his teeth. The only answer he made was to say, "It's your fault your mother's ill."

The words were like a knife in my chest. I could scarcely breathe, staring across the table at him. My skin crawled. He took another drink from his tankard. A piece of parsnip fell from his beard. I closed my eyes and swallowed. "How can you say that?"

He glared at me for a moment, then shrugged. His eyes wide, what was left of his blond hair unkempt. "Because it's true."

Guilt clutched at my throat. I ran to the cupboard, pulling my wool blanket over my head. Tears streaked my cheeks as I heard him leaving the house.

That night, I tossed and turned, checking on my mother every hour until my father came home, smelling of drink. The straw itched my back. Outside, dogs howled. I closed my eyes tight, my chest full of an ache I knew no physician could cure.

I woke up before dawn. Mother was still asleep, unmoving, so I went into the garden to finish harvesting the leeks myself. It had been a long time since I was in the garden alone. One of the legs of the wooden bench my father built when we first enclosed it had come loose, so the seat was tilted. The sun had barely risen, and the garden wall was tall, so most of the garden was in shadow. As I knelt in the shade beside the leeks, a thrush hopped down from the tree outside the crumbling wall to catch an earthworm. As he hopped back up to the wall, singing sweetly, I envied his good cheer.

Soil scattered to the grass as I shook off the leeks. The chickens, hearing me work, clucked their way out of their coop. They pecked my skirts. The rooster was nowhere to be seen. Since Mother fell ill, I realized, no one had fed them any leftovers, so he was probably down the street somewhere looking for food.

Resolving to feed them soon, I wondered why my father blamed me for my mother's illness. Did he, like the townspeople, think I caused the fever? Did he think I cursed the tanner too? The idea made me angry. I had been fond of the tanner. He was a kind man, my mother's friend. Some dark urge compelled me to wish that I was what everyone thought I was. It would serve them right if I went to the city gate at twilight—arms out, beneath the full moon—and called the mist down on all of them.

Then I caught myself, and my heart swelled with guilt. I said a brief prayer for forgiveness. When I was finished, I couldn't stop looking at the three pebble-crosses beside the herb garden, which marked the graves of my three elder brothers who'd been born dead. Mother often sang to them while she gardened, a lullaby she said her mother taught her. I saw her in my mind's eye, planting a seed in her lucky gloves full of holes.

As I piled the leeks in my skirt, her song haunted me:

"Sleep until morning, my dear one,
Housos leaves honey and sweet eggs.
Hera brings blooms, blue and red."

I sang the song to myself as I gathered my skirt, my voice catching with sorrow. All I wanted was for Mother to get well.

There was a sound coming from the back of the house, so faint it could've been the wind itself. My mother's voice. *"Haelewise?"*

I rushed through the back door, dropping the leeks all over the floor of her room, hands and knees covered in dirt. Mother had propped herself up on a pillow. Sunlight poured over her arms. "How long was I out?"

"Two days," I said, rushing to hug her. Tears welled in my eyes. "I was worried you wouldn't wake at all."

She tried to swallow. *Water*, she mouthed.

I hurried to the well and drew up a bucket. Much of the liquids I'd given her had dribbled down her chin.

She drank the cup dry three times before she spoke. "I don't even think I dreamed."

"I need to ask you about something Father said."

Her eyes narrowed. "What?'

"He said your illness is my fault."

"No no no. It most certainly is not!"

"I feared it before he said it. If it's not true, then tell me where you went the night before you took ill."

She reached for my hand and squeezed it in an attempt to reassure me. Neither of us spoke. "Your father is like the physician, asking about poison vapors and sins, looking for something to blame. This illness isn't your fault. It's the same illness that took your grandmother."

I had only vague recollections of an older woman, thin and matronly in an apron, with an ample bosom and a full head of dark hair. It was so long ago that I couldn't even picture her face. All I remembered was that she was kind, and her home had been full of pastries and apples. I blinked the memory away and tried to think. "Why does Father blame me, then?"

Mother sighed, sadness glinting in her eyes, then patted the cot beside her. "That's a long story. Have a seat."

I sat cross-legged on the bed, as I had done so many times when I was little. She reached for my hand and squeezed it, meeting my gaze, as if whatever she was about to tell me was important. Sadness glinted in her eyes. "Your father—" she started, then stopped, as if she were measuring her words. "Your father has been angry with me a long time. What have you heard of the wise woman who lives in the tower in the forest?"

I met her eyes, confused. "What does she have to do with this?"

"Give me a moment. Tell me what you know of her."

I thought on everything I knew. "Some say she is an old woman, stooped and hideous; others say she's an ogress. They say she lives in a tower near Prince Albrecht's castle, deep in the darkest part of the forest. They say no man can see inside the stone circle that surrounds the tower, that once men step inside, their vision fills with mist. They say she knows the old ways, how to make a philter to start and stop a belly's swell. They say a lot of things, Mother. There's nothing like a woman who lives alone to get stories going. Supposedly she kidnapped Princess Ursilda, and her father had to wear a wolf-skin to rescue her"—I looked up—"but you said that story was false."

My mother pressed her lips together tight, her face acquiring the strained expression she always wore when I asked about this story, but this time, I could tell she was going to push through whatever kept her silent. When she spoke, her tone was different from the one she usually used when she told a story. Not full of mischief with the act of tale-telling, but clear and matter-of-fact. "The wise woman knows the old ways, that much is true. And Albrecht really did wear a wolf-skin—his son Ulrich has it now, though he acts the Christian at court. But there was no 'rescue.' Ursilda's mother sent her to the tower to learn the old ways herself."

I searched my mother's face. "How do you know all this?"

"I heard it from the wise woman."

"When? What did you go to her for?"

My mother drew a deep breath, refusing to meet my eyes. I got the sense that she was trying to decide how much to tell me. When she finally spoke, her voice was haunted. "Don't tell your father I told you this, but I nearly died birthing the third of your stillborn brothers. After that, your father refused me. I went to the wise woman to get something to put a man to sleep, and something to make sure a living child came from what I did next."

Her admission horrified me. "*That's* how I came to be born?"

She nodded slowly. "The wise woman said that life could only be wrought from life, that there would be a cost. I felt the toll on my body then, but—"

"That's why Father blames me?"

Mother nodded again. "When my belly swelled, I told him what I had done, but he didn't believe me."

Outside, children were playing near the docks. The streets echoed with giddy screams.

"I'm thirsty," she said.

I left her to retrieve another bucket of water from the well. When I came back, she lay very still, white-knuckled, her eyes wild. My hand shook as I held the cup to her lips. The water only dribbled down her chin.

When Father came home, late that night, I was huddled with Mother in her cot. "She can't move," I told him. I couldn't keep the panic out of my voice.

He shrugged, dismissing my concerns, and sent me to bed.

I lay in the cupboard all night, restless, sleep eluding me until just before dawn. When I awoke, broad daylight striped the shutters and I could hear my parents talking softly in the back. I put my ear to the wall and listened.

"I've done what I've done," Mother was saying. "There's no turning back."

"Without consulting me, as usual. Doing whatever devilish thing you want—"

"I want to be buried in the garden," Mother said.

Her words were like a slap in my face. I blinked, my eyes filling with tears. Father cursed, slamming something—his hand, maybe—into the wall. All I could hear was the thud. Then footsteps, approaching the cupboard. He was angry, storming out. I panicked, shrinking into the corner. If he caught me listening, he would strike me, but there was no time for me to lie down and pretend to sleep. I sucked in my stomach and flattened myself against the wall. He will not see me, I told myself, he will not, he will not—

The cupboard walls shook as he passed, inches away in the dark. In the front room, I could hear him grabbing the cloak he wore on the water. The door slammed, and I took a deep breath, my fear subsiding. When I was sure he was gone, I hurried into the back room. Mother looked startled. "You're awake?"

"What did you do?" I asked, my voice catching in my throat. "Why were you talking about where you want to be *buried*?"

"Haelewise," my mother said, her face crumpling. "Come here." I sat down beside her. She made me look at her.

"It was just a precaution," she said. "In case something happens." I bit my lip, despondent. I knew she was lying.

The sunrise played tricks on the light, casting weird shadows over the bed. Mother's skin gleamed, pale and thin, stretched tight across her bones. She looked like an old woman, twice her age, her black hair on the pillow streaked with white. "Have I ever told you how your father and I met?"

I shook my head, having difficulty focusing on her words. "Why does it matter? You just told me you're dying."

Mother sighed. Her voice was thin. "Your father used to sell fish in the market. I would see him a few times a year when my mother and I drove our cart here to buy flour and other supplies, rare oils and spices. He was handsome, back then. Broad shoulders and a tapered waist, brooding eyes, beautiful golden hair." She closed her eyes, smiling faintly, as if she were seeing the younger version of my father in her mind's eye. Father was balding now, his belly swollen. "I didn't know, when I followed him into the linden grove that day, how wonderful it would feel to kiss him. Nor did I know how much what happened after that kiss would wreck my life. When I fell pregnant, my mother wanted me to drink a potion, but I married him instead." Her voice shook. "In the end, your brother was born dead."

I made myself breathe, trying to make sense of her story. Why was she telling me this now?

When she spoke again, her voice was so soft I could barely make out the words. "I've given up a lot for your father. We argued fiercely in those first months. He wanted me to be baptized." Her voice was full of regret. "Your father won the argument."

I pitied her. "But you still burn offerings. Visit wortcunners. Serve as a midwife."

She met my eyes. "It's not enough."

I did not ask her *enough for what?* I remembered the night the month before, when we were walking home from the birth in which both the fisherman's wife and her unborn child died. Tears had streamed down my mother's face, and her voice had risen with grief. There were things she could've done to save them, she confessed, if she didn't have to worry about being thought a heretic.

Her voice interrupted my thoughts. "What is Matthäus like?"

The question took me by surprise. "Why?"

"Just tell me."

I sighed. It was difficult to think of anything but the fact that my mother was planning her burial. The shock of it haunted me. And thinking about Matthäus made me sad. Since I saw him outside the tailor shop, he hadn't knocked on our door once. I suspected his father had forbidden him to see me. "Kind," I said finally. "Earnest."

Mother nodded. "That's how he seemed to me. Good. How do you feel about him?"

Her question conjured a lump in my throat. "I don't want to talk about it."

She watched my face carefully, measuring what I had just said. "His mother came by before you woke up. His apprenticeship will be over soon. Mechtilde said he wants to ask for your hand."

Her words knocked the breath out of my chest. The shock was palpable, almost too much for me to bear. I must've gone pale as a ghost.

"Haelewise, are you all right?"

"He what?" I said finally, realizing I had stopped breathing. I closed my eyes and made myself draw a deep breath. "Did you just say Matthäus wants to *marry* me?"

She nodded encouragingly, a delighted look on her face. "You like him."

"God's teeth, yes. I can't stop thinking about him. But his family is so wealthy. I'm pretty sure after what happened in the square, his father forbade him to see me." My voice caught. "I'm about as fertile as the dirt beneath the tanner's barrel. Even my own soul disdains my body, Mother. I dare not think it would interest anyone else."

"Oh, Haelewise—" She took my hand and pulled me close. "You're beautiful. Mechtilde says he's fallen for you. She's trying to convince her husband to allow a love match."

"He'll never agree. Not now."

"There's a cure for your spells, Haelewise. Your grandmother—" Her voice trailed off. She looked thoughtful, almost pensive. Finally she nodded, deciding something. "Bring me some water."

When I returned from the well, she patted the cot. I brought her the water and sat next to her. The cot was warm, the blanket scratchy beneath my legs. She hugged me close, resting her chin on my head. "Did I ever tell you the tale of the golden apple?"

I shook my head.

Mother took a deep breath. "In stories old there was a mother whose daughter was plagued with fevers. The girl burned so hot that the mother nearly died while the girl was in her belly. She burned so hot that when the girl was born, she was born nearly dead. But the mother held the girl to her breast anyway to nurse her. The mother wept tears of joy when the girl began to suckle."

There my mother paused, taking a deep breath. I let my head fall against her shoulder. I closed my eyes, feeling sleepy and comforted, the way I had when she held me as a girl. She put her arms around me, pulling me close. As I waited for her to go on, I breathed in the faint scent of anise and listened to the beat of her heart.

"As the girl grew older," she went on, finally, "her mother sought far and wide for a cure to her fevers. They consulted with every alchemist, every sorceress and physician. They brought the hermit from the hovel by the sea. The priest. The bishop. Nothing worked."

Mother stopped again, for a moment, catching her breath. I couldn't help but wonder if she was making this story up. It seemed too close to her efforts to cure my spells.

Outside, a peddler called out, hawking his wares. The room seemed suddenly chill. I pulled the wool blanket over my legs.

"In the end," Mother went on, finally, "it was not a healer who cured the girl. It was the girl herself who found the cure in a plant that grew just outside their doorstep. This plant bore tiny golden apples that shriveled as winter came, filling the air with a heavenly scent. The day the girl ate one, once and for all, her fevers left."

As she spoke these last three words, her voice rose, slow and steady, like a pack horse ascending a rocky path. Then she swallowed, as if her throat was dry. I handed her the cup of water. "Are you saying we've looked in the wrong places for my cure?"

She shook her head and drank.

"You think the cure has been here all along?"

"I'm only saying, sometimes, the cure grows just outside your door, if you look for it."

"What?"

She set down her cup. "Go get me the aniseed pot. There's something I've been wanting to give you."

Mother kept aniseed in the cupboard to make the seed cakes she ate after dinner. The seeds rattled as I brought the pot to her. She removed the lid and stuck her hand into the seeds. The scent of anise filled the air as she took something out, an old key, then shook her head; it wasn't what she was looking for. "Hold this," she said. She fumbled around inside the pot again, then shook the seeds from a tiny black stone figurine.

"Here." She held it out. "This used to belong to your grandmother."

I examined the figurine. The black stone had been carved into the shape of a woman holding a child, but no one would mistake her for the Blessed Mother. She was a bird-woman, naked with heavy breasts and wide hips. Her face was strangely shaped, grotesque, with protrusions on the sides of her face and wide-set eyes. She had wings and a beak. "What is this?"

"A good-luck charm. Put it somewhere safe. That key too. I don't know what it's for, but you might need it. Don't let your father, or anyone else for that matter, find the charm. They'll tell Father Emich, and he'll call you a heretic."

Mother had impressed upon me young the need to keep her faith secret. I hadn't even told Matthäus about the offerings she burned, the curses she muttered, the incantations to chase away bad luck. She was afraid to tell me much because she didn't want to put me in danger. When I was very small, a Frenchwoman who preached the gospel of Mary Magdalene had been stoned in the street. Mother's faith was far more heretical.

I looked closer at the figurine, carefully shaped from a soft black stone. She felt slippery almost. She had taloned feet like an eagle. Her hands were three-fingered, thumbless. She felt oddly warm to the touch. I met my mother's eyes, awed. "You used to say your goddess dwells in things, in the hidden powers of root and leaf—"

"Haelewise. I've broken my promise to your father a dozen ways today. Please don't ask me to do it again."

I sighed and closed my mouth.

"Everyone goes on about the pleasure of the act," she said, suddenly, as if caught in a separate thought. "And there's truth to that. There is. But the best thing about it is the children who come from it." She put her hand on my chin, turning my face to meet hers.

I nodded, a lump rising in my throat.

"You have brought me such joy, do you know that?"

CHAPTER FOUR

I slipped the key and the bird-mother figurine into my pouch where my father wouldn't find them and examined the charm each night when I laid down to sleep. Sometimes, if I stroked her curves, her black stone warmed under my fingers, and the air seemed heavier than before. She was fascinating to look at, simultaneously hideous and beautiful. Enthralling. She hinted at a world outside the bishop's wall, where Mother's beliefs might be accepted, where my fainting spells might not be seen as evidence that I was possessed.

Each night, I rubbed her curves, whispering prayers for my mother's cure. Not that the prayers did anything. Some nights, as I lay in my cupboard, I confess, my faith faltered. I wondered if my father's and mother's gods were like the *kindefresser*: stories people told to influence other people. But every time I was seized with doubt, I remembered the veil I sensed between worlds, the souls I sensed moving in and out of bodies. There was a secret world that shimmered behind the world we knew. I had felt it. I wrapped my fingers around the bird-woman and felt her power.

As the weeks passed, Matthäus didn't knock on my door. He certainly didn't propose. I began to feel foolish that I'd allowed myself to believe my mother's gossip. She had probably just been trying to make me feel better.

Word must have spread that I attended the birth of the miller's son instead of my mother. No one else came to summon Mother for a birth. As autumn turned colder, she slept more and more. From time to time, she lost the ability to move her limbs. When she was awake, her voice blew through the house, a whisper, a faint breeze. She lost her place in speech, glancing up in confusion.

Father became the thud of boots on the floor. I waited longer, each day, for the tinkling of his *holpfennige* in the jar. He said not a word to me as he came in, though he always put food on the table when he did. Fresh-caught whitefish I seared over the fire and ate in clumps, a hardened half wheel of cheese.

The autumn vegetables ripened. I pulled carrots and cabbage, leeks and onions, and soaked them in brine. I straightened the pebbles on my brothers' graves when they were disturbed by animals.

One afternoon in October, there was a knock on our door. Mother was sleeping, as usual. She didn't stir. When I saw Mat-thäus at the threshold, my heart fluttered. I hadn't seen him since my mother mentioned his intentions. I caught myself wondering if he was there to propose and quashed the thought, embarrassed.

When I let him inside, he scanned the poppets on the shelves in the front room. He'd never set foot in our house, despite all the times he'd knocked on our door. The rush lights on the table sputtered. A breeze swayed the beads in the window, casting light on the floor. In the corner, a rat twitched its nose. Shoo, I wanted to tell it. Get back in your hole!

"How is your mother?" he asked.

"Not well."

He sighed, pulling a strand of wooden beads from his pouch. "My father doesn't know I'm here. I had to sneak out while he was on an errand."

I tried to hide my disappointment. I had been right all along. His father didn't want him to see me. Why did our mothers think his father would accept me as a daughter-in-law?

"My mother and I wanted to give you something," he went on. He put the beads in my hand and closed my fingers around them, his hands lingering on mine. "They're called paternoster beads. We received several as a gift from the Duke of Zähringen, and we thought you might like one. You use them to pray the paternoster over and over, counting the repetitions. The duke says that God is more often moved by repeated prayers."

His touch made me dizzy. I opened my hand. The beads were beautiful, smooth pearls of wood. They had an unearthly weight. "Are you sure you want to give me these?"

"They're a parting gift of sorts, unfortunately. I have to accompany my father on a trip. He says we won't be back until the beginning of Lent."

"Oh," I said softly. Lent was four months away. "Where are you going?"

"The Duke of Zähringen is giving a feast in Zürich. He wants his whole family fitted with new clothes. Everything kermes-dyed, bright red, embroidered with eagles from his family crest." He took my hands in his. "When we come back, things will be different. I promise. I'll come by more often. I'm going to talk to my father about you on the trip."

Shame filled me. I pulled my hands away. "What will you say?" My voice shook. "What can you?"

He met my eyes, his own full of pain. "The truth," he said softly. "That you are important to me."

I thought again of what my mother said, that he wanted to marry me. A sob rose, unbidden, in my throat. I swallowed it and looked away. The rat was watching us from the corner, flicking its tail.

Matthäus held my gaze. "My mother and I have been working on him, but—" He shook his head. "Well, you know how fathers can be."

I made myself nod.

He embraced me for a long moment, his arms wrapped tight around me. His shoulders had gotten so broad. I longed for him to kiss me. "Get out of here," I said, pushing him away so I would stop thinking about it.

Laughing, he brushed my hair from my forehead. When he saw

the tears in my eyes, he moved to go, not wanting to cause me further pain. "I'll come by as soon as we get back. I promise."

As the door fell shut behind him, the rat scurried back into its hole.

The paternoster beads were an unexpected comfort. I put them in my pouch with the bird-mother charm, which I ignored more and more as the weeks passed. Maybe it was because the beads were a gift from Matthäus. Or maybe it was because, unlike the charm, I didn't have to hide them from my father. I carried the beads with me during the day so I could use spare moments to pray for my mother. Each night in my alcove, I whispered the paternoster, counting repetitions on the beads until I fell asleep.

One morning, Mother was feeling well enough to talk, and I told her about Matthäus's visit. "How did it go?"

I sighed. My troubles would only burden her. I tried to think of a way to explain without upsetting her. "He's going with his father to Zürich. The Duke of Zähringen is hosting a feast. He won't be back until Lent."

"Did he say anything about his intentions with you?"

I avoided her gaze, hoping to change the subject. "He's going to work on his father on their trip. I'll know more when he returns."

She nodded thoughtfully, fingering the blanket. After a moment, she looked up. "If his father won't give you his blessing, did you know you could have a wedding without a priest?"

That got my attention. "How?"

"You hold each other's hands, make a vow. There is power in the words themselves." She took my hands and squeezed them. "Look at me, Haelewise. This is important."

Her gaze was so intense, I wanted to look away.

"Their way is not the only way," she said. "Remember that."

As the weeks passed, Mother's condition worsened. Her forehead burned. She slurred her words. She was always too cold, or coughing when our fire filled the hut with smoke. By December, her skin was yellow all over. Her eyes looked like they would pop out of her skull. She was bloated, cheeks swollen. She couldn't get out of bed. It was clear by then that whatever she was fighting wasn't the fever that was going around, which either passed or killed its victims within days. I prayed fiercely for her recovery, fingering the paternoster beads a dozen times a day. Father petitioned the bishop to send a priest to administer a blessing, but so many people had come down with the fever, there weren't enough priests to see everyone.

One morning, I stood at her cot, wringing my hands, uncertain what to do. She had been unable to move for hours, and her breathing was labored. On the table next to the bed, the calming draught the physician had left us glowed. I poured twice the usual amount into a cup and pressed it to her lips. It was like a balm. In an instant she was calm. Her eyelids drooped. She slept.

When she woke, she could move again. Smiling, she chanted a children's rhyme in her odd little whisper. "*Five, six, witch. Seven, eight, good night.*"

Her eyes wet and bright, she petted a wrinkle in the wool blanket and looked at me. "It's beautiful," she cooed. "Do you see it? A beautiful kitten!"

What could I do but pet it with her, a rift opening in my chest?

That afternoon, she had another spell of paralysis. They seemed to be growing more frequent. Her eyes darted, frightened, around the room. I gave her more draught and she slept.

Hours passed, this time, before she woke. When she did, the kitten was back. I petted it with her, asking what color it was. She told me blue. I thought it strange how much she laughed.

At sunset, she complained that she was hot, though the first snow of the year had fallen that day. By the time darkness fell, it was so cold that the fire in the front room barely kept the back warm. I tamped it down, peeled off her blanket, and opened the shutters to let in the cold. Over the street, the sky was moonless, a mess of stars. The cobblestones were covered with a thin dust of snow. I wet a rag and pressed it to her forehead. At length she slept.

When her eyes opened, the light in them burned. "Haelewise," she whispered, barely able to shape the word. "I'm leaving you something."

When her voice trailed off, I reached for her hand, panicked, wondering if she needed more of the draught.

"You have the gift—" she croaked. She opened her mouth, once, twice, like a fish, trying desperately to finish whatever she had wanted to say. She glanced down at her chest. After a moment, she mouthed two words, slowly, carefully: *the gift*. Her eyes went wide. A familiar tension snapped the air in the room taut. The veil lifted. My breath caught. I squeezed her hand. "Mother."

But she only stared, wide-eyed, at the rafters. Her expression terrified, her small lips pursed in an O. After a moment, her hand went limp in mine.

No. The word repeated itself in my mind. No no no—

I knelt beside her, clutching her hand tight, begging her not to leave me behind. I felt a diminishing, a pull from the next world. I watched my mother's mouth, her chest, praying for her to take another breath.

The dew that rose from her mouth was silvery, the color of water, a whisper-wind. I shivered as it passed through me on its way out of this world. My vision blurred with tears as the tension in the air collapsed. All that was left was the cold coming in through the window and my mother's body on the bed. My mother but not, her body but not. A yellowed face, glassy green eyes, swirls of graying hair.

After a while, my eyes stopped seeing the body before me, and I was aware only of the memories replaying themselves in my head. Everything my mother ever did for me, the songs she sang, the tales she told, the alchemists and healers she sought out. What she taught me about how to tell winter is coming, when the spider returns to its chamber, and how to read the meaning of birdsong in each season. Sometime later—I have no idea how long—I heard a sound behind me. Father stood in the doorway. He'd lit the rush lights in the front room. I could see his shadow-shape, blocking the light. I couldn't be sure how long he'd been there. He stood without moving, his hand on the doorframe. Then he took off his cap and bowed his head.

He knew. Relief poured through me. It would've been horrible to have to tell him. After a moment, he walked in, boots pounding the floor. Up into the rafters he stared, crossing himself. His lips moved, his expression unreadable as he said a prayer. He wouldn't meet my eyes. When he walked out, the front door slamming behind him, a terrible guilt crept into my heart. I remembered his accusation that I was the cause of my mother's illness. Out the front window I could see him moving quickly, with purpose, down the street toward the square.

I closed the shutters, then went to the cupboard to lie down, shivering with cold. I shoved the paternoster beads and the bird-mother charm into my purse, where I wouldn't have to look at them. I knew I was supposed to think my mother's death was part of God's plan, but instead, I felt betrayed. Hundreds of times, I had prayed the paternoster, and every one of those prayers had been ignored. My father's god was no better than my mother's goddess, whose "good-luck" charm, I could not help but think now, was nothing more than a glorified toy.

I didn't expect to sleep. I couldn't stop thinking about my mother's body in the next room. Her last words about leaving me something, about my having a gift. None of it made sense. Hours passed before I slept, but eventually I managed to slip out of myself. I dreamed I was cooking, throwing spice after spice into a cauldron full of ooze that smelled like onions and earth. As I stirred it, I understood it was a magical remedy. I brought a ladle of it to my mother, who still lived in the world of the dream. She drank it and got out of bed.

When I woke, it took me a moment to realize the dream wasn't real. I stared at the ceiling. My eyes burned. My heart pounded in my ears, and the smallest of sounds, a *whoosh* of sadness, strangled itself from my throat.

Time was like an endless ribbon that night. It unspooled, wrapped itself around me. Bound so tightly to each moment, I could scarcely breathe, lying on the straw in the dark cupboard. Even the rats in the walls seemed to have slowed their scrambling.

Years passed, or so it seemed. I paced the front room. Out the window, the sky was black, moonless. Stars fell, outside, in the form of snow. I went half mad before I heard the *thunk* of my father's boots, before I smelled the scent of spirits when he ducked in our door. He didn't say a word to me, but I found that I could sleep with him home.

It was noon before I woke. The house had a sweet smell, like that of some spice mixed with pine. Pushing my feet into my slippers, I tiptoed into the back room to find my mother's body gone. There was no blanket on the cot. Even the mat was stripped from its frame.

In the front room, straw smoldered in the fire ring. The house was uncomfortably warm, the air thick with smoke. My father sat at the table in the same clothes he'd worn the night before, his boots and fingernails caked in mud. There were puddles on the floor. On the table was the physician's censer, in which a single brick of charcoal glowed. A fine powdery smoke rose from it, filling the room with that sweet scent. Father nodded without speaking, his eyes going to the back door. When I looked out, I saw that the snow over the garden was firmly packed.

The sight of that snow, glittering in midday sun, destroyed me. He had buried her without me. "How could you?" I said, coming back to the front room, my voice breaking.

He stared at me, his expression vacant. Too numb, I realized, to reply. I wanted to ask whether he'd found a priest or buried Mother himself. Then I saw that the jar at the door was empty of *holpfennige*.

All this time, he had been saving for her funeral rite.

CHAPTER FIVE

T hree weeks after my mother's death, on Christmas Eve, I stared into the empty cupboard. I cursed myself for forgetting to feed the chickens. I hadn't seen them in weeks, and Father had asked me to cook Christmas dinner. It would be so simple to go into the woods beyond the south gate and shoot a pheasant, but the guards would accuse me of poaching if I tried to bring it back through the gate. Mother always used the *pfennige* she earned from selling poppets to buy ingredients for feast days. The thought of selling them without her wrecked me, but so did the idea of eating Christmas dinner alone.

The unfinished poppets leered at me from the shelves, their faces blank orbs of cloth. They would look like hobgoblins if I tried to finish them; I had yet to learn how to use a needle without pricking myself. But Mother had finished a dozen poppets before she fell ill. Selecting a Pelzmärtel doll from one shelf and a princess with a fishnet veil from another, I put them in a sack and paused at the door.

The physician's warning to stay home echoed ominously in my ears. On the peg by the door hung my mother's cloak. Bright blue, dyed her favorite color by a wortcunner that we hadn't seen in years. The dye incorporated several secret ingredients, Mother said, for good luck. Everyone else in town wore the more fashionable dark blues the dyer made. It was tempting to put on her cloak—sometimes I wore it at home, just to be enveloped in her scent—but the blue color would give me away.

Into the cupboard I went to put on my wimple and tattered gray blanket, which would hide my face if I wrapped it around me like a hooded robe. I hated the fact that I had become such a pariah. All I'd wanted since I was little was a simple life—a husband, children to cuddle and tell wonder tales, to work as a midwife. None of it seemed possible anymore.

As I walked to market, my stomach growled. The air smelled of pastry and sweetmeats. Children played in the street, throwing snowballs. Peddlers cried out, selling spice cakes and wine for Christmas Eve. The sun shone, pale and cold on the bright snow, so white it pained my eyes. Beside the stable scene that had been erected in front of the minster, a crowd of marketgoers had gathered to listen to a group of choirboys dressed as shepherds, who were singing in the language of priests. I stopped to listen, keeping my distance so no one could see my face. The song stirred something in me, a blurry memory of a Christmas Eve when my parents and I had stopped to listen to a similar choir. The memory made me so sad, I was startled when the song ended and everyone began to disperse. As the crowd streamed past, I held my breath, hoping no one would recognize me.

"Poppets!" I made myself call in a singsong voice, tugging my hood further down over my face. "Poppets for sale!"

Several children, apparently bored by the performance, came straightaway. Their mothers followed. In no time at all, I sold the dolls. No one saw through my disguise. As I purchased the ingredients for Christmas dinner, I saw a man who looked like my father strolling arm in arm with a blond woman who resembled the widow Felisberta from church. As they drew closer and I became certain it was them, I pulled down my tattered hood. My father didn't notice me as he passed, his bald head glinting in the winter light. The widow and he were drinking something from their tankards, and her three little boys were skipping and eating spice cakes behind them. My stomach turned to see my father walking with someone who wasn't my mother and her children. I hurried away, unable to bear the sight, turning to the spice cake I'd bought for comfort.

Behind the minster, I saw two young wives on the steps, wearing wimples and kirtles. Doves danced at my feet, flapping their wings. "What makes you so sure she could cure the fever?" the first woman was saying to the second.

"She's a holy healer," the second answered. "I heard she's writing a book about the healing properties of plants."

"She would never come this far. All the way down the Rhine."

"Still. I would lay odds that she could do it. They say God works through her. She has visions. She writes them down."

"She sounds like a manly woman."

The second woman laughed. "I heard she's building an abbey herself. A fortress, with a river to carry away ordure and filth. She cured a woman in Bingen with fits."

I nearly choked on my spice cake. "Who are you talking about?"

The women turned to look at me.

"Mother Hildegard," the first wife said, peering at me.

I noticed for the first time their brightly dyed kirtles, the stilted way they spoke *diutsch*. Their long, ribboned braids, which my mother called corpse-braids because they were extended with hair from the dead. They were courtiers' wives. The first woman peered under my hood. "Aren't you the midwife's girl?"

"The one who cursed the tanner?" The other squinted at my face. "It's her. Get back!"

My heart beat in my throat. "I didn't curse anyone!" I shouted as I ran away. My feet pounded the cobblestones. I didn't stop until I ran out of breath in the alley behind the furrier's shop. Hunched and wheezing, I chastised myself. It had been foolish to address the women at all. As I caught my breath, I shivered. The air seemed to thin. Not now, I thought. Not here—

But happen it did. I felt the pull. My soul left my flesh.

When I came to, I was on my back in the slush, my hood fallen from my face. The furrier's sons had seen me faint. "You shouldn't be out," the younger boy sneered, blocking the alleyway, making the same gesture the miller's sister had in the square. "You'll loose your demon on someone else."

I stood, a flurry of fear in my stomach. The elder son leered and nudged his little brother. Following their gaze, I saw the budding swell of my breast, exposed by a rip in my dress. I had been so preoccupied with my grief that I hadn't noticed my own blossoming. I felt myself blush as I covered my chest.

The elder brother advanced on me, his muscles taut, like a snake about to strike. I leapt in the other direction, pushing his little brother out of my way, so that he slipped and fell face-first into the snow. As I fled the alleyway, I saw the blood, a beautiful red bloom on the snow where his nose smacked the stones.

On Christmas Day, Father walked home with me from Mass. As soon as we arrived at the hut, we washed our hands, and I sat down at the kitchen table to chop the ingredients for dinner. Father didn't speak at first. He only stood by the window watching me, the winter sun shining at his back, making a too-bright halo around his scalp.

"You'll be needing a woman's shift soon," Father said, watching me chop. "It's about time. What are you, sixteen now?"

I nodded, embarrassed.

He fished some *holpfennige* from his pouch and set them on the table, then pulled a bag of candied fruit from his pack and set them beside the coins. "I thought we should have something sweet, since it's Christmas."

His thoughtfulness took me by surprise. I noticed the shadows under his eyes, the sadness in his tone. All the sorrow I held inside me threatened to tumble out. "I miss Mother so much," I said suddenly. My voice shook.

Father sighed. "Don't despair, Haelewise. It's ungodly."

"It's only been three weeks."

He looked at me sharply. I racked my brain for something neutral for us to talk about. All day, as I cooked, I had daydreamed about making a pilgrimage to Hildegard's abbey. "What do you know of Mother Hildegard?"

He shook his head derisively. "A woman? Building an abbey, curing disease, writing holy books. She might as well be a character from one of your mother's stories."

"I thought she might be able to cure my fainting spells."

"She damn well might. They say she can do everything else. But Bingen is awful far. How would you get there?"

I sighed. Not how can I help you get there, but how would you do it yourself. "I'm still working that out."

Father sighed, going to the cupboard for the physician's censer. He filled it with charcoal and powder and brought it to the fire. It clattered on the table as he set it down, the crosses carved into its side leaking a familiar fragrant smoke.

"What are you doing?"

"Cleansing the house."

"Of what?"

He frowned. "Your mother's sins."

I couldn't believe my ears. Did he blame my mother for her illness? Did he think God struck her down for her "sins"? I shook my head, trying to shake these thoughts from my mind, but I couldn't. Outrage filled my heart.

Father looked away, watching the smoke swirl from the censer and up through the roof holes.

I thought of what he said about blaming me for my mother's death. I wanted to scream at him. "Would you please tell me why you think me responsible for Mother's illness?"

He pulled his gaze from the smoke, his thoughts clearly elsewhere. After a moment, he opened his mouth, then closed it, as if he were trying for once to measure his words. "What I should have said was I blame your mother for your demon."

I stared at him, waiting for him to explain.

The words tumbled out of him, as if he had wanted to say this for a long time. "You know the upbringing your mother had, deep in the dark forest north of town. Your grandmother whispered wicked incantations. When we first met, there was a darkness, a wildness in your mother. After I asked her to marry me, she vowed to forget all that, but your mother never was one for keeping her word. All those unnatural remedies she got for your spells in secret, the unholy incantations she muttered under her breath. Don't think I didn't hear them. When I stopped sharing her bed, she even broke our wedding vows." He hesitated, watching my face, his eyes going wide. "Mother of God!" he thundered. "Did she tell you everything?"

I shook my head. I didn't want to betray her trust. "I don't know what you mean."

"Damn it, Haelewise." It was clear he didn't believe me. He grabbed my hand across the table. His temper flared, as it always did when I refused to do as told. His fingers pinched my wrist, twisting my arm. "Don't lie to me. What did she tell you?"

My eyes watered. I made myself still, counting the holes in the censer. Its smoke tickled my nostrils. It was pungent like a spice, but impossibly sweet, recalling scents I'd smelled in the market as a girl. Cinnamon and anise, fennel and sage. Whatever he was burning was like none and all of them.

"That she visited the wise woman to get a potion."

He let go of my wrist, looking oddly relieved. "Is that all?"

My chest tightened. I made myself nod. "I swear it."

He sighed with relief, closing his eyes. It was a moment before he spoke, his voice matter-of-fact. "I have something to tell you. Do you remember Felisberta? From church?"

My heart beat in my ears. Felisberta was the name of the blond woman I had seen him with in the square. I nodded, afraid I knew where this was going.

"Her husband died of the fever. She has three sons. Her kin have abandoned her. Father Emich has encouraged me to marry her."

My stomach dropped. I could scarcely breathe. I thought of how much my mother had given up for him.

He couldn't meet my eyes. "I'd ask you to come with me to live with her, but she's afraid of your demon. She has her boys to think of."

His words shocked me. I had endured his fickle feelings for me all my life, but I didn't think he would be *this* cruel. Not only was he replacing my mother, but he was going to leave me behind because his new wife didn't want me in her house? No other girls my age lived by themselves. "Have you given any thought as to what this will mean for me?"

"I'll visit once a week. I'll bring fish and cheese. It won't be much different from the way things are now."

I stared at the wall, with a choked feeling in my throat that lasted all through Christmas dinner. As my father babbled about Felisberta's virtues, my eyes watered. The fish and candied fruit stuck in my throat. I kept thinking of the Frenchwoman who was stoned in the street for preaching the gospel of Mary Magdalene. If my father abandoned me and I had another spell in the square, the townspeople would burn me at the stake.

I spent Christmas night in a sort of stupor, trying to come to terms with his abandonment. I kept wishing stupidly that my mother were still alive to comfort me, or that Matthäus would hurry up and come home.

Father came back the next day with Felisberta, driving a cart hitched to an old gray ass. They took almost everything—all of our chairs and trunks—leaving behind only the earthenware jars in the cupboard, the kitchen table, the pallet where I slept, and my mother's trunk. Felisberta tried to take that too, but when she bent down to sift through it, Father stopped her. "That belonged to Haelewise's mother," he told her, his voice gruff with kindness. "Leave it for her."

Tears stung my eyes. My heart swelled. After everything he'd done, I still wanted his love, even though—or perhaps *because*—I knew how rare it was. As soon as they left, I went through the trunk, eager to find out what my father wanted me to have. It was filled with my mother's old linen dresses and smocks, most of them dyed her favorite shade of blue. My heart broke when I brought the fabric to my nose and breathed in her scent. There was a wimple she had discarded because it was torn. A pair of old boots. And beneath that, a small wooden box carved with a simple pattern. Pulling it out, I tried to open it, then realized it was locked.

A lockbox? I didn't know we had one.

The key from the aniseed pot. When I inserted it into the lock and turned it, the lock clicked. Inside, I found a tarnished gold hand-mirror wrapped in a blue silk cloth, its handle engraved with strange symbols and birds. Awed, I remembered the shoemaker's story about seeing the queen with one of these. Why would my mother have one? How would she own something so expensive?

Unwrapping the cloth, I saw that the looking glass had been smashed.

The lake began to freeze the next week, the tidepools near the docks whitening with thin scrims of ice. The winter before, I'd enjoyed stamping on them on daily walks. But since my run-in with the furrier's sons, I was reluctant to leave the hut. I spent most of my time sitting in the garden and trying to make up recipes for meals from what little food I had available at home. More than once, I heard a nine-killer shriek its hellish song from the garden wall, and I crept up and shot it—though the bird, in truth, was too small to eat.

From time to time, I took out the smashed hand-mirror and wondered how much about my mother there was that I didn't know. I fantasized about traveling to Hildegard's abbey. If Matthäus convinced his father to let him marry me, they might be able to afford to send me to her abbey for a cure. Every time I went to market, I took less-traveled streets, checking frequently that my makeshift hood hid my face. I avoided the street with the furrier's shop, choosing the street with the tailor's shop instead. If I saw Matthäus's father inside, I would know that Matthäus had returned from Zürich. But it was always his mother within. At night I dreamed that he came home and knocked on my door with good news: His father had agreed to a love match. And just like that, all my troubles were gone, that is, until I awoke.

At first, Father kept his promise and visited once a week for dinner. He brought food to share, smelly cheese and salted fish. But as time passed, he began to forget. Sometimes he forgot the cheese, other times he forgot the fish. One day, a few weeks before Lent, he showed up empty-handed and left when I didn't have anything to cook. I realized I'd have to buy ingredients myself if I wanted to eat with him.

The next day, disguised in my old blanket-cloak, I sold another completed doll to buy food. As I was purchasing flour, I saw a new face, a town crier I'd never seen before. A big man, ruddy-faced, his voice too loud as he moved from group to group with a scroll. Each time he moved to a new cluster of people, he spoke to them, eyes flashing, expression animated, too far away for me to hear. Each time he finished his speech, there was an exchange: I saw one woman give him a wineskin; another gave him a kiss. After that, he lowered his voice. The women gasped at what he said next, and the crier moved on. When he approached me, the look on his face turned my stomach. I picked up my things to go.

"Where you hurryin' off to," he slurred, following as I rushed down the street that led from the square. I could smell the wine on his breath. "Don't you want to hear the news from his imperial and royal majesty? I'll read the official decree tomorrow, but you can learn it now, if you earn my favor—"

"I have nothing for you."

"It's about the princess."

Something inside me snapped. Selling the poppets had been nerve-racking; by now, I had no patience left. "Leave me alone."

His expression hardened. He grabbed my arm and yanked me into an alley, twisting it behind my back. Too late, I realized my mistake. The crier expected to get what he asked for or else. As the crier pushed me into the wall, my eyes fell on the seal on his scroll: a golden shield with a pattern of black lions. The king's sigil. When he kissed me, I closed my eyes, wishing my soul would leave my body.

"That's how it works," he sneered. "Favor for information. Understand?"

I nodded, glaring at him. He let go of my arm.

"Princess Frederika has fled the castle," he growled. "She's headed this way. If you see her, King Frederick commands you to report it immediately, on pain of death."

CHAPTER SIX

T he last few weeks before Lent were miserable. I was hungry. I was lonely. I was afraid to go out. But I had to sell my mother's poppets to buy food until the spring vegetables ripened, so go out I did, stealing to the market in my tattered blanket-cloak. I smudged my face and clothes to make myself unattractive to bachelors so I would be dismissed as a beggar or worse. I found out soon enough there was freedom in such a disguise. Once I had sold all of the poppets, no one noticed me. Not nobles, not merchants, not even children playing in the streets.

By Ash Wednesday, there was nothing left on my mother's shelves but Gütel and a few unfinished poppets that wouldn't sell. Dolls without clothes, jesters without arms, blank-faced princesses with half-finished crowns. I would make a mess of them if I tried to finish them by myself. It was barely light out when I tied my hair back, pulled on my blanket, and hurried out to see if Matthäus was back from Zürich. Spring had yet to chase away winter's chill, so early in the morning. Even in the blanket, it was freezing.

My heart fluttered when I turned onto his street. How I prayed he was home. It had been so long since I'd seen him. Maybe he would have good news for me about his father. His house stretched above the tailor shop, its roof piercing the gray sky. Staring up at it, I couldn't help but wonder what it would be like to live there with him. Their house wasn't stone like the houses of nobles, but it had a dignity of its own. The crossbeams, the thatching. It had six large windows, a staircase, and two floors.

As I drew near, the orange cat we'd saved as a kitten—now a

huge tomcat, missing an ear from street fights—pressed himself against my legs, purring. I petted him absent-mindedly, looking for a pebble to throw at the window of the upstairs room where Matthäus and his brothers slept. The pebble clattered against the shutters. My breath puffed up in desperate, frigid clouds. "Hsst."

Nothing happened for a moment, apart from the sleet that fell on my nose. Then the shutters opened and Matthäus leaned out in his nightcap. The sight of him was like a balm. Relief washed through me. My breath caught in my throat.

"Haelewise? Is that you?"

I tried to master my feelings. "Can you come down?"

"Of course." Three smaller faces appeared beside his. I heard his brothers protest as Matthäus told them to get back to bed.

When Matthäus opened the door, my stomach fluttered. Had he been this tall when he left for Zürich? Had I forgotten how good-looking he was? Even disheveled in his nightshirt, brown hair falling into his eyes beneath his cap, he was startlingly handsome. When he smiled at me, my hopes soared. I had missed him so much.

"I wasn't sure it was you," he said, nodding at my clothes.

I looked down. "I didn't want to be recognized."

"I'm so sorry about your mother," Matthäus said. He pulled me to him, his eyes haunted with sorrow. "Mother told me last night."

In his embrace, my grief arose from where it had been lying in wait. My eyes burned, and I felt myself crumple in his arms. I wanted him to hold me like this forever.

"I'm so sorry," he whispered, pulling back to look at me. "I know how close you were. I'm going to miss her too."

I didn't know what to say. There was a knot in my throat. I wiped my face with the blanket, suddenly aware that my nose was running. "When did you get back?"

"Only yesterday."

"I'm sorry to wake you," I said, trying not to sound desperate. "The chickens flew away. I forgot to feed them. I need help finishing the last of my mother's poppets so I can sell them to buy food."

"Your father isn't providing for you?"

"He married the widow Felisberta."

Matthäus's eyes widened with anger. "*Married*—so soon?"

"Aye," I said curtly, my own anger at my father rearing up. "Mother died in December. He moved into her house the day after Christmas. I've been living alone, selling poppets for money."

"He didn't invite you to move with him?"

I shook my head, pressing my lips together tight.

The sympathy on his face was unbearable. Suddenly aware of how wretched I must seem, I lifted my chin. "I wouldn't have gone if he did."

He shook his head. "Let me go tell my father."

As soon as he went inside, I wiped my face carefully with the blanket. I smoothed its cloth, wishing I had worn something more presentable. I'd become so used to leaving the house in this blanket that I hadn't spared a thought for how he would see me.

As I waited for him to come out, the street grew visibly lighter. I thought about how Matthäus had promised to see me as soon as he got back. The fact that he was taking so long, that he hadn't come to see me right away, did not bode well. If he'd fixed things with his father, wouldn't he have come to tell me right away? By the time he came back out, my heart was full of dread.

He'd changed into his day clothes, put on his overshirt, and stuck a needle in his cape. His expression was difficult to read. "Sorry that took so long. It was hard to convince him to give me the morning off."

My heart fluttered. I opened my mouth to ask whether he'd talked to his father, then decided I wasn't ready. His father's reluctance to let him help me this morning was a bad sign.

We started the walk back to my house, our footsteps echoing through the largely empty street. The only other person we saw was a woman emptying a chamber pot.

"I'm sorry I didn't come to see you yesterday," Matthäus said. "I wanted to, but my father was insistent I see someone else first."

"Who?"

"Phoebe of Kürenberg."

I knew of the Kürenbergers. They owned estates in the foothills of the mountains in the northern forest and a beautiful cottage on the banks of the lake.

"Did she need to be fitted?"

He heaved a great sigh. "Unfortunately not."

"Why did your father want you to meet with her?"

He looked pained. Dread knotted my stomach. I had to ask. I couldn't wait any longer. "Matthäus. Did you talk to your father?"

"Haelewise—"

"What aren't you telling me?"

He couldn't meet my eyes. "The conversation didn't go well."

I knew he was going to say something along those lines, but hearing him say it was devastating.

"I'm working on it," he said quickly. "I promise—"

My thoughts whirled. All that hoping I'd done, all that praying. I felt like I was going to be sick.

"Haelewise, I mean it. I'm trying to get through to him. My mother's on my side."

He met my eyes.

I took a deep breath. "Thank you for telling me."

A long moment passed before either of us spoke. Our footsteps echoed on the cobblestones.

"I missed you," he said finally.

The look on my face must've been wretched.

After a moment, he changed the subject. "Did you hear about Princess Ursilda's wedding?"

"No," I admitted, trying hard to keep my voice even.

"Her father finally convinced a prince to marry her," Matthäus went on. "The wedding is next week. Father finished her dress yesterday. He won't stop joking about sewing wolf-fur onto the sleeves to match her brother's coat."

Matthäus kept up a stream of chatter about the wedding, and eventually I regained my faculties enough to pay attention. King Frederick would be attending, and he'd ordered a dress for his runaway daughter in case she turned up. Apparently Ursilda and Frederika were friends, and Frederika had been betrothed to Ursilda's brother, Prince Ulrich, before she fled.

That detail caught my attention. I stopped in my tracks. Prince Ulrich with the wolf-skin? "No wonder Frederika ran off!"

Matthäus nodded. "I know."

"Why would he promise his daughter to Ulrich?"

He sighed. "I can only guess that he doesn't believe the stories."

When we got to the hut, I started a fire, then set out the unfinished poppets on the table with my mother's scraps. Bald princes and princesses whose legs were unstuffed, half-clad dukes in sad little capes and nothing else. We planned out seven poppets and began sewing dresses and trousers, threading yarn into scalps. I kept pricking myself with my needle and cursing. The third time it happened, Matthäus stopped me, putting his hand on mine. "Haelewise, will you grant me a request?"

I looked up at him, hopeful. My skin tingled where our hands touched. The look in his eyes said he felt it too. He opened his mouth, his expression dazed, then closed it. His thoughts were clear on his face. He wanted me, and not only that: He was surprised by the strength of his desire. I took his hand in mine and clasped it tightly, smiling at him, praying his request would have something to do with *us*.

But then, as he looked down at our hands, something shifted inside him. "Give me the needle," he said, pulling his hand back, his expression resigned.

A moan of protest escaped my lips.

"You can't sew," he said, laughing, turning his attention to the task at hand. "Tell me a story instead."

I turned away so he couldn't see my disappointment. You can easily entertain him, I told myself, you're good at this. I forced myself to focus, to think about the kind of story that would be best for this moment. I knew Matthäus liked stories inspired by real-life nobles, stories about illnesses cured and injustice made right. But bitterness poisoned my thoughts. All the ideas that came to mind were tawdry yarns that I knew he wouldn't like. Scandalous stories that ended badly. I wasn't in the mood to please him.

Resigning myself to a story I would enjoy telling, I smirked and began the tale. "In stories old, there was a beautiful young queen who couldn't have children. She shared her husband's bed every night for years, but her belly never swelled."

Matthäus blinked at the reference to sex, freezing in the act of threading his needle.

I leaned in closer toward him, our shoulders almost touching, eyebrows raised, my voice an earthy whisper. "The queen drank the royal healer's teas. She prayed. She tried all the herbs the king's monks gave her, all the tricks the midwives recommended, but her belly stayed as flat as a board. Eventually, she heard rumors the king would seek an annulment. She sent for a witch from the forest who knew the hidden properties of plants. In secret, the queen asked the witch for a draught that would help her conceive. 'Life can only be wrought from life,' the witch told her in her raspy voice. 'There will be a cost.'"

Matthäus sat up perfectly straight. Part of me felt bad. I understood what I was doing. Using my body to remind him of his feelings for me. Intentionally trying to throw him off balance, telling him a tale that would disturb him. And yet, I couldn't make myself stop. I was angry, deep down, that Matthäus hadn't stood up to his father, angry that his father was keeping us apart.

"The queen didn't care," I said, defiant. "There was nothing she wouldn't give up for a child. The witch made her an unnatural elixir. That night, she kept the king awake for many hours."

By this point, Matthäus had gone completely still, his face bright red. There was a part of me that enjoyed it.

"The next winter, her belly swelled big and round. She laughed and sang. She was hot all the time, no matter how cold it was. When her time drew near, it became difficult for her to sleep. She stayed up all night, embroidering tiny dresses, sitting on the sill with the window open, gazing out. One night while she was sewing, she pricked herself. A droplet of blood fell to the snow. The blood spattered, and a flower grew where it landed. Bright red, it was, the most *frightful* rose."

Matthäus watched me, puzzled about where the story was going, but I could see that a part of him was entertained despite himself. A faint smile haunted his lips. I focused on the interested part of him—that part deep inside, which loved stories for their own sake—and spoke to it.

"From the petals of that rose there came a fairy," I pushed on. My voice rose. "A wicked nymph with hair the color of night and skin the color of snow. Her hair was a tangle of black thorns, and her lips were blood-red. She sang a terrible tune:

> *"Life from life! Snow White is my name.*
> *Your child will die in three days' time*
> *unless you make it her name too."*

He looked taken aback at the fairy's threat, setting down his needle. "By thunder," he swore. "What did she do?"

I smiled, triumphant that my tale had grabbed him. "She cried out. Her ladies-in-waiting came running. But the fairy had vanished by the time they arrived, leaving only the rose. Barefoot, distraught, in her nightgown, the queen rushed outside to pluck the flower. Only by the time she got there, the rose was gone. When she returned to her chamber—her toes covered in snow, her breathing labored—she had her first pangs. Her labor lasted three nights before the midwife finally told her to push."

Matthäus leaned forward, waiting for me to continue. I smiled at him, proud that my storytelling had made him so enrapt.

"The queen was so exhausted by the time the baby came that she thought she couldn't go on. When she finally held her daughter in her arms and saw the strangeness of the girl's features—her white skin, her red lips, her black hair—she knew what she had done: traded her own life for that of the girl. She drew the child to her breast to nurse, her eyes full of tears."

Matthäus stared at me, horrified.

I held up my finger. "She called for the king and told him they had to name the child immediately. Snow White, she insisted, so her sacrifice wouldn't be in vain. Then—her heart breaking—she fell into a swoon. She died the next day."

Matthäus dropped the poppet he was holding.

I waited an appropriate time before I went on. I had learned this from my mother, from the bishop's physician. A death is significant, important. A death requires a pause. "The king didn't take his wife's death well. His grief made him weak. Within a month, he was remarried. His new bride, Golden Braids, was a powerful witch who had preyed upon him in his grief. She carried a gold hand-mirror in which she could see the whole of the kingdom. She wore a magic yellow shawl made from her own hair."

I made my eyes widen with the alarm I knew Matthäus would feel at the queen's unnatural magic. Every good story needs a villain of some sort, and I was still angry about Felisberta. I saw no reason not to choose the stepmother for this one.

"As Snow White grew more beautiful, the aging Golden Braids became envious. The girl's lips were red. Roses blushed in her cheeks. She reminded the king of his late wife, whom he still seemed to mourn. When the girl turned twelve, Golden Braids convinced the king to promise Snow White to a wicked prince. Unbeknownst to the king, the prince turned into a wolf on the night of every full moon."

I paused here, overwhelmed, falling into the story, sympathizing with the characters. The grieving king. The fairy daughter. For a moment, I almost sympathized with the queen. "Snow White fled the castle on horseback, black hair twisting behind her. The king asked the queen to use her mirror to find her. But the queen lied to him, saying the mirror only showed mist. In truth, the queen could see Snow White in the mirror: The innocent girl lay in a clearing, fast asleep. After the king went to bed, Golden Braids closed her eyes and murmured a spell that made the night-birds hungry. The evil queen watched in the wonder-mirror, as night-herons and owls flew into the clearing. They hovered above Snow White, landing in the branches of nearby trees. The queen kept chanting the incantation, until there were hundreds of birds in the clearing. She didn't stop until the birds pecked Snow White to death."

Matthäus gasped.

"That's it," I said, my voice flat. "That's the end."

Matthäus paused, sitting up straight. He picked up the poppet he had been sewing and stared at it as if it were a foreign thing. For a long moment, he was silent, examining the poppet. Then he went back to sewing, his voice taking on a thoughtful tone. "Call me a fool. I don't know. Only a fool expects all to turn out well in life. But I prefer tales that give the listener hope."

CHAPTER SEVEN

Matthäus didn't come back to my hut for a long time after that. Whether this was because of his father or my story, I didn't know. I was terribly lonely without him, deeply regretful that my bitterness had gotten the better of me. I turned my story over and over in my mind, wishing I had told it differently.

The blooming of my mother's garden, that spring, nearly brought me to tears. Every time a new stem burst from the earth, my head filled with memories of kneeling beside her, learning how to plant seeds or identify seedlings. Each new stem bore a name she had taught me. Endive and spinach, sprouts and asparagus. Sometimes I heard the music of her voice as she taught me their names, sweetened by a mother's love for her daughter, and my heart broke. Other times, the sight of a new cluster of seedlings infuriated me. How dare they thrive—so steadfast, predictable—after their gardener was plucked from the earth?

These betrayals were closely followed by an uprising of flowers. Bloom after bloom of dainty blue primrose, followed by turnip flowers and frothy yellow lady's mantle. There were new seedlings everywhere, as if turning the earth had inspired old seeds to grow. Turnip and parsnip grew too close to the wall. Each morning, I stood over them, wrapped in my tattered robe, wondering where my father had laid my mother to rest. Was her head beneath the spinach or the primrose? Did the lilies grow over her toes?

One morning, when I went out to weed, I noticed a new plant I didn't recognize among the lilies, a plant for which my mother never taught me a name. A green stem, twisting up from the soil, with a single purple bud on its tip. Within a few weeks, another plant of its kind sprang up beside it. The next week, more appeared. By May there were dozens of them, scattered across the back of the garden. Strange bushes with leaves like wild lettuce, a bouquet of tiny purple buds at their centers. Light-thieves, my mother would've called them. Weeds. I couldn't bring myself to pull them up.

By summer's end, they were everywhere, healthy cabbage-like bushes with huge leaves a foot tall and three feet wide. At the center of each where the flowers once bloomed grew tiny nutlike globes, wild green fruit like none I had ever seen before. As the weeks passed, the berries grew larger, their skins turning yellow.

What happened next should have come as no surprise. Matthäus was over a year older than me, eighteen, nearing the end of his apprenticeship. I hadn't seen him in months. Phoebe of Kürenberg was twenty-one or twenty-two. If her father didn't marry her off soon, it would be too late. When the priest announced Matthäus's betrothal to Phoebe during the marriage banns, I was standing in my usual spot behind the rail at the back of the church, near the beggar who often sought alms on the minster steps, where I wouldn't accidentally sit next to anyone who would recognize me. As soon as the priest said the words *Matthäus, son-of-Heinrich-the-Tailor*, I was struck with the worst headache I'd ever felt.

I clutched the rail, white-knuckled. The beggar met my eyes. "A marriage," he breathed. "Is that what drives you away?"

"Away?" I whispered. "Where would I go?"

He didn't answer.

The priest droned on. The church swam around me. I felt nauseated, as if my body wanted to reject what my ears had heard. Calm down, I told myself. Of course Matthäus is marrying the Kürenberg girl. Did you think that you had mesmerized him, somehow, with your blind-bat eyes and dazzling wit? How could he possibly convince his father to let him marry *you*?

Somehow I made it through the service. Afterward, I saw Matthäus leaving with Phoebe, her wheat-colored plaits wound around her head like a crown. She wore a rich green dress that clung to her hips. She was a woman, much more so than me, that was clear. Never before had I hated anyone so much.

When I got home from church, for the rest of the day, I couldn't eat. I couldn't sleep. There is a limit to the amount of loss one person can take; I had already endured more than my share. It seemed unjust for the world to take Matthäus too. It was as if the gods were testing me to find out the limit of what I could take.

The next morning, exhausted, I went out to the back garden to try to make peace with what had happened. I thought I would sit on the broken bench and say a prayer. I'd hoped sitting outside among the plants and vines and stones would calm me, but instead I found myself haunted with memories of my mother. Sitting on that bench, I remembered a spring day we were turning the earth for planting, when a family of robins jumped down from a nest they had made in the back garden wall. The robins had fluttered down, fluting and warbling, to search the freshly dug earth for worms. One of them landed on her skirt, and Mother's laughter had been brilliant.

Searching the garden wall, now, I saw that the nest was long gone, the robins nowhere to be seen. The garden had never been large or well groomed, but I had let it go wild over the summer now that Mother wasn't here to take care of it. The stones of its wall were covered in moss and vines, and several rocks had come loose. The sod we'd pushed into the gaps between stones each year had eroded, leaving holes through which you could see the docks behind the house. It occurred to me that if I didn't intervene, it was only a matter of years before the wall would succumb to the ravages of time. It appeared that nothing in the world could escape that fate.

As I was contemplating this, I heard a muffled sound: a voice calling my name. "Who's there?" I called over the wall.

"Matthäus."

My chest went tight. The last time I'd seen him, I was wearing a tattered blanket. Here I was again, a mess, my hair unkempt, my boots covered in dirt. I tried to think of a reason to turn him away, but couldn't. I went inside and opened the front door a crack. I could see him on the other side, his dark hair straying into his gray eyes. So handsome, I wanted to jump in the lake.

"I came to explain my betrothal."

"You don't owe me anything."

He met my eyes through the crack, his expression pleading. "My father arranged it."

I narrowed my eyes. "What's she like? Your intended."

"Phoebe has a terrible temper and a cruel laugh. She's pregnant with another man's child."

"She's what?" I opened the door.

He stepped into the front room. "She was engaged to another man, who ran off. Her father made an offer mine couldn't refuse. A title. A cottage on the lake. Favor with the bishop-prince."

I shook my head. "Another man's child?"

"I don't want her." He brushed his hair back from his face, completely unaware of how handsome he was. "I wish it was you instead."

It was the one, the only thing he could have said to win me over. I took a deep breath. We stared at each other, becoming conscious of the space between us. He took my hand and squeezed it, then stepped close enough for me to see the green flecks in his eyes. "When my father demanded I court Phoebe, I was furious. But he said he would disown me, prevent me from working as a tailor altogether, if I didn't go through with it."

Listening to him say all of this now, when he was already betrothed to someone else, was torture. "Why are you telling me this?"

He was quiet for a long time. "You want me to say it?"

I could hardly look at him, it hurt so much. "Whatever it is, yes."

Silence filled the room. When he finally spoke, he looked at his feet, his voice husky with feeling. "I have to marry her, but I want you."

At first I wasn't sure what he meant.

He looked up at me furtively, his embarrassment clear on his face. "I've missed you terribly," he said. "I know my father's plans for me have hurt you, but I can't imagine my life without you. My father said we could provide for you. We met a physician in Zürich who said he could cure your spells."

Provide for me? A physician in Zürich—

I realized, suddenly, what he was offering. He wanted me to be his mistress. The realization was like a bucket of cold water poured over my head. "*What?*"

"My father said he doesn't care what we do, as long as I marry Phoebe. He even spoke to Phoebe's father about it."

I gaped at him, unable to make sense of what he was saying. My lips had gone dry. My thoughts were tangled.

"What does Phoebe think of this arrangement?"

"She couldn't care less. She only needs a husband so her child isn't a bastard."

I stared at him dumbly.

"It's a way for us to be together."

I took a deep breath. "It isn't, though."

"Why not? We could even have children."

A wild anger streaked through me. "I want a *family*, Matthäus. No one would let someone's mistress into their house to attend a birth. Our children would be bastards! Have you thought this through at all?"

My voice was shaking.

He blinked at me. Clearly, he hadn't considered it from my perspective. "No," he admitted. "I'm sorry. I guess I haven't."

"Leave," I said, walking to the door and opening it. "I can't stand the sight of you right now."

He looked positively shattered as he walked out.

The truth was, I didn't want to cry in front of him.

Two weeks later, he knocked on my door again. This time, I made him wait. I washed my face and pulled on one of my mother's shifts from her trunk, a beautiful bright blue kirtle with a ribbon that would emphasize my waist. I pulled my braids out from under my wimple so he could see them. Then I opened the door partway. "What do you want?" I said flatly.

"I'm sorry." He looked miserable, like he hadn't slept since we last talked. There were dark shadows under his eyes; his expression was tortured. "I should've thought more about what I was suggesting."

I glared at him. He deserved a couple sleepless weeks. There was no way he'd had as difficult a time as I had. "You should've."

"I understand that you can't accept, Haelewise. You deserve a proper husband. Unfortunately for me, I can't be that for you."

He waited for me to respond. When I didn't, he went on.

"I made you something."

He shrugged off a pack I hadn't noticed he was wearing, withdrawing two fur boots and a madder-red bundle of cloth. A dress, I realized as he held it up, dyed my favorite color. With an embroidered neck, a petticoat sewn into it, and bell-shaped sleeves with golden trim. Lacing down the sides so it could be tightened to fit my frame. "It's beautiful," I breathed, despite myself, awed. It was like a sunset trapped and shining in cloth.

He smiled nervously. "I worked on it every night, after I finished at the shop. I hardly slept."

My thoughts raced. "Matthäus. I don't understand."

He reached into his pack again and pulled out a madder-red cloak with a deep embroidered hood. He pulled it up so I could see it. The trim of the hood shimmered, golden. So fine, each of its threads seemed to shimmer with magic. I touched the trim, the brooch—I'd never owned a brooch—overwhelmed, suddenly, at the beauty of his gesture.

"Matthäus. Why would you make me a dress?"

"I love you." He said the words simply, matter-of-factly, as if there could be no argument against them. There was no show of emotion, no grand gesture, but there were tears in his eyes. When I saw those tears, for the first time, I understood the torment that gave birth to his proposal. He loved me. Everything stopped when I understood this—my breath, my heart—I swear, even the sun and the moon stopped moving. He wanted me as badly as I wanted him, but he saw no way out of marrying Phoebe.

My anger at him began to thaw. "I love you too," I said softly.

He met my eyes. "Come to the wedding."

I gawked at him. My mouth went dry. "Why would I do that? Why would you want me there? Are you mad?"

His expression was pleading, almost ashamed. "I want to look at you as I speak my vows."

His words hung in the air. Otherwise the hut was silent. My lips parted, and a tiny gasp escaped my mouth. Something inside me cracked open.

He reached for me, but I moved out of his grasp, afraid of what would happen if I let him touch me. I didn't trust myself.

"Come to the wedding," he said again. "Please."

"I don't know if I can bear it," I said, my voice husky with feeling. "Let me think on it."

CHAPTER EIGHT

The night before the wedding, I went down to the docks to bathe. I was as anxious as I would've been if I were the one getting married. I couldn't stop thinking about Matthäus's offer. On one hand, it was impossible. I couldn't bear to share him with another woman, and I was already such a pariah. There were women in town who lived alone—so-called widows and maidens—who we all knew were anything but. Everyone gossiped. The children sang dirty songs. I would be shunned and called a whore.

On the other hand, I *wanted* to be with him. Deep down, I wanted it more than anything. With my mother dead and my father gone, Matthäus was all I had left. How could I survive by myself with no trade, no way of earning money? Could I really live off the garden and the food my father would forget to bring? He had never even taught me to fish.

At the lakeshore, I peeled off everything but my underthings, thankful the lantern-light was scarce. Mud squished between my toes as I steadied myself on the edge of a dock. Wading in, I cleaned my fingernails to ensure they would be clean. I wet my hair and scrubbed my arms until my flesh was raw. For a moment, I was aware only of the stars, the cold water numbing my skin. Then I remembered what was happening tomorrow. Chills bloomed on my skin, and I felt a pull.

The next thing I knew, I was choking on the muddy lake bottom. I coughed, gasping involuntarily, before I could control my movements enough to stand upright.

Unsteady, I grabbed the dock. My limbs were numb. My lungs

burned. The tide slapped the dock. I closed my eyes, felt the mud between my toes, and thought about how foolish it'd be to try to live alone. I couldn't even bathe without endangering myself.

Back home, I undressed before the fire, then warmed my hands and brushed out my hair. Firelight leapt around the room.

When my shift was dry, I decided to try on the dress and cloak Matthäus had made. I wanted to see myself the way he would see me tomorrow, if I decided to go to the wedding. The linen of the dress sighed as I pulled it over my head. The fabric hugged my small breasts as I laced the sides. I smoothed it down over my belly, then pulled on the cloak, the golden trim glittering on its sleeves. They were tight at the top, with long and beautiful pendant cuffs. I wanted to cry. How could I watch Matthäus marry someone else?

When the door creaked open, I was asking this question of the crackling flames. "I thought I'd check on you—" Father was saying as he turned the latch. He trailed off in midsentence. "Hedda," he breathed as the door clapped shut behind him.

I turned, confused that he had spoken my mother's name. "Father? It's me."

Apart from the firelight, the house was dark. "I know," he said, but there was something about his tone. He stepped into the light, frowning at me, his expression stern. "Where did you get those clothes?"

I looked down at my cloak. He'd called me by Mother's name. When had she ever dressed in fine clothes? I tried to call up my memories of my grandmother's house, but my memories of my grandmother were shadowy flashes. An ample bosom, dark hair. Shiny apples she kept in her apron, a cauldron bubbling with stew. There was no telling how wealthy she was.

"Answer me."

"Tomorrow is Matthäus's wedding. He made this for me to wear."

Father stiffened. "At what cost?"

"As a gesture of friendship," I stammered. "I didn't have anything appropriate."

He eyed me, suspicious. "Why would you even want to go? I thought you wanted to marry the boy yourself."

My face grew hot.

Father gave me a knowing look, shaking his head with disapproval. "What is it the wise women in your mother's stories say? There is always a cost."

I was up so late that night, trying to decide whether to go to the wedding, my body nearly made the decision for me. I slept until the church bells rang, when there was barely enough time to dress. But I knew, as soon as I opened my eyes, that I would go. I wanted to hear Matthäus speak his vows to me. I hurried to get ready, pulling my new clothes over my head and pulling back my hair.

Then I rushed down the street toward the minster. Mass had already started. I could see the top of Matthäus's head next to Phoebe's blond braids in the Kürenberg pew. The sight of them together made my heart ache. As the priest droned on, all I could think about was how much I hated her. I found myself unable to do anything but glare at her, beset with hate.

After Mass, I hurried outside. A crowd gathered on the steps to see Matthäus and Phoebe's union blessed. Doves cried out mournfully, as if they shared my feelings about the event. Matthäus exited the church first in a fine corded shirt and pants, distracted, his eyes methodically searching the crowd. Phoebe followed him, her dress whipping in the wind, a long gown with an elaborate blue-and-gold-patterned neck and a high, gathered waist that failed to hide her belly's swell. Her pale hair looked thicker than usual, and her cheeks bore an awful salmony glow. I couldn't stop staring at her. That could have been me, a small voice inside me kept saying, that could've been me—an unholy chant—only I would be carrying *his* child.

My hands shook with rage as I watched the priest make his way down the steps toward her. I remembered holding the miller's son, the first child I'd ever delivered, how I wanted to steal him away. If I didn't agree to be Matthäus's mistress, I might never have a child of my own. And if I agreed, our children would be shunned.

As the priest began the ceremony, the crowd fell silent, and Matthäus's expression grew frantic. Soon the priest was asking them to speak their vows. Phoebe made her pledge in a flat voice, as if she was resigned to her match. When the priest asked Matthäus to speak his vows, there was a long pause as he scanned the crowd. When he finally saw me, relief flooded his face. He looked at me as he repeated the vows, despite saying her name. My cheeks grew hot, but I didn't look away.

And then the priest was blessing their union, braiding the traditional blue ribbon around their wrists. A polite cheer went up as the newlywed couple walked together down the steps, their families swarming around them. Matthäus's mother, smiling and laughing, embracing him. His father, slapping his back in a gaudy new coat and tunic, strutting like a rooster. I hated that man so much. I threw myself into the parade of revelers who were heading toward the feast. Down the cobblestone street I went toward the north side of town, reluctantly following the colorful band of revelers in bright clothes, richly dressed.

Matthäus's new estate was the Kürenberg cottage on the banks of the lake near the city gate. Under the dark gray sky, the place looked almost ominous, built of jagged gray stones. The lake glittered behind it. The garden was lined with a high wall made from the same stones as the cottage. Gray rocks of uneven size and shape curved up into an entryway. The wooden door mounted to it was open, but its hinges were heavy. Its face was carved with a portal shaped like the sun.

Following the others inside, I heard the sound of strumming, of laughter and talking, a man's singing voice. In the corner, a young

man not much older than me held a finely crafted lyre. He was
flamboyantly clothed in deep-green velvet. Garb so fine, he looked
like he'd stolen it from a prince. A minnesinger. I had only heard
about them in stories. I had never been at an event fancy enough to
hire entertainment.

I felt uneasy as I surveyed the garden. It was dotted with a dozen
tables bedecked with ostentatious garlands and feathers and wreaths.
Carefully pruned spindle plants lined the walls. Through a porthole
window you could see the waves rolling in off the lake. As I looked
for a seat, a peacock feather drifted to the grass, flashing an outra-
geous blue, and I felt an intense wave of resentment. All this wealth
was what made Phoebe so attractive to Matthäus's father. If I were
this rich, he would've matched his son with me in an instant.

But my stomach was growling, and I could smell the promise
of a colossal feast—sausage, mustard, sage and saffron, sweetbreads
and puddings—so I lined up behind the other revelers at the basin
to wash my hands. Then I found a small table in the corner nearest
the gate and seated myself, immediately setting about tearing one
of the garlands near my seat to angry shreds. It took me a moment
to realize what I was doing, to recognize my anger and force myself
to stop. I reached into my coin-purse and fingered the charm, saying a quick prayer to any god who would listen that I wouldn't
punch anyone in the face before I had something to eat.

My prayer was interrupted by the sound of more music.
Strummed with the minnesinger's quill, the lyre made a rippling
sound that reminded me of leaves in wind. It was maddeningly
beautiful. The voice of the young noblewoman who stood up at
the table beside the minnesinger was pure and clear:

> *"I raised a wild falcon with my own two hands*
> *Strong and gray-feathered, he marked my commands*
> *Until I removed the stitches from his eyes*
> *And he soared away to find a new guide."*

The minnesinger kept glancing at the newlyweds with a bemused expression. Phoebe and Matthäus looked uncomfortable. Phoebe's hand went to her mouth. A low murmur arose from the crowd, as the singer continued her song. The guest seated next to me, a gray-haired woman in silk, tittered. The blond woman across from her chuckled, her lips twisting up in a smirk. "How many suitors has Phoebe run off now?"

The old woman coughed. "The first disliked her temper. The second discovered the third..."

I smirked. "The minnesinger. Who is he?"

The old woman snorted derisively. "Ludwig of Kürenberg, of course. You must be here for the groom." She adjusted the brooch at her throat and turned to the blond woman. "At least their first-born will have noble blood."

The blond woman laughed. I gritted my teeth and turned toward the music. The next song began with a dying strain that made me sigh before the minnesinger even opened his mouth. I knew the melody from the street performers in the market: It was a common song about lovers who had known each other since childhood. When Matthäus caught my eye from the center table, I realized he must've requested it with me in mind. Tears stung the corners of my eyes. I hid my face in my goblet, taking a long draught of honey-thickened wine to hide my sorrow. The liquid warmed my hands and throat as it went down, tasting of expensive spices and a cheer I did not feel.

By the time the song was over, my goblet was empty, and a woman hurried over from the kitchen to fill it. As I sipped my second cup, other servants began to bring out more food than I had ever seen in one place. A dozen types of sausage with mustard for dipping, roasted goose, venison, candied quail, and even roasted boar. I couldn't help but stare at the poor beast's tusks. There was even roasted peacock, offered with its iridescent blue feathers reattached to its skin, fanning out in a fantastic array. My hunger overtook my envy as the plates were passed, and I quickly set to gorging myself. After the meats came giant bowls of fruit. Pear slices wet with piment, so soft and pulpy they seemed to melt in my mouth. An almond bread pudding, so rich and sticky it was like a delicious glue. As I was devouring my pudding, my mouth so full I must've resembled a squirrel, I caught Matthäus watching me. Embarrassed, I swallowed it as quickly as I could.

As the last dish was passed around, the minnesinger stood and wandered the tables, asking for requests. Just as I sank my teeth into a blackberry tart, he nodded, cleared his throat, and spoke. "I have been asked to sing both a wedding song and a funeral song," he said. A group of men at the next table hooted and slapped their thighs, until the women beside them glared at them. After the conversation I had just overheard about Phoebe, I understood the joke. "Something holy and something wicked. Something innocent and something wise." The minnesinger threw up his hands in mock frustration. "You are a difficult crowd!"

The gray-haired woman beside me laughed.

"There is a song I've been working on that might be all those things except holy." He crinkled his nose, glancing at Matthäus. "It's based on a new tale, never before sung. The groom would not reveal his source."

A murmur issued from the crowd. From the center table, Matthäus caught my eye again, trying to tell me something. Face burning, I buried my face in my cup.

The minnesinger held up his lyre and struck it with his quill, making it hum as he walked back to his place at the garden's edge. "The tale of the runaway princess!"

I nearly choked on my drink. Was this *my* tale? The one I told Matthäus? Did he arrange this for me? Everyone began talking at once. I heard snippets of what the blond woman across the table whispered to the woman beside me: "New song—Princess Frederika—Prince Ulrich—"

When the din died down, the minnesinger struck his lyre again, strumming out a melody both whimsical and sad. It sounded like a love song one moment, and falling snow the next. Folks set down their food, finished what they were eating, and grabbed their drinks. I did the same, gulping the last of my second goblet of wine, confused. Why would Matthäus tell the minnesinger my tale? I thought he hated it.

A hush fell over the garden, as the minnesinger sang the first verse:

> *"The queen at the window with needle and thread,*
> *Seven years, childless, has shared the king's bed.*
> *In sorrow, she pricks a soft finger against barb.*
> *Into the snow falls a red drop of blood."*

When he finished, the garden was quiet but for the distant rolling of thunder. Outside the wall, we could hear the tide washing the lakeshore.

How strange it was to hear my story sung by another. I stopped eating. My hands fell limp in my lap. Matthäus caught my eye again, and this time I grasped the meaning of his glance. He understood why I had told him this story. He understood and forgave all my envy, my hurt. He knew how much I loved telling stories. He'd arranged this performance for me as a gift.

For a brief moment, my thoughts cleared, like a sudden patch of sky on a cloudy day. My spirits lifted. Then the moment passed. What did it matter what he thought of me, when she was the one sitting with him?

With a sigh, I turned my attention back to the minnesinger, who was now singing a verse about the blood-rose fairy. Everyone around me had stopped in the middle of eating, hanging onto his words. The women at my table. The men at the next table who had hooted at the minnesinger's jokes. They gasped when Golden

Braids arranged the princess's marriage to the wolf-prince. They cheered when the princess fled the castle.

Two feelings warred inside me. No one would ever listen to me like that, a poor girl without noble blood. And yet, this was my story everyone was listening to, my story these nobles were waiting to hear with bated breath. I stole a glance at the center table. Phoebe was just as enraptured as everyone else. A secret glee rose up in me that I was going to see how she reacted to my horrific ending. It gave me great pleasure when the night-birds descended on the princess and Phoebe's plump face went white with shock.

My glee was short lived, however, as she turned to Matthäus to whisper something in his ear. Whatever she said, he reacted with contrition. He bowed his head and said something with an apologetic expression, like the dutiful husband I realized he would soon become. Anytime she needed him, he would be there for her. That was just the kind of man he was. How long could he play-act such love before his feelings became real? One year? Two? The thought that he would grow to love her stung.

As the music died, the woman beside me whispered something to her friend about how foolish the real princess had been to flee this match. Since the annulment had made her a bastard, Ulrich was about as good as Frederika could get.

Her friend nodded in agreement. "The rumors about Ulrich are idle peasant talk. I saw him outside the cathedral once, giving alms to a beggar. He's a good Christian."

The minnesinger bowed, and several men lifted their tankards. "Again!"

The minnesinger shook his head and launched into a ballad honoring the men who had just died, far away, in a bloody battle. As he strummed his lyre, Matthäus began walking around, thanking people for coming. When he got to my table, he smiled formally and squeezed my hands. Then he leaned close and whispered in my ear. "Come see me at the shop tomorrow."

I nodded quickly, meeting his eyes, as he moved on to the next table.

Before he could finish making the rounds, the storm clouds opened over the garden. Big fat droplets bounced into my empty goblet. "My dress!" the gray-haired woman next to me snapped suddenly, standing up, looking down at a smear of blue on her skirt. She pulled her coat over her head and hurried away from the bench. I looked down at my new clothes, wondering if I should seek shelter too. It would be an excellent excuse to quit this place.

The drops hit the table with loud smacks. The rest of the revelers began to get up. At the center table, I could see Matthäus helping Phoebe over the bench. I looked away before he could catch me watching and hurried outside. "Forgive me," I muttered to no one in particular, then splashed my way home through the mud and the rain.

CHAPTER NINE

To unravel is not human. It is the nature of poppets and pet-ticoats to come undone. And yet, the night of the wedding, it was as if some unholy seamstress pulled the thread that stitched me together. Lying in my cupboard, I had no idea how to stitch myself together again. Every time I closed my eyes, I saw Matthäus and Phoebe in the garden. I saw him helping her over the bench to get out of the rain. I tried to focus on the way he'd spoken his vows as if to me, the gestures he'd arranged, but I couldn't stop seeing him with her.

Hoping for comfort, I took the bird-mother figurine from my pouch, inspecting her strange curves. I remembered the day my mother gave her to me. How soothing it had been to lay my head on her chest, to listen to her stories, to enjoy the faint scent of anise that always surrounded her. That night, I felt her absence as keenly as the day she died. Matthäus's wedding would have been so much more bearable if I still had her to comfort me.

I didn't sleep, that night, until the sun was almost up. I spent the night dreaming up dark stories. There was one about a violent bridegroom, and another about a wolf in the wood.

When I woke around noon, I was hungrier than I'd been in weeks because of how well I'd eaten the day before. I went into the garden to see if any more of the autumn vegetables had ripened. There were no new vegetables, but the yellow berries on the new plants, the light-thieves that had overtaken the back of the garden, had grown quite large. I wondered if they were edible.

I plucked one of the golden fruit, overripened and shiny with dew. Its sweet scent overwhelmed me. It reminded me of apples. A golden apple, I thought with awe, remembering my mother's tale.

My heart leapt. The small fruit glittered with frost. Her words swam back to me. *I'm leaving you something.* Did she plant these herself?

There was never any question about what I was going to do. My mother had made it clear. The golden apple was a cure for my spells. The fruit was like nothing I'd ever tasted. Sweet and soft and pulpier even than the pears at the wedding feast. I took another bite, then another, shocked at the sweet tang, the softness of its flesh made crisp by frost. I made myself eat slowly, savoring the taste. When I reached the mess of golden seeds at its core, one of them got stuck in my teeth, and I stopped. It tasted terrible.

I inspected the seed-core, struck by how clear my vision had become. I could discern every crystal of frost, every whorl and tangle in its pulp. All around me, the dying plants of the garden sparkled with tiny droplets of frost. I saw detail for the first time in the branching veins of leaves.

Was this fruit a cure for my eyesight too? I turned my gaze to the sky to see if its brightness still made my eyes ache. For once, I didn't feel the urge to squint. My heart soared. I wanted to tell someone.

Matthäus. I was supposed to meet him at the tailor shop. I had almost forgotten. I pulled the cloak Matthäus gave me from its hook. Down the street I hurried toward the market, giddy about the new details I saw in the world. The texture of every dead leaf. The cracks in the cobblestones zigzagging in sharp relief. I was so elated, I forgot to avoid the furrier's shop. As I approached the alley behind it, the furrier's older son swaggered out of the back door. His eyes were bloodshot. A blister marred the side of his mouth.

"Haelewise?" he said with a sneer. "Why are you dressed like that?"

Footsteps, behind me. Turning, I saw the younger brother sauntering around the side of the shop. I noticed, for the first time, his dark lashes, the cold hard blue of his eyes. "That's a fine cloak. Come inside and show us what you did to get it."

I looked down at my outfit and knew what he thought, what anyone would think when they saw these clothes. My cheeks burned that I was actually considering it, that I was on my way to see the married man who had given me this cloak. I clutched the purse at my hip, desperate, praying I would escape from this alley with my virtue intact. And just like that, it happened again. My fingers tingled, and I felt a telltale shiver. The next world drawing close. Not now, I thought. No no no—

But instead of the pull I feared, the balance shifted in the opposite direction. The air grew heavy with possibility, the way it did during a birth. I heard a humming sound, an unearthly woman's voice rushing into my ears. *Use their lust*, she hissed with an almost demonic amusement.

I froze, terrified that the demon my father thought haunted me had finally spoken. The alleyway came back into focus. The younger brother's leering smile. The elder boy's footsteps behind me. Demon or not, I wondered if the advice would work. What other choice do I have, I thought. I made myself smile at the younger brother, trying to hide my nervousness. He eyed me. I adjusted my bodice.

"I would actually love a new fur," I whispered, approaching him, forcing a lascivious smile.

The younger brother smirked, surprised, reaching out to pull me to him. As soon as he did, I twisted. His hand swept empty air, and I ducked behind him out of the alley, scraping my knee against the wall. He cursed as I darted away, my hood falling down around my shoulders. The last thing I saw before I darted into the crowd was the humiliation on his face.

Back in the relative safety of my hut, I couldn't stop thinking about the voice I'd heard in the alleyway. Had eating my mother's apple conjured a demon, or was it my mother's goddess? I wanted it to be my mother's goddess, but I knew so little about her, there was no way to tell. I pulled the bird-mother from my coin-purse and set her on the table, inspecting her for some clue as to her nature. Her breasts, her wings, her talons were so strange. When I closed my eyes, I swear, I thought I could feel the air thickening with possibility around her, as if she were pulling something from the next world. Powerful, whatever she represented, but her nakedness, her *fierceness*, concerned me. What kind of goddess would advise a woman to use men's lust to her advantage? I wanted to trust her— my mother worshipped her, after all—but I was afraid my father was right, and my heresy had summoned a demon. A demon with a hissing voice, who was amused by men's embarrassment.

The idea both attracted and repulsed me, which was unsettling in and of itself. As the hour grew late, I put the figurine back in my coin-purse, deciding against telling Matthäus about the golden apples. How could I tell him about the cure without mentioning the voice it had allowed me to hear? And telling him about the voice would scandalize him. He was much more like my father in his beliefs than I was.

The next morning, I ate the only food available to me for break-fast: golden apples. I fingered the bird-mother figurine in my coin-purse, wishing I knew what god or demon she was connected with. I brooded over Matthäus's offer, hoping he would come to see me since I'd failed to visit his shop the day before. But he didn't come.

Soon enough, I was starving for something other than fruit. I decided to go into town and trade my last poppet for food. I could stop by the tailor's shop on my way back. I stood at the shelf where Gütel sat for a long moment before I took her down. She glared at me, one-eyed, her expression full of scorn. "Don't look at me like that," I told her. "I have no choice."

I smoothed her woolen hair, straightened her ribbons, and picked two brown glass beads from the rope that hung beside the window.

I pulled out the black one that remained on her face and sat down to sew her new eyes on. It took me an hour and several pricked fingers before I was satisfied.

Down the street I walked into town with Gütel in my sack, wrapped in my tattered blanket, simultaneously enthralled and afraid at the new details I saw in the world. The change in my eyesight was even more apparent than it had been the day before. The market square was brighter, finer, more intricate, as I moved warily through it, praying I would remain unrecognized for the time it took to sell Gütel and buy cheese and sausage.

At the edge of the market, the furriers' sons had gathered a small crowd around them: the tanner's sons, the cobbler, the blacksmith, the miller's cousins. The elder brother's words drifted toward me. "A succubus possessed her—" he was saying. "Haelewise begged us to lie with her."

Shock and anger filled my breast. "Liar!" I cried before I could think better of it. "I did no such thing—"

Everyone turned. "It's her," the tanner's son shouted, making the demon-warding sign. The crowd around me parted, giving me a wide berth. The gesture spread from the tanner's son to the people around him, hand to hand to hand.

"She'll curse all of us!" the elder brother shouted.

A darkness animated the crowd, a fear intensified by all the deaths the fever had wrought. The tanner's, my mother's. Terrified, I looked for an opening in the crowd to escape.

A gaunt woman with haunted eyes, the tanner's widow, called out, "Stop her!"

The crowd pressed closer. A bitter-browed man took a step forward, picking up a stone. "The fever is her fault!" he shouted, holding it up.

Folks nodded, searching the ground for stones. If I waited any longer, I knew what would happen. I rushed forward, pushing the tanner's widow out of the way, fleeing as fast as my legs would carry me from the square. Behind me, I could hear people shouting, calling me all manner of names. A thousand footsteps, coming fast. The banging of doors as people rushed outside to join the chase.

I raced home as fast as I could, slamming the door, pushing the table against it so no one could batter their way in. I bolted the shutters, breathing heavily, listening for the sound of the mob I knew would come. And then, as I was pushing my mother's cot against the back door, there it was, a pounding on the front door, the furrier's sons shouting for me to come out and pay for my fur. "Feverbringer," someone shouted. "Heretic!" A child's voice, thin and high. "*Witch!*"

I crawled under the table and sat with my back to the door, shaking, fighting an irrational urge to put my fingers in my ears and pretend they weren't there. After a moment, I heard an animated conversation taking place outside, some kind of argument. I couldn't make the whole thing out, but I had a sinking feeling based on the few words I could—words like *burn* and *oil*—that someone wanted to smoke me out of my hut. Eventually, a man's voice I didn't recognize ended the argument.

"It's not worth it," he called out. "It could spread to the docks."

The murmurs of agreement were a relief, until I heard what the voice said next. "Let's post a watch. You and you, stay with me. We'll get her the next time she comes out."

For hours, I sat under that table, back against the door, trying to figure out what to do. Should I leave town? Go to Matthäus for protection? Both possibilities seemed far-fetched. I would have to pass the watch they'd posted outside to do either. From time to time I could hear men talking in the street. Barely audible conversations, too faint to tell what they were about.

Eventually I came out from under the table to look for something, anything, I could eat to stop my hunger pangs. I found a handful of aniseed at the bottom of the pot, which I sucked seed by seed, distracting myself with their sweet taste. When night fell, I lit a rush light and sat at the table, watching it burn. I couldn't sleep. I kept peeking through the shutters at the dark street, wondering if the men were still out there. As the hour grew late, my thoughts turned again to the voice that had spoken to me in the alleyway. My mind whirled with fears that it was a demon—one of the lamia or lilit—that my prayers to any deity who would listen had invited into my heart. I didn't fall asleep until late.

When the morning sun shone through the cracks in the shutters, I woke with a new resolve. I had to leave town. I tried to summon the courage to open the shutters and see if there was anyone in the street. It occurred to me that perhaps it would be safer to peer through one of the gaps in the stones of the garden wall. I went to the back door and stood there for a long time. I was afraid one of the men who were watching the house had climbed into the garden. When I finally opened the door, I found a bright autumn day, the pale sun shining quietly over the garden wall. Peering through a tiny gap between stones, I could see two men in the street, watching the house.

Backing slowly away from the gap, I retreated to the bench behind the house. The sound of the lake lapping the docks soothed me, as I tried to figure out how to slip out of town. Should I clamber over the garden wall? Steal a boat? My father had never taught me to row. If only I could fly away on the back of some beast like the witch they thought I was. But even if I could, I had nowhere to go.

At sunset, when the air filled with the smell of bonfires and the festive sound of bells, I heard a group of children come down the street, laughing and singing a Martin song, and I realized it was Martinmas. The memory that swam back to me of singing that song with my father was too painful to dwell on for long. I talked to my mother beneath the earth, her goddess in the beyond, fingering the figurine in my coin-purse. I rubbed her black stone absently, praying desperately for guidance on how to escape.

It must have been around midnight—the moon bright, a few days past full—when the figurine grew warm under my thumb and my skin bloomed with chills. I braced myself for a fainting spell, but instead, I felt the air grow heavy with possibility like it had when I heard the voice behind the furrier's shop. The air trembled, as if something was coming. What, I didn't know. A soul? A voice? Then, ghostly tendrils began to unfurl into existence all around me.

I shivered, watching them drift up like smoke from an invisible fire. They grew thicker, glimmering and whorling, coalescing into the shape of a woman kneeling in the dirt.

My mother. She was straightening one of the golden apple plants, wearing her lucky gloves and the bright blue cloak I'd seen moments before inside on its hook. I rushed to her, calling out, "Mother!"

She looked up from the weeds and beamed at me, her face joyful as she opened her arms. I jumped into her embrace. The ghostly feel of her arms around me was a balm. She murmured my name, over and over, pressing her face into my hair. My eyes teared up, as her scent enveloped me. Earth and anise. After a moment, she pulled back from me and frowned. When her lips began to move, it took me a moment to decipher her voice. It hummed, barely audible, like the low buzzing of bees. "You ate the golden apples," she was saying.

I blinked the tears from my eyes, nodding, overwhelmed by a sudden thought. "Was it you who spoke to me?" My voice was soft with wonder. "I thought it was a demon."

She didn't acknowledge my question. Her voice grew deeper, louder. "You have to leave town." She gave me a warning look— half angry, half afraid—the same expression she wore when she spoke of the *kindefresser*.

I tried to explain, choking back sobs. "The townspeople want to stone me. They're keeping watch for me outside."

Her expression softened. "Don't cry. You have your whole life in front of you." She wiped away my tears. Her smile was gentle. "You're going to have children, tell stories, become a midwife. You're going to find your purpose."

"I will?"

She nodded. The air shimmered around her. The mist had begun to drift into the garden. It swirled around her, moonlit, glowing. "There's a whole world outside the wall."

"How do I get past the watch?"

"There's no one out there now. The Martinmas festivities distracted them."

"But where do I go?"

"Find the wise woman in the forest near Ulrich and Ursilda's castle. She needs an apprentice."

I searched her eyes. She was looking at me with such love.

"Haelewise—" She smiled at me, radiant. "I loved you more than life itself." Her eyes glistened, and her voice caught. Then her smile began to waver with uneasiness. The air snapped taut, and I felt a diminishing, a pull from this world into the next. My mother searched the air, frowning, panicked. She shook her head, once, twice, and reached out.

But before she could pull me into an embrace, all the tension in the air collapsed. The mist rushed back into the next world, taking her with it.

CHAPTER TEN

I fell to my knees, kneeling in the place my mother had knelt in the dirt. My heart sang with relief. The voice that spoke to me was my mother's. She had come back to visit me as a ghost. The world of her stories was filled with such apparitions, but I had never expected to see one in real life.

Reaching out to touch the golden apple plant she'd straightened, I wondered what she meant when she said I'd find my purpose. The leaves of the plant rustled, springing back at my touch. I picked up the bird-mother charm, touching the tiny infant she held in her arms. I remembered how right it felt to hold the miller's son, his weight, the need I felt to take care of him. I felt a sudden longing for the children I would one day have.

When Matthäus married, I thought I'd lost my chance, but I should've known better. I was brokenhearted about losing him, but—of course, *of course*, he wasn't the only path forward. If seeing the wise woman was the first step toward making the life I wanted happen, I would go to her. I would ask to become her apprentice.

Determined, I went inside, put on my new cloak, and packed my things: a comb, a water skin. My quiver and bow. The shattered mirror. The rest of the fruit from the garden. I counted two dozen. I wanted to keep eating it. I picked one of the leaves from the plant so the wise woman could identify it. My sack full, I tied my drinking-horn to my belt, then turned my mind to the problem of how I would make it through the market without being recognized. There was no one outside here, but the market would be different, and how would I get through the gate?

In the back room, I rummaged through my mother's trunk until I found a forgotten pair of britches, a man's tattered tunic, and a cloak at its bottom. At the market, no one looked twice at a boy in ragged clothes. I took off my new dress and cloak and headscarf and pressed them into my sack. I wrapped my small breasts tight with a length of fabric, then pulled on the tunic and britches.

My hair, I thought. I found my comb, untangled my knotted locks, and braided them, thinking I would use my knife to cut the plait. But when I put on my father's cloak, I saw that tucking the braid into my tunic hid it. I didn't really want to cut it.

I hurried outside before the watch returned and set out toward the city gate. In the dark square, I only passed a single group of revelers leaving a tavern. Seeing only a boy in tattered clothes, they didn't even nod. I was beneath their notice.

As I approached the shadowy shape of the Kürenberg cottage, I felt a pang in my chest. I couldn't leave without telling Matthäus goodbye.

The garden gate was unlocked. It creaked as I pushed it open. As I slipped in, the orange tomcat who had apparently followed Matthäus to his new home rubbed his face against my legs. The sight of him made my heart ache. Giving him a pet, I checked both upstairs windows. There were no candles burning, no lights. But it looked like someone was awake downstairs. The shutters were open. In the window, I could see the flicker of candlelight.

I peeked inside, where Matthäus appeared to be sewing, needle in mouth, alone among a sea of scraps. It was simultaneously soothing and heartbreaking to see him like that. My childhood friend, my love, now someone else's husband. From my vantage point, I couldn't see the whole room. I took a deep breath. *"Matthäus,"* I hissed, ducking behind a spindle-plant in case anyone else was in there with him. He didn't react. I said his name again. He came to the window alone, peering out in his nightcap. I stepped out from behind the spindle-plant and waved. At first he looked alarmed.

I pulled down my hood, shaking my head. "It's me."

"Haelewise?" He laughed. "By thunder! What are you wearing? Why didn't you come to the shop yesterday?"

"Come out. I'll explain."

He closed the shutters. The flickering light behind them disappeared. A wave washed the shore behind the house. After a moment, the garden door opened, and he walked out, handsome as ever, holding the candle. But for the first time, looking at him, I saw the life he *couldn't* offer me.

He gestured for me to sit with him at a table and held his candle up to look at me. "Your eyes," he said, his voice full of awe. "They're beautiful."

I didn't understand, then, what he meant.

Nervous, I reached for his hand across the table. He met my gaze, his gray irises bright in the candlelight. Hopeful. I could tell he thought I was going to accept his offer. I looked down at our hands. "I'm leaving town," I said quietly. "I couldn't go without saying goodbye."

He set down his candle. "Leaving? Where will you go?"

"To see the wise woman."

"The one who kidnapped Ursilda?" He looked horrified.

"My mother said she didn't. I heard she wants an apprentice."

"Oh, Haelewise," he said, his eyes glowing with disappointment. "There'll be no convincing you to stay?"

I shook my head, tight-lipped, then felt a perverse need to make him understand. "I was almost stoned yesterday. A mob chased me home."

His eyes widened. "Are you all right?"

"The worst injury was to my pride." I sighed. "I'm going to find somewhere else to live, someplace I'm not despised."

His face fell. "Lord have mercy upon my soul." He stared at me, as if he couldn't decide what to say next. Finally, he sighed. "May I kiss you? Just this once?"

My heart stopped. Part of me wanted to scream at him that he didn't deserve it, but another part wanted that kiss so badly it hurt. "Just this once," I said finally.

His lips were soft, and they tasted of salt. I was startled at the depth of his want. The rest of the world fell away, and I forgot where we were, who I was. There was only *us*, there was nothing but the weight of our shared desire. I don't know how long we kissed. It wasn't until his hand brushed my thigh that I remembered—he was married. His pregnant wife was upstairs. I couldn't do this.

His eyes stayed closed for a long moment after I pulled away. His face was full of longing. Then he looked at me, understanding. He didn't speak as I stood up to go.

When I left the garden, the door creaking behind me, he was still sitting, silent, at the table.

I only looked over my shoulder once. He was watching me go, his eyes flashing with regret. I made myself focus on the road that led to the city gate, ignoring the regret that was rising up inside me to meet his. The sound of the lake lapping the shore mocked my heartache.

As I walked toward the north gate, I made myself focus on the problem before me: I had to get past the city guards. If I spoke to them, my disguise would be ruined. After some thought, I decided to make myself swagger like the furrier's sons. One foot in front of the other, tough, chin up. I nodded as I approached the gate as if our exchange would be an annoyance, my expression carefully nonchalant.

The guard nodded, fooled, and let me pass through the gate. The water glittered with moonlight on either side of the bridge. For hours, I encountered only shadows, the shapes of birds sleeping along the lakeshore. As the night turned gray with the coming dawn, the footpath turned west into the forest, away from the lake.

I paused before I stepped onto the footpath. Mother told so many stories about this part of the woods. It was supposed to hide strange animals and fae, the *kindefresser*, the source of the mist, Prince Albrecht's castle on the cliffs. The wise woman's tower.

I took a deep breath and turned down the trail. Elder ash and tangled oaks huddled over the path where it entered the forest, as if the trees were dancing together, holding hands. Following the path, I was surprised at how quickly the shadows closed around me. The canopy of leaves overhead was thick, almost impenetrable. Very little light filtered through.

I walked that path for so long, I lost track of whether it was night or day. Eventually in what must've been afternoon, I shot and ate a rabbit and slept beneath a firethorn bush.

It wasn't until I woke that night that I saw the giant raven, barely visible, in the branches of a spruce tree. *Kraek*, it called, looking right at me, eyes flashing amber. *Kraek!*

Those eyes, I thought, chilled. I no longer believed in the *kindefresser*, but I had been superstitious about amber-eyed ravens since the one in the grove took Gütel's eye. Was this the same bird, or were there many? The thing flitted from tree to tree, croaking. I got the sense that it wanted me to follow it.

"Shoo," I told it, my voice shaking. The bird croaked again, then took off down the path. The needles of the fir trees shivered. As the path wound uphill, the backs of my calves began to burn.

Just before dawn, I heard distant noise. The call of a trumpet. The howling and baying of dogs, growing nearer. My mother and I had encountered hunting parties long ago, when we used to walk in the woods. This part of the forest belonged to Prince Albrecht. The only nobles hunting here would be he or his son, Ulrich. I didn't want to meet either of them.

I climbed the tallest tree I could find. Sap stuck to my gloves. Branches snapped beneath my boots. I wrapped my cloak tight about me and looked around.

To the north, I saw the distant shape of the shadowy castle on the cliffs where Prince Ulrich lived, surrounded by the misty bog in the valley that was supposed to be full of fae. The sight of the castle gave me a chill. I thought of what my mother said about Ulrich changing into a wolf when the moon was full. It had seemed far-fetched by the light of day, but now I couldn't help but wonder what moon phase it was. The moon was waning, nearly a half moon now.

East of the castle, the sun was edging the treetops on the horizon with a dim pink. No sign of the source of that noise.

To the west, a blanket of trees spread out green and dark. The dogs howled again, closer than before.

There was movement below. A stag bounding through the mist. An arrow struck my tree with a *thwack*, the green feather at its back vibrating with the force of the shot, and I froze.

Hounds bayed in scattered unison, their sound growing louder. I tightened my knees around the top of the tree trunk, holding my breath. Below, the alaunts flew past—snarling and ravening, so fast they were like gray ghosts—too focused on the stag to notice me. I sighed, relieved. The baying faded as I heard the relaxed clip of hooves on dirt, a low sound, the chatter of men behind them.

Out of the mist two young lords trotted into the clearing. Their horses were thick gray things, well-groomed, legs splattered with mud. Green banners zigzagged over their necks. Behind them, a page boy rode a third horse, carrying a green banner with the wolf that was Albrecht's coat of arms. Prince Ulrich, I realized. One of these men must be him.

There, at the back of the group. Black-haired, broad-shouldered, in a mangy coat of wild gray fur on a jet-black horse. The wolf-skin. His expression was determined, his eyes a cold bright blue. He was striking, with black hair, unlike the monster I'd imagined, but there was something predatory about his eyes. As he drew closer, I recoiled, sensing something very *wrong* in the air around him. I clutched my trunk, holding my breath, willing him not to look up.

Trailing behind him on a dappled horse was a woman several

years older than me. She rode into the clearing, gazing up at the moon, contemplative. She wore a long black mourner's cloak and a modest headscarf that hid her hair except for two red braids. The braids swayed as she rode, and her green eyes glistened with tears that streamed down her freckled cheeks. She was beautiful in an unearthly way. There was an aura of wildness about her. "I shouldn't have let Father talk me into coming out," she said, guiding her horse to catch up to Ulrich, her voice fluttering. She smoothed her cloak over her belly. "I don't feel well."

"Father was enacting the physician's orders," Ulrich snapped. "You're far too melancholy for a woman in your condition. The air will do you good."

She didn't answer for a moment. When she replied, her voice was apologetic. "Yes, brother, of course."

Ulrich turned toward his sister. I couldn't see his face, but his voice was barely audible, his tone condescending. "I understand that *you* are a slave to your womanish whims, but *try* not to allow them to disrupt my hunt. The business with Frederika has me snappish. I need the diversion."

She nodded quickly, her headscarf shifting around her shoulders. When she spoke, her voice fluttered with false cheer. "Perhaps I simply need nourishment."

Ulrich turned to the page boy. "Mark this spot, boy. We'll finish the chase after Ursilda has her meal."

The page jumped down from his horse with a flag.

"The southernmost pavilion is just ahead," he told Ursilda, kind again, as if nothing had happened. In the distance, among the trees, I could make out the faint lines of wooden beams. "Can you make it that far?"

His sister nodded silently and followed him.

They led their horses far enough away that I could no longer see them, but close enough that their voices still carried. The sound traveled so well, I was afraid to climb down until I started to nod off and feared that I would fall. The forest is still dark, I told myself, as the men's voices rose. Slowly, I climbed down, testing my steps as I went. The last branch on the way down snapped.

The men went silent. A horse whinnied, nervous.

I winced.

"Did you hear that?"

"The stag?"

"Come with me." Ulrich's voice, cold. "Both of you."

Twigs snapped on the forest floor. The sounds grew nearer. A torch flickered to life. My heart pounded in my ears.

"You don't think Zähringen has spies all the way out here."

Zähringen? The duke who gave Matthäus those paternoster beads?

"I told you," Ulrich hissed to his man. "Zähringen has been furious ever since the king promised to give me Villa Scafhusun."

Although his voice was low, I could hear satisfaction in it, the pleasure he took at the other man's misfortune.

I heard a twig snap nearby. "Get out of my forest!" Ulrich snarled, so close I froze, holding my breath. "Or I'll tear you limb from limb."

A chill ran down my spine. I bolted, hood falling from my face, braid flying behind me.

I looked back only once to see their surprise. None of them had expected a girl.

CHAPTER ELEVEN

A way from the clearing I fled, ducking under branches, weaving around tree trunks. Twigs leapt out to scratch my arms, my face. I heard the sound of crackling leaves behind me, the sound of Ursilda crying out. "Rika!"

I didn't stop to find out what she meant.

Trees bumped up and down. I ran until I almost ran into that raven again, perched in another spruce. The great bird stared me down, its amber eyes glowing like newly fired glass. The bird flapped its wings, commanding my attention, then took off toward a string of boulders that jutted from the ground like teeth.

The circle of stones that surrounded the wise woman's tower. It had to be. My skin tingled as I drew close. Preparing to pass between two of the stones, I had the distinct impression that I was crossing a threshold. There was a great power zapping from stone to stone. Inside the circle, the next world was so close, I could feel a presence enmeshed with the air. A living shadow. The mist, I thought, that makes men blind.

Through the trees, I could see the raven land atop a large stone wall. Beyond it, a vine-covered tower stood cloaked in silvery tendrils of mist. The tower looked ancient, cobbled together from wood and rock, older than old. The stones that made up its face were huge, weatherworn, crumbling, and covered with vines. Its high roof was a thicket of branches tied with rope, shrouded in mist.

The raven eyed me from its perch, watchful, then circled the tower and flew out of sight. I followed it, shadowing the stone wall, heading toward the tower, my heart beating in my throat. The wall stones were cold against my palm, silent in their pact with the dark. Passing a wood-braced portal, I peered through it into a huge shadowy garden, a dim thicket of bushes and vines and weeds. At its far end, rows of plowed earth sat waiting for spring. In the center, grotesque stone figures danced. Skeletal shrubs twisted. Closer to the tower, a huge birdbath stood. Taking it in, I was overcome with a shiver of fear and familiarity, the hairs on the back of my neck standing on end.

It seemed too quiet as I circled the tower, looking for a door or window, cursing the noise my feet made. The opening I found was narrow and tall, the kind of caged window used in fortifications— a slot made for shooting out, instead of looking in.

Dim firelight flickered within. As I crept nearer, my nostrils tickled with smoke. I saw dozens of talismans hanging inside the window, paper rustling, beside a wicked-looking bone amulet and the dried-out skin of a snake. The sight filled me with fear.

Behind the bars, an old woman dozed beside a dim hearth, head resting on her shoulder, a bit of spittle shining at the edge of her mouth, iron-gray hair pulled back. About twice my mother's age, old enough that her skin hung loose around her neck. Her kirtle was brightly dyed, her bosom large, her dark hair roped loosely into white-ribboned corpse-braids like the courtiers' wives wore.

She's a wealthy midwife, I tried to tell myself. A country noblewoman. There's no reason to be afraid.

Then my foot snapped a twig, and her eyes popped open, glowing a hazy amber. I froze, and my heart skipped a beat.

"Well, what have we here?" the old woman said, standing up from her chair to peer through the bars, pushing the talismans and such aside. Her expression was kindly, but her *diutsch* was stilted, and she drew out her words as if they took great effort to shape. Her eyes glittered that hazy amber, and my chest tightened as she looked at me. I heard my mother's voice in my head. *Don't let the kindefresser snatch you away—*

The prince's trumpet sounded in the distance. The old woman shook her head and moved out of sight. I could hear my heart beating in my ears. Some feet away, a door opened. "Hsst," she said. "Ulrich is hunting. Come inside."

What else could I do but follow her inside, though I couldn't shake the feeling that I was escaping something bad into something worse. The tower was dark. Shadows played on the floor. Our footsteps echoed on the stones. The area around the door was filled with earthenware jugs. Farther in, I could see the rest of a large circular room. Candles guttered along the walls. Furs littered the floor. A manuscript sat on the table next to a vat of ink. The rounded walls were rimmed with shelves of books. I blinked at them, surprised at the display. The only books I'd seen before were the ones the priest used at Mass.

Beneath one of the guttering candles, a grid of eerie phials glowed in a cabinet, a collection even larger than the alchemist's. A giant raven perched beside them, settling his wings. I thought he was the one who led me here until he turned toward me and I saw that his eyes were black. Herbs and dried vegetables, ropes of garlic and onions, hung from the beams of the ceiling. Across the room was a table, a cauldron, a wood oven. Behind that, a shadowy set of winding stairs led to another floor.

Reluctant to leave the doorway, I removed my hood. The running had loosened my braid. She broke into a wide grin, beaming at me. "Well, if it isn't Hedda's girl, Haelewise."

I stopped in my tracks, unsettled, wondering how she knew my name. Mother must've come to see her about my spells. There was no other explanation.

I set the thought aside. "And you, what are you called?"

"Mother Gothel, by most."

"Gothel," I tried. The word tasted odd on my tongue.

"My birth name is Kunegunde, if you prefer. Would you like something to eat?"

As soon as she asked, my stomach growled. I hadn't eaten anything the day before but the rabbit. Kunegunde smiled. The faint smell of bread wafted from the oven, as if it had been freshly baked in the middle of the night—as if Kunegunde had *known* I was coming.

The thought made me shiver. A cauldron hung over the glowing hearth.

Kunegunde followed my gaze. "I hope that hasn't burned."

She got up to stir whatever was in the cauldron. As she did, I detected the rich smell of beets, leeks and turnips, garlic and parsnip. Some kind of meat—not fish, but dark, like mutton or venison—and a strange scent, a spice I'd smelled before. That spice. A memory came back to me. Not long before the wall was built, my mother went on a long journey to purchase midwifery supplies. She told my father she needed to buy a rare oil. They had a huge argument about it; he said everything she needed for births could be bought in town. She went on the journey anyway, leaving me with my father for four days. When she came back, she gave me a leaf-wrapped package: a delicious meatcake, a new remedy for my spells. It was one of the few curatives my mother gave me that tasted good, and it'd kept my spells away for a month. It smelled *exactly* like the spice in this cauldron, an exotic scent I hadn't smelled before or since. She must've purchased that meatcake here.

I remembered how excited my mother was for me to try that meatcake and was overcome by a fresh wave of grief. I had to work to keep my voice calm. "How often did my mother come here?"

"Once or twice, perhaps? Maybe more." Kunegunde stirred whatever was in the cauldron without looking up.

"She died last winter," I whispered. The words caught in my throat.

Kunegunde looked at me then. There was sadness in her eyes, as if she remembered my mother with great fondness. "I heard she was sick."

Tears wet my cheeks. How had she heard that all the way out

here? How many folks came to her? In town everyone thought of her as dangerous, Ursilda's kidnapper. I remembered a merchant who called himself Gothel, a cloth-trader we had met in the tailor shop. "Was Gothel your husband's name?"

She chuckled softly. "I have no husband. Gothel is the name of this place."

She broke the loaf from the wood oven into two crusts and filled them with stew. She didn't bother, I noticed, to carve them with a cross. She placed the food on the table near the fire ring and nodded for me to sit. I did, forcing myself to eat slowly, the bread warming my palms, though I wanted to tear into it. It was the most delicious stew I'd ever tasted. Savory with garlic and herbs, the strong flavor of beets. The meat I'd smelled was rabbit, though it was far more delicious than the animal I'd roasted in the wood. There was a crunch to it, a glaze with bitter hints of that spice.

"Is there something I can help you with?"

I squared my shoulders, gathering my courage, deciding it would be best to state my intent outright. "I came to offer myself as an apprentice."

She laughed, at first—a startled, merry sound—raising her eyes to the heavens in what looked like a prayer of thanks. I smiled, certain that my mother was right and she was going to take me on. But after a moment, Kunegunde's expression changed, and all of the joy faded out of it. She looked at me with a weary sadness. "I'm not sure you would be safe here."

My stomach dropped. "But the tower—the mist. I have nowhere else to go."

"The mist isn't infallible. There are ways around it."

"I was almost stoned in my hometown. I already understand something of the healing arts," I said, hoping that would make me more attractive to her. "My mother was a midwife."

"I know that," she snapped, her mood shifting quickly, as if my assumption that she didn't infuriated her. Her eyes flashed.

I blinked. My surprise must've shown on my face.

She froze, realizing how harsh she had just sounded. "Forgive me. It's just—your mother came to me more than once. I remember my clients. Aren't you tired? There's an extra bedchamber on the second floor. I'm cross when I don't get a full night of sleep. We should talk after both of us rest."

"I would be grateful to sleep here," I said slowly, still startled by her sudden temper.

She led me upstairs, chatting amiably about how dark the room would be with the shutters closed, how comfortable I would find the bed. She spoke quickly, as if she was trying to distract me from her outburst by a steady stream of chatter. "Here you are."

The bedchamber had a tall narrow window, brightened by the gray light of dawn. Against the wall was a luxurious cot with linen sheets, a coverlet, and a feather-stuffed mattress. Never had I slept in such a fine bed. My eyes must have gone as round as coins. "Thank you," I breathed.

Kunegunde nodded and excused herself, saying she needed to lock up downstairs before we slept. "The hunting party."

After she left, I went to the window and looked down over the walled garden. One of the smaller ravens was washing its wings in the birdbath. As I watched, the food I'd eaten and my long journey caught up with me, and I was overcome with a sudden wave of exhaustion. I battened the shutters and lay down, my need for sleep warring with my fear that Kunegunde wouldn't accept me.

I reached into the pouch on my belt and pulled out the bird-mother figurine. Please, I prayed, rubbing her curves. Please let me stay. The figurine grew warm in my palm, thrumming softly, thickening the mist in the air around me. The mist swirled, wrapping itself around me, caressing my arms. I shivered, tears in my eyes—tears of happiness, tears of grief—the same way I'd felt when my mother visited me in the garden. The effect was so soothing, I smiled, drifting off into that space between sleep and waking, a sort of dreamless trance. After a while, I thought I heard my mother's voice. Not demonic this time, but gentle. *Visit the next mountain*, she hummed.

I jolted upright so fast, the bedroom swayed around me. I couldn't tell if I had been awake or dreaming.

CHAPTER TWELVE

Midday light brightened the room. For a moment I didn't know where I was. Then it came back to me—the forest, the stone circle, the tower. The mist I'd sensed early that morning, comforting and beautiful. I could still feel it at the edge of things. Sitting up, I saw two ravens perched on the sill, watching me, their black eyes glittering with intelligence. How long had they been watching me? Had Kunegunde opened the window? A third bird, the larger one—though his eyes seemed to be black now—soared down to perch on the sill alongside them. The way he gazed at me, measuring me up, unsettled me.

"Shoo," I told him. He didn't budge.

The shutters creaked as I closed them on all three birds, pushing them out. Barring the window behind them, I could hear them flapping their wings and croaking. I closed my eyes, enjoying for a moment my renewed privacy. Then I remembered the voice I'd heard before I fell asleep. I must've dreamed it. If I hadn't, my mother's advice puzzled me. Why should I visit the next mountain? I had just gotten here.

Wafting up the stairs was the smell of pig meat, the sound of fat sizzling over a fire. How long had I been asleep? Did Kunegunde have time to slaughter a pig? I found the bird-mother charm in my coverlet, slipped her into my pouch, and went downstairs. On the first floor, Kunegunde stood a few feet away from the fire, keeping an eye on the sizzling meat while she read from a tome. Dark colors leapt off the page. Ruby red, deep blue, a gold so bright it glowed. "I set the table outside," she said without looking up.

"Outside?" The day before had been cold enough to require a cloak.

Kunegunde nodded, putting the book away and flipping pig meat onto a plate. It smelled delicious.

I followed her to the door that led into the garden. The basin where the raven had bathed the night before was encircled by a bed of overgrown thorns. The birds were currently nowhere to be seen. Here and there around the birdbath stood the statues I had seen the night before. A naked woman, her arms covered in vines and dirt. Several chipped grotesques, terrible half-human creatures with snouts and horns. Fearsome things, effigies of heathen gods like my mother's Pelzmärtel dolls—or the figurine, I thought suddenly. Along the back wall I saw the trees I'd noticed earlier, glowing with firebright red apples. The ground beneath them was littered with leaves as gold as coins.

The legs of the table crooked to the cobblestones, knobby, the face of the table whittled smooth. In the center of the table was a basket with half a dozen boiled goose eggs. Before each of our chairs was a bowl of sops. Near the table, a fire pit glowed, blazing with a comfortable warmth. Kunegunde set down the plate she was carrying with slabs of pig, and we sat. Over her shoulder I could see a spider greedily spinning her web. "You make a good lad," she said, nodding at my tunic.

"This smells delicious."

Juice and fat filled my mouth, greasy and salty, as I began to eat. I was ravenous. The meat and eggs in particular were incredibly tasty. We settled into a contented silence, enjoying breakfast. After a while, I smiled at her nervously, gathering my courage to bring up the purpose for my journey here again. "My mother said you want an apprentice. Is that not still so?"

"I do," she said quietly, her expression strained. I could tell she was measuring her words. "I'm sorry I didn't express myself adequately this morning. My last pupil—things didn't end well."

I remembered the story my mother had told me about Ursilda. "No one is going to come after me. My father won't even notice I'm missing for a week."

Her eyes flashed with an anger so intense, it scared me.

"Even if he managed to figure out where I went, he certainly doesn't have a wolf-skin," I joked quickly, trying to lighten her mercurial mood.

"It's not that," she said. She closed her eyes and drew a deep breath, though when she spoke next, her voice was tight. "I would love to take you on as my apprentice, but these woods are dangerous. If you stay here, you have to promise not to leave the stone circle."

"I can do that," I said eagerly. "What trade would I learn?"

She nodded and cleared her throat. "I could teach you wortcunnery, midwifery. I could teach you to read and write. I could teach you the old ways—"

My breath caught. "I would like that very much."

The largest raven soared down suddenly from wherever he'd been hiding in the garden. Croaking, he looked at me with glittering black eyes as he tried to hop up on the table. "Have his eyes changed color?"

"There are three of them." The bird croaked as if in agreement. She laughed. "Erste does what he wants."

After that, we fell silent, enjoying our food. For the rest of the meal, she watched me thoughtfully. It was almost as if she wanted to ask me something, but she kept thinking better of it. I didn't feel comfortable enough to ask her what.

By the time we finished breakfast, there was grease all over my tunic. After I helped her bring the leftover cheese and eggs downstairs to the buttery, Kunegunde suggested I bathe in the brook. Although the sun was stronger than it had been yesterday, she said tomorrow would bring frost. Today might be my last chance to bathe in the stream. She gave me a rag, a clean tunic, and a cake of something she called soap, then held the tower door open. "The brook is over there," she said, pointing north. "Through those trees. There's a pool just this side of the stones."

I nodded, ready at that point to agree to anything.

"I'll be at the window, listening. Call for me if you need me. Rush straight back to the tower if you hear anyone."

"I will."

Outside, shadows played beneath the trees, patches of darkness and sunlight. I weaved in the direction she'd pointed. The trees were thick and tall, the shadows dark even by daylight. As I looked for the stream, I heard movement in the brush around me, unseen animals running from the sound of my feet. My skin tingled as I approached a segment of the stone circle that surrounded the tower, and an unseen force stood my hair on end. Walking along the inside of the circle, I searched for the pool, listening for sounds of the hunting party I'd met the night before. Would they still be about? The only thing I could hear was the she-goat, bleating from the tree by the barn. It was warmer than it had been the day before. I couldn't see my breath in the air. Then I heard the sound of water ahead. The brook.

Soon enough I saw the sun glint, golden, on a stream that ran through a clearing into the trees ahead. The brook was wide, only ankle-deep, bubbling and burbling over a rockbed before it tumbled into the perfect bathing hole. I froze as I approached the waterfall. A mother deer and her child were drinking. The doe looked up at me with big brown eyes, then nudged her spindle-legged child and bounded into the trees.

The pool sparkled, crystal clear. Small fish darted at its bottom. It was the kind of place my mother would've loved. All at once, a memory came back to me of splashing with her in a place like it when I was small. For a moment I was a little girl again, laughing with her in the sun. Then the moment passed, and I found myself standing alone at the edge of the pool, my heart filling with grief. The watersong, idyllic sun, and darting fish did nothing to improve my mood; in fact, they seemed almost to mock it. As if that weren't enough, while I was unraveling my braid, a collared dove lit on the branch of a nearby pine and began to sing, as if I had stumbled into the ballad of some cut-rate minnesinger.

"God's teeth," I groaned, unwrapping the cloth I had stretched around my breasts and removing my underthings, in a hurry to finish my bath.

A brief gust of wind made me shiver as I stepped into the pool. The water was cold. Not so cold that I stopped midstep or winced, but cold enough that I knew I would have to make this quick. The waterfall tinkled, and the sun glittered with a maddening cheer on the water's surface as I waded in. I wet my hair quickly, rubbing myself all over with soap like Kunegunde had told me to do. That task completed, I began to wash my hands. As I worked, I noted how smooth my skin was. Even my fingernails were clean. When I was finished, I used the towel to dry myself, noticing a few wispy hairs on my groin.

Gradually, I became aware of a feeling that I wasn't alone. First there was a shiver on my neck, then the hairs on my arm rose. I stood in my towel at the water's edge, conscious of a faint noise. The distant baying of hounds.

I snatched my clothes and ran back toward the tower. Kunegunde opened the door as she saw me coming, dripping wet, nearly naked. "The hunting party again?"

I nodded. "I think so."

Her eyes widened. "They didn't follow you, did they? Was Albrecht with them?"

I shook my head. "I didn't see them. Last night, it was only Ulrich and Ursilda."

Kunegunde took a deep breath, clearly frustrated. "Only? Ursilda knows how to find the tower. She could've been leading her brother here."

"Have they come back since Ursilda was taken?"

Kunegunde went silent. She pressed her lips together.

"Give me those clothes. I'll wash them for you. There's a dress that should fit you in the trunk, along with a comb you can use to tame that bird's nest of hair."

In the trunk I found the items she described. The dress was sewn from tightly woven linen. It fit almost as perfectly as the dress Matthäus had tailored for me. It took me almost an hour to dress and comb out my hair. As I worked, I realized I should ask Kunegunde about the golden apples. She was known to be an excellent wortcunner; there was a good chance she would be able to identify the plant. If that conversation went well, I thought, I could ask her about the bird-woman next. She had just admitted that she practiced the old ways.

As I went downstairs with my sack, she looked up from the tome she was reading at the table. I asked her if I could get her advice about something. When she nodded, I pulled a golden apple from my sack and held it out. "Do you happen to know the plant that bears this fruit?"

She stiffened. Her eyes went to the fruit and back to my face. I couldn't quite read her expression, but I could tell she was concerned. "Yes," she said. "Where did you find it?"

"Dozens of these plants grew in our garden this year." I set it down in front of her, eager to get more information from her. "The fruit seems to be a curative. Two days ago, I tried one. Afterward, there were changes in my vision, and—I take it you know about my fainting spells?"

She nodded, slowly, as if remembering.

"Since I started eating the fruit, they've changed."

I had her full attention now. She cleared her throat. "How?"

"Usually my soul leaves my body, and I faint. Now, instead, I hear a voice."

Kunegunde closed her eyes, rubbing her temples, as if she had been stricken with a sudden headache. "What does it say?"

"Many things," I said. "Last night, she told me to visit the next mountain."

For a moment she didn't respond.

"Do I need to pay your fee before you'll tell me the plant?"

She shook her head without opening her eyes. "No. Your mother already paid. I never charge twice for the same complaint."

"What is it, then?"

"Set the fruit down," she said without opening her eyes. "Carefully. Try not to get any more on your skin."

Slowly, I did as she asked.

She opened her eyes to confirm that I had. "Don't touch it again. I'll be right back." She disappeared into the entryway and came back with a jug of water, a sack, and the soap. "Wash your hands," she said. "Scrub them. It will clean any residue from the fruit off your skin."

I washed my hands while she retrieved a pair of gloves, putting them on before she picked up the fruit to examine it.

"What is the plant? Is it poisonous?"

"Do you have more?" She nodded at my sack.

Careful not to touch them, I poured the rest of the golden apples onto the table. Two dozen, a bit bruised from the long walk in my sack. Kunegunde's eyes widened as she saw how many there were. "How many of these have you eaten?"

I thought about this, growing nervous. "Several. Is that bad?"

She nodded anxiously. "This fruit can be dangerous in such large quantities. I'm going to give you a draught that will expel the poison." She walked over to the apothecary cabinet, from which she retrieved sysemera, rue, and betony—my mother had used those herbs—and began pounding them with a mortar and pestle. She poured out the resulting juice and told me to drink it.

As I did, she slipped the fruit one by one into her sack. With each fruit she took, I felt a loss. I could hardly stand to watch.

When Kunegunde had put them all in her sack but one, she took

off the gloves and used the washing water and soap to clean her
hands. My stomach heaved, and I threw up in the chamber pot.

When I was finished emptying my stomach, she went to the shelf
to retrieve a tome, which looked like it was going to fall apart any
minute. "This is a speculum detailing all the plants of the Roman
Empire and their properties."

She opened it to a page that contained an exact replica of the
plants that grew in my garden. Someone had carefully illustrated
one from leaf to root. There were the faded green leaves Mother
had straightened, the violet flowers that bloomed at its center, the
small golden apples it bore. All of the colors were faded, as if they
had been painted by hands long dead. Beneath the plant, underground, the illustration showed its root, a malformed shape like a
man. I looked closer at the book. On the opposite page, the same
border swirled around a block of text. "Look here." She pointed to
the first word on the page, whose beginning letter looked like two
mountains, side-by-side, outlined in black. "This word names the
plant. *Mandragora*, although most folks around here call it *alrūne*."
She pointed again. "This is a description of its properties. That
speaks to the root's ability to bring sleep. This discusses its healing
properties, its attractiveness to demons, how much is needed to
poison the blood. But this is all about the root."

"It says nothing of the fruit?"

Kunegunde shook her head. "What color are your eyes usually?"

"Black," I said. "Why?"

She left the room. I leaned over the hearth, rubbing my hands
over the fire to combat the draft from the window-slot. When she
returned, she held a hand-mirror. It was tarnished gold, decorated
like the smashed one I had taken from my mother's trunk, but its
face was smooth. As Kunegunde held it out for me, the image on
the metal changed, the tan of her fingers becoming the burnished
brown of the ceiling and then a golden-pink version of my thumb
as I touched it. The blurry shape of my reflection stared back at

me, my cheeks still red with cold from my bath, my wild black hair curling from my scalp. I turned the mirror this way and that, trying to see my features in more detail. I had never seen my face reflected back at me whole. I resembled my mother a great deal. The only thing that set me apart from her was my eyes. My eyes. I opened them wide with disbelief. There was a faint circle of color around my pupils. "My eyes are golden."

She nodded, putting on the gloves again.

She used a small knife to cleave the golden apple on the table. Untangling a seed from the glistening pulp, she cut it in two. From her apron, she produced a small circle of glass, which she held over the seed-halves. In the glass her eye loomed large. I could see the veins that laced its white, the twitch of her pupil as she looked at the kernel up close. "This fruit is overripe. Having hung on the vine so long, it could've taken on properties of the root." She put the glass circle and fruit away, then glanced back at the book, removing her gloves. Her expression turned dark. "I mentioned the demons the plant attracts earlier. Are you sure the voice you heard is one you want to hear?"

She searched my face, her eyes filled with judgment. Anger reared up in my throat, and I had to work to master my expression. Kunegunde had no way of knowing the voice I heard was my mother's. I hadn't told her. "I'm sure," I said, unable to keep a tremor out of my voice.

She watched my face for a long moment, sizing me up. "Your mother gave you something before she died, didn't she?" She held her thumb and forefinger apart just far enough that the bird-mother would fit between them. "A figurine about this tall."

I stared at her. How did she know? My thoughts whirled. If I told the truth, would she take the figurine away like she did the fruit? "What?" I said, pretending confusion. "No."

Her eyes narrowed, as if she didn't believe me. "You must stop eating the alrūne," she continued after a moment, her tone matter-of-fact.

"Different plants possess different amounts of poisons. If you eat the fruit of the wrong vine—" She shook her head. "I can give you a powder made from dried gooseberries and a few potent herbs, which won't make you susceptible to demons. It'll cure your spells. I could even cure your sensitivity to light—"

"I don't want to stop hearing the voice," I said, interrupting.

She frowned at me. "You don't believe it is demonic."

"No."

Her face fell. "If you like, I could add a touch of alrūne to the powder. A small amount that wouldn't threaten your life."

I thought about this. I needed to trust her. I had nowhere else to go. Her eyes were eager, as if the thought of my safety was important to her. "All right."

She looked relieved, getting up. "I'll make it now."

"Do you think you could add something to the powder to bring on my menses? I'm almost seventeen years old, and I still haven't bled."

She considered. "I can't put anything like that in the powder, but I can concoct an oil that might do the trick."

That night, Kunegunde insisted we lock up the tower. For the months I was there, we would do this every night of the week leading up to and after the full moon. She said Ulrich wore the wolf-skin most often around the full moon when its power was at its strongest. Tonight, like last night, she said it was especially important since we knew the hunting party had been near. She locked the bottom door, barring it shut, and she locked up the garden. The downstairs window-slots were caged, but she carefully barred the upstairs shutters too.

Her fear was contagious. By the time I went to bed, I was afraid to open my bedroom window. I wondered what had happened during Ursilda's "rescue" to make her so paranoid. As I tried to sleep, I listened for the sound of the hunting party, but all I heard was the wind. I wondered how Kunegunde knew my mother gave me a figurine. It must be part of what allowed me to hear my mother's voice. Kunegunde must know how it worked.

I pulled the figurine from my coin-purse, inspecting her. The air seemed weightier around her, just as it had the night before, and the mist seemed to thicken around her. Closing my eyes, I rubbed her until I could feel my mother swirling faintly around me, enveloping me like she had the night before. I thought I smelled the faint scent of anise. The same comfort filled me, the same relief. After a moment, the figurine warmed beneath my fingers, as if she couldn't contain all of the power she drew from the next world. I lay there, perfectly still, basking in my mother's presence.

When my sense of her faded, I looked at the figurine in awe. Who was my mother's goddess? What power allowed my mother's spirit to come to me like this? The bird-mother stared back at me, silent, refusing to answer. Her body language was motherly, compassionate, but she was undeniably fierce too. Her beak, her talons, her wings, the child in her arms, her naked breasts and hips. She seemed foreign from all I'd been taught to think of as holy, so monstrous and so sensual. She embodied aspects of motherhood that I'd never thought of as sacred—mother-greed, fury, the animal urge to protect, and lust. I had fought against those instincts in myself because my father had taught me they were sinful. The bird-mother was no Virgin, that much was clear, but that didn't make her a demon. I rubbed the figurine, willing my mother to coalesce and answer my questions, but my only companion that night was the mist itself.

I must've fallen asleep with the figurine in my hand.

CHAPTER THIRTEEN

On the morning of my second day at Gothel, I awoke to find that my things had been moved. On top of the trunk at the foot of the bed, my sack and pouch were laid out, everything I had brought with me arranged in neat little rows. My bow and arrow. The broken mirror. The sight of the figurine, glistening black in the morning sun, filled me with dread. Kunegunde had found her and moved her. She knew I had lied to her. I sat in bed for what seemed like hours, staring at my things, dreading that Kunegunde would cast me out when I went downstairs.

When I finally got up to get dressed, I found a phial filled with oil and a pouch full of powder laid out neatly beside the other things on the trunk. The remedies Kunegunde had promised. Had she come in to give them to me, only going through my things after she saw the figurine in my bed? I shouldn't have lied to her.

The powder tasted bitter. The oil was umber, like dried blood, and it smelled almost bestial. I smeared it on my groin as she'd instructed me the night before, then pulled on my dress, gathering my courage, and marched myself and the figurine downstairs.

Kunegunde was reading a tome. She looked up and met my eyes, defiant, as if she were daring me to lie to her again.

"Thank you for the curatives." I held the figurine up. "I see you found this. I was afraid to admit to you that I had it. My mother warned me never to show her to anyone."

"Mmm," Kunegunde said, turning a page, her voice cold.

"Do you know what it is? How it works?"

Her expression was indignant. "I don't know why you think

I'm going to be honest with you, when you haven't been honest with me."

"I'm sorry, Kunegunde. I apologize for lying. I didn't want you to take it from me."

"Too little, too late."

"Why does it make you so angry that I have it?"

"It's not that. It's the fact that you lied to me about it." She eyed the figurine in my hand, her expression hurt. "Get that thing out of my sight."

Her tone was so scornful, I turned around immediately to go upstairs and put it away. She barely spoke to me for the rest of that morning, and when she did, her words were full of a frosty reserve. I could tell she was angry, punishing me. I wanted to make my lie up to her, but I didn't know how.

After lunch, when she excused herself for a nap, I decided to slip out of the tower and shoot something for dinner in an effort to make her happy with me again. I hurried with my bow to the bathing pool just inside the stone circle. I hid in a bush beside the clearing, waiting for some unlucky animal to try to quench its thirst.

Soon, a family of swans flew down into the water: a cob, a pen, and three cygnets. I couldn't believe my luck; I hadn't eaten swan since the bishop built the wall. My father had loved it when my mother used to make *schwanseklein*; the soup was delicious, his favorite meal. I knew the recipe.

The swans were so graceful with their long white necks; for a moment, I watched them, transfixed. Then they took off all at once, and I cursed, leaving my hiding place to go after them. I paused at the edge of the stone circle, hesitant, but my desire to make things right with Kunegunde won out over my obedience.

As I crossed the threshold, my limbs tingled and I felt the spell zapping between the stones, but the feeling was more muted than it'd been the day before. The swan family was waddling down the bank a ways off. I let my arrow fly and the cob drooped, the other birds flying away in a terrified cloud of white feathers. I hurried along the bank to retrieve him.

As I was plucking his feathers, I heard Kunegunde calling me from inside the stone circle, her voice panicked. *"Haelewise?!"*

I rushed back through the circle, forgetting all about my plans to surprise her, worried that something had happened. She was standing by the pool, the fear on her face quickly shading into anger as she saw the half-undressed bird in my hand.

Her eyes flashed. "Where did you go?"

"Down the brook a ways."

"Outside the circle?!"

"I'm going to make *schwanseklein* for dinner."

She pressed her lips together tight. I braced myself for her to yell at me. But she was too angry even to raise her voice. She gave me a warning look that reminded me of my mother's expression in the garden when she warned me that I had to leave town. "Come in and get dressed," she hissed. "Now. I don't think you understand the gravity of the situation."

After I put on my clothes, she sat me down at the table. I braced myself for an unhappy discussion. "I'm letting you stay here on two conditions," she said, her voice dripping with condescension. "First, you must tell me the truth. Understand?"

I nodded.

"Second, you can't leave the circle without me. I can't emphasize this enough. I take it you know the story about Princess Ursilda."

I nodded again, eager to win back her trust.

"When Ursilda's mother sent her here, Albrecht was on a campaign with the king. When he returned and found out where she was, he was irate. Not because he's Christian, though he pretends to be at court, but because he knew I would cure the fear he'd beaten into his daughter, that I would help her grow strong enough to defy him. After he took her home, he told the king I kidnapped her and convinced King Frederick to issue a writ for my death."

I must've looked horrified. "That's a harsh punishment for tak-ing someone in with her mother's permission."

"Albrecht is wicked. The wolf-skin has belonged to the men in his family for centuries. It's warped them." She met my eyes, her expression pointed, her voice low. "Sometimes, peasants traveling through these woods go missing."

I swallowed, overwhelmed with two emotions at once—a childish pride that she wanted to protect me, and fear at what she was saying about Albrecht. I remembered the *wrongness* I sensed in the air around Ulrich when I saw him wearing the wolf-skin, and I shivered.

Later that afternoon, when Kunegunde invited me to go for a walk, the day had been going so terribly, I was thrilled. She said it was safe if we left the circle together because she would be there to protect me, and she was out of some important herbs. I followed her toward the edge of the stone circle, hoping she would take the walk as an opportunity to talk, but my attempts to strike up a con-versation with her were met only with grunts. The sensation of the spell zapping between the stones as we passed through the circle seemed even weaker than it had in the morning.

Giving up on conversation with Kunegunde, I tried to content myself with enjoying the beauty and wildness of the woods out-side the stone circle. The mountainside was wilder even than the dark forest I'd walked through to get here, teeming with foxes and stags and rabbits, a thousand types of rare and poisonous plants and mushrooms that grew in the shade. It was as if the mist encouraged everything it touched to grow.

The sunlight, in the rare instances that we stumbled into it, didn't bother my eyes much. Although I had eaten no alrūne that day, the gooseberry powder seemed to treat my sensitivity to light. Eventually, we came across a mossy tree, and she told me to help her gather some of the moss. As I put the moss in our basket, she pointed at a thick stand of fernlike plants my mother had taught me young not to touch. "What's that?" she asked.

"Poison hemlock," I said quickly, eager to show her what I knew. Hemlock bore pretty blooms earlier in the year, but this late all that was left were a few dried seed heads, which the wind had yet to shake loose.

She nodded. "You know the plant. Even this time of year. Your mother taught you well. Hemlock is useful in tiny doses, but too much can cause vertigo and death. Recite that back."

I smiled hopefully at her and repeated it, though I already knew those facts. As we walked, she continued teaching me the names and uses of plants. Some of what she said that day my mother had already taught me, but there were new lessons too. There were many plants in this part of the forest that I'd never seen before. As we walked, I felt relieved, grateful that her anger with me seemed to be thawing.

CHAPTER FOURTEEN

W e fell into a routine during the rest of my first week at Gothel. In the mornings, Kunegunde sent me hunting—as long as I promised to stay inside the stone circle. I shot a hare, a pheasant. One day I even shot a goose. Kunegunde spent hours roasting the birds. I found it odd how much her recipes reminded me of home, but I didn't dwell on it. Each prize I brought back to the tower seemed to make her happier with me; she said she was eating better than she had in years. In the afternoons, she set about teaching me my letters and numbers. As a child, I had never even dreamed that I would have the chance to learn to read. I found it fascinating, how the written letters on the page corresponded to the sounds of speech. I loved reading so much. Soon, while Kunegunde studied, I was sounding out the words of a speculum on local flora, which Kunegunde had written herself using a faint brown ink she made from crushing local vegetation. Kunegunde seemed impressed with my memory for sounds and the pleasure I took in words. While she read, I spent hours turning the pages of that speculum, learning its pictures by heart.

I marveled over Kunegunde's striking illustrations of huszwurtz and wolfsgelena, over the vines that spiraled around the borders of its pages. Vines and thorns and exotic flowers. Monsters and gods that resembled my mother's poppets. I recognized Wodin and Cupid, Pelzmärtel and Lamia.

As the days passed, I stopped noticing the tingling inside the stone circle, the mist in the air. When I rubbed the figurine at night, my sense of my mother grew fainter and fainter, until my heart began to ache with longing and disappointment.

One night, when I had been at Gothel about a week, I rubbed the figurine's curves in bed at night and felt nothing. No thrumming, no mist, no indication whatsoever that the figurine was more than a stone carving. For a heartbreaking moment, I questioned whether there had ever been anything special about her, whether I'd conjured my mother's ghost out of the madness of my grief. But no, Kunegunde had promised she would add enough alrūne to the powder that I would still be able to hear the voice. Perhaps she had forgotten? I tried to think of some way to ask her about it, but I was wary, since the figurine was such a touchy subject.

"Kunegunde," I said as I walked downstairs the next morning. She was working on a manuscript at the table. "May I ask you something?"

She kept writing. "Just a moment." Her quill looped over the parchment, darkening the page with indecipherable symbols like the ones on the hand-mirrors. After a moment, she looked up, clearly irritated that I was disturbing her work. "Yes?"

"I can't feel the mist anymore," I said, working hard to keep my voice even. "The mist that surrounds the tower. When I got here, the air was thin, and it was everywhere. But now, the tower feels like an ordinary place. Can you sense the mist too? Did something change?"

"No," she said, setting her quill down on the table, her agitation growing. I couldn't tell if she was frustrated about being disturbed or about my question itself. She took a deep breath, obviously working to stay calm. When she spoke, her voice had a forced quality. "I can't sense the mist anymore either. Not most days. It comes and goes. Think of it like a scent. Once you smell it for a while, you forget it's there."

I nodded slowly. That seemed like a logical explanation. I thought for a moment, trying to figure out what was still bothering me. "I can't hear the voice anymore either. Did you forget to add the alrūne to my powder?"

"Of course not," she snapped. "I told you I would."

"The figurine is different too," I said tentatively, watching her face, worried that I would upset her by mentioning it. "It used to hum, but now—"

"Same principle," Kunegunde said, a warning note in her tone, the words so clipped I knew she would snap if I pressed. "Nothing to worry about."

The next afternoon, the wind blew so strong it shook the last of the red apples from the tree in the garden, and we put our books away to get ready for the storm. "Batten the shutters," Kunegunde said, putting on her apron to walk outside. "I'll be right back. Tonight will mark the last new moon of autumn. We'll bake apple *strützel* and make an offering. I think we have enough aniseed."

"*Strützel*," I said eagerly. Mother and I had always made *strützel* around this time of year too. She said it was a traditional recipe to celebrate the beginning of the darker half of the year. As Kunegunde went outside, I hurried through the tower, latching the shutters, while Kunegunde gathered the fallen apples from beneath the tree.

When she came back in and handed me a firebright apple from her apron, I realized—all at once—who she was. The dark-haired, ample-bosomed woman from my memory, the grandmother my father had told me was dead.

The apple shone, red, in her palm.

I took it from her dizzily as everything fell into place. The sadness Kunegunde showed when I told her my mother died. The huge garden. The memory of swimming with my mother in that pool. No wonder my mother had told me to come to Gothel.

"What is it, Haelewise?"

The apple rolled out of my hand and under the table.

Kunegunde followed it with her eyes. "Cat got your tongue?"

"You're my—" I wanted to say the word *grandmother*, to run to her and embrace her, but as soon as Kunegunde realized what I was going to say, her eyes flashed.

"*Anasehlan!*" she shouted, raising her hands. Her voice lilted with the rhythm of my mother's voice when she swore in the old language. The spell echoed through the air, snapping with power. My chest collapsed, and a terrible force sucked all of the air out of my lungs. I couldn't breathe. My hands went to my throat.

Seeing my fear, her expression turned regretful and she lowered her hands. The action released me. I gasped for air.

"We can't speak of that," she said. "Your mother made me swear. There is blood-magic involved."

I nodded, slowly, though I was more focused on trying to recover my breath than understanding. Once I could breathe again, I worked to regain my composure, reflecting on what she had said. Outside, the storm raged. Wind whistled unhappily around the tower. "Blood-magic?"

She shook her head fiercely. "You're not anywhere near ready to learn about that. You just got here."

When I was recovered, we set about making the dough for the *strützel*. She seemed truly concerned about my well-being. She kept apologizing, asking me if I felt all right. She smiled at me as we worked the dough, calling me "little one," the same name my mother had called me, and I realized that must've been her pet name for my mother.

I couldn't believe I hadn't noticed their resemblance before. As I watched her braid the dough, I saw shadows of my mother in her—the way she pressed her lips together tight to discourage talk about a subject she didn't like, the way she flicked her wrist when she braided the dough—and I longed to grow close to her like a granddaughter should.

While the *strützel* baked, we made dinner: the goose I had shot that morning, the mushrooms I had picked on the way home. We roasted the goose over the hearthfire and cooked the mushrooms in the cauldron in the goose's fat. We made spiced wine, seasoned with anise and a hundred apple slices. She said the meal needed to be good; the new moon was a time of transition, when the otherworldly weather changed and prayers drifted naturally into the next world, so tonight we would set out food as an offering to the Mother.

I didn't understand what she was saying about the otherworldly weather, but the idea of making an offering to my mother's goddess with my grandmother brought tears to my eyes. I remembered all the times my mother and I had burned offerings back home when my father was out. I wondered if the ritual would allow me to feel the mist again, so my mother would be able to come to me as she had on my first nights here, and I felt a wild stab of hope.

Thunder cracked and boomed while the goose finished roasting, and waves of rain crashed into the shutters. Kunegunde carved a spiral into each of three hollowed-out bread crusts, covering each with goose and apples and cheese and the delicious-smelling mushrooms. In a basket, she set one of the crusts, arranging *strützel* in a pretty ring around it. Then she walked to the door of the tower and set it on the ground outside. I stood behind her, watching, hopeful and eager.

When she bowed her head, I bowed mine too.

"Mother," she said, reaching for my hand. "Everything we do, we do in your name. Take this food as our offering. Bless us with enough firewood to stay warm and enough clients to eat well this winter. Keep the tower safe."

My eyes watered at the simplicity of her prayer, and my heart swelled with hope. For a moment, I thought I could feel the mist gathering, an otherworldly presence, but the sensation was so subtle, I wasn't sure. Then it passed, and my heart broke. I reached out, trying desperately to feel it again, but it was gone. Kunegunde stood silent beside me—eyes closed, back straight—her expression transfixed. Clearly, she felt something that I couldn't. When she opened her eyes, a sob leapt from my throat. The disappointment was too much for me to bear.

"Haelewise. What's wrong?"

I crumpled into myself. "I couldn't feel it. I know you said that happens, that it's like a scent, but I could tell you *did*."

Kunegunde led me over to the chair beside the hearthfire and made me a cup of caudle to settle my stomach. Leaving the food on the table uneaten, she sat in the chair beside me. I sat there for a long time—eyes closed, filled with a sadness so heavy I couldn't even lift a finger. After a while, I knew there were sounds coming out of her mouth, but I couldn't bring myself to make sense of them.

"*Haelewise*," she said again. This time, I snapped out of my trance. "It comes and goes. There's no controlling it. This was supposed to be a happy night. What can I do to cheer you up?"

I thought for a long time. My thoughts were sluggish with disappointment. It took me several sips of caudle to rouse myself from it and recognize that I could use her offer as an opportunity. Groggily, I rummaged through all the questions I had for her, trying to decide which one to ask first so I could best capitalize on her pity. If there was ever a time to ask about the bird-mother, I decided, it was tonight. I made my voice small. "Will you tell me about the figurine? Do you know why my mother had it?"

Kunegunde went very still. For a moment, I was afraid that I had pushed her too far. Then she took a deep breath. When she spoke, her voice was measured. "Your mother, like me, worshipped the ancient Mother, who's been forgotten by a world obsessed with the Father."

"That's who the bird-mother represents?"

Kunegunde nodded.

"Who is she?"

"She has many names. She is worshipped in secret everywhere the dove flies, here and in the East, as far away as Rome and Jerusalem."

"What does it mean to follow her?"

She took a long drink of wine. "To protect women and their knowledge. To hold the natural world sacred. To learn the hidden powers of root and leaf and the creatures of the earth."

"Why does she take the form of a bird?"

Kunegunde leaned back in her chair. "That's a difficult question. I'm not sure if anyone knows for sure, but every effigy I've ever seen of her depicts her as a bird-woman. I've always thought she is more like the mist in the forest, or a living shadow, or the ants that will eat that offering we just set outside."

I nodded, drawing a deep breath, alarmed by her comparison of the goddess to crawling insects. I dismissed the thought, mulling over the rest of what she'd said. She'd ignored the most important part of my question. I needed to know how to use the figurine so I could conjure my mother again. I made my voice childlike, small. "What is the figurine? How does it work?"

For a split second, I thought I saw her wince. Then her expression went blank. "It's just a charm," she said, as if the question was silly. "Something you carry around for good luck."

Frustration filled me. I knew she was lying. The figurine had something to do with why I could hear my mother's voice; otherwise, how would she know I had it? Her refusal to tell me what she knew, what I desperately wanted to know, infuriated me, but I was afraid to confront her after the spell she cast on me earlier. I closed my eyes, deciding to pretend to believe her for now, racking my brain for a way to approach the subject more indirectly. "Are there many who worship the Mother?"

Kunegunde's voice went hard. "Not anymore. We have to worship in secret. The world of men is wicked, Haelewise. Full of royals and clergymen so afraid of losing power, they'll execute anyone who stands up to them."

I waited for her to go on, but she fell quiet. The fire crackled. "The spell on the stones. How does it work?"

Flames leapt in her eyes. "I don't know. It's been here longer than I have. As for how it works, this is a thin place. The spell draws its power from the mist beyond the veil."

"A thin place?" I said, confused. "Like what I feel during births and deaths? But permanently?"

"Yes." She shifted in her chair, still watching the fire.

How could my ability to sense something so powerful fade in and out? It didn't make sense. The sluggish disappointment that I'd felt earlier returned, making my head foggy. Suddenly it was hard for me to think again. I took a deep breath, trying to decide what to ask her next, fighting my mental torpor.

"How does a place become thin?" I asked finally.

It was a long time before she took a sip of her wine and spoke. "The same thing that makes the veil thin anywhere. Births, deaths, the presence of gods or ghosts. In places like this, the veil has thinned so many times that it has become worn. The boundary between this world and the next is permeable."

"What happened here?"

Kunegunde shook her head. "I don't know. Nor did the wise woman who lived here before me—I asked the same question when I first arrived. All I know is those aren't ordinary stones, Haelewise. They're graves. I suspect they belong to women. That whoever cast the spell did so to protect the women who remained."

CHAPTER FIFTEEN

Winter fell soft and quiet over the tower, covering the wood in a great white hush. As the days grew cold, Kunegunde acted more and more as a grandmother would. She began checking that I wore my cloak when we went on walks. She made me more powder and fertility oil when I ran out. From time to time, she called me "little one." These gestures brought tears to my eyes, though her temper was still short and her falsehoods complicated my granddaughterly affection. In early December, when my mother would've told stories about my birth and remarked that I was a year older, Kunegunde said nothing, and I found myself haunted by a great sadness.

That winter would be the coldest I've ever lived through, and I've lived through many a winter in my long life. There was snow and snow and more snow, as if the gods wanted to erase every living thing from the forest, to unmake its capacity for life. The wood turned black and white, an intricate latticework of branches and snow. The birds, aside from the ravens Kunegunde kept, all but disappeared. Snowbanks drifted, and we woke to the hoofprints of stags. Frost edged the leaves of the holly bush. Winter berries ripened, as red as blood. Without the reminder of services, the days blended together. Kunegunde celebrated no saints' days, marking only Yule, the shortest day of the year. Her midwinter ritual involved spiced wine, a roast of lamb, and a hearthfire built of logs smeared with lamb's blood that raged into the night.

On the night of the first full moon after Yule, I woke with the sense that there was someone outside. Opening the shutters to peer down into the garden, I saw Kunegunde bent over the birdbath, chanting over the ice that glistened within it. What in the world is she doing, I thought, remembering the rumors about the queen whispering into her hand-mirror.

Her corpse-braids hung down either side of her waist, white ribbons glowing silver, her expression fixed with intense concentration. She was perspiring, murmuring something under her breath. When her lips stopped moving, the ice flashed with colors that were not a reflection. After a moment, they coalesced into the shape of a giant wolf leaping through a wood. The beast was impossibly large, made of shadow. Everything about it seemed wrong. Even at this distance, I knew immediately what it was. Ulrich, in the wolf-skin.

She was using the birdbath to scry on him.

When I gasped, Kunegunde looked up as if she had heard the noise. I jumped back from the window, resolving to get a closer look at the basin in the morning.

The next day while Kunegunde was working on her manuscript, I slipped into the garden, looking over my shoulder to make sure she hadn't followed. When I was sure I was alone, I walked casually to the birdbath. It was waist-high, carved from faded stone. There were hairline cracks in its walls, not deep enough to let water out. All over the inside of the bowl were faded symbols like the ones on the mirrors and Kunegunde's manuscript. Was my mother's mirror for scrying too? How had it shattered? Had Kunegunde given it to her?

Back inside, Kunegunde was still hard at work illuminating a page of her manuscript. The border was decorated with dozens of images of birds in flight; indecipherable black symbols looped and curled all over the page. Some of the birds were outlined in a faint golden sheen. She was making her way down the page, gilding them. Her quill glistened with a gold leaf suspension, which I had seen her make with stag's glue.

Watching her, it occurred to me that my mother *spoke* this language, that she had probably been able to *read* it. Suddenly I was overwhelmed with an urge to touch the symbols, to feel them under my fingers, to shape them with my tongue.

"Is that the old language?" I breathed. "It's on your mirror and the birdbath. It must be."

Kunegunde was making a thin line of gold down the wing of a bird. "Yes," she said absent-mindedly, without looking up.

"Will you teach it to me?"

"Someday," she said. "When you're ready." But there was a guarded note in her tone, a warning, and I understood she meant that someday was a long time away.

During what must've been one of the first days of February, the ravens began acting strangely during our afternoon reading. All three hopped down from their perches on the shelves and croaked noisily. As we looked up from our books, they headed toward the caged windows and flew out. "Someone is approaching the circle," Kunegunde said.

"Is their hearing so subtle?"

"No, but their sense of smell is." Kunegunde got up to go to the door and look out. "People seldom travel this far in winter. Who-ever this is must be desperate."

The visitor the ravens escorted back was an ashen pregnant woman in motley robes and furs who looked like she must've begged for the two large wheels of cheese and bread loaves she offered us. She kept looking over her shoulder at the ravens as she stood on the threshold, like she was afraid of them.

When we shut the door behind her, she relaxed and explained her situation. She'd experienced no pangs, though she expected to have her child last month. Her midwife couldn't help her. She had begun to feel poorly and was afraid for her life. Kunegunde took her coins and let her in. "How long since you felt the child move?"

"Almost a week. Several days at least."

"When did you last bleed?"

"Late March."

Kunegunde frowned. "That is too long. If the child hasn't died yet, it will soon. From the color of your skin, I'm sorry, I fear it already has."

The woman nodded grimly. "My midwife said as much."

"We'll start with gentle herbs. If that doesn't work, we'll try pennyroyal."

Kunegunde told me to ready the hearth area and make the caudle. I didn't say anything, but I agreed with Kunegunde that this wouldn't go well. I couldn't feel what I usually felt before the birth of a living child, the tension in the air. Either the woman's labor was nowhere near starting, or her time had already passed. I began making the preparations—hanging tapestries over the window-slots, lighting candles on every surface—reliving all the times that I made these preparations with my mother.

My eyes were wet by the time I got the fire going and hung caudle over it to warm. As I watched the fire, trying to collect myself before I turned around, my sadness gave way to a hollow ache, an anger in my breast. My mother should still be here, I thought as the flames crackled. I should be apprenticed to her.

When I told Kunegunde I was finished, she asked me to get the snakeskin I'd seen hanging before the window and a particular paper talisman. She hung the talisman around the woman's neck and tied the snake around her belly as a birthing girdle. Then she told me to rub rose oil on the woman's groin, and get tosh and primrose oil from the cabinet so that she could prepare a draught.

As I handed her what she'd asked for, I couldn't help but feel morose. I had seen my mother use a similar brew to bring on labor, but I doubted it would do much good today. As the woman sipped the concoction, Kunegunde murmured something under her breath—a chant or prayer—and reached under the woman's skirt. I was shocked when she pulled her hand away, her expression turning hopeful. "The babe may only be too cramped to stir."

I turned around so they couldn't see my skeptical expression. I had never attended a live birth when I didn't sense tension in the air. As the hours passed, my pity for the woman grew. I listened to her tell Kunegunde about her past labors as we waited for the draught to take. We drank the caudle. The sun set, the shadows in the tower grew deeper, and my anger at Kunegunde ebbed. As I watched the woman cradle her belly, it occurred to me that Phoebe would've given birth by now. I wondered if Matthäus regretted his choice to obey his father. Did he still hate Phoebe? Did he miss me? The idea that he might be stuck in a loveless marriage pleased me, I confess.

I lit the lanterns on the walls. Midnight came and went, and the skin of the world refused to grow thin. When it was clear the draught and caudle had done no good, Kunegunde gave the woman pennyroyal. Within an hour, her pangs were so intense that her round face shone with sweat. Each time she experienced a pang, I felt terrible for her. Usually by this time in labor, the skin of the world was stretched so tight, it was ready to split open. The only time I had felt nothing like this was before a stillbirth.

I rubbed the woman's back with peppermint oil as my mother had taught me to do, whispering words of comfort. When the woman's water broke, Kunegunde told me to melt some snow. I did as she said, though I was sure there would be no live baby to bathe. As the woman's pangs came faster, Kunegunde told her to bend, rock her hips, and remove her skirt. When she did, I thought I saw the shape of a foot kick the surface of her belly. I watched her skin until I saw movement again, shocked.

"God's teeth," I said, forgetting to hide my disbelief. "You were right."

Kunegunde saw it too. "The child is alive, but breech. We have to turn her."

The woman nodded, a determined look coming over her face.

A terrible alarm filled me. It was one thing not to be able to sense the mist at the edge of things here, but if the child was alive, I should be able to feel possibility in the air or a pull into the next world. I had been able to sense that all my life. Kunegunde set to work massaging the woman's belly with the same technique my mother used. She told me to prepare a bath and get the goat's horn with the cloth teat in case the mother had trouble nursing. I did everything she said to do, unsettled.

It was another hour before Kunegunde said the baby was in position. As the birth drew near, Kunegunde instructed the woman to squat on the floor beside a nest of clean linens and rags. The woman screeched as she pushed the child out into Kunegunde's hands, then crumpled to the floor. The baby was larger than any I'd ever seen with a full head of dark hair. Wriggling, balled-up fists. A girl. I was so startled by her movement that when Kunegunde handed her to me, I froze.

"The throat," she said. "Didn't your mother teach you to clear the throat?"

I nodded. The child opened her eyes, shocked and silent and still. I reached into her mouth, waiting for her soul to whoosh past me as I did. But nothing happened; the air in the room was still. The baby gasped all the same, batting yellow-rimmed eyes as she began to mewl. I could scarcely breathe as I smoothed her fuzzy black hair. Why hadn't I sensed her soul?

"See the yellow eyes, the shallow breath?" Kunegunde asked me from where she squatted next to the crumpled woman. "It's the pennyroyal. Bathe her. Swaddle her, while I bring her mother to. The best remedy for that is mother's milk."

The warm water on the baby's skin made her quiet. Her eyes searched mine, wonder-struck, as I cleaned blood and mucus from her hair. She looked to be an ordinary child with an ordinary will. I was rattled that I couldn't sense her soul. When I pulled her from the water, she screamed. I swaddled her until she calmed again. Rocking her to and fro, humming, swaying my hips, I remembered the way I felt holding the miller's son. I was happy the baby appeared to be healthy, but other than that, I felt *nothing*. Despite the fact that I held a child in my arms, I felt utterly disconnected from the work I had always loved.

The babe started crying again. Be quiet, I wanted to scream.

"She's hungry," I said, irritated, raising my voice so Kunegunde would hear.

My grandmother held a cup of water to the mother's lips without answering.

"Kunegunde—" I said, indignant, trying to catch her attention.

Kunegunde continued to ignore me, focused on helping the woman up.

"Another girl?" the woman said when she was finally upright, eyeing her baby weakly from the pile of rags where Kunegunde had propped her up. She patted her chest.

I brought her the infant, my throat tightening with fear. She settled the girl expertly at her breast and pulled aside her robe. The babe went silent immediately, her small mouth seeking out the nipple. The woman closed her eyes and leaned back, relief on her face. I glanced at Kunegunde, who shook her head and mouthed the word *later.*

"Stay the rest of the night," Kunegunde told the woman, who nodded gratefully. "Both of you need rest."

On the way to bed that night, Kunegunde slipped into my room, shut the door behind her, and sat beside me on my bed. In the other room, I could hear the woman cooing to her baby. Kunegunde lowered her voice. "What upsets you, little one?"

"Did it seem to you that there was something strange about that birth?"

Kunegunde looked puzzled. "Only the child's too-long making in her mother's womb and the pennyroyal. Why do you ask?"

"Can you sense souls?"

Kunegunde cleared her throat. "How do you mean?"

"Usually during a birth, I sense possibility in the air, the trembling of the child's soul. This time, I felt nothing. My ability to sense the next world, the movement of souls. The thing that made me a good midwife. It's vanished."

She watched me steadily. "Ah, yes. That happens sometimes. Like I told you before, it comes and goes. As you grow older, the gift can fade. You can still be a good midwife without it."

"Why would it fade now? It's always been reliable."

"Who knows how these mysteries work?" she said, getting up, squeezing my hand. "You did well tonight, little one. I'm exhausted. Let's talk more later."

There was something strange about her tone, her eagerness to go to bed. I could tell she knew more than she was letting on. "Good night," I said helplessly.

As I listened to the sound of her footsteps going upstairs, I felt powerless. Why was Kunegunde hiding things from me? How could I make her tell me what she knew? I needed to know what was happening to me.

CHAPTER SIXTEEN

That night, I dreamed I was a great black bird with talons, searching for something in the wood. I landed in a tree beside a clearing, where a masked rider sat astride a horse bearing Prince Ulrich's banner. The rider dismounted, unsheathing a silver dagger to menace a black-haired woman in ragged clothes who had fallen in the snow. As he advanced on her, I knew with certainty that he was going to kill her. I dove at him to protect the woman, to peck out his eyes, to tear him apart.

Jolting awake, I could feel a faint voice rushing in from the next world, an indecipherable hiss too faint to hear. I knew that my mother was trying to tell me something, that the dream was an omen. But for some reason, I couldn't hear what she was trying to say. I rubbed the figurine, praying, but nothing happened. I was so frustrated about my inability to understand the message that I couldn't get back to sleep. The sounds of the baby's cries and her mother's feet on the stairs didn't help things.

By the time I came down to breakfast, frazzled from lack of rest, I decided to ask Kunegunde about it. "I had a nightmare," I said, sitting across from my grandmother. There were goose eggs and bread in a basket on the table. The mother had gone home.

"What about?"

"I'm a bird, soaring over the wood, looking for something. Down below, I see a woman being menaced by a rider with Prince Ulrich's banner. He's about to kill her with a silver dagger. I swoop down to tear him apart with my talons."

She watched me steadily, her expression shocked.

"At the end of the dream, I hear the voice that spoke to me before, trying to tell me something."

Her expression darkened. "Tell you what?"

"I don't know. That's what's frustrating. I feel like I'm supposed to do something, but I have no idea what."

She watched me for a moment across the table, very still. Fear flashed on her face, though I could tell she was trying to hide it. "You should pay no attention to such dreams," she said angrily. "I told you, the voice that speaks to you is the voice of a demon."

"I told *you*, I don't believe it is."

She glared at me. "I've been putting a touch of alrūne in your powder like you asked. You remember what I showed you in my speculum. Alrūne attracts demons."

"Forget it," I said, deciding to drop the subject. I was too tired for an argument.

That afternoon, Kunegunde and I went for our daily walk into the forest. The snow was already a foot deep, enveloping the bottom of the stones in the circle as we passed through them. I hadn't felt the spell on the stones in months, and the absence of the sensation made me resentful. Outside the circle, the whole world had gone quiet, an icy hush of powder and wood. As our boots crunched the snow, I thought I heard something—a snap of faraway twig, amplified by the cold. Meeting Kunegunde's eyes, I froze in place. The voices we heard next were distant, echoing across the snow. She held out her arm to stop me from bolting, but there was little danger of that. "Be still," she hissed now, reaching into her satchel to put something in her mouth. She chewed it quickly, swallowed, and chanted under her breath.

"*Leek haptbhendun von hzost. Tuid hestu.*"

Her body crumpled to the snow, and her eyes rolled back in her head.

Looking down at her, I wondered if this was how I looked when I swooned. When I knelt down to shake her, she didn't respond.

After a moment, Erste zoomed down through the canopy of leaves toward us, his eyes flashing amber. He perched before her on the snow—eyes fading to black—and her eyes popped open. "Kingsguard," Kunegunde said dizzily. She reached out to a nearby tree to steady herself. "Princess Frederika must be nearby. Help me back to the tower."

There was snow on her corpse-braids and kirtle. I took her arm, steadying her, so shocked I could barely form words. "What just happened?"

"Let's go," Kunegunde said, a look of worry coming over her face.

"What did you do?" I asked again. "What *was* that?"

"Help me back. Now. I can't risk being seen. Remember what I told you about the writ for my death?"

I started moving toward the tower. "Tell me what you did."

She spoke slowly, breathing heavily as we went, as if it took great effort. "Everything that is done can be undone. Even the place-ment of soul within flesh. That chant loosed my soul. Once freed it entered Erste, and we flew through the trees to find the source of the noise."

I blinked at her, unable to grasp what she said. "You saw them yourself?"

She glanced uneasily into the trees. "From the branches of a nearby spruce, through his eyes." She nodded at the bird on her shoulder. Wind whistled through the pine needles.

My thoughts raced. If her chant loosed her soul, then I truly had lost the ability to sense the movement of souls. Why not, I thought angrily. I had lost everything else. The ability to hear my mother's voice. The ability to sleep through the night.

I stamped through the snow after her.

We hurried back toward the circle, my mind running through what my mother had said about the *kindefresser*. She could take any form. All the amber-eyed ravens that had come to visit me when

I was a girl. God's teeth. What was it Kunegunde said when I first arrived here? That Erste did what he liked. That bird had led me to her tower. Kunegunde had led me to her tower inside him. "Do you do this often?"

"No," she said, her breath coming in huffs. "You can't go far. You can be killed, just as you can in your own body. It's a risk to inhabit a bird."

When we reached the tower, Kunegunde washed her hands and had me help her upstairs to bed, warning me that she might not wake for a while. That night, I lay in my bed, mulling over what I had learned. My father would've run from what I'd seen that day, or at the very least demanded Kunegunde have an exorcism. I remembered what she said when I first arrived at the tower, that the alrūne would make me susceptible to demons. Was she truly afraid of demons or was she putting on a show to make *me* afraid of them?

My gift had started fading almost as soon as I got here, when I told her I heard a voice, and she started making me take the gooseberry powder. How could I trust that she put any alrūne in my powder at all? What if she put something in it to suppress my gift instead?

I pulled the bird-mother charm from my pouch and ran my hands over her curves, but nothing happened. Nothing had happened in months. I closed my fingers around her in the dark, her stone cool on my palm, and prayed for guidance.

There was no call to breakfast the next morning. I woke to the sound of Erste rapping the shutters. This had happened before when Kunegunde closed the shutters of her window upstairs. I tried to ignore him, burying my head under my pillow. "God's teeth," I said. "Go away."

For a while, the rapping faded. I must've fallen asleep until I woke some time later to the sound of croaking. It sounded like a frog had died and was using dark magic to resurrect himself. I groaned and got up to open the shutters. Erste flew in and soared up the stairs into Kunegunde's room.

The bird gone, I sat on my bed, watching the sunlight pour through the open window. Why had my mother told me to come here, if Kunegunde was the kind of person who would give me something to suppress my gift? What was Kunegunde hiding?

By the time I headed downstairs for breakfast, my chest was tight with frustration and bitterness. As I heated yesterday's rabbit stew, all three ravens descended upon me, flapping around and begging for meat and bones. I tossed them my scraps, disgusted, unable to apprehend why Kunegunde kept such scavengers around.

It took me all morning to complete the chores we usually did together. After Kunegunde's deception, I found myself feeling incredibly resentful about the extra work. By the time I fed the geese cabbage and leftover parsnips—the mother and father honking greedily, the goslings pecking at my hands—I was indignant.

My boots sank in the drifts as I walked back to the tower. I shivered as I opened the door. Then I stomped upstairs to the sloping chamber where Kunegunde slept on the third floor, hell-bent on figuring out what she was hiding.

Beside the bed, Kunegunde's purse bulged with whatever she'd eaten before her soul left her flesh. I tiptoed toward the chair to see what it was. Kunegunde didn't stir. The object in her purse was yellow and wrinkled. So shriveled, it took me a moment to recognize it as the husk of one of my golden apples, which Kunegunde must've set out somewhere to dry in the sun.

I stared at it in disbelief. Kunegunde had sworn the alrūne would make me susceptible to demons. She had told me not to eat it, and then she had eaten it herself? My heart filled with outrage.

She lay still on the bed, asleep, huddled under her blankets. In that moment I hated her, pure and simple. I wanted to hurt her back.

I slipped the alrūne back into her purse so she wouldn't know that I knew. Then I left her room to wash my hands. Afterward, I sat in my bedroom, trying to fathom what this discovery meant. Kunegunde didn't want me to hear what my mother was trying to tell me, enough that she lied about the danger the alrūne represented, and I was pretty certain she was putting something in the powder to suppress my gift. I thought of the way Kunegunde's eyes flashed when she spoke of the world of men. Did she want to keep me here, the way my mother tied a keeping string around my wrist when I was little? Was she afraid my mother would tell me to leave her?

My stomach sank. That had to be it. On my first day here, I'd admitted that my mother told me to visit the next mountain, right before she took the alrūne away.

I spent the rest of that day trying to decide what to do about my newfound knowledge. I wondered what was on the next mountain, if I could go there without Kunegunde knowing. That evening, I picked up the pouch of gooseberry powder that sat on the small table beside my cot. The pouch was small, inconsequential in weight. I remembered a petal-picking song from when I was little. *Will I or won't I*, it went. *Shall I or shan't I?* After a long moment, feeling defiant, I put the powder away, deciding not to mix it with my evening drink.

Kunegunde woke an hour or so later, when she padded downstairs in fur slippers and a heavy robe. Lantern-light leapt along the walls. The fire crackled in its ring. I was sitting at the table, examining a page from her speculum. Before me was a half-drunk cup of wine. As the day drew to a close, my anger had only increased. The effect was tiring. After supper, I had read the labels of the earthenware jugs in the entryway and made some spiced wine to calm myself. By the time she woke, I was on my third cup.

She peered into my drink as she sat down beside me, then poured a cup for herself. "How long was I out?"

"A full day." My voice was clipped.

"Expect it, if I do that again. It takes effort for a soul to settle back into a body. You need rest. Did you feed the ravens?"

I nodded, silent.

"The pigs and geese? The goats?"

"Everything we normally do," I said flatly.

She took a sip. "What's wrong?"

Anger rose in my throat like bile. I wanted to confront her, to call her out on her lies, but I was afraid she would cast me out. I felt trapped. The words tumbled out before I could think better of them. "You know *everything* about me. My parents, my upbringing. My spells, my nightmares. You expect me to trust you, to obey you, to believe everything you say. But I know nothing about you!"

Kunegunde met my eyes. She didn't respond for a long time. For a moment I didn't know if she would. I thought she was going to ignore my grievance completely and drift off to sleep. Then she nodded, once, stretching her hands over the fire, the flames giving her fingers a reddish glow, and met my gaze. "How about I tell you the story of how I came to keep this tower? Would that help?"

I glared at her, my indignance slowly giving way to curiosity. Finally, I nodded.

She smirked, shaking her head at my hesitance. Then she took another sip of her wine and leaned back in her chair, closing her eyes. After a moment, I heard the slow tumble of her voice. "My parents marked me for religious life when I was small. I wasn't their tenth child, but I had spells much like yours, and they thought holy life might keep them in check. When I was ten, they sent me away to live with a devout widow, who immediately set about remedying the holes in my religious education. Also there was a girl who wished to be an anchoress, and another young woman by the name of Hildegard."

After everything else she'd lied about, I was dubious. "You knew Hildegard as a girl."

Kunegunde nodded. She leaned back in her chair, sipping her drink, staring into the flames. "She was like a sister to me. She was often ill, but when she was well, we roamed the countryside, playing in the wild places of the estate. We both felt the world itself was sacred. She was obsessed with what she called its *greenness*, the force that dwells in all living things. She was always so sure about the vows we would take. She said she was destined from birth to be the Lord's servant. I did not share her faith. I found the widow's lessons constricting. The memorization of psalms, the obsession with purity and cleanliness. I preferred to spend my days in the woods, listening to the calls of wild animals and birds. The lessons did nothing to stop my spells, which still struck without rhyme or reason. The widow consulted with healers, giving me remedies. As I grew older, and my body blossomed, I dreamed of escaping the life my parents chose for me, of finding a husband and starting a family. When Hildegard was ill, I spent my days gathering flowers in the forests and fields. I dreamed of running away from the widow's manor. One of my favorite places was a hyssop field with a brook running through it on the edge of the estate. In summer I used to take off my boots and wade in the stream, breathing in the hyssop's bitter mint. It was there that I met a handsome lord from a neighboring estate who would often pass astride his horse on the other side of the stream. When I was alone, he spoke to me. If Hildegard was there, he only waved. He was so handsome, Haelewise. Broad shoulders, laughing eyes, and kind." She met my eyes, her own bright in the firelight, the loose strands of hair around her face glowing silver. For a moment, I could see the young woman she had once been beneath her wrinkled expression—in the wonder that lit her eyes and the wist in her smile. "I loved the way he looked at me, Haelewise, like my body was a holy thing. He worshipped me."

I searched her face, surprised to see her speak of love. The fire crackled between us. She smiled, her eyes faraway, caught up.

"Nearly every day at noon, he would pass on horseback, and Hildegard was often ill. If I was alone and I saw him coming, my spirits would lift. Sitting on opposite sides of the stream, we talked of everything: his father's statecraft, his siblings, how much I missed my family, my doubts about holy life. Something held us there and caught us, making us linger with each other by the stream. Over time, he became all I thought about. I believe that was true for him as well. There is a force, Haelewise, that draws lovers together. I could feel it every time we sat across from each other. A heaviness behind my eyes, a pulling toward him. It felt *right*."

I swallowed a sip of my wine, drawn into the story despite my anger with her.

"The day before we were to leave the estate and take our vows, the widow sent for the healer to examine Hildegard. Hildegard was getting over one of her illnesses, and the widow wanted to confirm she was well enough to travel. While we waited for the physician, I went out to the hyssop field, hoping to meet the lord and say goodbye. I fell asleep while I was waiting for him, as I often did. In that field, sunlight warming my eyelids, I dreamed that we were together." She met my eyes, her own feverishly bright, glistening that uncanny amber. "There was something about this dream, Haelewise. It sprang from deep inside me. Even now, I can't explain it. When I woke, I knew it was holy, a vision that would come to pass. Not long after I woke, he rode up. It was hot. Midsummer. I asked him if he wanted to walk barefoot through the stream to cool ourselves, to search the creekbed for pretty stones. I tied the skirt of my dress up, fully aware that the sight of my bare legs would distract him. I pulled up my hair, showing off the nape of my neck. He took off his boots, rolled up his pants, and took my hand." She paused, her eyes reflecting the firelight. "The widow would've whipped me if she saw me like that. Clothes and hair in disarray, skirt tied up, holding a lord's hand. It was exactly the sort of thing she was supposed to protect me from, but everyone was

always so worried about Hildegard, no one paid me any attention."
She laughed bitterly.

When she took another draught of wine, I had a sip of my own,
my doubts all but forgotten. By then, I was caught up in the suspense of her story, waiting for something to happen between her
and the lord, hanging on to her every word.

"I told him that this was the last time I would see him," she
said, "and he looked at me with such sorrow. I sat on a boulder
that jutted from the water and gestured for him to sit beside me.
When he did, my thoughts became fixed on the place where our
thighs touched. His nearness was like an incantation. It pulled me
to him. When I looked into his eyes, I understood what my body
knew already. I was *supposed* to kiss him. When I did, he went stiff,
surprised, but after a moment he kissed me back. I cannot explain
what happened next except to say that we kissed for an eternity.
And then—"

She stopped there to stare into the fire. Flames leapt in her eyes.
She went silent. I filled her cup, noticing the way the muscles in
her face had relaxed, as if she had kept this secret far too long. She
drank before she spoke again, and I could tell that she wanted to
linger over that moment. "It was beautiful, Haelewise. The most
sacred hour of my life. I don't regret one second of it. I can still see
the field in my mind's eye. Lilac flowers everywhere, humming
with hawk-moths, orange-winged. I pushed him onto that bed of
flowers. I remember the scent of the blooms beneath us, the color
of the sky above. The sky was blue, that day, perfectly clear. When
it was over, we lay together in those flowers for I don't know how
long, breathless. Then we said our goodbyes.

"When he was gone, I pulled the flowers out of my hair. I
cleaned my dress in the brook. I said nothing when I returned to
the manor. I held those moments close. The next day, we began
the journey to the abbey. By the time we arrived and prepared to
take our vows, my menses hadn't come." Kunegunde shook her

head, falling silent. When she spoke again, her voice trembled. "I was so happy when I realized I was with child. It was the perfect reason not to take the veil. The first thing I did was tell Hilde-gard. I thought—naïvely, of course—that she might be happy for me. But her loyalty to the laws of the Church far outweighed our friendship. She shamed me for my condition. She asked me why I had defiled my body. Mortified, the next morning before dawn, I took my horse from the stables and rode south. I went to see my parents, to confess what had happened, so they could go to the lord's family and offer him the dowry they had set aside for the convent. But when I told them, they shamed me just as Hildegard had, saying the lord wouldn't want to marry me since I had defiled myself."

She met my eyes. "I hated them for that. I still do. Condemning me for the one thing I knew I had done right. I fled, riding south without a destination. I slept outside, in barns, as I wandered the countryside. Female cooks sometimes took pity on me and let me wash dishes in exchange for a room. At one such inn, the cook told me about a Mother Gothel who was a friend to women in my con-dition. Hoping she would take me in, I set out to find her tower." Kunegunde met my eyes. "It was here that I gave birth."

I blinked, surprised to find that her story had reached its end. The night encircled us, the tower dark. The flames leapt in the hearth. I blinked, finding myself overwhelmed by her story. But as I turned the story over in my mind, all my doubts and suspicions about Kunegunde came rushing back. I thought of the dreams I had been having, the way Kunegunde insisted they were sent by a demon. If Kunegunde could have a holy dream, then so could I. Unable to restrain my bitterness, I frowned. "How did you know the dream was holy? That it wasn't demon-sent?"

Panic flitted across her face. For an instant, her eyes went wide and fearful, like the eyes of an animal caught in a trap. Then she mastered her feelings; her expression went as still as the ice in the birdbath. "I hadn't eaten any alrūne, little one. Remember what I showed you in that book? Alrūne is a spiritual poison. It causes *false* visions."

I only nodded, my anger simmering. There was no doubt now. She was lying to me.

CHAPTER SEVENTEEN

That night, I had the dream again. I woke the next morning unable to shake the vision from my head. When the dream world finally dissipated, I found myself more frustrated than ever that I couldn't hear my mother's voice. She was trying to tell me something, I was convinced, and Kunegunde didn't want me to hear her. I sat up in bed, sunlight pouring through the stripe between the shutters, blanket soft on my legs. The bright light made me squint.

God's teeth, I thought, searching for my mother's shattered hand-mirror. There was a shard large enough at its center for me to see my eyes. When I looked into it, my suspicions were confirmed. The golden color that the alrūne had given my irises had been replaced by a deep red. The gooseberry powder, I realized. And now, the black of my pupils looked like it was starting to swallow the red up. If I continued not taking the powder, my eyes would be completely black soon. How could I hide that from Kunegunde? I would have to avoid her gaze as much as possible and hope she didn't notice.

I remembered what my mother said in the garden: that I would find my purpose. Whatever that meant, it had something to do with her goddess, these dreams I was having, her faith. I resolved to find where Kunegunde hid the alrūne so I could hear my mother's voice again. Eating the alrūne would also make the difference in my eyes less noticeable.

The downstairs room was gloomy enough that I could spend that day shadowing Kunegunde, helping her experiment with a remedy from an ancient tome that she hadn't tried before. I tried to avoid meeting her gaze directly as much as I could. Fire leapt in the hearth, and her ravens roosted on the upper shelves, startling me each time they croaked. I pretended to be interested in wortcunnery, watching carefully whenever Kunegunde opened a drawer in the apothecary cabinet or one of the earthenware jugs near the door. Wherever she had stashed the alrūne, it wasn't in the drawers or jugs she used that day.

By evening, I was exhausted from all the deception and frustrated that I hadn't figured out where she kept it. I did not put the powder in my evening drink. When the ravens started swooping at the shutters to get outside, like they often did when there was someone in the forest, I let them out and volunteered to follow them to see what was there.

"Don't leave the circle," Kunegunde reminded me.

Outside, the sun was sinking over the horizon. The last tendrils of daylight were turning pink. The ravens soared away from the tower, sounding their awful deep-throated cry again and again. I followed them into the forest. The wind bit my face. I fingered the bird-woman in my pouch as I walked into the trees, praying that whatever ill omen their calls predicted would not apply to me.

As I neared the brook, I paused, realizing that I could feel a faint tension, a possibility in the air again. Relief coursed through me. It was as I thought. My gift hadn't vanished. Kunegunde's gooseberry powder had stolen it from me.

As I neared the edge of the stone circle, I slowed, trying to decide whether to break Kunegunde's rule. Then something came over me. At first I didn't recognize the source of the shiver. I thought I was just cold. Then I felt the tension in the air, the pull. My soul lifting from my skin.

I woke on my back in the snow, a dull ache in my head. A fainting spell? Now that I had stopped taking the powder, things were back to the way they had been before. I could sense the next world, but without the alrūne, I couldn't hear the voice. I had to find out where Kunegunde had hidden it so my mother could speak to me again. Was she trying to tell me something now? Did she want me to go see what was out there, like she wanted me to visit the next mountain?

Ice snapped beneath my boots as I rushed to the edge of the circle, my frustration spurring me on. It was a relief to be out from under Kunegunde's watchful eye, though this part of the forest was unnaturally dark. When I passed through the stone circle, my whole body tingled. A wild laugh bubbled from my throat. It was wonderful to feel like myself again, to have these sensations. I hurried into the forest after the birds, boots crunching the snow. Again I felt the trace of a shiver prickling the back of my neck, but when I turned to look over my shoulder, I could see only shadows.

"Who's there?" a feminine voice asked behind me.

I whirled around, surprised, despite the fact that I had suspected someone was out here. A girl about my age, maybe a little younger, stood a few paces away, leading a white horse with a large basket around its neck. She had wild dark curls that refused, like mine, to be tamed by her braids; she was dressed in a faded woman's shift and skirt and wimple under dirty furs. Her face was eerily similar to mine. Her pale skin was covered in dust, but she held her head high, as if she had noble blood. In the twilight, her eyes glinted a pretty hazel with bright golden flecks. There was only one other person I'd seen with eyes that color: back home, years ago, beside her mother on a white horse. Princess Frederika. But the princess was years younger than I was, and this girl seemed about my age. Then I remembered how old, how *brave*, the princess had seemed all those years ago on her mother's white horse, and I knew. It was her. "*Your highness.*"

The princess looked over her shoulder uneasily, lowering her voice. "Surely you mistake me for someone else. Who are you?"

"Haelewise, daughter-of-Hedda-the-Midwife."

She looked skeptical. "You sure are finely dressed for a peasant."

"You sure are humbly dressed for a princess."

She frowned.

I could tell she didn't want to give up the pretense, but I was so certain. "I saw you with your mother at a parade. On this horse!"

She laughed, despite herself, searching my face. "By the breath of the gods. You resemble me so much, it's like staring into a mirror."

I gazed at her. She was right. We were about the same height—I was short, and she was a little tall for her age. The resemblance would've been even more pronounced if I were still eating the alrūne, which would've made my eyes gold. "We could be sisters."

"You wouldn't happen to want to marry Prince Ulrich for me, would you?"

My eyes widened. I shook my head, holding up my hands.

She laughed again—loud and wild—and I realized she was kidding. I had spent so long in Kunegunde's tower, I didn't know how *not* to be suspicious. The princess's horse was near enough now for me to see her big brown eyes. I approached the horse in an attempt to change the subject. "Your horse is beautiful."

"Her name is Nëbel."

The horse sniffed my hand and opened my fist with her muzzle, as if to see whether it held a treat. Her nose was cold against my palm. Her huge pupils glistened, inky black, in the dark. When she discovered that my hand was empty, she let out a nicker of protest. "She's friendly."

"She's known nothing but kindness since she was a foal. I saw to that. She's the finest horse in the kingdom, aside from her fearfulness."

I looked at the horse's broad white chest, her rippling muscles. It was hard to imagine her afraid of anything. The creature snorted, meeting my eyes. I turned to Frederika. "What are you doing in this part of the forest?"

She drew back, her expression instantly mistrustful. "Who sent you to spy on me?"

"No one. I—"

"My father? Ulrich?"

I held up my hands. "I'm an apprentice to a local wise woman. I swear it. Our animals were acting strangely, so I came to see who was out here."

"Do you mean Mother Gothel?"

I nodded.

"I've been searching for her tower for ages." She lowered her voice, looking over her shoulder again into the trees. "It's been two moons since I bled. May I follow you back?"

I hesitated. Frederika was a noble, the daughter of the king who had issued a writ for Kunegunde's death. She was the betrothed of a man my grandmother hated more than anyone else. But the tower was supposed to be a haven for women in Frederika's condition. Kunegunde was such a recluse. What were the chances that she would be able to recognize Frederika in these clothes? And why in the world, with all the secrets Kunegunde was keeping from me, should I worry about being honest with her? The idea of lying to my grandmother filled me with pleasure.

Explaining that we would have to hide her identity, I led Frederika back toward the tower. We could use our likeness to our advantage and introduce her as my cousin. We would call her Ree.

At the edge of the stone circle, Nëbel whinnied, pulling on her reins, eyes wild. "The stone circle," Frederika said. "I'd heard of it, but—" She whispered in the horse's ear, then pulled her inside the circle. "By the devil," she swore. "This place is so thin, it's making her nervous."

Can she feel the thinness herself, I wondered, or is she only commenting on the horse's behavior?

Nëbel pranced anxiously, whinnying and blowing air through her nose. By the time we reached the tower, the horse was calmer. The spell, I thought, the one that zapped between the stones. That was what was making her nervous. I helped Frederika tie the horse outside, then led her into my grandmother's home with her basket.

Kunegunde was so absorbed in her writing, she didn't notice that anyone had come in with me. Only Erste looked in my direction when I opened the door, dark eyes glittering from his perch.

"What was out there? A wolf? A fox?" Kunegunde said without looking up.

Frederika stepped forward, clearing her throat. "Mother Gothel?"

Kunegunde looked up. "Do you know this girl?"

I avoided her eyes, grateful the tower was so dim at night. "This is Ree, my cousin on my father's side. She was wandering the forest, looking for the tower."

Kunegunde looked from Frederika to me and back. "Cousins. You look like sisters. You say she's your father's kin?"

I nodded, perhaps a bit too eagerly.

She shook her head. "Well, girl? Out with it. What do you want?"

"It's been two moons since I bled," Frederika said quietly.

"Ah. What did you bring as payment?"

Frederika peeled back the linen that was covering the basket. Inside were several blocks of goat cheese, a large sack of flour, a walnut bread wrapped in cheesecloth, some quinces, and several pounds of dried blaeberries. "Is it a difficult spell?"

"Everything that is done can be undone," Kunegunde said, her voice matter-of-fact.

She nodded at the basket Frederika offered—it was enough—and gestured for her to set it on the table. Then she retrieved the manuscript she was always working on from its place on the shelf and turned to a page that had yet to be illuminated. She lingered over it for a moment, reading, then excused herself to go downstairs to the cellar.

While she was gone, I inspected the indecipherable symbols on the page, awed, realizing the manuscript Kunegunde had been working on all this time was a spellbook. Frederika settled into the chair by the fire ring, her expression melancholy.

In a moment Kunegunde came back upstairs with a lockbox. She fished out a key from a drawer in the apothecary cabinet, which she used to unlock it.

Inside were about three dozen alrūne fruit, the ones I'd brought to Gothel and more, dried like the one I had found in her pouch so they wouldn't rot. Also within were several misshapen bulbs that looked like the plant's root in the drawing she had shown me.

My heart stopped. There they were. Finally, I knew where she was keeping them. I had to work to keep my breath regular.

Kunegunde took out one of the roots with a rag, closed the box, and locked it. I watched her closely as she put everything back, memorizing the locations—the key in the drawer, the lockbox in the cellar—though I was anxious about the prospect of stealing the fruit back. I would have to be careful how much I took.

Kunegunde caught me watching and raised an eyebrow. "Make yourself useful. We need pennyroyal, lavender, thyme. A cup of snow and some rope."

From her chair, Frederika watched me move around the tower, collecting the items Kunegunde named. When I'd collected all of them, Kunegunde suspended the cup in the ropes above the fire ring. She stoked the flames so the snow would melt. After a while, she called Frederika over. She had her knot the rope around the alrūne root, then drop it into the cup, whispering strange words. "This chant binds the root to the child in your belly," she explained. "You're certain you want this?"

Frederika stared into the cup, measuring her words. "I want the child, but I can't foresee a life where I will be able to care for it."

"Isn't that always the way?"

Frederika looked grim, her expression uncertain.

"The potion has to steep overnight. What if we start the spell now, and you can decide tomorrow whether to finish it? It will cost you either way, mind you. The ingredients—"

Frederika thought for a moment, then nodded.

"Sprinkle in the herbs."

She did as told.

Kunegunde turned to me. "Do you want her to sleep in your room?"

I nodded. The prospect of putting off the spell set Frederika at ease. We talked with Kunegunde awhile, spinning stories about my father's family. We play-acted brilliantly, making up anecdotes about all the times we had played together as youths. Our appearances weren't our only likeness; our minds worked similarly. We had never met before this day, and yet somehow we were able to improvise these stories seamlessly, finishing each other's sentences. It was exhilarating.

As soon as we went upstairs, we shut my bedroom door and stared at each other in awe. It almost felt, by then, that the stories we'd made up were true. I pulled the shattered hand-mirror from the trunk so we could indulge in a moonlight comparison of our faces. She touched the symbols with her fingers, looking at me wordlessly, before she turned her focus to our reflections. It was difficult to see with all the cracks in the glass, but we had the same round face and curly black hair, the same high cheekbones. Our noses were a bit different, as were our eyes—mine were almost fully black now, and hers were that gold-flecked hazel—but apart from that, the resemblance was undeniable. We giggled and called each other cousin for long after we heard Kunegunde go to her room. Eventually, when we settled down in bed, I asked Frederika why she ran away from the castle, and she told me the story. As I suspected, it had all begun when her father promised her to Ulrich.

"Why would he promise you to such a man?"

She shook her head. "He doesn't believe the stories. Hardly anyone noble does. Father says they're wives' tales, peasant talk. Ulrich can be so charming at court. He strutted like a peacock into our castle and convinced my father—*my father*, the king and Holy Roman Emperor—to give him my hand. Ulrich boasted about the safety of his castle, swearing he would protect me with his life.

My stepmother tried to tell my father what he's really like, but my father didn't believe her. He swore it was a good match, since my mother"—Frederika blinked, her voice catching—"since the annulment made me a bastard. He *thanked* Ulrich and promised him Scafhusun for his fealty." She shivered again. "I wish I could stay with Daniel."

"Daniel is the father of your child?"

She nodded, telling me about the boy with whom she had fallen in love, a young Jewish man who lived in a nearby settlement. They had been handfasted in secret months ago.

I was so shocked at her description of Daniel that I had trouble paying attention to what she said next. Nobles sometimes married merchants, as Phoebe had married Matthäus, but a high princess carrying the child of a Jewish peasant was beyond belief. When I was little, the synagogue in the next town had burned down in the middle of the night. Father said God set the fire, but Mother said it was set by wicked men who wanted to drive the Jews out of the city.

"He would make such a good father," Frederika was saying.

"How did you end up in his settlement?"

Her voice was tired. "When the nights grew too cold, I couldn't sleep in the forest anymore. I had to find a place to stay. A place that didn't have any connections to my father. I was following the trade route west, when I met a trader on his way to the Jewish settlement. It seemed perfect. Small. No priests, no princes, and the kingsguard wouldn't think to look for me there."

I looked at Frederika anew, realizing for the first time how clever she was. She would have to be to escape her father. People said he was the same way.

"I didn't mean to fall in love with Daniel." She sighed. "It just happened."

Empathizing, I told her about the woman Matthäus had married, how he wished he could marry me instead, how I'd refused to be his mistress. "I couldn't do it," I said, surprised at the bitterness, the anger in my voice. I sounded like Kunegunde when she spoke of the Church. "I couldn't bear the shame."

She was watching me closely. "You cared for him a great deal."

I went silent for a long time, staring into the dark, all the feelings I had tried to suppress threatening to bubble out. "I did," I admitted, finally, my voice carefully controlled. "But it wasn't enough. I need to be respectable to work as a midwife. I want children, a real family of my own."

Frederika fell silent. I thought on what I'd said, realizing it might be unkind to speak of my longing to be a mother when she was trying to decide whether to end her pregnancy. When I apologized, she went sullen, despairing at the plans her father had made for her. Eventually, she changed the subject to the spell Kunegunde would cast in the morning, which seemed to fascinate her in theory if not in effect. When she confessed that her stepmother had taught her a few incantations, I remembered the rumor about the queen whispering into a hand-mirror, and my breath caught. "You've been learning the old ways?"

Frederika nodded slowly, startled by my eagerness.

I tried to rein it in. "Does your father know?"

"Absolutely not. It was all in secret."

Her boldness inspired me. She had learned the old ways in secret, run from her arranged marriage, hidden from her father in these woods, and here I was afraid to sneak into an old woman's lockbox. "I've got to do something," I said, getting up. "I'll be right back."

"All right." Frederika wrapped herself in the blanket.

Down the stairs I crept, listening for movement above, enjoying the fact that I was defying Kunegunde. The ground floor of the tower was silent apart from my footsteps. Embers glowed in the fire ring below the draught that was steeping in the cup. I went to the apothecary cabinet and opened the drawer where Kunegunde had put the key. Lighting a small candle, I tiptoed downstairs into the cellar. The candlelight flickered and hissed as I passed through the archway into the dark. I surveyed the room. Where would she put the lockbox? I checked behind the barrels in the buttery but found nothing. I checked the crates in the corner with no success. As I was searching the shelves, I stumbled slightly on an uneven stone. Kneeling down to remove it, I found the lockbox buried beneath the floor. I could hear the dried fruit rolling around noisily inside it and swore an oath of joy.

Unlocking it, I took out three dried fruit—hopefully not enough for her to notice—closed the box, and locked it, holding my breath as I put everything back. It was only after I had returned the lockbox to its hiding place in the cellar and the key to its drawer upstairs that I could breathe again. I broke off a piece of the dried alrūne, ate it, and wrapped the rest in a cloth, feeling defiant. Blowing out the candle, I was conscious of the need to wash my hands. I did so as silently as I could, then tiptoed back upstairs, feeling more than a little self-righteous about my theft of what had been mine in the first place.

When I slipped back into the room, Frederika was lying on her side, as if she had fallen asleep. I hid the alrūne in the bottom of my sack and lay down, trying to remember where we were in our conversation. While I was thinking, she turned over to look at me.

"I'm glad you're here," she said. "It's good to have someone to talk to."

I smiled. "You don't have to decide right away whether to cast the spell. I bet Kunegunde would let you stay here longer."

"The kingsguard are closing in. If they find me like this—"

"No man can see inside the circle. You're safe here."

"Ulrich can," she sighed. "If he's with them—"

Moonlight striped the cracks of the shutters with pale light. Her eyes brimmed with tears.

CHAPTER EIGHTEEN

When I woke the next morning, Frederika said she had been up all night thinking. Daniel's parents had demanded that she come here, but she didn't think she could go through with the spell without talking to him. If Kunegunde agreed to let her stay another night, she wanted to know if I would be willing to go with her to talk to him. She was afraid she wouldn't be able to find her way back to the tower without my help. When I told her how Kunegunde had forbidden me to leave the circle, Frederika said we could sneak out. It was only an hour or so away on horseback, she said. We could go there and back in one night if the weather was good.

"All right," I said, eager to win her trust. "I will."

She smiled and told me to call her Rika, before we went downstairs. On my way out of the bedroom, I got out my mother's hand-mirror and checked my eyes. My pupils had stopped enlarging, and the thin circle of red around them was becoming coppery. Close enough to how they looked when I was taking the powder that Kunegunde was unlikely to notice. Thank the gods, I thought. The day before had been exhausting.

For breakfast, Kunegunde was making some sort of pastry with the quinces and cheese Rika had brought. All three ravens were roosting on the ceiling beam above her, greedily watching her cook. They weren't making a sound, but the sight of them filled me with unease. Had they been up there the night before, I wondered, when I sneaked downstairs? Had Kunegunde been watching through Erste's eyes when I stole back the alrūne?

Following me into the room, Rika inhaled the scent of the sizzling dough, then gagged and put her hand over her mouth. "Sorry," she managed to say, as she scanned the room for an exit. Morning sickness. I led her into the garden, where she expelled the contents of her stomach in a snowdrift.

In a moment, her queasiness passed. "That's been happening more often lately."

"It's most common in early pregnancy. If you decide to keep the child, it'll likely run its course in a couple months."

She laughed ruefully. "I can't wait."

My eye fell on the birdbath a few feet away. I checked over my shoulder to make sure Kunegunde or her birds hadn't followed us out. Then I brushed away the snow that had collected on the birdbath until the symbols were visible. Gesturing for Rika to come closer, I lowered my voice. "Have you seen anything like this before? These are the same symbols from the hand-mirrors and her spellbook."

She moved closer to inspect the basin. I watched her face for signs of recognition. A moment passed before she looked up at me. Her gaze was steady. "That's a water-*spiegel*."

"Did your stepmother teach you to read those symbols? Where did the old language come from? Who speaks it?"

She pressed her lips tight. "I cannot say."

"Why not?" I said, meeting her eyes, my stomach filling with dread. Was she going to refuse to tell me about the old ways too? The words tumbled out. "Rika, that hand-mirror we used last night was my mother's. She died last winter. I know the symbols are the old language, but Kunegunde says I'm not ready to learn about it. She's hiding something—"

"I'm sorry about your mother," she said, cutting me off, her face a mask. Her reserve was infuriating. "But I can't help you. I feel better now. Let's go in. I'm getting cold."

She headed back for the tower before I could stop her.

I blinked, watching her go, feeling slighted. Why wouldn't she tell me what she knew? She was so sure of herself. It was easy to forget she was the younger of us two. I re-covered the birdbath with snow, wondering how I could get her to trust me. By the time I'd finished and gone inside, Rika was explaining her reticence to Kunegunde. My grandmother was listening, pressing quinces and cheese into dough.

"I understand," she said when Rika went quiet, turning to meet my friend's eyes. "It's a difficult decision."

"Too difficult to make lightly," I said. "Could she stay with us while she decides?"

Kunegunde glanced from me to Rika, her brows furrowed. "There's no reason you have to make a decision today. We can finish the spell tomorrow or in a week. I suppose you can stay here until then."

Frederika looked relieved. "That is gracious of you."

Kunegunde turned back to her cooking, her voice suspiciously gentle. "I was once in a situation much like yours. This place was my haven. I feel obligated to return the favor."

That afternoon, in our room, Rika told me a funny story about the night after she and Daniel were handfasted in secret. They had sneaked away from the settlement, and his mother caught them half-clothed in a cave. Daniel's pants were around his ankles, and I was giggling uncontrollably, when Kunegunde called for us to come down, furious. When we went downstairs, she was sitting stiff at the table before her spellbook. Her voice tight, she told us to go to the clearing near the pool to pull up some rapunzel root for a pottage stew, but I was pretty sure she only wanted us to go because she couldn't focus on her writing due to the volume of our laughter.

Rika acted chastened, probably afraid Kunegunde would cast her out, but I was eager to leave the tower with her.

Rika retrieved Nëbel from the stable so the horse could get some exercise. As soon as we were out of earshot of the tower, she went back to telling her story. I made myself listen carefully as we followed the stream, keeping an eye out for the wilted rapunzel shoots that would mean the root was beneath the surface. The stream was half frozen, a thin scrim of ice around its banks. But the farther we got from the tower, the more difficulty I had focusing on her story. When she finally finished, I scanned the trees to make sure the birds hadn't followed us out. "Please. Rika. Tell me what you know of the old ways."

She froze for a moment, then shook her head. "I would like to, but I cannot. I'm sorry, Haelewise."

Her refusal made me angry. "I won't tell anyone."

"That doesn't matter. I swore an oath of secrecy."

I tried to think of a way to get her to trust me, racking my brain again for some way to prove myself. The bird-mother charm. It had been so important to Kunegunde. Perhaps it would prove to Frederika that I could be trusted. I pulled the figurine from my pouch. "My mother gave me this."

Rika's eyes widened. "Your mother. Who was she again?"

"Hedda-the-Midwife."

Rika shook her head; she didn't recognize the name. "May I hold it?"

When I nodded, she took it from my hand, turning it over in hers. "Haelewise, these are *rare*. The Church destroyed most of them. Have you shown this to anyone?"

I shook my head.

"Don't. They would burn you at the stake." She handed it back. "The only other person I know who has one is Ursilda."

I gazed down at the figurine, her breasts, her wings, her talons. "It's an effigy of the Mother, isn't it?"

Rika met my eyes, again, measuring my expression. After a moment, she nodded.

"My mother made offerings to her in secret," I said. "Please. I want to understand her faith."

Rika sat down on a boulder beside the stream, setting her empty basket on the ice. "How do you not know of the faith when you have a figurine? Do you know what *she* is for?"

I sat down next to her. "My mother called her a bird-mother charm. Once, when I rubbed it, I conjured her ghost."

Her eyes widened. "You have the gift."

"What?"

"The figurine calls the next world close. For those who have the gift, that means the ability to see the dead."

"She spoke to me too."

She looked at me more closely. "You're eating the alrūne."

I nodded. "I need to learn how to use the figurine to conjure my mother. I miss her so badly."

She watched me steadily. "I wish I could help you. All the figurine does for Ursilda is increase the potency of her prayers."

"And what of the alrūne?"

"It allows my stepmother to cast spells, to use the water-*spiegel*."

"For scrying?"

Rika thought for a moment, considering. Finally, she nodded. "A circle of women use them to watch the world."

My breath caught. "Do you think my mother was a member of this circle?"

"If she had one of those—" Rika nodded at the figurine. "She was."

My heart stopped. Ice cracked under my feet. Everything went still. For a moment, the wood was so silent that I thought I could hear the heavens circling the earth. My mother had not practiced her faith alone. There was a circle of women out there who were like her. She must've been a member before she married my father. She had a whole life—a life of meaning and magic—that my father had made her give up.

"*Rika*," I said, my voice wavering with emotion. I tried to control it, but I was angry at my father, at Rika for refusing to answer me. "Tell me what you know about the circle."

"I can't."

"I need to know who my mother was."

"I've never even heard her name."

I stood up, unable to contain the anger that was coursing through me. For a moment, the only sound was that of my footsteps as I paced, back and forth, alongside the stream. Then I whirled on Rika, and the ice split beneath me with a loud *crack*. "Was Kunegunde part of the circle?"

She met my gaze, nodding slowly. "But she left after the king issued a writ for her death."

I thought about this. "You and Ursilda, your stepmother, the three of you, you're part of this circle? And my mother and Kunegunde were too?"

Rika took a deep breath. She stood up. "I'm sorry, Haelewise. I've already said too much. I'm not supposed to say *any* of this to someone who hasn't been initiated. And you have not."

"I've never had the chance. My mother died before she could tell me of her faith. Please."

"Haelewise, I can't say. Stop asking me to break my oath."

Her refusal to answer me was so maddening, I didn't speak to her for the rest of our walk.

I stayed angry at Rika for the rest of that afternoon, outrage cold in my breast. I couldn't stand the fact that she knew something about my mother and wouldn't tell me. I was jeopardizing my livelihood, my home, by lying to Kunegunde about who she was. She owed me as much. As we ate supper that evening, I resolved not to help her anymore until she told me about the circle. It would be foolish to risk angering Kunegunde by sneaking out. I had no place else to go.

That second night, it was late before we heard Kunegunde shuffling to her room. As soon as we heard the door shut, Rika moved as if to get out of bed. "Not yet," I whispered. "She'll catch you leaving."

"Me? Aren't you coming?"

I shook my head. "I've thought better of it."

Rika looked stricken. Her breath hitched. When she spoke, she sounded desperate. "Haelewise. I can't go without you. I won't be able to find my way back."

"I'm sorry," I whispered. "Kunegunde will be furious if she finds out I've left the stone circle. I'm risking enough already."

She looked pained. "Haelewise," she said, her voice breaking. "You don't understand. I would tell you if I could. But I swore a blood-vow. I can only speak of the circle to others who have taken the oath."

Remembering the look on Kunegunde's face when I tried to call her *grandmother*, I felt my resolve begin to falter.

"Haelewise," Rika said, her voice trembling. "Come with me. I'm going to see him, no matter what."

Uncertainty pulled at me. If I didn't go with her, she might not be able to find her way back. She might be forced to have the baby, and who knew what her father would do to her or Daniel if he found out? Guilt nagged at my conscience.

"I need your help," she begged. "Haelewise, please."

I led her downstairs in a resentful silence and slipped on my cloak. Outside, the clearing around the tower was still and quiet, the snow glowing an eerie white. The night was bitter cold, and the rising moon seemed too bright for a waning half. The night seemed to energize Rika, but I hated the romance of the moonlight and gleaming snow. It occurred to me to wonder why the natural world never reflected *my* emotions. I always seemed to be at odds with it.

As she showed me how to mount a horse, I was silent. I climbed atop Nëbel behind her, listening to the hard crunch of her hooves on the snow. Outside the stone circle, we rode in silence. When she finally spoke, she tried to chatter about a neutral subject, asking questions about the herbs Kunegunde used for spellcraft. I answered only with noncommittal grunts.

Eventually we approached a mountain with a well-worn trade

route leading up and around the side of it. When Rika turned Nëbel up the path, my heart stopped, and my breath caught in my throat. This was why my mother told me to visit the next mountain. She wanted me to meet Rika. To learn about the circle.

As we rode up the path, I asked my mother to forgive me for not heeding her advice before.

Nestled partway up the side of the mountain was the settlement: a ramshackle hall and stable, set far enough back from the cliff, you couldn't see them from below. On either side of the hall I could see a drab building I suspected was a makeshift synagogue. Scattered among the trees were dim huts of varying sizes, each of their roofs covered in snow.

We tied Nëbel to a tree just outside the cluster of buildings. There was a scarlet firethorn bush with about half its leaves left near the hall, which Rika asked me gingerly if I would wait behind. I squatted behind that bush, feeling foolish for what felt like hours, though it must have been a half hour at most. While I waited, I thought about all the times people had kept things from me, snapping leaf after leaf from the bush, tearing them into shreds.

When I had torn all the remaining leaves from the part of the bush where I crouched, I reached for the figurine in my coin-purse, praying for my mother to speak to me again. I knew it was probably too soon since I stopped the powder and started the alrūne, but I needed her guidance. I had lost my way.

For a long moment, nothing happened. Then I thought I felt the figurine warming subtly beneath my fingers. I thought I felt the air growing taut, the mist gathering faintly around me. A subtle fog— barely perceptible, dewy. I couldn't tell if I was imagining it.

I closed my eyes, chasing after the sensation. A faint gust of wind tousled my hair, and I imagined it was my mother's hand. After a moment I thought I could feel her presence, smell the faint scent of anise in the air. My eyes brimmed with tears. My anger melted, and everything shifted around me: The stars above shivered with beauty; hoarfrost glittered on the firethorn; the night air rippled with cold. Everything I was upset about melted away.

It was just enough hope to renew my faith. Staring down at the nest of broken leaves I had made, I could feel my determination returning. There had to be a way to convince Rika to tell me what I needed to know.

By the time Rika came back, breathless, I knew what I was going to say. Her hair was mussed, and there were leaves in her hair, her eyes feverish with the desire to talk to me. "Daniel said it's my decision whether I want to have the baby, that a living woman's needs must take precedence over the unborn. He says a child's soul doesn't enter its body until it takes its first breath. He called it the breath of life. Is that how it works? You must know."

I nodded slowly. "That's how it works, yes. A child's soul enters its throat when it takes its first breath. I've seen it."

She nodded, determined. Then she took my hands, looking me in my eyes. "Thank you for coming, Haelewise. You've been so good to me. I don't know what I'd do without you."

Her gratitude brought tears to my eyes. I felt bad for denying her before. "Of course."

"I still don't know what I'm going to do."

"Rika," I said, my voice full of urgency. "Could I take that vow? The one you took. The oath."

Her eyes widened. Her whole countenance changed.

My voice shook. "I want to join the circle."

Rika's expression turned solemn. "All right," she said. "I will find a way to make that happen."

I could hardly believe what I had heard. "You will?"

"I swear it. When I leave, you're coming with me. Once you take the vow, I'll tell you everything," she said, speaking the words with such conviction that I believed her.

CHAPTER NINETEEN

A week passed, and I was still waiting for Rika to make her decision. I was getting antsy. On the one hand, I wanted to take the oath as soon as possible, but on the other, I didn't want to rush her. I had given up waiting for her each night as she sneaked out of the tower to see Daniel. Now that I'd led her back once, she said she could find her own way home to the tower. The clearing where they met was halfway between the two mountains, so she didn't have to travel far, but she was always gone hours.

Sometimes, I fell asleep as soon as she left, dreaming my inscrutable dreams. I woke in the middle of the night, my skin itching with feathers, my mother's voice humming in my ears. Her message continued to elude me, though the words were becoming louder and clearer. Other times, while Rika was gone, I couldn't sleep, and I spent hours brooding over my own feelings. Rika was right when she said I cared for Matthäus a great deal. Beneath my bitterness at his marriage was an undeniable wellspring of love. If I lived outside the Christian world in the forest, perhaps I would be less ashamed for acting on it. If wherever we went when we left the tower was close enough, perhaps I would go to him.

Every night, I ate the alrūne. Every morning, I checked my eyes in the shattered mirror. I was trying to limit the amount I ate so I could reap the benefits of the fruit without my eyes growing so bright that Kunegunde would notice. I took care not to get too close to her or look her straight in the eyes.

Rika and I spent most of our days gathering herbs and plants for Kunegunde inside the circle. As I went about my chores, I imagined a time after Rika and I left the tower when I was part of the circle. I would eat the alrūne every night, use the figurine to conjure my mother, and watch the world in a water-*spiegel*.

One night, when Rika had been at Gothel almost two weeks, my head was so full of these thoughts that I was unable to sleep. When Rika came back, I was still awake. "Where will we go when we leave the tower?" I asked her, sitting up in bed.

"I've been trying to figure that out," she said. Her cheeks were flushed from the cold and she was out of breath.

"Have you decided if you're going to have the baby?"

She nodded, taking a deep breath. Her voice shook with feeling. "I love Daniel so much. I want a family with him."

"I could help you with the birth. We just need somewhere to go, somewhere your father and Ulrich can't find us."

Her eyes brightened, and she looked hopeful for the first time in days. "It would have to be a thin place like this so we could cast a spell strong enough to keep my father and Ulrich out."

"Could you cast such a spell?"

"No. But you could once you join the circle. Or you could learn—"

"Do you know of another thin place?"

"No," she said excitedly. "But I know someone who might. Let me think about this."

She must have stayed up for the rest of the night, planning our next step. Before I fell asleep, I watched her for a long time, arms folded, deep in thought. I wondered if she inherited her personality from her father or if it was the product of growing up in a castle; I had never met a young woman as reserved and strategic as she was. Still, she was only human. By the next morning, her lack of sleep over the last two weeks was catching up with her. There were dark circles under her eyes, and she fell asleep at breakfast. I saw Kunegunde watching her closely and panicked. I could tell Kunegunde knew something was up.

That night, Rika said she would talk to Daniel about our plan. After she sneaked downstairs and left the tower, I heard the shuffle of Kunegunde's footsteps. My grandmother peeked around the open doorway into our room and saw me lying alone in our cot. "I thought so."

I blinked up at her, not sure what to say.

"She's putting us at risk, coming and going like this. Ulrich could see her and follow her back."

I closed my eyes. "You and I leave the circle together all the time. Rika is careful. She only goes out at night."

Kunegunde's eyes narrowed. "Rika?"

My anger turned to panic as I realized what I'd just done. Kunegunde wasn't stupid. Rika was too close to Frederika.

"I thought you said her name was Ree."

"That's a nickname I call her."

Kunegunde's expression tightened. She watched me silently from the doorway. Then she chuckled with a perverse amusement and went upstairs.

CHAPTER TWENTY

Three times, I've tried to chronicle this part of my story. Three times, I've failed and scraped my shame from the page. The language I learned as a girl—this language we all speak—doesn't have the words to describe what happened next. *Diutsch* is a language of things, a song of mud and brick and stones. I'm certain the old language would work better to describe these ill-starred events. It was a language of mist, a song of wind and prayer and smoke. But the old language has only survived in spells and oaths. I have no choice but to write these clumsy words onto this page. This try will have to do, whether I fail or no. May the Mother forgive me. If I scrape the parchment further, there won't be any left.

Rika was so late getting back, the night Kunegunde discovered who she was, that I fell asleep before she did. The next day was the worst of my life, a day I would curse for years to come. That morning, I dreamed I was a bird for the final time. Everything was the same as before. The masked rider. The girl. My urge to protect her. This time, however, when I woke, I could finally hear the words my mother spoke to me: *Protect the princess.*

When I jolted awake, I knew who the girl in the dream was.

The side of the bed where Rika slept was empty. There was only a faint impression in the feather-mattress where she'd lain. I hurried downstairs to find Kunegunde in the kitchen reading. "Where's Ree?" I asked, my voice frantic.

"Gone," Kunegunde said, her voice hard.

"What? Where?"

"She changed her mind. She said she was going back to the next mountain to the father of her child."

The idea made my breath catch, though I didn't believe it. Kunegunde had driven Rika out. I fought to swallow my anger.

"How long ago did she leave?"

"An hour, maybe two."

I rushed to the caged window to look out. A white blanket of
snow had already spread itself over Rika's footsteps.

I made myself draw a deep breath. I had to find Rika and warn
her. Where would she be? The clearing between the two mountains, where she met Daniel at night. The clearing where my dream
took place. "My stomach hurts," I said. "Do we have any hellebore?" I knew we were out. "I could use a purgative."

"No," Kunegunde said through clenched teeth, grabbing her
cloak. She was on to me, and she wouldn't let me leave without her.

Outside, the world was a tangle of black and white. The trees at
the edge of the clearing were glittering and black, sharp with icicles.
The sky had gone as colorless as fear. The wind blew in gusts, scat-
tering the snow. Flakes spun in the air. I tightened my cloak about
my neck and pulled on my gloves, preparing myself mentally to run.

As we stepped into the wood, the wind whipped my cloak and
cleared our path. "There it is," Kunegunde said, pointing into the
shade just inside the tree line where the black hellebore grew. I pretended to look for the cluster of white flowers.

Kunegunde threw out her arm to stop me from moving forward. The same gesture she made weeks before when we heard the
kingsguard. I followed her gaze to a stand of spruce where a fox
was scurrying up a snowbank. A small red beast, thin-legged, with
a pointy nose. There was something strange about its posture, the
way it raised its muzzle to sniff the air. Its eyes were wild. "It flees
something," Kunegunde said.

The fox leapt, heading east, and I heard a faraway sound. Long
and high, piercing. A scream. My heart thudded with panic. It
sounded like Rika's voice.

"Be still," Kunegunde hissed. She pulled a dried alrūne from her pouch and took a bite without bothering to hide it. She gave me a stern look, then muttered the same chant she had spoken before. *"Leek haptbhendun von hzost. Tuid hestu."*

As I wondered what the words meant, I felt a numbness in the tips of my fingers. My scalp began to tingle, and I felt my soul trembling in my flesh. God's teeth, I thought with horror, as the spell pulled my awareness, unwilling, from my body. Everything that is done *can* be undone—

For an instant, I was nothing. Or rather I became light and shadow, mist and wind, nothing and everything at once. Then I was soaring over a sea of spruce in the body of that bird, the trees swimming dizzyingly below me. The next mountain rose in the distance, amid an endless sea of trees. At first there were no words in that mind-space, only the buoying currents of wind, the un-settling sensation of soaring on them. Far away, the faint sound of echoing voices. The strong scent below of horses and men.

We dove toward the voices. *We.* It took a moment to understand it, but there was indeed a *we* in that mind-space. It was not only me experiencing these sensations; there were other souls with me inside the bird. Our thoughts and feelings were all mixed up. A disturbing disappointment at the living quality of the horses and men. Erste. It was hard to tell where his thoughts stopped and mine began. Another mind was there with us, too, a third. A more com-plex mind, filled with more complex thoughts and a rage so bright it burned. Kunegunde.

The world jerked and we landed on the lowest branch of a spruce. The clearing where we had landed was covered in snow. At its center, Rika stood in her tattered clothes and braid, clutching an arrow that had pierced her thigh. The bright red feather at its back quivered as she inspected the wound. *Rika*, I screamed, my heart breaking. The word came out of the raven's mouth, transformed into the call of a bird. *Kraek!*

Rika looked up, panicked, the arrow dropping to the snow.

At the edge of the clearing, a masked man looked up in the middle of dismounting his horse. He saw the bird in the spruce tree, then returned his focus to Rika. His horse wore Prince Ulrich's colors, just like it had in my dream: a green and black banner emblazoned with a wolf. He advanced on Rika, eyes blank above his mask. "Faithless girl!" he sneered. "Which of those filthy peasants did you lie with? What village is he from?"

Rika went silent, tears streaking her cheeks.

"We saw you with him. Who is he?" The masked man sounded furious on his master's behalf. "Say his name!"

She shook her head fiercely.

"How dare you betray your husband?"

Rika backed away from him, stumbling into a snowdrift. That was when I noticed it, as the man marched toward her. The tension in the air. As he drew closer to her, so did the next world. When he tore off her necklace, I knew it was time to descend upon him in a whirl of feathers. This was it. The scene from my dream.

But as Erste drew himself up to heed my will, Kunegunde made known her will to stay put. No no no, I thought, correcting her. We have to attack. The world shuddered as the bird shook its head, unable to sort out the two contradictory commands. By the time we could see, the masked man had unsheathed his dagger, a wicked silver thing with an emerald-studded hilt. The raven-mind was fascinated with the blade. He couldn't take his eyes off it.

The man held the dagger over Rika's breast. She tried and failed to stand, to flee. She shivered, her lips moving in prayer. "*Xär dhorns*—"

The scream that filled our mind was mine. A silent thing, at first, pure thought, a wordless expression of horror. Then it became bird-sound. *Kraek!*

The man looked up, Rika's necklace swinging in his hand. For a moment, I worried he would recognize us somehow, that he would grab his bow and shoot at us. But he only turned, shaking his head,

and dropped the necklace into his pouch. Returning his full attention to Rika, he plunged his blade into her breast.

Her mouth opened in a soundless scream. Her eyes widened,
darting and wild. Her body went limp. Blood trickled from her
lips. Grief filled my heart as I watched her soul leave her body, a
pale wisp of breath, and dissolve into the next world.

The man inspected Rika's hands, retrieved his dagger, and
chopped off a finger. The tension in the air collapsed.

Rika lay dead on the snowdrift, a slow circle of blood seeping
from her chest. The only sound, for a moment, was the sound of
falling snow. As the man sheathed his dagger, the wolf insignia on
its pommel cap glinted in the sun. I tried to turn our gaze toward
Rika's body, my grief flowing into that mind-space like a river
with no place to go. The bird made a strangled sound, and the
image began to twitch from one side of our vision to the other, as
Kunegunde made felt her desire to go.

No, I corrected her again. Wait—

The conflict set the bird free to do what he wanted. He dove
toward the dagger. The man swatted at us, as Erste used his talons
to pull the dagger from its sheath.

And then Kunegunde regained control, lifting us up over the
trees toward the bodies we'd left behind, the weight of the blade
making our flight far less graceful than before. Horror-struck, I
tried without success to turn us around. The next thing I knew we
were lurching into the snow beside our crumpled bodies. I could
feel Kunegunde pulling herself out of the bird's body, and Erste
too, becoming one with the mist. For a terrifying moment, I animated his body alone, before I willed myself out—

When I opened my eyes, I was lying on my side near the stand
of spruce, my sack open in the snow. I couldn't move. My arms and
legs were numb. Ants seemed to march over my skin. I was filled
with such grief that I lay unmoving in the snow, giving myself over
to the deadening cold.

When I finally looked up, I saw Kunegunde kneeling a few feet away, wobbling as she tried to support herself. Before her, Erste was splayed out, the dagger forgotten nearby in the snow. When she saw me looking at her, she cried out, her voice slurred. "What have you done?"

I couldn't have answered if I'd wanted to. My tongue was stuck to the roof of my mouth. But her selfishness shocked me. Here she was, mourning a bird, when we had just watched Rika die?

After a moment, I managed to push myself halfway up only to fall back into the snow. I tried again. I felt dizzier than I had ever felt.

"You stopped taking the powder," she mumbled, peering at me. "You stole the alrūne. I should've noticed. Your eyes—"

I shivered, managing slowly to stand and draw a deep breath. Something snapped in my chest, like the ice on the banks of the lake at the beginning of spring.

"How could you run Rika off?" It was becoming easier to form words. My tongue was prickling.

"We were supposed to report seeing her on pain of death. If the king found out we harbored her—"

"She's dead because of what you did."

Kunegunde chuckled softly. "Better her than us."

Her callousness horrified me. I screamed at her. "She's dead, Kunegunde. That man stabbed her in the heart."

"I saw."

"You lied to me about the alrūne. You gave me a powder that stole my gift."

"Your gift? Is that what your mother called it?" Kunegunde's breath puffed in frozen clouds from her lips. "Our souls aren't properly moored in our bodies. That's why our souls leave our flesh. It's why we can sense the next world when it's close. Have you been hearing voices again? Is that why you wanted to attack that man?"

My mouth dropped open. "Yes, but—"

"Demons are notorious meddlers in politics. They don't care

about peasants' lives. That man could've killed us. We were bound in the body of a bird. He had a bow!"

"You take the alrūne yourself!"

Kunegunde opened her mouth to speak, but no sound came out. She closed her eyes, as if willing herself to be calm. When she finally spoke, her voice was tight. "You don't understand how dangerous the world of men is. I'm right to silence that demon until you learn enough to protect yourself. If you enter whatever squabble is happening on the next mountain, you'll get *hurt*."

"It's not a demon," I said flatly. "It's Mother. The voice that speaks to me is Mother."

She stared at me. Her amber eyes glittered in the pale light. There wasn't a single sound in the whole wide wood. "Do you know why your father told you I was dead?"

I blinked at her, stunned. I shook my head.

"That scar your mother had on her cheek. How did she tell you she got it?"

My memory of that scar, the discussion I had about it with the physician, seized me. It felt like I was choking. "A hunting accident."

Kunegunde smiled a tight smile. "There was no hunting accident. Your mother was here when Albrecht came for Ursilda. That scar is a wound he dealt her as she was trying to lift the wolf-skin from his back."

I gaped at her with disbelief. No wonder she didn't like to talk about that story.

"It festered. It took six weeks for me to nurse her back to health. Your father blamed me. He didn't think it was safe for your mother to visit. And the truth is, he's right. It won't be safe here until I find a way to destroy the wolf-skin."

I grabbed my sack. Snow pricked my face. An energy filled me, thawing my blood.

"Haelewise. What are you doing?"

"I'm going for a walk. I need some time to think."

I turned and went quickly; I had to find someplace for that energy to go. The trees stood, skeletal, unmoved by my anguish. I wavered between blaming Kunegunde and myself.

My eyes burned as I walked. I would have to leave Gothel. There was no question about it. But leaving Gothel would put me in a worse position than I had been when I left home. With Rika dead, I had nowhere to go. No way to join the circle.

Despair struck me, so hard I didn't know what to do. I fumbled for the figurine in my pouch, wrapping my fingers around her smooth stone, willing my mother to appear to me again. Mother, I prayed. Guide me.

The words floated up to the sky with the last of my hopes.

For a moment, nothing happened. The world was still. The stone of the figurine stayed cold. Then its stone began to warm and my skin began to bloom all over with chills. I felt a heaviness, a weight in the air. The next world drew close, and I heard a hum.

Seek Hildegard, my mother whispered.

I fell to my knees in the snow, relieved that my mother had finally spoken to me again. I blinked back tears, looking anew at the frozen wood. The firs seemed to sparkle with my gratitude.

But as I thought further on this advice, knees freezing in the snow, my mother's words began to baffle me. Why on earth would she tell me to seek a Christian abbess? How in the world could someone like Mother Hildegard help me find my purpose?

The only purpose I felt now was a desperate need to see Rika's killer punished. Rika, my only true friend. Though we had known each other only briefly, she was like my sister. When I was with her, I had felt *known.* A certainty coursed through me, pure and sharp. I understood what I had to do, my heart full of a cold resolve.

I hurried back to retrieve the wolf-dagger from the snow where Erste had dropped it. I could use it as evidence against Ulrich.

My grandmother was slowly packing the snow atop what I

presumed was Erste's grave. She looked exhausted. Every time she moved, she had to pause to catch her breath. A few feet away, the dagger glittered, its blade glinting silver on a snowdrift. I took a deep breath. "I'm leaving Gothel."

Kunegunde looked incredulous. "Where exactly do you think you will go?"

"To make sure Rika's killer is brought to justice."

Kunegunde's eyes widened. She looked genuinely worried. "Haelewise, no. You're a peasant woman. It'll be your word against Ulrich's. He's a noble. No one will believe you."

It was clear she believed what she said, but I knew she was wrong. I could feel it in my bones. "I must."

"And then?" she scoffed. "Where will you live if not here?"

"I don't know," I said, remembering my mother's advice. The abbey might be the only place that I *could* go. My hands shook. My temple pounded, and my temper flared with anger at Kunegunde, at Ulrich, at the baffling cruelty of the world. Kunegunde understood that cruelty, so she had withdrawn to her tower. But burning in my heart was a new resolve. I wanted to fight it.

"Your mother would want you to stay here with me where you're safe."

"She told me to see Mother Hildegard."

Kunegunde's face went white. "Haelewise, no. A peasant girl like you will never get an audience with her. Everyone talks about how great she is, how wise, how holy, but all she's interested in is power, currying favor with archbishops and kings. She has to abide by the rules of men, the rules of the Church. Your word will mean nothing to her."

"My mother—"

"Haelewise." She met my eyes. "Your mother is dead."

The dagger glittered in the snow between us. For a moment, I fantasized about using it against her. When I spoke, it was through gritted teeth. "I never want to see you again."

I dove for the dagger and ran, the frigid air burning in my lungs. Kunegunde moaned, behind me, trying to follow. Her age seemed to make her more susceptible to the exhaustion that came from the movement of our souls.

I knew I could grab my things and leave before she got back to the tower. Inside, I gathered my belongings: clothes, knapsack, bow and quiver, mirror, the alrūne I had stolen back, a bread crust, a few quinces from the cellar, what was left of the fertility oil. I checked my coin-purse for the figurine—it was there—and filled my drinking-horn with water. I wrapped the murderer's dagger carefully in cloth and tucked it in my sack, hoping it would be useful to prove what Ulrich had done. Then I changed into my own clothes, swiped a few coins from the jar where Kunegunde kept her fees, and hurried into the forest.

As I followed the footpath north, I could hear Kunegunde calling my name. Her voice faint, drifting on the wind. For a moment I felt loss: of the kinship we shared, of the closeness I had once wanted to feel with her. A small voice in the back of my mind made itself heard, the old voice that made a mockery of my every choice. Where will you live, if not at Gothel? I pushed the thought down and continued doggedly north, Kunegunde's warning not to get involved in royal affairs echoing in my head.

Certainty did not, it seemed, belie fear.

After I gathered more evidence against Ulrich, I would make it my goal to see that he was punished. The obvious course was to go to the king, but there was the decree. I would have to lie about the fact that she had been staying at Gothel, not to mention the vantage point from which I witnessed her murder. The king was supposed to be a brilliant diplomat. What if he saw through my lies? Perhaps that was why my mother wanted me to seek Hildegard. If I could get *her* to believe my story, she could help me convince the king to take my word over Ulrich's.

Onward I went, past pine trees and snowdrifts. When the wind blew, the snow was blinding. I chuckled when I realized it had finally happened—for the first time in a long time, the weather matched my mood. As I walked, I began to feel a creeping exhaustion, the sort of tiredness that cannot be ignored. The same tiredness that made Kunegunde sleep for a day the last time she sent her soul into the bird. It was catching up with me.

I didn't even make it to the clearing before I started to fall asleep on my feet. Snow filled the air. Wind whistled through the trees, tempting me to lie down in the snow for what might be my final sleep. But I forced myself to trudge on for Rika's sake. I was relieved when I came upon a hollow in a tree trunk where I wouldn't face the full force of the wind. Wind whistled around it, singing a ghostly song—a faint howl like the faraway cry of a wolf. On another day it would've frightened me, but I was so sleepy, I didn't care. Snow dusted my nose and eyelashes as I crouched down to enter the dark hollow. The sun had set. I could barely keep my eyes open.

Inside, I wrapped myself in my cloak and my tattered blanket. The bark was cold against my back, and my blanket didn't do enough to warm me. I didn't know if the hollow would be safe. Still, I had little choice in the matter. This was better than sleeping in the open, where I might be discovered by hunters or worse.

I thought of Rika in my last conscious moments before sleep.

CHAPTER TWENTY-ONE

T he sleep that enfolded me was dark and deep. I woke once, terrified, unable to move my arms or legs. My skin prickled all
over, numb again, as if it were crawling with ants. When uncon-
sciousness retook me, I dreamed that my mother was still alive,
and I was living with her again in our hut. I don't know how long
I slept before I sat up, reaching out, expecting to feel the wall of
my cupboard, opening my mouth to call for her. When my fingers
touched cold bark, the nightmare of everything that had happened
came rushing back.

My mother was dead, and so was Rika. I lay unmoving in that
tree for an endless moment, trying to come to terms with those
facts. When the world of my dream finally fell away, I pulled out
the bird-mother figurine, a lump forming in my throat. "*Mother,*"
I whispered aloud. "Are you there?" An eternity passed while I
waited for an answer. It must've been an hour or more before I ate
a bite of alrūne and crawled out of my hollow.

It was light out, although the gray skies and endless snow made
it difficult to tell the time of day. I headed in the direction of the
clearing, or where I thought it was. But without a raven's ability to follow a scent, I couldn't be sure. I stumbled upon a couple
of clearings, but all of them were empty. Eventually, I realized I
would need Daniel's help to find the right one.

The skies had cleared by then, and I could see that the sun was
setting. The snowstorm had passed. When I reached the settlement, a woman in a tight headscarf stood atop the hall beside the
synagogue, knocking snow off the roof with a broom. I hid my

bag under the firethorn bush where I'd waited for Rika, my heart lurching with grief. The woman on the roof stared at me, her expression too far away to read.

I headed toward the hall. As soon as I opened the door, I felt a blessed warmth. A fire crackled near the entrance, the heat warming my hands and cheeks. A festive array of dried vegetables hung from the ceiling around the fire: garlic and parsnips, ginger and turnips, some dried herbs too far away for me to identify. Beyond that were four long tables. Well-worn. Faded decorations swayed from wood beams, the old purple of wild violets, the dark red of wild rose. Rush lights flickered on the walls. In the far corner, a woman in a looser headscarf, brown wool skirt, and tunic was stirring a cauldron over a fire ring, humming softly, her hair in a long auburn braid. Noticing her relaxed posture, suddenly, I dreaded telling her why I'd come.

The door creaked as I let it fall shut behind me. The woman with the auburn braid turned and saw me standing before the door. She backed away, her eyes wide with fear, calling out in a language I didn't understand.

I was puzzled at first, racking my brain for an explanation for her reaction. Then it hit me. Daniel must've found Rika in the clearing while I slept. This woman thought I was a ghost.

It was heartbreaking to be mistaken for Rika now. I held up my hands. "My name is Haelewise, daughter-of-Hedda-the-Midwife," I made myself say. "Rika was staying with Mother Gothel and me on the next mountain. I witnessed her murder."

The auburn-haired woman's eyes widened. She studied my face. "Your eyes are different," she said. "Brighter."

The door opened behind me. The woman with the tight headscarf hurried in, her hair completely hidden beneath it. She gawked at me, then turned to the auburn-haired woman, her face pale.

"It's not her," the auburn-haired woman said. "She's a friend Rika made at Mother Gothel's."

The woman with the tight headscarf walked over to me slowly, her face full of fear. She touched my arm, my cheek, my hair. I didn't move. "Why do you look so alike?" she asked. "Are you kin?"

It took me a moment to answer. "No, but she was like my sister."

The auburn-haired woman poured some ale for me from a barrel. "Stay," she said. "Any friend of Rika's is a friend of ours. Eat with us."

She rang the dinner bell, and the woman in the tight headscarf withdrew to one of the tables, her face pale. The other villagers and their families began to trickle in, helping themselves to the cauldron of stew, sitting down at the tables with their bowls. Many of the men were wearing hats. They stared at me as they passed, murmuring among themselves, giving me a wide berth.

When everyone was seated with their stew, the auburn-haired woman introduced me to everyone as a friend Rika had made on the next mountain. After that, the whispering stopped and the bearded man who sat next to the woman in the headscarf led everyone in a blessing in a language much different from *diutsch* or the language of priests.

It was strange to be eating with so many others. I had become accustomed to eating with Kunegunde or by myself. Back home, no one ate together like this except in taverns, and if I'd gone inside a tavern, I would've been run out.

I tore into my stew. I hadn't eaten in over a day. But I had only finished half of it before a memory of Frederika lying dead in the snow came back to me unbidden. I pushed my bowl away.

The hall around me was a welcome distraction. At the next table, the woman in the tight headscarf—whose name, I learned, was Esther—kept glancing at a handsome boy who was staring into the fire at the back of the hall, his eyes shining and dark. He looked so stricken that I knew he must be Daniel. In Esther's gaze, I recognized a mother's love for her child and felt an ache.

As I watched, Esther stopped eating to bring Daniel a cup of something to drink, but he wouldn't take it. She brushed his hair back from his forehead, but he jerked away, too angry to accept such comfort. No matter who went over to try to talk to him, he wouldn't speak. Several of the villagers tried, but he just sat there, staring into the fire. Eventually, they went to the bearded man seated next to Esther, who had led the prayer over the meal.

"It's time, Shemūel," they said. "We can wait no longer."

Shemūel shook his head, but the men protested further.

"Your son has gone mute. We must decide without him."

"We can't just leave the girl up there without a funeral."

Up there? Where in the world did they put her?

His mother glared at the man who said it, then got up to talk to her son. When she came back, her mouth was tight with resolve. "He won't speak," she told Shemūel. "I suppose they're right. It's time we decide."

Someone passed a jug around our table, and everyone began to refill their cups. I refilled mine, my head swimming with a thousand thoughts. Was Daniel too stricken to lead me to the clearing? Should I leave this place now with the dagger and go to Hildegard without waiting for additional evidence? A few men stepped outside, loosening their pants to relieve themselves. All was quiet, except for the sound of tankards thudding against the table. At the next table, Esther and Shemūel looked at each other. Then Shemūel cleared his throat and stood, straightening his hat. "Frederika was untruthful. She led us all to believe she was someone she wasn't."

A few of the older women at their table nodded.

"She put our community in danger," Shemūel went on. "Hiding here from the king, telling us she was a common orphan. Seducing my son when she was already engaged to a prince. When Daniel told us who she was, I was afraid."

It was difficult for me to hear Frederika spoken of this way. I wanted to stand up, correct him. She didn't seduce him. They were in love. Why were they blaming her?

"Still," one of the men at another table said. "She lived with us for months. She fed and groomed our horses. She had stains on her robes from making our food."

"Aye," the auburn-haired woman said, nodding. "She took Daniel's place in the stables when he rode to market. She was good with the mules. Their eyes sparkled when she went into the barn. They hold their heads high, now. She convinced every one of 'em he was a horse."

Laughter echoed through the crowd.

"But she was not Jewish," Esther said.

"Nor was she Christian," another woman spoke up.

"Let her father decide how to bury her!" Shemūel called.

The whole room was silent then. You could hear the shifting of cloth beneath the tables. All eyes were on Esther and Shemūel. They stayed quiet for a long time. After a while, there was the sound of folks drinking and shifting on the benches.

Shemūel looked deep in thought. "If the king finds out she was living here," he said finally, "we'll all be put to death."

Murmurs rippled through the crowd.

"She was shot with a Zähringer arrow."

"Do you think Zähringen was jealous of Ulrich's betrothal?"

I tried to swallow the sob that leapt from my mouth without much luck. Everyone turned to look at me. I wiped my eyes and stood. "I was there," I said, raising my voice. Rush lights crackled and sputtered on the walls. "Frederika was staying with us at Gothel. Yesterday, I saw a masked man attack her. He used one of Zähringen's arrows, but his horse bore Ulrich's banners, and he cursed her on Ulrich's behalf. He asked for the name of her lover. When she wouldn't tell him, he killed her."

Esther's eyes widened, then fluttered closed, her mouth moving in prayer. People began to nod, murmuring. "That's why her finger was missing. The killer took it as proof to take back to Ulrich."

"Frederika was like my sister," I went on, my voice ringing out. "I want to make sure Ulrich is punished. I have the dagger his man used to kill her. If anyone knows anything more about what happened, I urge you to come forward. I'm going to Mother Hildegard of Bingen for guidance on how to tell the king."

Everyone began talking at once. Then the door opened and a little boy rushed in. "Prince Ulrich comes!"

Esther's eyes went wide. "Loose Nëbel!" she told Daniel, her voice urgent. "Hide!"

Daniel nodded and hurried away. In the silent hall he left behind, I thought I heard the distant whicker of a horse.

The hall emptied as if it were on fire, everyone rushing to hide themselves inside their huts. As I left the hall with everyone else, my anger mixed with fear. It unsettled me, fluttering anxiously in my chest. All around the settlement, lanterns were going out, one by one, and doors were slamming shut. My heart thudded. I looked up at the sky, wondering what form the prince would be in tonight, trying frantically to remember the moon phase.

A waxing half moon shone down, ghostly and white.

Esther stood outside the nearest hut—hers, I guessed—watching the receding form of her son. As the sound of carriage wheels and horses grew louder, she closed her eyes and mouthed a silent prayer, reaching for her husband's hand.

When the groaning cart finally crested the path into town, pulled by Ulrich's great black horse, I could see that it was painted black, as were the terrible spikes that extended from it to the horse pulling it. From a distance it almost looked as if the cart were made of shadow. The only colors were the faint gold and green accents that decorated its joints. As the cart drew closer, I saw Prince Ulrich seated beside the driver, drinking lustily from a horn. He wasn't wearing the wolf-skin tonight. He was dressed in clothes so fine, they would put a duke to shame. A beautiful surcoat dyed deep green and black, the colors of his house. His eyes flashed as he looked up, that cruel blue, and his shining black hair hung around his face.

Behind him sat an older woman and his sister, Princess Ursilda. The princess's face glowed in a wimple and black hooded cloak. Very pregnant, hands resting on her belly, dark circles under her green eyes, her face freckled and gaunt.

A muted excitement flitted through me. Ursilda had a figurine; she was a member of the circle. Then I felt a stab of guilt.

"Frederika!" Ursilda cried when she saw me, her eyes lighting up. The elder woman helped her out of the carriage. "You're alive! We heard you were dead!"

Ulrich whirled around to follow her gaze. When he saw me, his eyes filled with horror and fear. He stared at me, shocked speechless.

The idea that I could cow him made me smile. Let him think I was a ghost.

Ulrich made a small noise, something between a moan and a gasp. I leered at him, taking a perverse satisfaction in his fear.

Behind the carriage, four guards in fine green surcoats brought up the rear on powerful steeds. Their hair was oiled, and they were so well dressed, they looked more like courtiers than strongmen.

"Who—what—how?" Ulrich stammered.

Ursilda stepped into the torchlight, the older woman following her. When she saw me up close, her expression crumpled. "Brother," she sobbed, desolate. "That isn't Frederika."

The older woman accompanying her took her hand. "Ursilda. Calm down. Breathe. For the sake of the child—"

Ulrich searched my face again, relief flooding his expression. He handed his page boy the torch, then walked a circle around me, inspecting me like a farmer inspects cattle, prodding my hips, my face, my hair. His breath smelled sickly sweet, like my father's when he had been drinking. I hated him then with all my heart. His cruel blue eyes, his black eyelashes. Every lock of his shining black hair. "So similar," he smiled. "Who are you? Why are you here?"

I froze. If I opened my mouth, the only possible thing that would come out was an ancient curse. The wind blew a mist of tiny snowflakes. They glittered red in the torchlight.

He turned to Esther, his expression guarded. "Frederika is dead, then, as the message said." He looked closer at Esther, her tight headscarf, her husband's hat. "What the hell was she doing in a Jewish settlement?"

"She wasn't here," Esther said, head bowed. "I found her body yesterday in the wood—with one of Zähringen's arrows in her thigh. We moved it to a cave atop the mountain so her remains would be safe until you got here."

Ursilda cried out and stumbled into the arms of the older woman beside her, a sorrowing sound in her throat. The older woman comforted her, whispering into her ear.

Ulrich's expression darkened. He peered at Esther as if seeing her for the first time. He clenched his fists, and his face went white. "What were you doing in the wood?"

Esther paled. "Looking for herbs. This girl might have more information," she said, nodding at me. "She witnessed the murder."

I whirled on Esther, panicking. Why was she telling him that?

"What did you see?" Ulrich asked me through his teeth.

I swallowed my fear. It would be foolish to admit what I saw to the man who ordered Rika's murder, unless I wanted to be next on his list. I cleared my throat, trying to disguise my loathing and sound subservient. "Very little, your highness. The snow was thick."

Ulrich glared at me, then snarled. "We will speak of what you saw after the body is recovered. Fix the killer's face in your memory. Recall every detail you can."

I made myself nod.

Ulrich turned to Esther. "Take me to her body."

Ursilda's caretaker addressed the prince. "Your highness, I don't think your sister can manage the ride up the mountain."

Ulrich turned to Esther. "Woman. She's right. Get my sister some nourishment and a warm place to rest."

"Yes, your highness," Esther said, bowing, already turning toward the hall. "Of course."

I watched Esther lead Ursilda and the older woman away with apprehension.

My anger returned as the guards escorted me up the winding path on a mule, the valley beneath the settlement stretching out white and silent. I hated every one of Ulrich's men, their banners, the snowflakes glittering on the flanks of their horses.

The night was still as we made our way up the wild mountain path, the only constant sound the scratch of hooves on hardened snow. The half moon hung in the sky, eerie and white. The snow gave the mountain an unearthly glow. From time to time, weapons clinked in the guards' sheaths. Daniel and Esther led the way, followed by Ulrich and his entourage, and me. My mule was a stubborn thing that kept stopping and starting, occasionally refusing to move. The first time this happened, Esther doubled back to coax my mount. A single lock of shining dark hair fell from her head-covering as she worked. She blushed furiously and tucked it back under her scarf.

When the mule was moving again, she made sure Ulrich and Daniel weren't in earshot, then hissed, "Do not speak of Daniel to Ulrich—"

"Why did you tell him what I saw? You put me in a difficult place."

"I wanted to draw his attention away from my son. Forgive me. I didn't think it through. When we found out Frederika was pregnant, and who she was, Shemūel and I ran her out. I was the one who told her to visit Mother Gothel. We had to get her away from him."

I tried to hide my anger but couldn't.

"If the king found out a common boy, a Yehudi boy, got his daughter pregnant—" Esther's face went pale. "I wanted Frederika away from here before she started to show. Please. Say nothing of my son to Ulrich."

"I have no desire to get anyone killed."

She searched my face, desperate for some sign that she could trust me, before she rode away.

The next time my mule stalled, Ulrich doubled back, still drinking from his horn. His eyes flashed as he trotted toward me on his horse. Esther tugged on the reins of her mule, following him—to eavesdrop, I presumed. Ulrich's great black horse looked impatient, hot air fuming from its nostrils.

"Who are you?" the prince said.

I swallowed the hate that rose in my throat. "My name is Haelewise, your highness," I said in the stilted *diutsch* Kunegunde spoke. If I were a noblewoman, he might have mercy on me and let me go. "I grew up south of here. Forgive me. I'm not accustomed to speaking with men of your rank."

"I doubt that very much." He narrowed his eyes, as if he thought my innocence was an act. "What were you doing in my forest— alone—a pretty girl like you?"

I gripped the reins of my mule tight, knuckles white. "I beg your pardon, your highness. I am only a girl who saw trouble in the forest near her family estate."

"What is your house?"

"I am a Kürenberger," I lied, remembering that they had estates in this area.

Ulrich fell silent, his expression dark. I made myself lower my eyes with deference.

"Whoa!" Daniel called out from his horse up ahead. "We're here!"

"We will continue this discussion later."

He kicked his horse's flanks. I caught my breath as he turned toward the cave, all my hatred for him rushing back up. I pulled my cloak tight. The wind was fierce, but it was not responsible for the chill I felt.

The cave that had become Frederika's tomb appeared at first to be nothing more than a deep shadow along a ridge. But as we processed toward it, I began to make out details. Jagged rocks that rose like teeth out of the snow, the behemoth boulder that had been rolled in front of the cave to protect it. As the guards began talking about how to move the boulder, I thought of Father Emich's stories about the miracle of Easter and felt a wild, irrational hope that we would find Frederika inside alive.

As the guards worked to move the boulder, Daniel hung back. I watched Ulrich dismount from his massive black horse, my thoughts racing.

I slid off my mule, nearly losing my footing on the uneven ground, as the villagers pushed the boulder aside. Wind howled into the cave. A bat flew out, alien and black, that most unholy of birds. The villagers ducked, covering their heads.

The bat soared away from the cliff like a tiny demon, disappearing into the star-studded night. I shivered, unable to shake the feeling that its appearance was inauspicious, though I was fairly certain it was neither alite nor oscine.

"Wait here," Ulrich called out sternly, his voice cold. He nodded at Daniel, who was gazing at the cave with a stricken expression. "Except you. Come with me. And bring that torch."

He made Daniel go into the cave first, torch sputtering.

Foreboding filled me as I watched the torchlight disappear into the maw of the cave. I stamped my feet, watching the cave mouth, my heart breaking as I imagined Rika's tomb inside it. Then Ulrich was leaving the cave, his expression grim. I hated him so much.

"Bring her down," he shouted bitterly to the guards, mounting his horse.

Esther stared at him, eyes wild, as he galloped past us down the mountain path.

I turned back toward the cave reluctantly. I wanted to pay my respects before the guards carried away Rika's body, but the cavern seemed ill-omened.

Inside, Daniel was bent over a shadowy, still shape. When I approached, he glanced up at me, eyes flickering red and wide in the torchlight. As my eyes adjusted to the light, Rika's body came into view on the stone at our feet.

Hoarfrost silvered her black braids. Blood and rime flecked her lips. Her hazel eyes were glassy, unseeing. She must've lain in that clearing a long time before Daniel found her. Her body was encased in ice so thick, it looked like glass.

As I looked down at her unmoving body, a terrible guilt over-whelmed me. This is my fault, I thought. I could've stopped this.

The stars spun overhead with the snow as we made our way back down the mountain. Ulrich's guards spoke in hushed tones, watch-ing me, as they carried Rika's body down. I wanted to tell them the truth about Ulrich, but I knew they wouldn't believe me. No man would trust the word of a woman over the word of a prince, even a woman he thought was noble.

Daniel rode beside me in silence for much of the way down, his mule knocking up and down on the path. When the guards fell far enough back to be out of earshot, I lowered my voice. "Could you take me to the clearing tomorrow when the sun is up?"

He looked horrified. "I never want to go back there," he said, too loud.

I glanced behind us. The guards had seen us talking. They were speeding up their pace. I spoke quickly, my voice low. "I want to see if there's any more evidence against Ulrich."

His eyes widened, and he breathed deep. He thought for a long moment and nodded. Then the guards were upon us and we fell silent.

When we arrived at the settlement, the guards loaded Frederika's body onto a cart and ushered me into the hall. They were careful not to let me out of their sight, as if I were a precious object, a jeweled crown or a royal cup that might be carried off. Someone had kept the fire in the hall burning, and the rush lights on the walls were still lit. A group of villagers was clustered at a table, talking in hushed tones. Ulrich was nowhere to be seen. Ursilda was sitting alone by the fire, wrapped in furs. As I approached, she stared into the flames, her expression blank, hands cradling her protruding stomach. Red curls frizzed out from under her wimple.

I sat down next to her, realizing this would probably be my only chance to talk to her alone. It was terrible timing. Too soon. She was grief-stricken.

"You must've loved Frederika very much," I said softly, reluctant to disturb her.

She looked up, her face almost as pale as her wimple. Tears made the freckles on her cheeks glisten. She stared into the flames, not meeting my gaze as she spoke. "Is it true? That she was staying with you at Gothel?"

I cursed inwardly, wondering how she knew that. One of the villagers must've told her. Esther, I realized, remembering who had led her back to the hall. Clearly if I had wanted to keep Frederika's stay at Gothel secret, I shouldn't have told her. Fear knotted my stomach. I made myself nod, hoping Ursilda hadn't told anyone else. "Have you mentioned that to your brother?"

She shook her head. "I haven't seen him."

"Could I beg of you not to tell him? Or anyone else?" I looked down at my feet. "If the king finds out—"

She blinked. "The writ."

"I would be in your debt."

"Ulrich becomes livid when I mention Gothel anyway. Even if you hadn't said anything, I wouldn't have." She went back to staring into the fire.

"Were you and Rika close?" I said, testing the waters.

"I've known her since I was little. I stayed—" Ursilda's voice heaved, and she appeared to choke on the words. When she finally spoke again, her voice was a whisper. "I stayed with her for months when the king first married her stepmother. This is a great loss. My second lately. My husband died last year. When I saw you, I hoped—"

She trailed off, unable to finish the sentence. My heart broke for her. Her own brother had done this, and she had no idea.

"I cared for her too," I said quietly, my voice breaking.

She met my eyes and nodded. "What were her last days like?"

I wanted to tell her about our plans, about Daniel, how happy, how in love she had been. How she seemed to float into our room each night after seeing him. But speaking of that might put Daniel in danger. "She was happy."

Ursilda tried to smile. "I'm so glad to hear that," she said, her voice choked. The flames crackled. She reached out her hands, warming them, then wiped her freckled cheeks with a handkerchief. "I would like to talk further. But the stress of this day—I'm sorry. I must rest. Could we speak again in the morning?"

My heart sank. I wanted to talk to her about the circle now. I couldn't wait. "Ursilda. Forgive me for bringing this up at such a delicate time, but we might not have another chance to speak alone." I took a deep breath, and the words came tumbling out. "Rika told me you follow the old ways. She said you have one of these." I pulled out the figurine. "Could you tell me how to use it?"

Her eyes widened. She whirled around to see if anyone had seen. "Put that away!"

I slipped it back into my pouch.

"Where did you get that?"

"My mother gave it to me."

"Your mother? Who is she?"

I opened my mouth to answer truthfully, then stopped myself, uncertain. It would be more prudent to use the same house name I had given Ulrich in case they talked about me, though I would prefer to be honest. "Hedda of Kürenberg, may she rest in peace."

She looked at me with interest. "I'm sorry for your loss."

"Ursilda. I need to ask you something. Please—" My voice was full of want. The flames leapt in her eyes. They were deep green, the color of spruce trees. I willed her to understand how much this meant to me. "I want to take the oath. Rika had promised to give me a place to live, to help me join the circle. Now I have nowhere to go. My mother was a member, but she died. I used the figurine, once, somehow, to conjure her, but I haven't been able to do it again. I need—"

"This is too much," Ursilda interrupted me. "I'm sorry. I can't do this right now. What is your name again?"

"Haelewise of Kürenberg."

She nodded. "I will send for you in the morning. We can talk further then."

I took a deep breath. Again, I wanted to push, to make her understand *now*. If she didn't send for me tomorrow, I might never have another chance to talk to her. But I couldn't risk it. I had to respect her grief. "Of course," I made myself say. "It can wait until morning. Please don't tell your brother what I told you. The writ—"

"I won't," she promised. Squaring her shoulders, she called out to the woman she had brought with her. "Irmgard, help me to the carriage. I need to lie down."

I watched as the older woman helped her out, praying that Ursilda would call for me tomorrow as she promised. The finely dressed guards stood on either side of the door, glowering, daring me to try to follow them out.

Not long after Ursilda and Irmgard left, Ulrich came in to sit at the table nearest the fire. As I watched him stare into the flames, my heart hardened. My whole body stiffened with hate. I swallowed my anger, reminding myself that I only had to be civil to him this one night. As soon as I talked to Ursilda in the morning, I would ask Daniel to take me to the clearing and leave.

Esther hurried in to offer him a pitcher, the scent of wine filling the air. I watched her curtsy obsequiously. "My deepest apologies, your highness," she said, bowing low. "This wine is the best we've got."

Ulrich sneered, as if he was disgusted by the poverty of his accommodations, but allowed her to fill his tankard. When she finished, he drank from the cup, then wiped his lips with the back of his hand. As soon as he set his tankard down, Esther refilled it. She wants to keep him happy, I realized. She's afraid he knows about Daniel and Frederika. Ulrich took another drink. Seeing me, he signaled for me to come over and sit with him. I swallowed my hatred and went.

He took another deep draught from his cup as I sat down beside him. "Tell me everything you saw."

My eyes went to the silver dagger at his belt; my heart beat faster. The dagger's pommel cap had the same wolf insignia as the one I carried, but accusing him now would do nothing but get me killed.

"How was the killer dressed?"

I made myself meet his eyes. He was testing what I knew to see if he should have me killed. My heart thudded in my throat. "I think he wore a leather jerkin, your highness," I lied, "though I can't be sure. The snow—"

Ulrich watched me, slamming his tankard down on the table, his face red. Liquid splashed over the brim. His eyes flashed, ghastly. "Could you not see the horse's banners?"

"No," I lied. "The snow was too thick."

"Not even their colors?"

My mouth was dry. "Forgive me, your highness. I heard a commotion in the clearing from far away. When I arrived, the killer was leaving. All he left was a Zähringer arrow in her thigh."

"I don't believe you," Ulrich said. He upended his tankard, drinking deep, until all the liquid inside was gone. He set the tankard down, wiping his mouth with his sleeve, his jaw set.

My thoughts raced. Had my story not been good enough? Was he going to kill me anyway?

Someone cleared their throat. Esther had come by with the pitcher. "More, your highness?"

Ulrich stared at her blankly as if he hadn't heard what she said. Then he nodded, and Esther began to refill his cup. When she was done, he took another long draught. He set his tankard on the table, staring at me. His hatred was red-hot, glowing, like iron worked by a blacksmith.

He grabbed my wrist and twisted it, and the hall was no more. My mind went white.

"You're going to admit what you saw," he said. "Then you're going to give me a list of everyone you told."

I turned to hide my face, terrified. I thought of Kunegunde's warnings about Ulrich and his father, how the wolf-skin had made the men in their family wicked. Nothing in my life had prepared me for this conversation.

Ulrich called to Esther. As she approached, he leered at me, and his dark eyes flashed with a loathing so fierce, I had to look away. "Bring a cup for the girl. No, a whole pitcher. Two. Her tongue needs loosening."

Esther curtsied and went away. I didn't want to drink. I was too afraid. I could slip up, make a mistake. Even in the din of the busy hall, I could hear my heart pounding.

Esther returned with the pitchers, meeting my gaze, apologetic. She filled my cup. Ulrich glared at me. *Drink*, his eyes said.

The wine warmed my throat as it flowed down to my belly. The liquid sloshed, dark, in its cup.

When Ulrich spoke next, his outrage was palpable. "Clear the room," he called to the guards, snapping his fingers.

The sound echoed, and I suddenly wished that I were anywhere else. Before I could move, the door slammed on the other side of the room. We were alone.

Ulrich smiled at me fiercely when he saw my eyes on the door. "Tell me what you know."

I froze. Time seemed to slow. I thought of the dagger I had stowed in my sack, wrapped in cloth. I wanted desperately to stab him with it, but his guards would know I had done it.

"I have, your highness. I'm sorry, I don't understand."

"Very well, then. Drink your wine."

I made myself do as he said.

He pulled me over to the fire where I'd sat with Ursilda earlier. The light from the hearth danced in his blue eyes.

Ulrich stoked the dimming fire with the poker. Orange flames flared from the embers. The hall brightened. The tip of the poker glowed bright red. He stared at the tip, considering it. "Are you afraid of me?"

The sob in my throat hardened, and I shook my head no.

"You should be." He leered, then put the poker down and grabbed my hand. I was too terrified to pull away. "Now. Tell me what you know."

When I didn't answer, he pulled me into his lap. "Perhaps you need persuading," he said. His breath was rancid-sweet, his kiss violent. I could feel his desire for me pressing my leg. I wanted more than anything to escape it. As I tried to wriggle free, my thoughts went to my mother, how desperately she had tried to protect me. I wondered, a strange calm coming over me, if she was watching over me now. Would she be disappointed that I didn't go straight to Hildegard, or proud that I had been brave enough to try to seek evidence?

My mother. The figurine. I reached into my pouch. Mother, I prayed, rubbing the smooth stone desperately. Guide me.

My skin began to tingle, and the next world drew close. *Rōtkupfelīn*, my mother whispered.

Thoughts raced in my head. Rōtkupfelīn was the name of the girl in one of my mother's tales. The story went that she met a werewolf on her way to her grandmother's, who encouraged her to stop to pick flowers along the path. The werewolf beat Rōtkupfelīn to her grandmother's, ate the old woman, and crept into the old woman's bed to wait for her. But when Rōtkupfelīn got there, and the werewolf asked her to get into bed with him, she escaped by telling him she needed to go outside to relieve herself.

I gasped, understanding. If I was coy with him, he might believe that I didn't suspect him. I made myself look into Ulrich's eyes. "You sent them away?" I whispered in a playful voice. "So we could be alone?"

He nodded, confused at my overture. His thoughts were clear on his face. Maybe she *didn't* see anything. My ploy was working. "I did," he said slowly.

I leaned back slightly so I could slip my arms out of my cloak. As the fabric hit the floor, I met his eyes, conscious of the way the dress fell over my small breasts and hips. "The common folk tell stories about you where I'm from."

His gaze slid down from my face to my curves.

"Is that so?" he said. "What do they say?"

I made my eyes wide. The hall was still but for the crackle of the fire. "That you turn into a wolf on the night of the full moon. Are the stories true?"

"Indeed," he said, chuckling, as if he were play-acting.

I forced a smile. Brave, I told myself. Be brave.

He slipped his hand under my shift. I made myself sigh with false desire, then opened my eyes. "I think I've had too much wine," I giggled, wiggling. "I'm so sorry, your highness. I need to go outside to relieve myself."

He shifted on the bench. "Go," he said, irritated. "Come right back."

I straightened my dress, put on my cloak, and went with him to the hall door, my heart pounding in my throat. Ulrich barked at the guards. "The girl has to piss."

I hurried behind the firethorn bush near the hall where I'd hidden my bag. As I crouched out of sight of the guards, gathering my courage to dart into the trees, I heard footsteps. A second later there was movement in the shadows, and I heard Esther's whisper from behind a nearby tree. "Did you tell him about Daniel?"

"Of course not. He's wicked. He—" My voice broke.

Esther met my eyes, her expression full of guilt.

"I tricked him into letting me outside. I'm about to run."

She nodded gravely and pressed something into my palm. "Please. Take this with you. Frederika gave it to Daniel. I'm so sorry I told him you saw the murder."

I peered at the object, a heavy circle of gold. It was a ring, bright and cold, set with a hundred glittering pale jewels. Diamonds. I had never seen one before. "Esther. I can't—"

"Aren't you going to an abbey? To see a powerful abbess?"

I nodded.

"I bet they would take you more seriously if you give them that. Besides, I don't want Ulrich to find it in my hut. He'll know she's been here." She pointed farther into the woods where silver fir trees sagged with snow. "Daniel loosed Frederika's horse back there. Find her, quickly, and ride far away."

I thought of Ursilda, the talk we were supposed to have in the morning. Daniel's promise to take me to the clearing. My heart sank. There was too great a cost to stay.

I grabbed my bag and slipped into the woods. The night was cold. My heart hammered in my throat. It was only a moment before I heard the shouts of Ulrich's guards behind me. I searched the trees frantically for any sign of the horse. In the distance I could see a ghostly equine shape standing next to what had once been a stream, head bent over the ice.

"Nëbel," I hissed, my voice panicked. She looked up, her eyes liquid and warm, her body tense. I fumbled in my sack for one of the quinces I had taken from the cellar at Gothel, holding it out. "Do you remember me?" I whispered in a more soothing tone, approaching slowly, willing myself to ignore the commotion at my back.

The horse stayed put, watching me silently, eyeing the quince. When I was close enough, I fed it to her. She snorted a soft greeting. I reached for her reins, then mounted her as Frederika had taught me. She whinnied in surprise. I squeezed her flanks with my thighs and nearly fell, she took off so fast.

CHAPTER TWENTY-TWO

I rode Nëbel away from the settlement as fast as I could, my heart-beat thudding in my ears. Down the mountain, ducking under branches and weaving around trees. When Nëbel slowed to pick her way through a dense thicket, I held my breath. I could see torchlights bouncing behind me. "Halt!" a deep voice shouted. "Haelewise of Kürenberg, I order you to halt!"

"What is she riding?" a man shouted.

"Is that Frederika's horse?"

It wasn't until Nëbel took off again that I could breathe. As we neared the bottom of the mountain, I could hear riders getting closer behind me, see their torches growing brighter. When we reached the valley, I turned Nëbel to follow the old footpath that led north into the bog. Nëbel was strong and fast without the trees to slow her, but the prince's men were better riders than I was. They were gaining on me.

Desperate, I reached into my coin-purse for the figurine, wishing, praying for safety. I searched the woods for a place to turn, but there was nowhere the riders wouldn't see my hoofprints and follow me.

And then it happened. The figurine grew warm beneath my thumb, and I thought I saw a shimmer in the bog below. It was so faint, I thought I might be imagining it, but peering down into the trees, I could make out a silvery shape. A ghost-woman, beckoning me into the trees. My mother.

I turned Nëbel sharply into the bog, pressing the horse's flanks with my thighs, trying to catch up with her. A lump in my throat, a wild need to see her after all that had happened. She was so far ahead, I could only see her in glimpses. Now a shadowy figure in the distance, now a luminescent ball of light.

She flew through the bog ahead of me, veering north. No matter how hard I pushed my horse, she always seemed the same distance ahead—shimmering, weaving between trees, leading me deeper and deeper into the forest.

Behind me, blessed snowflakes drifted down, vanishing my trail. No matter how hard I rode, I couldn't catch up. After a while, the noise of galloping horses behind me grew faint. I could only hear a single rider—far behind me—see the light of a single distant torch. I kept going, following the glimmer of my mother. From time to time, I checked behind me.

When I could see the torchlight no more, I searched the forest in front of me, desperate, and realized I could see my mother no longer. She was gone.

A rift opened up in my chest, and something yawned in my throat. A moan so low, so terrible, I didn't think it was my own.

I kicked Nëbel's flanks, urging her forward, refusing to believe my mother was gone. But the light never reappeared. After an hour or so, my arms and thigh muscles began to ache. By dawn, I was too tired to ride any longer. I crept into an abandoned hut and pulled the horse inside so she wouldn't be spotted, closing the shutters of the only window.

I was so tired, I almost forgot to eat the alrūne and smear the fertility oil on my groin, but the pressure of the dried fruits against my hip reminded me. Once upon a time, I had been angry with Kunegunde for taking them from me, but now I was grateful for her foresight. If she hadn't dried them, the fruit would be rotten by now, and I would likely be dead.

As the gray morning sun shone through the holes in the roof, my thoughts turned to the circle I would probably never join, the life my mother left behind. What was it like for her to be a part of that circle? How often had she looked into the water-*spiegel*? Did she learn incantations like the ones Kunegunde spoke? Why would she agree to give that up?

I pulled the figurine from my pouch and stroked her curves. In the gray light, she seemed almost to glow. Father had forbidden Mother from telling me so many things. No wonder she told stories. They were the only way she could tell me the truth. The amber-eyed *kindefresser*, who took strange forms and lured away children—that was my grandmother. The golden apples growing just outside the castle—the alrūne. Her stories were like the words she whispered to me now. They were warnings. They came true.

It was almost midmorning before sleep found me, and what sleep I got was fitful. Terrified that one of Ulrich's riders had caught my trail again, I was awakened often by simple sounds: the call of a bird, snow crunching under the foot of an unknown animal. When I awoke undiscovered at sunset, my fear subsided somewhat, but I didn't by any means feel safe.

Before I left the hut, I wrapped my breasts, put on my boy's rags, and tucked my braid under my tunic so I wouldn't be recognized. Outside, I apologized to Nëbel and darkened her white coat with dirt.

I knew how to find the abbey. Head west through the mountains, then follow the river north. The woods were dark as I searched for the river. The only sounds were those of animals—the calls of owls, the distant yips of foxes, the occasional roars of stags. When I found the river, I decided I wouldn't follow the shoreline in case Ulrich's riders were watching the riverbank. Instead, I would shadow it from inside the trees.

I filled my drinking horn full of river water—it was clear here, there were no towns close by—then hurried back inside the tree line. As I guided Nëbel through the wood that first night, keeping the gleam of the river to my left, I found myself haunted by

Frederika's last moments. I found myself reliving, despite my best efforts, the unwilling kiss I'd suffered the night before. Anger burned in my heart, cold and white, at the man who was responsible for both.

When the gloom over the forest lifted, exhausted from riding, I tied Nëbel and curled up under the leafless boughs of an elderberry bush. Its branches were tangled, as if the horns of a hundred stags had grown from its trunk. Laying my head on my sack, I ate a bite of the alrūne, wondering how to approach Hildegard. If I told her anything close to the truth, she would think I was possessed by a demon like my father and everyone else in Christendom.

I fell asleep before I could reach a decision.

Grief is a funny thing. It comes in fits and starts. As I rode the next evening, all of my grief for my mother, for Rika, came rushing back. Soon enough I was crying into Nëbel's mane, turning the dirt I had smeared on it to mud. I was tired of my hair catching on twigs and branches, tired of hiding from Ulrich and his guards. My skin crawled when I thought of what had almost happened the night before last.

The forest was thick. The moon was waxing toward full, but barely any starlight or moonlight shone through the branches. Shapes leapt out of the dark. The night surrounded me, broken up only by the sounds of night-creatures scurrying away, the sounds Nëbel made as she moved. Hooves on dirt, the flap of a tail, a soft whicker, the windy sound of her breath. She was a good horse, calm and sweet, until she sensed a storm coming just before dawn. Then she became unpredictable, nostrils flaring, wild-eyed until I whispered calming words in her ear.

I had a lot of time to think as I followed the river north. I found myself wondering what Matthäus was doing. I imagined him lying with Phoebe, their babe in a cradle beside their bed. He was so dedicated to doing the right thing, I was sure that he would grow to love Phoebe simply because a man was supposed to love his wife.

Perhaps I had been foolish to turn down his offer. How simple it would have been to live out my days as his mistress. What a comfort it would've been to have someone to love, to not be caught up in the treacherous affairs of wolf-princes and princesses.

Such thoughts thickened my mind-fog, feeding my saturnine mood. I built proverbs in my head in an attempt to distract myself: *Blessed is the snow that hides my path. Blessed is the lie that saves a life. Blessed is the woman who helps her kind.* I repeated them like incantations, in the hopes that they would fill my thoughts.

Seven days into my journey, at sunrise, when I could ride no more, I found a hollow tree in which to rest. The forest was warming quickly, as spring set in and I left the mountains behind. I still hadn't decided what to tell Hildegard. In my most hopeful moments, I wondered if there was another reason my mother wanted me to seek her out. It seemed unlikely that the abbess would know something of the circle, but it wasn't impossible.

Mangled roots pressed my bottom as I unwrapped the band I was still wearing about my breasts. Settling in, I took out the figurine from my coin-purse and prayed, rubbing her curves, but her stone remained cold under my thumb. Since the night I'd escaped from Ulrich, I'd prayed over and over for my ghost-mother to return, but she hadn't. Although I had kept taking the alrūne, it seemed that I was completely alone in the world. After a while, I gave up and wrapped myself in my blanket, my thoughts turning again to Matthäus.

I was wondering what he was doing now—saying his morning prayers, getting dressed to work at the tailor's shop—when I heard a soft melody nearby: *hah-mama, hah-mama.* Looking up, I saw a collared dove peering into my hollow. Was I sitting on her nest? As I felt around for it, I had an idea. I had only ever watched Kunegunde send her soul into a raven, but the dove was relatively large. Nowhere near as big as Erste, but if I ate the alrūne and spoke the right words, I could fly in her body to see Matthäus.

My heart lurched. The urge to see Matthäus welled up inside me. Matthäus, my oldest friend, my love. Even though I wouldn't be able to talk to him—to see the face of someone who loved me would be a balm. Kunegunde had warned me that you couldn't fly far or be gone from your body long, but I was willing to take that risk.

I searched my memory for the words that had loosed Kunegunde's soul. In trying to decipher their meaning, I had learned them by heart. Pulling one of the dried alrūne from my sack, careful not to disturb my avian visitor, I took a nibble of the fruit. Then I stammered the words my grandmother had spoken. "*Leek hapt—*" I started, a tingling in the tips of my fingers. "*Leek haptbhendun von hzost. Tuid hestu.*"

My skin crawled. The air went taut. I could feel my soul beginning to lift from my skin. As before, there was an in-between moment—when I became part of the mist—and then I was inside the dove.

Through her eyes, I could see my body crumpled inside the tree. Being inside the dove was different from being inside a raven—the dove-mind was calmer. I felt only a quiet hunger as she scanned the earth for seeds. I pictured us flying, lifting up out of the forest toward home. And then we were moving, soaring up, with a faint sense of avian surprise that we were doing so. Up, up, up over the greening blanket of the wood, southeast toward the lake glimmering pink with dawn. It should've been enthralling, soaring like that toward home, but I felt only an ache for Matthäus, and a nagging fear that I would see something I didn't want to see.

When the city wall rose up beneath us, I pictured us pulling down. The dove obeyed, floating down over the wooden wall toward the Kürenberg estate. We landed on the garden wall, where a sea of clothes had fallen in the process of drying on the clothesline. Here goes nothing, I thought. I hopped onto the shutters of the room where I had seen Matthäus sewing my last night in town. The shutters were closed. We had to pry them open with our beak.

The sewing room was a mess. Fabric scraps everywhere, pin-cushions, cloth. On the floor was a half-made tunic still attached to an abandoned needle and thread. The trunk he kept by the wall was open and spilling with fabric. It looked like Matthäus had been searching for something, and he hadn't had a chance to clean up.

What had disturbed his work? I wondered, pausing to sense where he was. I heard no movement in the other rooms, sensed no sign of life. Cautiously, I flew through the house. No one was there. Upstairs, I found two rooms with empty beds—one with the cradle and one without.

The whole house looked like it had been ransacked, as if someone had been desperately searching for something. There were broken dishes in the kitchen, trunks open in each room. Cups on the table, clothes on the bed, a half-empty horn of curdled milk in the cradle. If Matthäus had simply traveled with his father, the house wouldn't be such a wreck.

Something had happened.

Fear overtaking me, I soared as fast as the dove would take me toward his father's shop to find out what. Speeding over roofs and alleyways, I saw the city waking up. Women emptying chamber pots from the night before, opening shutters to let the warmth in, oblivious to the ensorcelled dove passing overhead. I fluttered down to light on the windowsill of Matthäus's parents' room above the tailor's shop. The shutters were open. Inside, his mother sat in bed in her nightcap, eyes red from crying. His father sat next to her, his forehead wrinkled with anxiety. For a long time, they were silent, and I wondered if they would ever say anything.

Then his mother shifted in her seat. "It's been almost a week."

"I don't know what you want me to say. He didn't even tell Phoebe he was leaving."

"It's unlike him to vanish like this. He's been hurt. I know it."

"If he doesn't come back soon, we'll petition the bishop."

"What can the bishop do if the guards took him?"

Guards? I stared at them, shocked. Why would the guards take
Matthäus? I waited for them to speak further, but they fell silent as
if they had reached a familiar impasse. His mother looked stricken.
His father looked irritated. Without thinking, I cursed under my
breath. The words came out of the dove—*hah-mama*—catching his
mother's attention.

"*Heinrich!*" she breathed, clutching her husband's arm. She
pointed at the bird. "Its eyes—"

"Holy father protect us," her husband prayed when he saw, his
expression horrified. He jumped out of bed and rushed at us, flapping his blanket. "Shoo! Get out of here!"

I flew back to my hollow quickly, afraid that I had already
strayed from my body too long. As I lay there, watching the dove
wander dizzily from my den, I couldn't stop thinking about Matthäus's disappearance.

The next night, when I continued my journey to the abbey, I
scanned the trees for birds I could use to fly home again. I needed
to know why the guards might have taken Matthäus. But I came
across no birds large enough, that night, to cast the incantation.
Only tits and nightjars. Tiny things.

I resolved to find out what had happened to Matthäus as soon as
I went to the king.

Over the next few nights, I planned what I would tell the abbess.
I deliberated over every detail, rehearsing my speech as I rode. I
must have looked a sight, muttering to myself in my tattered boy's
clothes on my muddy horse. I felt ridiculous, talking aloud when
there was no one else to hear. Even the foxes seemed to judge me
from their dens.

By the twelfth morning, I could see the abbey and the city it
overlooked across the river. The sight filled me with foreboding,
making me so nervous, I could barely eat the hare I shot and cooked
over the fire. I was terrified of entering the city, even disguised as

I was. What if Ulrich's men were looking for me there? What if one of the villagers had told him I was headed to see Hildegard? Hoping my disguise was good enough, I used one of Kunegunde's coins to pay for the ferry across the river.

It was strange to be out and about by daylight. The ferry ride made me queasy. I had become accustomed to my only company being foxes and porcupines, glow-flies and the strange bats that soared from the mountains at night. Now there was laughter and yelling and talking. As we crossed, I watched the wheel of the mill near the abbey slowly turn in the river.

At the wooden city gate, there were merchants shouting their wares. The guards eyed me, suspicious of the oddly feminine peasant boy on his muddy mare, but they allowed me to pass through the city gate.

Inside the city, my heart stopped thudding quite so loudly. Before me I found a wet street lined with narrow rows of houses. Muddy rivulets streamed downhill. Spring had come earlier here. As I rode through the city toward the abbey, a cat streaked by, thin and covered in scabs. Screaming children streamed past, playing at chase. One of them limped. Another's face was covered with boils. All of them were skin and bones. I saw new spring gardens, here and there, the plants wan little buds. Sickly looking hens, half-dead goats. The prices in the market were outlandish: eight *pfennige* for freshly caught pike, five *pfennige* for a wheel of cheese. Even the fishmonger looked desperate.

I wondered who was buying food at these prices, if no one was allowed to leave the city gates here, as was true back home. The woods here were plentiful. It had only taken me an hour to shoot and cook the hare I had for breakfast. As I passed through the market, the spires of the abbey rose up on the other side of a smaller river, pale and glittering, like the spires of an enchanted castle from one of my mother's tales. The red bridge that led across the river was beautiful up close, constructed of red and gray and tan bricks.

Sunlight glinted on the river. Crossing the bridge, I saw a grassy path rutted by cart wheels and hoofprints that led to and from several wealthy-looking estates.

Then I saw them in the distance—two of the guards I'd seen with Ulrich on the mountain. Well-coiffed, hair oiled, in black and green surcoats, Ulrich's colors. My stomach dropped, and all the dread I had been carrying deep inside me returned. They were standing guard halfway between where I stood and the abbey gate, talking, huge swords at their hips—waiting for me. How was I going to get past them?

I thought of the deserted hut where I'd slept a few days before and wanted desperately to turn my horse around and go back. Instead, taking a deep breath, I made myself pull down my hood over my bright eyes and ride nonchalantly toward the abbey gate, already spinning the story I would tell them.

The guards glanced up at me, stepping into the path to stop my progress. "Halt. State your name and business."

My heart pounded. I pulled on Nëbel's reins and cleared my throat, making my voice as low and gruff as I could. "My name is Eckert, sir," I said merrily. "Eckert, son-of-Hildebrand-the-Baker. I'm on my way to the mill."

The taller guard eyed me. The shorter one grunted. "We're looking for a young noblewoman with long black hair and golden eyes. She's riding a white horse. We have reason to believe she's traveling to this abbey. Have you seen her?"

I made myself scoff. "*Golden* eyes, you say?"

"We've seen it ourselves."

I snorted. "What, is she magic? Like the goose who laid golden eggs?"

"Get out of here," the taller guard said dismissively.

I laughed as if I found their assignment uproariously funny and pressed Nëbel's muddy flanks with my thighs. She moved on. Behind me, the taller guard groaned to his partner.

"This is a fool's errand."

"Hardly. She's one of the duke's spies. She's implicated in the murder. If we find her—"

I nearly choked as I rode on and their voices behind me grew faint. Ulrich was telling people I was a spy?

"I wish we could've gone with the body. This is tiresome. At least the others get to meet the king."

I could scarcely breathe. The other guard's answer was finally too low for me to hear. My body was tense, and there was an ache behind my eyes. My teeth hurt, I was gritting them so tight.

When I turned the corner, the porterhouse stood beside the gate. Behind it I could see a stable and a half-built structure that was swarming with stonemasons and carpenters, which looked like the beginnings of a church. The outer abbey was still under construction. Beyond the half church was a dock. In the rapids beyond it was the mill I'd mentioned to Ulrich's men, a ways past the abbey. I kept riding past the porterhouse, as if I were going toward the mill.

When I reached the mill, I kept riding. About half an hour from the abbey, I found a bank where a bend in the river made a relatively secluded pool. Trees grew along the bank, offering a bit of privacy. Shivering in the cool spring air, I led the horse into the water to clean her off first, then ducked underwater to unwrap my breasts and undo my braid. The water was demonically cold, as if it had sprung from some frozen part of hell. As I scrubbed the dirt from my skin, I felt a hatred for Ulrich—his overweening sense of his birthright, his arrogance, his lies.

When both of us were as clean as I could manage, I tied Nëbel to a tree so she could graze and I could put on my shift. I thought of Matthäus as I let the sun dry me, praying that he was alive and well, that nothing had happened to him. When I was dry, I pulled on my fine clothes and tied back my hair beneath my wimple. Then I put on the ring Esther had given me, which I planned to offer when I presented myself. The diamonds glittered brightly in the sun.

I mounted and squeezed Nëbel's flanks with my thighs. Toward the abbey we went, the queasiness that had stricken me earlier returning. My mouth went so dry as I approached the workmen that I had to take a drink of water from my horn. My heart thudded in my throat. I made myself turn as quickly as possible from the river toward the porterhouse so the guards wouldn't see me when I went around the bend.

And then I was inside the gate. The porter looked up, confused. "The lady is traveling alone?"

Noblewomen didn't, I realized. I should've known he would ask about that. I met his eyes, knuckles white against Nëbel's reins, and spoke in stilted *diutsch*. "My escort met misfortune."

"Of what sort, miss, if I might ask?"

I groped for a response. "Robbers. Four days north of here."

His eyes widened, as he nodded. "You've traveled far."

"This ring is all I have left to my name." I showed it to him. "I've come to speak with Mother Hildegard."

His eyes grew large as he inspected the ring, and he bowed his head. "What should I call your ladyship?"

I thought long and hard before I answered. I had labored over the decision whether to be honest about who I was for a week. It was a gamble to use my name, but it was a gamble not to. "Haelewise of Gothel," I said finally, praying he couldn't tell I'd never spoken the words in my life. But they were true, at least. I had lived for over three months at Gothel. I'd played there as a girl. My mother grew up there, and my grandmother lived there still.

The porter nodded, taking Nëbel's reins and tethering them to a nearby pole. "Lady Haelewise," he said, holding out his hand.

I smiled at him, nervous, his gesture catching me off guard. After a moment, I took his hand, dismounted, and followed him inside, where dim stones flickered around a hearth. He nodded at a register on the table. "Do you write, miss?"

I nodded, grateful Kunegunde had taught me how. The date on

the register said in painstaking letters: *March 4, The Year of Our Lord 1158*.

"Would it please you to set down your name?"

Haelewise of Gothel, I wrote in my unpracticed script.

"I'll stable your mount. Then we'll get you upstairs."

I listened to the *clip-clop* of Nëbel's hooves as he led her away. While I waited for him to return, I turned the pages of the register, fear fluttering in my throat. Noble name after noble name cluttered its pages. I swallowed my fear, trying to convince myself I was not at risk, that my mother had told me to come. Then I saw the frontispiece of the register. It was emblazoned with the king's seal.

God's teeth, I thought. I've ridden here on his dead daughter's horse.

CHAPTER TWENTY-THREE

My hands shook as the porter led me over stepping-stones that dotted the muddy ground. I could feel my falsehoods threatening to collapse around me like the roof of a burning building. I might be safe as far as Nëbel went—white mares weren't too uncommon—but I had shown the porter Frederika's ring. For all I knew it could be some famous bauble everyone who was anyone knew about. Following the porter up a narrow stone stairwell to the upper level, I tried my best to swallow my fear. There were no rails. Our boots made a nervous music as the porterhouse and stables and half-built church dropped away below, but I was less afraid that I would fall than I was that someone would see through my disguise.

At the landing, a heavy wooden door prevented trespassers from passing through the upper abbey wall. Its iron knocker had been shaped into a grotesque, winged face. The iron looked black and smooth. The face sneered out—godlike, angry—as if to deter unwanted visitors from entering.

The porter reached for it to knock, the iron sounding loud and heavy against the wood. As we waited for the gatekeeper to answer, the porter cleared his throat. The sun shone hot on my clothes. A dizziness came over me, which I attributed at first to the height at which we stood and the social height I was trying to climb.

A panel slid open above the knocker. Through its bars, a face peered out. I could see only dark eyes, sliding over to the porter. "We are not expecting anyone," a woman said in a muffled accent unlike any I'd heard. "Who is this?"

"Lady Haelewise of Gothel," the porter said. "She seeks an audience with Mother Hildegard."

"Has she brought a letter of commendation?"

The porter looked at me. I shook my head, repeating the story I had told him, adding the detail that my papers were stolen during the attack.

The woman continued routinely. "God bless you and keep you from further ill, but this is a sacred place. We cannot let just anyone in. Are you here on pilgrimage?"

I shook my head. "I seek sanctuary."

"From whom?"

I bit my lip, remembering the king's seal on the register. "I witnessed something terrible. I can only tell my story to Mother Hildegard."

"She brought an offering." He nudged me. "Show her."

I held up the ring, terrified that the gatekeeper would recognize it. Like the porter, her eyes widened at the sight of it. Her face disappeared and the panel slid shut. My heart pounded while I waited to see what she did. I thought I heard the sound of keys jangling on the other side of the door. After a moment, the lock clicked. The door opened just wide enough for her to take the ring. Through the crack, I watched her turn it this way and that with tawny fingers. She opened the door. "It may be days before Mother Hildegard can meet with you, Lady Haelewise," she said. She wore a thin crown with a gauzy veil attached to its back, which cast a beautiful white haze over the black of her hair. Her robes glowed white in the sun, contrasting with her bronze skin. "We have standing orders not to disturb her. But we would welcome you to stay in the guesthouse as you wait."

As the sister let me into the upper abbey, my hair stood on end. The air inside the upper level felt taut. I closed my eyes, reaching out. The air was so thin, I could feel the next world enmeshed with this one, just like I could at Gothel, though I could sense no mist here.

This was a thin place. There was no doubt about it. What this meant for Hildegard and her Christian abbey I had no idea.

The sister, who told me her name was Athanasia, began naming each of the buildings we passed—the residential house, the abbess's tower, the cloister. All the buildings on the upper level, she said, had been completed just last year. The mill had been good to them, and Hildegard had hurried to make them comfortable.

I faded in and out, having difficulty attending to what she was saying. My thoughts kept returning to Ulrich's men on the path below, the king's seal on the register. What would the king think if he discovered me here with his dead daughter's horse?

Athanasia continued her chatter, pointing at a stone building, oblivious to my discomfort. "There is the infirmary. There, the garden." She pointed at a stepping-stone path, on either side of which a huge, healthy garden grew with green leaf-buds, a vast swath of growing nettle and dandelion.

I had never seen a garden so endless.

"The garden of remedies is behind it."

The guest cottage stood between the garden and the upper wall. It had one small window with battened shutters and a thatched roof. She opened the door, inviting me to hang my cloak on the wall. In the corner was a small table for eating or reading or sewing. There was a richly dressed bed where I could sleep, a pipe in the wall with a lever that brought water from the river, and a hearth with a cauldron to heat water for baths. I tried to nod casually, as if I expected such wonders, but in truth I was awestruck by the idea of a lever that could bring water directly into my room.

My expression must've betrayed my feelings. Athanasia laughed. "I always forget what a marvel running water is here. It was more commonplace in the East."

"Is that where you're from?" I asked, then wished I hadn't, fearing that my question would betray my unworldliness.

Athanasia turned toward the wall, her expression sorrowful. "I was born in Constantinople. My mother, God rest her soul, died there. I alone escaped."

I nodded, my breast swelling with sympathy. "God rest her soul," I said, meeting her eyes. "How long has it been? My own mother died not a year and a half ago." My voice trembled.

Athanasia crossed herself. "There are things of which it is best not to speak. Someone will bring dinner shortly. Vespers are in two hours. Do you wish to attend?"

I nodded slowly, wondering if it was expected.

"Very well," she said, moving toward the door, her veil trailing behind her. "When the bell sounds, step outside. Someone will come to escort you into the nuns' chapel. In the meantime, you will find soap and towels beside the tub. If you wish, there is time enough before the service to bathe."

I looked down at the things on the stool by the tub as the door clicked shut behind her. I took my mother's mirror from the sack and brought it to my face. In its metal, the shadow-shape of my reflection stared back at me, divided with cracks. My hair was frizzy beneath my wimple, my face covered with a thin film of river sediment. My eyes looked haunted, unearthly, still the same strange bright gold.

The mirror clattered as I set it on the stool and picked up the soap. It was similar to the cake I'd used at Gothel, but it had a more fragrant smell: like quince with hints of a spice I couldn't place. The hand towel was raw linen, embroidered with a pretty pattern around its edge. Working the pump brought water into the barrel beneath the pipe as if by magic. It felt good to make something happen, pressing the pump down and pulling it up.

I filled the cauldron, brought it to the hearth, and started a fire. While I waited for the water to heat, I thought of Matthäus, praying that he was safe. I couldn't get over his mother's mention of guards. Where had Matthäus gone? Why was his house in such disarray? Matthäus was an innocent tailor. Why in the world would the guards want him?

A possibility I hadn't thought of before occurred to me. What if Matthäus and Phoebe had quarreled, and Matthäus had left her? His father would be upset because they faced the loss of their new status. But why in the world would that involve the guards? I wanted to pull out my hair, it made so little sense. I hoped I could see the king quickly so I could make sure Matthäus was all right.

When the water was hot enough, I poured it into the tub. What a relief it was to sink into that water. The warmth soothed my aching muscles. The soap filled the air with the scent of quince. For a blissful moment, I forgot all of my fears. There was nothing but me and the water.

But as I scrubbed my skin, watching the dirt slough off and cloud the water, I thought of Ulrich, how no amount of soap would ever cleanse me of his touch. I thought of the guards below, who might at any moment realize I was already here.

When the knock sounded, I shot up. Bathwater splashed out of the tub. I slipped on its bottom, steadying myself on its lip—silent, naked, bathwater dripping down—certain that the guards had come for me. I scanned the guesthouse for a place to hide. Could I slip out the window?

"Miss," a muffled voice said from the other side of the door. "I brought the stew."

Feeling foolish, I sank back down into the water. "Come in."

The maid was a lay sister with a sly smile, straw-colored hair, and tan, weathered skin. She wore a traditional habit: simple robes unlike Sister Athanasia's. My stomach growled at the sight of the food tray she carried. "Tell me something," I said, trying to keep my voice calm, to pronounce each sound of each word like Kunegunde. "Are royals allowed up here? Guards and such?"

"Royals, miss?"

"I saw the king's seal on the register."

"The count who protects this abbey is the king's half brother. No men've been allowed on the upper level but Brother Volmar and the priest since construction was completed. Even the porter only takes visitors to the upper gate."

Relief flooded me. I closed my eyes. "Who is he? The porter."

Her voice was rueful. "I don't know. It's a post, miss. They change out every week."

"Why do you keep calling me *miss*?" I asked without thinking, relieved that the porter wouldn't be a close associate of the king.

A puzzled look crossed the lay sister's face.

I realized my mistake. A noblewoman would expect to be treated with such deference. "Please, call me Haelewise. What is your name?"

"Walburga, miss," she said with a curtsy. "I mean, Lady Haele-wise. Will it please you to eat this?"

She removed the cover of the food tray. A delicious-smelling stew steamed in a bread bowl. Beef, with carrots and parsnips. Garlic.

It took all my willpower not to jump out and dive for it. "Yes. Thank you so much, Walburga." I was starving.

I hoped the monk wasn't on the upper level then, as I was out of the tub before the door closed behind her. I wolfed down that stew, soaking wet, bathwater dripping down my skin. I didn't even bother to dry off until I was done. After that I dressed, taking the last nibble of one of the dried alrūne, noting that I had only two fruit left. I tied back my hair, pulled on the tunic, and paced, anxious to tell Hildegard what Ulrich had done.

When the bell for vespers rang, I waited for someone to escort me into the cloister. A light rain had passed over the abbey while I bathed. The leaf-buds on the plants in the garden glistened—hearty and green—in the sun. After a while, Sister Athanasia showed up to walk me to the cloister. She shook her head when I greeted her, lips tight. The keys on her ring jangled as she turned the lock.

The heavy door creaked as it opened. The cloister glowed with the pink light of dusk. The church inside was candlelit, painted

with murals. One depicted a young man on pilgrimage. Another
showed him lying ill, his mother beside his bed. Both were scenes,
I would later find out, from the life of the saint who had been buried in the crypt.

Near the altar was a door to the nuns' chapel. The tapers on the
wall flickered as I found a seat. No one else was here. Seven stacks
of psalters sat on the shelf before my pew. I picked one up, saw it
was written in the language of priests, and put it back. Soon the
sisters began to file in, all dressed like Sister Athanasia in crowns
and veils, the white fabric of their robes whispering as they moved.
Two dozen sisters, each carrying a candle, which she placed in the
holder on the wall as she passed, lightening the dim room in incre-
ments. None of the lay sisters, I noticed, attended the service.

Last in the procession was an elderly nun holding a taper larger
than the rest. Mother Hildegard. Recognizing her, I wanted to call
out, but I knew better than to interrupt the service. The abbess was
silvery haired with bone-white skin, and she wore a white robe
and veil similar to the other nuns. In the candlelight, as she placed
the taper in its holder, her eyes seemed to flash a very faint gold.
The effect was almost ominous. For a moment, I wondered if she
ate alrūne. Then she passed back into the shadows, smiling, and her
eyes seemed to fade to a more common pale brown. Perhaps I'd
imagined the brightness out of sheer hope and desperation.

A priest followed her in, swinging a censer of incense that
smelled like my father's church. The smoke floated to the ceiling
as he spoke a blessing, then led the sisters in an unfamiliar prayer.
When he was finished, Hildegard nodded at her daughters. Everyone reached for their psalters. Looking closer at the words below
each stack—*dies Lunae, dies Martis, dies Mercurii*—I realized they
were ordered by days of the week. I reached for one from the same
stack as the sister beside me and struggled to find the page to which
she'd turned.

An eerie instrument played a long tense note from another

room. Mother Hildegard waited for the sound to stop, then opened her mouth to sing. Her voice was like a bell, ringing out, walking up and down invisible stairs. The abbess's face shone in the light of the large taper, her eyes radiant—there it was again, that faint glint of gold—her whole aspect lit with joy. Her daughters began to sing with her, their voices following hers like echoes. After a moment, their faces lit up too, and their voices began to shake with feeling. I wondered if they could feel God's presence, although he was no more apparent to me here than he'd been in my father's church.

The service went on, the sisters alternating between song and prayer in the language of priests, their expressions radiant with joy. Jealous, I closed my eyes, reaching out to see if I could feel whatever they did, but despite the thinness of this place, I sensed nothing. Only an emptiness, the same disturbing *lack* that led me to resent going to church as a girl.

Tears stung my eyes. I had to work to master my emotions. I don't know why I expected to sense something, but the fact that I didn't made me inexplicably upset. The sisters sang on, joyful, turning a page of their psalters in unison, sending a chorus of whispers through the chapel. I set down my psalter, giving up on trying to follow along. Then I fumbled for the figurine in my coin-purse, rubbing her curves, reaching out to my mother. "*Why*," I prayed. "*Why did you lead me here?*"

CHAPTER TWENTY-FOUR

Mother Hildegard didn't send for me the next day or the next. She passed me sometimes, marching to and from the cloister gate, a wax tablet under her arm, barely registering my presence. There was no denying that her eyes had a golden tint outdoors—they shone a brighter gold in the sunlight—but I couldn't tell if that was from eating alrūne or just her natural eye color. Sometimes Brother Volmar, the elderly monk who served as her scribe, walked with her. I would be lying if I said I never had the urge to interrupt them, but no one else spoke to Hildegard when she passed, and I was only a lowly visitor.

I spent most of those first days waiting for Hildegard to call me. I avoided services, staying in my guesthouse except for meals. At night, I clutched the figurine, desperate to understand why my mother had brought me here. I rubbed the figurine, but it didn't thrum; it seemed to have no power within the abbey walls, despite the thinness of the air. I began to suspect that a blessing on the grounds by some high holy man—a bishop or an archbishop—kept it from working.

The suspicion strengthened my resolve to finish my business at the abbey as soon as possible. Thoughts of my audience with Hildegard began to possess me during mealtimes, making me too agitated to eat. Though I found them monotonous, I started going to services, willing the abbess to notice me. Time was passing. Ulrich was no doubt plotting to get away with what he'd done. My sleep was plagued with nightmares in which I never escaped him, or his men stormed the abbey. Nightmares in which the guards found and killed Matthäus. When I awoke from those, I tried to unravel what might've happened to him, but I failed to make any sense of what I'd heard. I reminded myself that I planned to check on him again as soon as I left court, but it didn't feel like enough.

One afternoon, when Hildegard passed me on her way to the scriptorium, her eyes were so bright, I became certain she was eating alrūne. If she was, it would explain a lot about why I was sent here. I found the garden of remedies Athanasia showed me and began searching its rows for alrūne plants. If Hildegard was eating the fruit, surely she would be growing the plants.

The garden was vast. In one area I recognized a number of seedlings—yarrow, bloodwort, and belladonna, all of which were used, I knew, in the healing of ulcers and wounds. The next patch was full of seedlings that grew into plants that reduced fevers: cinquefoil, watercress. There were pea plants and broad beans, thyme and rapunzel, lungwort and hellebore. In another area, I saw growing java pepper, lettuce, dill—plants that Kunegunde's speculum said tempered the desires of the flesh. Finally, I saw a whole patch of alrūne plants at the edge of the garden, lavender flower buds just beginning to peek out of the center of their cabbage-like leaves, and my heart leapt. There were dozens of plants. She had to be eating them. Why else would she grow so many? Maybe she would know something of the circle after all.

I became even more desperate to speak to her, but she didn't send for me, no matter how many services I attended or how often I tried to catch her eye. I became so frustrated, I wanted to scream at her during services, but I knew it would only hurt my cause. I tried to occupy my mind with puzzling out the language in which the sisters sang during services and read at meals. Unraveling the patterns and rules of the language distracted me. At meals, I asked Sister Athanasia questions about the devotional reading. Our whispers seemed to chafe at the sister who always sat beside Athanasia, a tall woman who wore her black hair tightly coiled beneath her veil, who found frequent reasons to touch Athanasia's hand. She pressed her lips together tightly when I asked Athanasia a question, stabbed her radishes, and sent me withering stares.

Athanasia seemed to enjoy teaching me Latin, nevertheless. After almost a week of mealtime conversation, I asked her to meet me in the afternoon, when her companion wouldn't, I presumed, be disturbed. I thought, perhaps, as the gatekeeper, Athanasia might have a special relationship with Hildegard, and if I impressed her, she might tell the abbess to see me sooner.

One day, Athanasia and I were strolling around the garden, talking about the day's psalms. A lay sister in plain robes knelt nearby in the dirt, humming to herself as she planted seeds in a barren area. "*In media umbrae mortis*," I said, stopping beside a row of cabbages, noticing the mournful sound of the phrase. "You say *umbrae* is shadow? And *mortis* death?"

She nodded, a curious look on her face. "Go on."

"*In media umbrae mortis*. It has a sorrowing sound."

"It does," she said, searching my eyes. "To match its sense."

"*Non timebo mala* is lighter. And *quoniam tu mecum es*—"

"How many times have you heard that psalm before?"

I felt myself flush. "Probably many, in church, before I knew what it meant."

"Have you ever thought of taking vows?"

I stared at her mutely. It never occurred to me that I might make the abbey my permanent home. Practically, holy life would offer me a home and safety from men like Ulrich, but the figurine didn't work here, my mother couldn't reach me, and the bald truth was I would break my vows in an instant for Matthäus.

Athanasia sensed my reluctance. "There is freedom in holy life. You might not think it true, locked up as we are from the rest of the world. But every morning I wake up here, I am freer than I ever was at home." Her voice trembled, and she met my eye.

I nodded, wondering what she meant.

"Hildegard is a forgiving mother superior. This is better, much better than the alternative. *Dominus regit me, et nihil mihi deerit.*" There were tears in the corners of her eyes. "Think on it," she said, with a solemn smile.

I made myself nod, reluctant to alienate her.

During the second week of my stay, a storm blew over the abbey, the clouds bursting as Walburga brought my breakfast. She barely had enough time to close the door behind her before lightning split the sky. As she hurried to batten the shutters, she almost spilled my water. Thunder seemed to shake the earth. Loosened by the sudden deluge, bits of thatch began to slide down the roof of the guesthouse. "Such uproar from the heavens," Walburga said, handing me a cup of rose water, her eyes widening with mock scandal. "Interrupting the construction. It's almost as if the Lord is upset with his architect."

I nearly spilled the draught, I laughed so hard. Everyone knew who had designed every inch of the abbey grounds.

Walburga and I had become friends during my first week at the abbey. Whenever she brought me food, we would gossip about life outside the abbey. She told me about the boy who wanted to marry her. I told her about Matthäus and my slow progress toward womanhood, the phial of fertility oil my grandmother made me that was almost out. Walburga seemed to think Hildegard could help with that, as well as replenishing my alrūne, which I told her I took to control my spells. She spoke of the abbess with an interesting mixture of awe and cynicism.

With everyone else, I took pains to be cautious during conversations. But Walburga was earthy, irreverent. She gossiped and told stories. Her upbringing seemed so similar to my own. Of everyone whom I met at the abbey, she seemed least likely to care if she saw through my disguise.

"What do you know of this place?" I asked her that day at breakfast. "What used to be here before Hildegard built her abbey?"

"Mostly farmland, miss," Walburga said, her voice turning nostalgic. "My parents still live in the farmhouse on the hilltop. There was a wood, thick with oaks and berries and birds. A field covered in dandelions. And here, where she built the upper level, there were the crumblin' ruins of the old abbey that housed St. Rupert's crypt." She looked thoughtful. "It was an eerie place, falling apart, an oak tree growing through the roof. My mother used to tell us to put our ears to the wall so the spirit of the place could whisper to us."

Her words made my hair stand on end. "What spirit is that?"

Walburga's expression turned inward. "I don't know, miss. They say this hill was once home to a Roman citadel. And before that, an ancient meeting place. Who knows what gods live here? There's an ancient shrine near the spring we use for holy water. My mother says Hildegard's plans to disturb it will bring bad luck."

I sat up straight, nibbling at a crust of bread, wondering if the shrine was the reason I was supposed to come here. "Have you ever seen it? This shrine?"

She nodded. "All the time. I used to play there."

"What is it like?"

"Quiet." She shrugged. "Unnaturally so. When I was little, we were afraid to make too much noise when we swam in the spring."

"What is it a shrine to?"

Walburga shrugged. "Some heathen religion. My mother won't speak of it."

That caught my attention. "But Hildegard wants to destroy it?"

Walburga lowered her voice. "Actually she wants to incorporate some of the stones into the cloister."

I blinked at her, surprised. First the alrūne, now this. "Really?"

"No one ever speaks of it except in Hildegard's secret language, but I think the archbishop won't give her permission."

"Secret language?"

"She calls it the *lingua ignota*. Hildegard only teaches it to her most trusted initiates, but I've picked up bits and pieces."

"Why would the abbess teach her initiates a secret language?"

Walburga gave me a look. "I wouldn't want to speculate *too* wildly, miss, but if I had to guess, I would say she has secrets."

I giggled. Thunder rolled, and another bit of thatch tumbled down the roof. "Nëbel," I breathed, remembering. "My horse. She's terrified of storms."

"Should we go down to the stable to check on her?"

"I'm afraid to leave the upper level. There are people looking for me."

Her eyes widened. "I could go for you."

"Would you?" I nodded, grateful.

While I waited for her to return, I pondered the shrine, the alrūne patch. What was Hildegard's relationship to the Mother?

When Walburga returned, her habit was soaking wet, plastered to her face and arms. The rain seemed hell-bent on flooding the garden. "Your horse is fine. The stablehand says she reminded him of a mare he cared for as a boy. He knew *just* how to soothe her, wrapping her in a blanket and tethering her tight."

Her words worried me. Had he tended Nëbel before?

"He said she must belong to someone filthy rich who could afford to be sentimental. Who's up there, he wanted to know. A princess? A duchess? I told him I didn't know your station. He had a good laugh at that, calling you the mysterious princess with the mysterious anxious horse."

My voice was small. "Did you give him my name?"

"Aye," she said, watching my expression. "Shouldn't I have?"

"I wish you hadn't. Is he close to the king?"

"Of course not, miss." Walburga stared at me, her brown eyes wide. "He's a peasant."

I closed my eyes, dread filling my stomach. If the stablehand talked, it was only a matter of time before I was discovered.

Walburga waited for me to explain.

"I need to see Mother Hildegard tonight," I said, meeting her eyes. I could wait no longer. "I witnessed Princess Frederika's murder. The horse you just checked on was hers."

That night, walking back to the guesthouse after supper, I found myself thinking about the shrine again, my belly full of pea soup and uneasiness. If this hill was sacred to the Mother, why didn't the figurine work here? Was the blessing on the grounds really so powerful? If Hildegard incorporated stones from a heathen shrine into the cloister, would that change things?

Someone called to me from across the garden. "Lady Haelewise—"

Approaching me was the lay sister Solange, whom I'd often seen on her knees in the garden, a fleshy woman in a plain habit with ruddy skin, dark eyes, and black hair. The sky behind her was moonless so early in the evening, dark and spattered with stars. An earthy odor accompanied her. "Mother Hildegard will see you now," Solange said.

Relief filled me. Finally. I hurried to retrieve the dagger from the guesthouse. Solange waited for me outside. As I walked out, I checked my reflection in the broken mirror, wrapping my hair in a scarf. My golden eyes flashed with determination.

My heart beat double time as Solange led me to the tower. My need to avenge Rika's death surged, filling me with clarity and purpose. The door opened into a stone hall, undecorated except for a shield leaning against the wall that was painted with the king's family crest.

I must've frowned. Solange laughed. "No love for the king, I see, miss. His half brother, the count, donated that shield a couple years ago when he took over as protector. It was meant for the porterhouse, but Mother Hildegard doesn't want to display it publicly. She says the only house we should show allegiance to is God's." Solange led me toward a winding staircase. "Mother Hildegard is upstairs."

Up the steps we went, our footsteps echoing past the second floor of the tower to the third. The keep was a circular room, sparsely furnished, with opulent arched windows. Two ornamental torches glowed on either side of the room, flickering, casting deep shadows over Hildegard's face. She sat in the center of the room in one of two chairs so richly dressed, they looked like thrones. As I entered the room, she looked up, though it was too dark to read her expression.

She looked smaller and thinner than she did during the Divine Office, as if her holy duties enlarged her. She dismissed Solange with a nod, then gestured for me to sit in the other chair. From my seat, I could see her face a little better, though she was still shrouded in shadows. "Forgive the dimness," she said with an apologetic smile. "I'm fighting a headache."

I nodded, thinking of the pain the light once caused me, and decided to get straight to the point. "I've come to seek your counsel, Mother Hildegard. I witnessed the princess's murder. I've been waiting to speak to you for a week."

The shadows prevented me from seeing her reaction, though I tried. The torchlight lit a halo of silver hair around her ears. "No one mentioned the reason for your pilgrimage to me until tonight."

There was a warning note in her tone. I realized, suddenly, how forward I was being. I closed my eyes, took a deep breath, and cautioned myself to be respectful. "The killer was Prince Ulrich's man, Mother. The arrow he put in her thigh was one of Zähringen's, but it was a ruse, I think, to implicate his enemy."

Hildegard was silent for a moment. I wished I could see her expression. "Why would the betrothed of the princess have her murdered?"

"I don't know," I said impatiently. "Does it matter?" Then I caught myself. I kept letting my anger get the better of me. "Forgive me. I *know* it was him. The killer berated her for betraying Ulrich, and he used a dagger emblazoned with his coat of arms."

I held out the cloth-wrapped dagger for her to inspect.

Hildegard drew a deep breath when she saw the bloodstains on the cloth. She set her jaw, taking the cloth from me. She murmured a prayer before she unwrapped the bloodstained blade and saw the wolf design on its hilt.

"I met Ulrich in the forest, and someone told him I had witnessed the murder. I tried to tell him it was impossible to see in the blizzard. He kept trying to get me to tell him everything."

She inspected the dagger in the torchlight. "But you escaped?"

I drew a deep breath, intending to tell her what happened, but the words wouldn't come. My breath hitched, something caught in my throat, and just like that, my composure shattered into a thousand fragments. The next thing I knew, I had gone to pieces like a clay pot dropped to a floor of stone. "He was going to take my virtue," I sobbed. "He wanted to kill me. I can't stop thinking about it. I have nightmares."

Hildegard wrapped the dagger and set it aside, reaching for my hand. "Would you like me to pray with you?"

I couldn't answer, the sobs were coming out of me so fast.

"*Ave Maria*," she began. Her skin was paper thin. Torchlight danced around us. "*Gratia plena...*"

As she said the prayer, I took deep breaths, trying to calm myself, paying attention. Had she chosen the Ave Maria for a reason? It was still too dark for me to read her expression, but she spoke the prayer reverently, with feeling.

Out the windows of the keep, the stars were so bright and so many that I wondered if I was looking at all the souls of heaven as they watched over the earth. I wondered if my mother was one of them. If Rika was one of them, watching, waiting to see if I would avenge her death.

"Mother," I said. "I want to take my story to the king. I want to make sure Ulrich is punished. But he has already gone to the king with a false story that implicates *me*. I need your advice. I have no idea how to get the king to take the word of a woman like me over the word of a prince."

Hildegard's eyes flashed. She massaged her temples. I could tell she sympathized with my plight. She was silent for a long time, longer than I expected would be necessary for her to consider my request, as if she was working something out. I wondered what it was. Finally, she nodded, deciding. "The emperor—you should refer to him as *emperor*—is due to hold court at a nearby palace in three weeks' time. I have an audience with him the week after Easter. I could take you to see him myself."

I took a deep breath. The stars shone over the river outside. "Thank you."

Her posture straightened, and she opened her mouth.

I could tell she was about to dismiss me. This might be the only audience I would have with her for weeks. I needed to find out about the alrūne, the shrine. But I couldn't just come out and ask. I thought fast. "There's another matter on which I would seek your help."

She leaned forward, raising her eyebrows. Her expression was so knowing, I feared she would see right through me to my low birth, my heresy. "And what is that?"

"I've heard you're a great healer. I take two remedies, and I'm almost out of both. One is an oil to bring on my menses. I haven't started them yet. The other is a fruit that stops the fainting spells I've had since birth."

"Fainting spells." She shifted in her seat. "What sort?"

I told her what my spells were like—how the air around me thinned, the next world drew close, and my soul left my skin. She watched me closely, something passing over her face that I couldn't quite read in the dark. I described all the cures my parents tried, all the herbalists and holy healers we'd visited, the prayers and blessings and exorcisms. "It wasn't until after I began to eat a certain fruit, last year, that my spells—" I stopped myself. The word I was going to say was *changed*, but I bit it off at the last minute. If I said *changed*, she might ask how, and I didn't dare mention the figurine or the voice because she might think me possessed by a demon. "That I was cured. The fruit was a cure."

She watched me closely. "What fruit?"

"My grandmother called it alrūne."

Her eyes widened and she leaned forward, checking my eyes. There was an uneasiness in what she said next. "You eat alrūne."

"It's a cure. When I eat it, I don't have fainting spells."

"Do you have it blessed first?"

I shook my head, puzzled. "I didn't know I should."

Hildegard was silent for a long moment, and I saw something pass over her face. This time, I was certain I hadn't imagined it.

I summoned my courage. "Mother," I said. "Forgive my boldness, but do you eat alrūne yourself? I've seen the way your eyes glint sometimes during services."

She sat up straight, alarmed. "Haelewise of Gothel. Who taught you this?"

"The princess." I met her eyes, telling myself to be bold. I had to know. "You didn't answer my question, Mother. *Do* you eat it?"

She was silent for a long moment. Then she laughed, shaking her head, clearly shocked at my forwardness. "From time to time, I do, yes. If you must know. It helps with my headaches. I always have it blessed first."

"Mother—"

She held up a hand. "The cardinal says the alrūne grew from the same earth as Adam. He says it carries the devil's influence. We must destroy the fruit you harvested improperly. If the bishop finds out you're eating it, you'll be excommunicated or worse."

I shook my head with a sudden burst of anger. I wouldn't allow anyone else to take my alrūne away from me. I had already made that mistake. "No," I said. "I won't."

Hildegard looked at me, startled. She watched me long enough that I realized how uncommon it must be for anyone to refuse her. Then she closed her eyes, as if she were listening to distant music.

After a moment, she smiled a sad smile. "What a strong will you have. You remind me of my old friend Richardis."

Her voice hitched, and she bowed her head, overcome. When she finally looked up, I knew from her expression that Richardis was dead.

"I'm sorry for your loss."

She nodded. "It's been years. I thought I could speak of her without—" Her voice caught. "Even after all these years, I am too attached."

The grief on her face was so great, it was difficult to watch. She balled her hand into a fist. Her knuckles went white. I heard the sound of them cracking.

After a moment, she regained her composure. "Your grand-mother. Who is she?"

I drew a deep breath. "You know her, actually. Her given name is Kunegunde."

"Kunegunde. I should've known." She gazed at me steadily, as if she was deciding whether to say more. Then she shook her head, pursuing a separate thought. "You resemble her in more ways than one. What color were your eyes when you were born?"

"Black," I said.

She watched me steadily. "Before you took the alrūne, did you have sensitivity to light?"

"Yes," I said. "How do you know?"

"I have it too," she said simply.

I blinked back at her, shocked.

She walked over to the wax tablet to write something down. She began writing on her tablet, muttering to herself in Latin. "*Oculi nigrim, pallid complexionis.* How old are you?"

"Seventeen."

She made a note.

"Might I ask what you're doing?"

"Cataloging your temperament." She put down her stylus. "I'll prepare an oil to bring on your menses. You're far too old not to have had them. It isn't healthy for all that waste inside you to keep building up. As for the alrūne, we have a number of the plants in our garden. I'll have Solange show you how to harvest them and cleanse them. I'll have her take you to the spring we use for holy water."

The spring? Near the shrine? I took a deep breath, trying to hide my eagerness to see the ruins.

"I'll prepare you a tincture from the root," she was saying. "There are no fruits, unfortunately, this time of year."

I nodded, disappointed. Of course there would be no fruit yet this time of year, but I had hoped they would have some dried. "Will the root have the same effect as the fruit?"

She nodded slowly.

"Does blessing the plant alter its effects?"

She nodded again. "Oh, yes."

"How?"

"You'll see." She smiled. "Forgive me. My headache grows worse. I will pray to He-Who-Is that your sleep tonight is untroubled. I'll send Solange in the morning with the oil."

CHAPTER TWENTY-FIVE

Back in the guesthouse, I stripped down to my shift and began my bedtime ritual—bathing, combing my hair, and getting into my bed, reaching into my sack to take a bite of alrūne. The act had become so habitual, I almost forgot that Hildegard had told me to stop. When I remembered, I sat up in bed, holding the fruit in my palm, trying to decide whether to heed her advice. Tomorrow, I would be leaving the abbey grounds. My mother might be able to speak to me beyond the wall. I went to bed without eating it, but my thoughts raced and I found myself unable to sleep until I took a bite.

The rap at my door as I dressed the next morning startled me. Solange stood outside the guesthouse holding an ampulla, stoppered and filled with a gleaming pink oil. "Here you go," she said, handing me the ampulla. "Mother Hildegard asked me to confiscate the rest of your alrūne to be destroyed."

A fierce possessive feeling surged in my breast, but I mastered myself quickly and made myself nod, going calmly to my sack. Fumbling through it for the alrūne, I decided I was unwilling to part with both of the fruits I had left. I smiled at Solange and handed her one with an obedient smile, leaving the other hidden at the bottom.

Solange told me to meet her after terce so she could show me how to harvest the plants properly and cleanse them at the spring.

As soon as Solange was gone, I lay down on my cot, pulled up my shift, and rubbed the oil onto my skin. The ointment was pungent, filling the air with the essence of crushed rose petals, white dock, and an unfamiliar scent. When my skin was slick, I smoothed my dress down and stared at the ceiling, a ridiculous hopefulness in my breast. I had long ago given up hope on Kunegunde's unguent, though I had been using it for months. To put my faith in another remedy was a self-deceit I thought I knew better than to indulge. All my life I had been going to alleged saints and healers whose miracles never quite came through.

But the heart is a traitorous thing. It wants what it wants. As I lay among the scent of rose and white dock, I allowed myself to fantasize about Matthäus. He and Phoebe had quarreled; he'd left their cottage in a rush to seek an annulment. When the bishop refused to grant it, he went to the king. The king was sympathetic, having sought an annulment from his first wife, Rika's mother. Matthäus went back home a free man, where I found him in the tailor's shop after I left court. I entreated him to come with me to my hut so we could talk in private. Soon, he was holding my hands in the cupboard, kissing me, and more. The rose oil had worked by then, and when I told him I had come of age, he asked me to marry him. It was such a pretty delusion, I didn't want to let it go.

On my way to the cloister for terce, I worried Hildegard would be able to tell I'd eaten the alrūne the night before. Then I realized I was being foolish. At Gothel, it had taken days for the golden eye color to fade completely.

When I met Solange in the garden, I pretended not to know where the alrūne grew. I let her lead me toward the patch. As we walked, I smelled the faint odor of parsley, the bitter scent of some impossible-to-identify budding green. Sunlight streamed through the clouds, glittering on the walking stones.

"The alrūne is over there," Sister Solange said, pointing out the patch I had seen before.

Remembering Athanasia's comment as we passed the plants that tempered the desires of the flesh, it occurred to me with amusement that if I wanted to stay at the abbey, I should probably sneak back out here at night and eat *all* of them.

"We have permission to harvest two plants," Solange said, kneeling before the bed.

The garden was quiet, apart from chattering birds. There was no one around but us. As I knelt beside Solange, squinting, I noticed the patch had a trenchant smell as if its soil had recently been turned with manure.

She nodded at the two largest alrūne plants. "These look like they have the most developed roots. To cleanse them, we'll have to leave the abbey. There's a spring on the other side of the hill. We'll leave the roots in its water for a day and a night so their impurities will be cleansed. Then, we'll have the priest bless them, and Mother Hildegard will make you a tincture."

I peered at the plants suspiciously, reminding myself I still had one dried fruit left if the root tincture didn't work.

When I met Solange's eyes, she smiled at me and pulled a pair of gloves from her bag. "Why gloves?" I asked, thinking about how many times I'd touched the fruit on the way here without wearing any.

"Alrūne is poisonous," Sister Solange said, smoothing the leather fingers of her gloves. So Kunegunde hadn't been lying. "The seeds are the worst."

My heart skipped a beat. "The seeds?"

She nodded.

The walk my mother went on the night before she took ill. Did she go looking for an alrūne patch to harvest wild fruit for their seeds? I remembered the lucky gloves she always wore to garden, how full of holes they were. If my mother handled the seeds when she planted them in our garden, that could have been what made her ill. "What are the symptoms of alrūne poisoning?"

Solange looked grim. "Yellow skin. Fevers. Swelling. A woman came to us, once, who ate the seeds by accident. Hildegard tried everything to flush the poison out. The juice of sysemera, betony, and rue pounded in a mortar, mixed with garden spurge and followed by a draught of hydromel usually works to expel any poison, even arsenic. But the woman was dead within three months. After we buried her in the cemetery, an alrūne patch sprouted from her grave. That's where we got these plants."

My mouth went dry. The earth beneath me began to spin. The sun beat down. Had my mother *eaten* the seeds? I remembered the tale of the golden apple, her request that she be buried in the garden. The alrūne patch that grew there the next spring.

She hadn't planted them. She had—

The truth was too difficult for me to bear.

Sister Solange saw the tears in my eyes and misunderstood. "It's a sad tale. That it is. God rest her soul. Agnes, her name was." A fly buzzed around her head. "It's not true, you know, what they say about the roots. They don't scream when you pull them from the earth."

I wiped my eyes with my shirtsleeve, attempting to get a hold of myself.

"I've harvested dozens. They never make a sound."

The spade she pulled from her bag was iron, the sort of fine tool a blacksmith forged in one piece. As Solange excavated the soil around the first plant's roots, I remembered the spade my mother used. A wooden thing with a knot of rope connecting handle to trowel. With my inner ear, I heard the song she used to sing while she gardened. *Sleep until morning, my dear one. Eostre leaves honey and sweet eggs*—

What would it be like to love someone so much, you would sacrifice yourself?

I must've stared into space for a long time. When I blinked and came awake, the abbey garden came into focus. Sister Solange's digging had exposed a root: a gray, misshapen thing. She reached into the dirt with her gloved hand to uproot the plant. There was no sound apart from the snapping of tendrils and spattering of dirt. The root was less human-shaped than the one in Kunegunde's book, resembling a gray carrot more than a man.

The second plant allowed itself to be harvested in silence too. Squinting, I watched her dust off a more typical specimen of the root with a knotted head, a trunk, tendril-like arms, and carroty legs. Solange met my eyes as she plopped it into her bag. "Is your mount stabled here? The spring is far enough away that we'll want to ride."

I followed her through the gate, swallowing my anxiety about leaving the abbey, trying to summon my earlier excitement that I would get to see the shrine. The next world fell away as we descended the stairs. I fell behind Solange, pulling my hood down over my face to hide not only my identity but also my tears.

We found Nëbel housed in the blessedly dim second stall, nibbling on a bag full of hay. The sight of her made my heart swell. Her whicker was kind, and her large eyes seemed to sympathize with the wreck that my life had become. "Did you miss me, girl?" I whispered.

She nuzzled my hand.

I remembered what Rika told me about how well she had cared for Nëbel. This was probably the longest she's been stabled without exercise, I realized, with a pang of guilt.

"Ho, there, miss," a voice from behind me said. "She's yours?"

I turned and met the eyes of the stablehand, a reedy man with ruddy cheeks.

"Beautiful thing, she," he said. "Anxious, but sweet as clover."

Solange cleared her throat, as if she disapproved of my chatting with him. "Bring us two caparisons and saddle cloths."

The stablehand nodded and disappeared. The caparison he brought for Nëbel was bright white. She stood still for him as he put it on her, followed by a bridle with well-ornamented bosses and reins and a saddle. She made a neighing sound as I stepped into the stirrups, flicking her tail at a fly as we rode out of the barn. Ahead of me, Solange sat astride a chestnut mare.

"The spring is north of here," she called back as we rode, "through the woods and up the hill."

My earlier excitement about the shrine was gone. There was nothing I could do about it. My mother's song echoed in my mind. I was glad Solange had ridden ahead of me so we didn't have to make conversation. I couldn't believe that my mother would take her own life.

I followed Solange through the woods, noting tearfully how the next world drew close as we rode uphill through the dense trees. As we approached the top of the hill, I realized I could sense the mist here, shimmering and soothing, at the threshold. Tears filled my eyes, and I smiled, despite the shock I'd just received.

Not long after I heard the burbling of water up ahead, we passed several stone slabs leaning against the trunk of a tree. Alongside them were stacked some fragmented blocks of stone and a crumbling dais. My hair stood on end as we approached, and I nearly jumped from my horse. I could see faded symbols on the stones. "Wait," I told Solange. She pulled on her reins.

I tethered Nëbel and walked to the stacked stone blocks. Some of them were marked with grooves shaped like birds in flight, which recalled the designs on my mother's mirror and the water-*spiegel* at Gothel. Behind them lay a cracked statuette of a woman. She looked like she'd been struck with a hammer, but her destroyer had been careless. Although her body had been fractured, I could still make out some of its parts. She was naked, and her breasts had once been large. In the rubble, I could make out wings, the remnants of her face. Her forehead and eyes were still intact. Staring into her eyes, I was stricken with anger that someone had smashed her likeness. It was sacrilege.

I turned to Solange, unable to hide my fury. "Who smashed this?"

"Brother Volmar, I believe, although it might have been the archbishop when he came to bless the grounds."

"Does Mother Hildegard really want to incorporate some of these stones into the abbey?"

Solange went pale. "How do you know of that?"

"I overheard a conversation."

"In the *lingua ignota*?"

I closed my eyes. "I've pieced some of it together."

"You just got here, miss!"

"Do you know what her purpose is in incorporating them? Why would she want to do that? She's Christian."

Solange wouldn't answer. She had gone pale as a ghost.

I glared at the smashed effigy of the goddess, outraged at whoever had smashed her likeness. The figurine in my coin-purse thrummed. The air went even more taut. My skin began to tingle.

When I touched the figurine, tendrils of mist began to unfurl into existence in the air around me, silvery whorls that caressed my face and arms. I was filled with the same love I felt when the mist embraced me at Gothel. So great, so wide, I gasped at the weight of it. But swirling beneath that endless love was a cacophony of feeling: outrage and ferocity, pride and power, greed and desire.

Put me back together, the familiar voice commanded, louder than I had ever heard her speak, her voice a furious hum.

The veil slipped shut. I worked to regain my bearings. The chaos of feeling haunted me, like a dream I couldn't shake off.

Put me back together? I thought finally. Me?

Solange was staring at me. I couldn't think, I couldn't speak, I couldn't even breathe, the insight hurt so much. I couldn't deny it any longer. I had been telling myself stories, all this time. The voice that spoke to me wasn't my mother. It was *the* Mother.

A low keen escaped my throat. I felt no joy that the goddess had come to me; instead, I was desolate that my mother hadn't. The apparitions, the voice, the mist, I thought. Was none of it her?

Solange hurried toward me. "Lady Haelewise? Are you all right?"

Sobs racked me, and I doubled over. It was as if my mother had died all over again. Nëbel whinnied, pulling at her tether, wild-eyed. "Whoa." Solange tried to calm her.

Solange reached for my hands, but I pushed her away. After a moment, the wave of grief began to subside. I took a deep breath, trying to master myself. "Forgive me," I told Solange. "I lost my mother not so long ago. My grief is unpredictable."

Solange nodded, her eyes widening. For a moment, I thought I saw a knowing expression, but I couldn't be sure, it passed so quickly. I wondered if she knew something I didn't.

She squeezed my hands and got back on her horse. "The spring isn't far."

Taking a deep breath, I mounted Nëbel and followed Solange, slouched atop my horse. We soon came upon a dense stand of trees where the spring burbled cheerfully, without regard for the terrible ache in my heart. Solange dismounted, then bent over the spring, pulling the alrūne from her bag. Hands still gloved, she tied them together with a small length of rope. Bubbles floated to the surface as she sank the roots down, weighting them with a stone. For some reason, watching the roots disappear, I had to suppress another sob.

"I'll come back tomorrow evening to retrieve them," Solange promised.

I followed her back through the woods, overcome by a desperate sadness.

I spent the next day in the guesthouse except for meals, tossing and turning in my bed. I couldn't stop thinking about my mother. My revelation at the shrine had dredged up my memories of her on her sickbed. The physician's red draught dribbling down her chin, the blue kitten I pretended to pet with her. I wanted desperately to believe it was *she* who'd spoken to me all this time, that *she* had appeared to me in the garden, but I didn't want to delude myself.

I was so sick with grief, I couldn't bear to speak to anyone. When Solange stopped by to let me know the alrūne roots were drying, I made her tell me through the door. I even asked Walburga to leave my meals outside.

When I poked my head out to retrieve my evening meal, the light hurt my eyes. I hadn't eaten alrūne the night before, knowing I'd be stuck in the abbey, where my mother—or *the* Mother—couldn't reach me. I knew my light sensitivity would come back, of course, but I wasn't ready for how upset it would make me. By the time I brought the food inside, I'd lost my appetite.

On the second day after I visited the shrine, my grief ebbed. I didn't feel well enough to leave the guesthouse, but I felt well enough to get out of bed. I spent the day reading a Latin primer Athanasia had given me, trying to make peace with what I'd discovered. Many times that day, I reached for the figurine and prayed to the Mother for comfort. I figured since it was she who'd comforted me all this time, perhaps she could comfort me now, but apparently, the blessing on the abbey grounds still made that impossible.

On the third day, Solange informed me that the roots were blessed and ready to be pulverized. She took me to the infirmary to show me how to pound them into a powder. She filled a phial with a tincture and showed me how much to take. I dissolved the tincture in a cup of water and drank it right away, hopeful that it would fix my sensitivity to light. An hour later, my stomach convulsed, and I had to run back to the guesthouse to use the chamber pot. The tincture restored a faint golden color to my irises, but I was queasy for the rest of the day.

The next morning, I couldn't keep down my breakfast. As I walked to prime, my head spun. The abbey seemed brighter. The air around me had been suffused with a dizzying light.

What happened next shouldn't have surprised me. My new curative was prepared by an abbess, and I was standing in a Christian chapel. But I had become so accustomed to the monotony of services, when I felt the chill, I was startled.

I straightened in my pew. The air felt weighted, tense, like the air before a lightning storm. The presence I sensed at the threshold was powerful, paternal, strong. A vertiginous light filled the chapel, filling me with a love that felt both ancient and welcoming. I knew immediately whose presence I was feeling—the Father—but it set me off-balance.

Help us, he commanded, in a voice as deep as thunder.

CHAPTER TWENTY-SIX

After prime, I felt light-headed, confused. I paced the guesthouse, unable to quell the nervous energy that thudded in my chest. Who did the Father mean when he said, "Help *us*"? My hands shook, and I felt inexplicably afraid, almost *suspicious*, of his presence. I couldn't explain my misgivings, but I couldn't talk myself out of them. The Father was supposed to be benevolent. His presence had seemed loving, kind, but my heart beat too fast when I thought of him, and the walls of the guesthouse seemed nauseatingly close. Instead of ecstatic, I found myself disquieted. The more I thought about it, the more I wondered if my experiences with my earthly father were responsible for my misgivings.

The insight did nothing to relieve my unease. Nor did it fix the nausea brought on by the tincture. By terce, I was so sick, I couldn't leave the guesthouse if I wanted to. Clutching the chamber pot, I tried to distract myself by thinking over what I'd learned about Hildegard, about the shrine. Considering the rapture I saw on the sisters' faces during services and the extent of the alrūne patch in the garden, I began to wonder if Hildegard was giving her daughters the tincture. I wondered how long ago the shrine was built, what the people who built it were like, and what had happened to make this place thin.

By that night, my queasiness had subsided somewhat, and I hoped the next day would be different. As I drifted off to sleep, I clutched the figurine. I still couldn't believe what my mother had done; memories of her continued to plague me. The Father's voice echoed in my head, but I couldn't make sense of his command. I prayed for the Mother to tell me what I was supposed to do at the abbey, how she wanted me to put her back together. Did she mean the broken pieces of her effigy, or something else? I begged her to send me these answers in a dream, since she couldn't reach me in waking life, but no such dreams came. Her silence—her absence here—gutted me. More and more, I wanted to leave the abbey.

The next morning, I poured a smaller amount of the tincture into my cup, but after I took it in my morning draught, the dizziness and nausea came back stronger than ever. The Father's light was no longer limited to the chapel. It was everywhere, unavoidable and vertiginous. It filled the guesthouse, even with the windows closed. A love so holy, so unconditional and accepting, it felt incomprehensible. I lay on my cot, the abbey going round and round, struck by a dizziness so strong I couldn't move.

On the second night after I started taking the tincture, someone knocked on the door of the guesthouse. My vertigo had faded as the sun set, just as it had the night before. I was already in bed, relieved the spinning of the guesthouse had stopped, my mother's figurine in hand. I dressed quickly, putting the bird-mother in my pouch where no one would discover her. Running a brush through my hair, I looked at my dim reflection in the shattered mirror. My eyes were wide. Palest gold. My black hair floated frizzy from my crown.

"Miss?" The door opened. It was Solange.

I put the mirror down.

"Mother Hildegard would see you now."

I put the mirror away and wrapped my head in a scarf. Out the door I followed her through the shadowy garden.

In the keep, Hildegard sat in one of the two chairs before an open window. The room was dark. All of the other shutters were closed. The torches on the wall weren't lit. From the landing of the staircase, I could see the waxing moon through the window. An iron lantern brightened the floor around Hildegard's chair. She looked at me, her face a mess of lantern-shadow. "You've been taking the tincture?"

I took a deep breath. "Yes, Mother."

"Do you feel him?"

I nodded, trying to hide my unease. "He spoke to me."

She broke into a dazzling smile, beaming, her face overflowing with joy and happiness. She patted the chair beside her, and I sat. "What did he say?"

"He asked for my help."

She reached for my hand and squeezed it, leaning into the lantern-light. Her eyes glowed the faintest gold. Her expression was kind, open. She smiled encouragingly. "I have prayed on your arrival here."

"You have?"

She nodded. "The Living Light spoke to me. He told me to take you in. When we go to the king, I will be better able to protect you if I can introduce you as a postulant."

My mouth fell open. Athanasia saying I should take the veil was one thing. Hildegard could actually make it come true. I stared at her, speechless. I was a terrible candidate for holy life. The Father's light unsettled me. I was more comfortable with shadow. I was filled with resentment, the desire for human touch, and revenge. I longed to have children, to join the circle, to live the life my mother couldn't. Offered another path, I found myself even more certain about the one I was following.

My feelings must've shown on my face. Hildegard's expression was disappointed. "You don't want holy life?"

The lantern flickered. I didn't. I knew this clear as day, but I couldn't afford to alienate her. I set the question aside, trying to find a safe way to explain my reservations. "Have you ever eaten *unblessed* alrūne?"

Hildegard fell silent. Her eyes widened.

The shock on her face made me feel defiant. "Why do you want to incorporate the stones from the shrine?"

Hildegard didn't respond. She drew a deep breath. Outside, the waxing crescent moon was bright. There were gossamer clouds drifting past it. After a moment, she sighed and met my eyes, lowering her voice until it was barely audible. "What I'm going to say next is not something I speak of freely. I only speak of it to my most trusted daughters. I'm only telling you now because I want you to trust me. Do you understand?"

I nodded, hopeful that she would finally unravel some of the mysteries that had plagued me here. "I won't tell anyone."

"Good," she sighed. She opened her mouth several times to answer, then closed it, as if deciding against a rhetorical approach. When she finally spoke, her voice was quiet. "I've always sensed a feminine presence at the edge of things, a holy greening power that makes things grow and heal. But that power never spoke to me until a year ago, when I forgot to have my alrūne blessed and started hearing a woman's voice at the shrine. The voice commanded me to incorporate the stones."

My jaw dropped. "You didn't think it was a demon?"

She started to laugh then stopped herself, as if she couldn't quite decide whether she found my question amusing. "That was *exactly* what I thought. Only the Living Light had ever spoken to me before that day. I prayed desperately to He-Who-Is to banish her. But instead of offering me salvation, the Lord struck me down with a grave illness. He punished me for questioning her. During the worst of this illness, while I tossed and turned, he sent me a vision of a woman enthroned in a wild forest. She was shadowy, winged, snakes coiled at her feet. She was clothed in swarms of golden bees. Her expression was almost *beatific* at first. I thought I was seeing St. Mary or the Church." Hildegard's expression turned inward, and then she shuddered slightly. "Then her expression turned *furious*. I understood that whoever—*whatever*—she was, she was the source of the voice I'd heard, and she was angry I wanted to disobey her."

Shadows? Wings? Bees? My mind reeled. My hands felt suddenly cold. I remembered what Kunegunde said about the ants that ate her offering, the buzzing of the voice that spoke to me. I opened my mouth but faltered, afraid to speak my thoughts aloud.

"I have seen many strange things with my inner eye, but that vision is by far the strangest." She shook her head, her eyes full of bafflement. Then she turned to me, her voice hesitant. "My illness persisted until I wrote the archbishop for permission to incorporate the stones. Then it ended, as quickly as it had come. Did a woman's voice speak to you here?"

I thought I heard eagerness in her tone. "At the shrine."

She nodded, once, quick. She had been expecting that answer. "What did she say?"

I drew a deep breath. "She told me to put her back together."

Hildegard's expression turned pensive, almost troubled. The moment stretched out so long, I wondered frantically if she saw something heretical in my answer, if she was going to withdraw her offer to escort me to court. Finally, she drew herself up, deciding something. "My offer still stands," she said, meeting my gaze. Relief coursed through me that I hadn't alienated her. "I was deeply saddened when your grandmother made the decision, so long ago, to—" She paused, searching for the right words, her voice measured. "To follow another path. She was like a sister to me. It is clear you are a seer. There are things I do not know about the history of this place. Perhaps you could help me to understand."

I stared at her dumbly. My certainty that I should reject her offer faltered. It meant something different now. The Mother had spoken to her. If she incorporated the stones, perhaps the Mother would be able to speak to me here. No matter what, I needed Hildegard's protection when I went to the king. My head spun. "May I think on it?"

Hildegard smiled. The wrinkles around her eyes crinkled. "Of course. It is a decision of great magnitude."

I was about to take my leave when I realized I had one more

question for her. Even with her protection, I was intimidated by the prospect of speaking at court. "I'm still uneasy about my audience with the king—or, rather, emperor. Would you consider teaching me how to speak to him so I won't say anything improper?"

A slow smile spread across Hildegard's face. "Of course. That I can do well, whether you choose to join us or not."

I stayed with her in the keep until late, talking about how I should carry myself, how an emperor would expect to be addressed. I told her about my likeness to the princess, and we came up with a plan to use it to my advantage. She made me practice my story over and over, correcting me, asking the questions the king would ask. "Tell the truth," she said, again and again. "Frederick is a brilliant diplomat. He will know if you leave anything out."

I tried not to think too hard about this.

CHAPTER TWENTY-SEVEN

Four days before my visit to the king's court, I found a rust-colored stain in my undergarments. Staring at it, I felt a new kind of vertigo. My stomach lurched with disbelief. The rose oil had worked. When I told Walburga, she squealed and clapped her hands, then offered to get me some blood moss to put in my undergarments. As I waited for her to come back with it, I sat on the edge of my bed, staring at the stained cloth, trying to sort through my feelings. I had been praying for this moment forever. I should've been ecstatic, but the happiness I felt was surprisingly distant.

As the day we planned to travel to see the king drew near, I agonized over my next conversation with Hildegard. I knew she would ask me for my decision about whether I would join the abbey, and I had no idea what I was going to say. My mind told me to agree to become an initiate so she could offer her protection, but my heart knew I wouldn't be satisfied with life at the abbey. Meanwhile, my dizziness and nausea worsened. The Father's light had become so bright, I couldn't see anything else. I began to doubt my ability to travel and tell my story to the king if my dizziness and nausea didn't subside.

The night before my audience, I lay in bed in my shift, agonizing over what to do. Since we were leaving the abbey, I wanted to go back to eating the alrūne from my mother's garden, but I was hesitant to break my word to Hildegard after what happened with Kunegunde. I eyed the tincture, wondering how small an amount I could get away with dissolving in my morning drink, how pointless it all was when the Father made me so uneasy. I thought of the miller's son, his weight in my arms—the way Hildegard had shuddered when she told me about her dream.

The fruit at the bottom of my sack called to me.

The next morning, when the sun peeked through the crack in the shutters, I felt better than I had in weeks. Instead of the Father's dizzying light, I felt only the closeness of the next world, the tension in the air. My only complaint was the nagging unease I felt about what I was going to tell Hildegard. Leaving the tincture untouched on the table, I turned my thoughts to what I would wear for my audience with the king. My best clothes, of course, the dress and cloak from Matthäus. I brushed my hair, counting a hundred strokes like the princesses did in my mother's tales. I wrapped the dagger in my sack and, saying a quick prayer, dropped the dried fruit and figurine in my pouch.

I checked my reflection in my mother's mirror. My brushed black hair was wild, frizzing out from my head in shattered waves. My eyes glowed much brighter than the day before, gold and frantic. In the deep red cloak I looked regal, strange, like the seer I supposed I had become.

When Walburga arrived, moments later, with my breakfast, she beamed when I invited her in. "You're feeling better, miss!" she said happily. "Just in time. Isn't your audience with the king today?"

I nodded, tearing into my food. I was ravenous. I hadn't been well enough to eat in weeks. But halfway through the meal, I was hit with a bout of nervousness that my lie would be found out.

"Lady Haelewise," Walburga said when I stopped eating. "What's wrong? I thought you felt better."

I met her eyes, trying to decide how honest to be. Her expression was open, completely without judgment. I lowered my voice. "I've decided to tell Mother Hildegard I'll take the veil."

"Why does that trouble you?"

"I'm already having second thoughts."

Walburga reached for my hands. Her whisper was almost inaudible. "You are wise to declare that intention before you see the king, no matter what."

I hugged her back. "Thank you for saying so."

She nodded, but her reassurance didn't relieve my unease.

"I'll see you when you get back," she said, hugging me on her way out.

There were tears in her eyes as she left the guesthouse. I watched her go, my own eyes wet. Some sixth sense made me fear I wouldn't see her again.

Grabbing my things, I found Sister Athanasia at her table in the gatehouse, reading an illuminated manuscript. She nodded when I appeared at the doorway, stood, and walked me to the gate. "Mother Hildegard is already downstairs."

The bolts made their solemn noise as she pushed them aside. Her keys jangled as she clicked open the lock. She held the door open, then whispered ardently, "Godspeed."

I hugged her, overcome by another wave of anxiety.

Athanasia must've read my expression. "Mother Hildegard wouldn't let you go if she wasn't certain she could protect you."

I smiled a sad smile, pretending her words gave me comfort, and stepped through the gate. The tension in the air dissolved, and I felt the next world fall away.

As I descended the steps to the lower level, my nervousness returned. On the lower level I was assaulted by the scent of manure emanating from the stable. When I lifted the door-flap, a horsefly buzzed out, and an even stronger variant of the smell hit my nostrils. I brought my sleeve to my face to mask it. The stable-hand stood before a stall, speaking softly to a dappled horse. "Lady Haelewise?" he said as he looked up. I nodded. "Your horse is ready."

Nëbel's eyes glittered when she saw me. She lifted her muzzle and let out a whicker, nuzzling my palm, snorting hot breath. She pranced, shifting her weight, as if she couldn't stand anymore to be still.

"It's good to see you, girl," I whispered.

She nuzzled me and whinnied again as I untethered her and led her from the stall. There was a nervous kick in her step as I put my bag on her tack and mounted her.

"The procession is waiting," the stablehand said.

His words brought me back to myself. I guided Nëbel through the door-flap. I took a deep breath, grateful for the fresh air. Clopping along the stepping-stones, we passed through the abbey gate.

Outside, four guards in leather jerkins waited on horseback. I smiled, hoping they would protect me if we ran into Ulrich's men. A fine carriage sat beneath the oak with black wooden wheels and golden accents. Draped over the top was a bright white canopy embroidered with a golden cross, darkened only by the shadows of leaves.

The abbey guards turned as we passed through the gate and Nëbel's hooves hit the steps. One of them gestured at the carriage. "Mother Hildegard is waiting."

I slipped off my saddle and handed Nëbel's reins to a guard. She whinnied in protest, tossing her head from side to side, and I was struck with a pang of guilt. I cupped her face with my hand and apologized.

The carriage door-flap rustled as I pulled it aside. Hildegard and Brother Volmar were waiting within. Daylight filtered through the canopy, illuminating the interior of the carriage. I sat on one of the benches, unsettled. Hildegard wore a black habit and scapular with a white wimple and black veil. No jewels, this day, no crown. She smiled at me. "Brother Volmar, this is Haelewise." She reached out to brush a blade of grass from the skirt of my cloak. "Haelewise, Brother Volmar is coming along so that record may be made of my audience with the emperor."

"Blessings to you," he said.

"And to you, Brother," I replied automatically.

"The business I have with the emperor is delicate," Hildegard said when I was settled in my seat. "He is displeased with a letter the pope sent him. He won't take what I have to say well. We're hoping your news will improve his mood. He has been trying to identify his daughter's killer for weeks."

I cleared my throat, wondering whether I'd misheard. "Pardon me, Mother, but did you just say the emperor is displeased with the pope?"

She frowned. "I did, in fact."

"That seems rather bold."

She laughed, a strange little trill. "He's a proud man. Have you made your decision?"

Here it was. I had known this moment was coming, planned for it, but now that it was here, I felt paralyzed by indecision. The moment stretched out. I closed my eyes, summoning my courage.

"I'll take the veil," I said finally, feeling uneasy about the lie even before I finished speaking it.

Hildegard didn't seem to notice, or perhaps she ascribed my anxiety to the weight of my choice. The love in her eyes, the joy, as she smiled at me, seemed almost infinite. "You have no idea how much this gladdens me, daughter."

Daughter. The word brought tears to my eyes, and my breath caught in my throat. Stilling my heart, I smiled back, trying to look as if I felt no guilt.

CHAPTER TWENTY-EIGHT

The towers of the palace cast long shadows as I got out of the carriage. Mother Hildegard climbed out after me, and Brother Volmar followed her, muttering grumpily about his aching bones. On the ride there, Hildegard had chattered on and on about life at the abbey, the steps of becoming an initiate. I couldn't stop wondering what she would do if she found out I'd only agreed to take the veil because I needed her protection. I fretted over every gesture, every word, every tiny sigh of acknowledgment, worried that each one might reveal my plans to flee her protection as soon as it was no longer necessary. By the time we arrived, the knot in my stomach was so tight, I was relieved for the excuse to get out of the carriage. The afternoon sun beat down on my arms as I stretched my legs, grateful. The heat was uncommonly strong, giving the world around me a summery haze.

I took Nëbel's reins, and she whinnied softly. I set my self-loathing aside, trying to focus on the palace in front of me. Well-armed kingsguard stood watch outside the gatehouse. They eyed us calmly at first, but a murmur passed through them as we drew near. One of the guards paled, backing away and crossing himself.

"A ghost!" he said, pointing at me. "Sweet Mother of God, a ghost!" He reached into his pouch and pulled out a holy cross. "*Pater Noster, qui es in caelis, sanctificetur normen tuum—*"

I took a deep breath.

Behind us, in hushed voices, two kingsguard began to argue about the identity of my horse.

The captain and two men left their stations to crowd me. "The princess!" one of them said, pulling on the fabric of my cloak.

"It can't be," said another. "We buried her over a month ago!"

Beside me, Nëbel brayed, nervous.

I feared for a moment that she might panic. My thoughts raced. Anxiety fluttered in my chest. Then I stilled myself, remembering what I was supposed to say. "My name is Haelewise of Gothel," I called out, my voice echoing, resolute. "I am not the princess, but a seer come to help avenge her death."

The captain paused, looking me up and down. The others quieted, waiting to see what he would do. The captain watched me, crossing himself, his face still pale.

I surveyed the crowd. "I foresaw the princess's murder. I have an audience with his imperial and royal majesty to tell him who killed her."

"The girl speaks truth," Hildegard called from beside me.

The captain nodded slowly, his men following suit. One of them went through the gate and came back with a bald man in dark stockings. The bald man's tunic clung to his round belly. "Mother Hildegard, I presume?"

She nodded, just barely, hands clasped before her.

"Let them in," he said. "The emperor is expecting them."

The captain muttered under his breath but let us pass.

We followed the bald man through the gate.

Grapevines coated the outer palace walls. The courtyard was dotted with statues and pools. Our footsteps echoed ominously on the stones. Atop the outer walls, more guards patrolled. At the end of the courtyard, a rectangular building rose from the stones, a narthex sheltering heavy wooden doors.

Inside, torches blazed, crackling, on either side of a hall. Their flames scattered shadows on the floor, which seemed to dance with a life of their own. On the dais were two thrones on which sat the middle-aged king with the fiery red beard and his golden-haired second wife. Rika's stepmother, one of the circle of women who worshipped the Mother in secret, her eyes bright gold. *Queen Beatrice.* She was here with him.

My heart leapt. Another chance to join the circle, I thought. I just have to find a way to speak to her privately.

Beatrice wore a pale-blue dress, crown, and headscarf. Her golden braids, glittering as bright as her eyes, hung to her ankles. As we approached, I realized the reason the braids shone as they did was that they were interwoven with thread spun from gold. She was far younger than I expected, barely older than me, though she carried herself as if she were older. Laughing at something the king said, she seemed at first like the ideal woman—beautiful, feminine, her face modestly draped with undyed linen—until I looked closer and saw the spark in her eyes, the *defiance*, as if she dared anyone in the world to cross her.

I prayed she would notice my eye color, my eagerness to speak to her. How in the world do I get her alone, I wondered.

The king wore a large golden cross around his neck, a black tunic, and a burgundy cloak with golden stockings. On his head, he wore a huge jeweled crown with a giant sparkling cross at the forehead.

When we reached the front, I knelt as Hildegard had advised. "Your imperial and royal majesty."

The king peered at me. He blinked, once, twice, then bellowed, his voice breaking with emotion. "Is this some kind of trick?!"

Hildegard and Brother Volmar bowed their heads. The abbess took a deep breath. "No, your imperial and royal majesty. This is the seer I wrote you about, Haelewise of Gothel. She came to me with news of your daughter's death. I didn't mention her appearance in my letter because I knew you'd have to see it for yourself. I believe her resemblance to your daughter is a sign from He-Who-Is to heed her words in your quest to avenge Frederika's death."

The hall was still. Behind us, guards shifted their stance uneasily, waiting to see what the king said.

"Look at me," the queen commanded. Something passed over her face when she looked into my eyes. "Her nose is different, Frederick. And her eyes are golden."

Hope surged in me. So strong, I almost forgot why I was there. It took everything I had to lower my eyes and turn to the king, returning to the speech we'd rehearsed. "I apologize for my resemblance, your majesty. I hope it is not too painful that I should come to you so soon after your daughter's death."

I watched through my lashes for his reaction. After a moment, the king nodded. "You may rise."

I stood. His eyes bore into mine. One of the jewels in his crown shone so brightly, it was hard to look at him directly. A dazzling red jewel with a strange white glow.

He shifted in his seat, his knuckles white against the arms of his throne, his jaw clenched.

The queen reached out to put her hand on his. He waved it away. "Tell us what you know," he said, glowering at me.

Bowing my head, I opened my mouth to begin the speech I'd practiced with Hildegard. "Your imperial and royal majesty, I throw myself at the mercy of this court. I am your most humble servant." I could see the king's eyes on me. My heart thudded in my breast. I reached for the figurine in my pouch, praying that I would get this right. "I bring difficult tidings. I dreamed of your daughter's death before she was murdered."

He clutched the arm of his throne. The queen leaned forward, watching closely. I met her eyes. I thought I saw something flit across her face again. A wordless prayer rose in my breast.

Then I turned my attention back to the king, focusing on what Ulrich had done, until I was conscious only of my hatred.

"In my dream, I saw a masked man," I said bitterly. "He stabbed a girl in tattered robes whose face I could not see. Taking the form of a bird of prey, I descended upon him to rip him apart with my talons. I had this dream every night for many weeks."

The queen's expression betrayed nothing.

I drew myself up. "It was not until I was gathering herbs in the woods, one day, near my ancestral home, that I saw the masked man come upon your daughter. Forgive me, your imperial and royal majesty. I didn't recognize her because of her tattered clothing. I understand now that she had disguised herself as a peasant. The masked man, I could see now, was wearing Prince Ulrich's colors. His horse bore Prince Ulrich's banners. I heard him berate her for fleeing the castle, for betraying her betrothal to Prince Ulrich. He shot her with a Zähringen arrow to implicate the duke, but the dagger he used was unquestionably Ulrich's—"

The king stood. "Did Zähringen send you here? We heard about a Haelewise who was rumored to be his spy."

Hildegard put her hand on my shoulder. "Show him."

I pulled out the cloth-wrapped dagger, kneeling and offering it up. "In his hurry to get away, the killer dropped the weapon. I bring it to you as proof."

There was movement behind me. After a moment, a guard took the dagger from my hands and brought it to the king. The throne room was silent as he inspected it. He went white when he saw the insignia on the pommel cap. "The arrow," the king shouted. "Ulrich brought us the killer's *head*—"

"He could've stolen the arrow," the queen said. "Beheaded one of his own men. All he and Albrecht care about is power. I told you!"

"They were betrothed. I promised him Scafhusun. Why would he kill her?"

The king's disbelief shattered me. I had hoped the dagger would be enough evidence. I tried to think of another way to convince him. If I told him that Rika had handfasted another, he would understand why Ulrich had done what he did.

"Rika married a commoner," I said softly, head bowed, apologizing to Rika internally. *Forgive me. Ulrich must be punished.*

"What?!" the king thundered.

I drew a deep breath. If I played this right, I could indict Ulrich and still protect Daniel. "Ulrich found out. He killed both of them, but he only brought you her body."

Hildegard stiffened beside me, alarmed that I had strayed from the story I'd told her.

The king turned from the queen to me. I averted my gaze. When he finally spoke, his voice was controlled, restrained and tight with anger. "Why didn't you mention this before?"

"Your imperial and royal majesty." I bowed my head. "Forgive me. I didn't think it relevant."

"Why did you tell Ulrich you were a Kürenberg?"

"I was afraid to give my real name. I knew he was the killer."

The king glared at me. "Two weeks ago, a Kürenberger came to us to report that Prince Ulrich sent guards to his home. He said they were searching for a Haelewise of Kürenberg, whom they claimed was a Zähringen spy involved in my daughter's murder. He said you were anything but. He wanted to clear your name."

My heart sank. Was *that* why Matthäus's house was in disarray? No, I thought. No no no—

"Where? What happened? Did you take him into custody?" I asked, my voice pitching.

"Why do you care, if you are not a Kürenberg?"

I closed my eyes, trying to swallow my guilt. All I could think about was Matthäus. I made myself focus on what the king had said. He had asked me a question, why I cared. I decided to tell the truth. "I regret that my lie may have caused harm to others."

"You should have come to us earlier. We already issued a writ for Zähringen's death. If he's innocent—"

"I apologize, your majesty," I said with a low bow, feeling a sudden pang for the man who'd given Matthäus the paternoster beads. "My failure to come to you sooner was a mistake."

A long silence ensued.

The king sighed. "Bring me Ulrich!"

As several of the guards hurried out, Hildegard cleared her throat. "Your imperial and royal majesty, I pray that my daughter has been helpful. As you well know, there is another matter about which I would speak to you. Could I beg your attention to it now?"

The king blinked as if he'd forgotten she was there. "We have no time for your sermons now, holy lady. The question of my daughter's murder must be resolved first. Guards!" The guards on either side of the dais stepped forward, awaiting his command.

"Lock her in the west chambers."

My heart fell. I was going to be imprisoned? I turned to Beatrice, desperate. "My queen," I whispered fervently, trying to catch her attention. She met my gaze, her eyes flashing, aureate.

I thought fast, searching for something to say that would pique her interest without revealing my heresy to anyone else. I had to get her attention. My thoughts raced. The stories about her upbringing, the sorceress who raised her. Perhaps Hildegard didn't know them. It seemed that nobles sometimes dismissed such talk.

I smiled at the queen, trying to seem obsequious enough that no one else would know what I was getting at. I curtsied. "It's an honor to meet you. My mother spoke highly of your grandmother."

Beatrice blinked, raising her eyebrows so slightly I couldn't tell if I was imagining it.

Hildegard looked at me quizzically, then shook her head, apparently dismissing my statement as an innocent compliment. She turned to the king. "I would wait with my daughter, your majesty, if that is permissible."

"We will allow that." He turned to his guards. "See that they do not speak alone."

CHAPTER TWENTY-NINE

Two of the kingsguard locked us in the windowless west chambers, a dark and echoing place with a stone floor. As the guards lit the torches that lined the walls, a ridiculously ornate table came into view in the center of the room. It was wood, adorned with intricate engravings, a painting of the king's crest in the middle. Benches lined the walls. There were three doors leading into other rooms, no doubt as richly dressed. I sat on one of the benches, awash in a sea of fear and guilt that I had put Matthäus in danger.

Hildegard sat across from me, her expression frustrated. When she turned to me, her expression was stern. For a split second, I was afraid she was going to ask about my comment to Beatrice, but that wasn't what she wanted to talk about. "Why didn't you warn me that you gave Ulrich the wrong name? We could've prepared."

I blinked at her. That mistake was the last thing on my mind. I shrugged, irritated that she seemed more concerned about losing leverage than anything else. For someone who claimed to serve the house of God alone, she seemed awfully preoccupied with earning the king's approval. But now, more than ever, I needed her protection, so I couldn't afford to show my annoyance. "It slipped my mind. I'm sorry."

"And your story about Frederika's commoner husband." Her voice shook with frustration. "Is *that* true?"

Meeting her gaze, I realized how dangerous that disclosure had been. A holy woman had to be truthful. I nodded, bracing myself.

Her eyes were pleading, confused. "Why didn't you tell me?"

I blinked. Where Kunegunde would've gone silent and cold, the abbess was offering compassion, a plea for understanding. Guilt lurched in my chest. This was nothing. If only she knew all the *other* lies I'd told her. I drew a deep breath, deciding the best course here was to tell the truth. This was the sort of falsehood even a holy woman would condone. "The husband is real," I whispered. "But he's still alive. I'm trying to protect him."

"Oh," Hildegard said, her eyes widening. After a moment, she nodded, once, dismissing the subject, and I knew my deception was forgiven.

After that, I withdrew to one of the bedchambers early, worried that, in my exhaustion and emotional state, I would make a mistake that would further rouse Hildegard's suspicions. As I undressed, I thought over my audience with the king, fretting over how badly it had gone. How long would we be here? Where was Matthäus now? Was he all right? Had my statement piqued the queen's interest?

In bed, I prayed for the Mother to send me guidance, but I heard no voice and received no vision. I rubbed the figurine's curves, desperate to understand why she'd gone silent now, when I most needed her. There was no blessing on these grounds as far as I could tell. I fell asleep worrying feverishly over Matthäus's safety, feeling inexorably lost. Since Rika's death, I had followed the Mother's advice as best I could. What mistake had I made to end up trapped in these chambers? Why had my audience with the king gone so utterly wrong?

We were locked in those chambers for days. Each morning, the guards brought food, and I asked them if Ulrich had been found, but the answer was always no. During breakfast, Hildegard chattered happily about my imminent vows, as if there was no question that I would come back with her. I tried to act eager, but my plummeting mood made it more and more difficult as the days passed for me to keep up the charade.

Hildegard and Volmar spent most of their time at the central table, the monk taking dictation for the speculum Hildegard was working on, which they said was an encyclopedia of the hidden properties of all the elements of God's creation. After the guards brought dinner, Hildegard spent her evenings in her chamber in contemplation. I could hear her muttering prayers beneath the door.

As the days turned to weeks, the queen did not come, and my hope that I had captured her interest faded. I became desolate, unable to keep up the pretense that I wanted holy life. When Hildegard chattered about holy orders, I nodded politely. Hildegard and Volmar became increasingly impatient. One morning, during the third week of our confinement, I overheard them talking in the next room when they thought I was still asleep. Through the door, I heard Hildegard express doubts to the monk about my commitment to my vows. She wanted to know if he had noticed my interest fading. When he said he wasn't sure, she expressed concern that Ulrich hadn't been apprehended yet. She said he must've gone into hiding, and perhaps it was time for them to leave this place. During breakfast, I caught her watching me, her faint golden eyes measuring me up, as if she could decipher my true nature with observation. If she left without me, I wondered, would the king relegate me to some far worse prison? Was she the only thing stopping me from being cast into a dungeon?

For the rest of that day, I renewed my attempts to keep up the charade of my commitment to holy life. I tried to make myself useful to Hildegard and Volmar. I sat with them as they worked on their speculum, asking questions, trying to project an appearance of interest in holy work.

Not long after the evening change of guard, I was sitting on the bench listening to Hildegard describe the qualities of a rose quartz to Volmar when we heard footsteps outside.

A key clicked in the lock.

The queen hurried in, golden braids wrapped around her head like a crown. My heart soared as she turned to the guards. She had come, finally, after all this time. "Go," she said, waving the guards out. "Cast your lots in the hall."

The guards left quickly, no doubt relieved to escape the monotony of their post.

"Forgive me, Haelewise," she said, her eyes proud, regal, gold. "I wanted to come sooner, but I had to wait until both guards were mine. Who are you, really?"

Relief filled my heart. I sent up a quick prayer of thanks. "My name is Haelewise of Gothel, your imperial and royal majesty. I am the daughter of Hedda-the-Midwife and a fisherman whose name I will not say."

"She's a postulant at my abbey," Hildegard added.

The queen met my eyes, her brow furrowed. "But you are one of us—"

Volmar narrowed his eyes, suspicious. "One of who?"

Beatrice ignored him, turning to me and Hildegard. "You eat alrūne. Both of you. I see it in your eyes."

"We take a tincture made from the blessed root," Hildegard corrected her, glancing at the monk.

"I asked you a question," Volmar reminded Beatrice. "Answer me."

Beatrice's laughter tinkled, growing louder as she turned to him, her smile tight. "Let me remind you that you are standing in an imperial palace. I am the queen and empress. I can have you arrested for the pleasure of it."

Volmar turned very red, veins pulsing at his temples.

Beatrice smiled prettily, as if she was satisfied with his mortification. Then she turned to me. "Haelewise, the suspense is torment. Are you one of us or not?"

I drew a deep breath. This was it. My chance. But I couldn't ask to join the circle in front of Hildegard without abandoning my charade. If the queen rejected me, I would be left with nothing.

"Haelewise?" Hildegard asked, concerned. "Why do you pause? What does she mean?"

I closed my eyes, a sudden pressure at my temples. "I'm not one of you," I said, looking up to meet the queen's eyes. My voice echoed. "But I wish to be."

The chamber was quiet for a long moment.

The queen laughed, joyful, her eyes full of delight. "*Mervoillos!* How do you know of us?"

"From Frederika and Ursilda."

"Haelewise?" Hildegard asked, distraught. "What are you saying?"

I sighed a great sigh and reached into my pouch for the figurine, though I feared that to do so would alienate Hildegard once and for all. But I saw no other option, and if the figurine would help me win the queen's trust, it didn't matter what Hildegard thought.

"My mother gave me this," I said, holding it out.

"What is that?" Hildegard said, eyeing the charm in my hand.

Brother Volmar grabbed it, eyeing it with contempt. "It's a heathen abomination, like the one we smashed at the shrine!"

Volmar showed her the figurine. I watched Hildegard's face as she recognized what he was holding. For a second, I thought I saw a very complicated regret. Then Hildegard's face became a mask.

"We must destroy this immediately," Volmar said in a matter-of-fact voice, setting it on the table, looking about—I presumed for something to smash it with.

The queen's eyes widened when she saw what Volmar wanted to destroy. "You most certainly will not," she said, then turned to me. "I *thought* you were one of us," she laughed, a tinkling sound like bells.

"Hildegard," Volmar said suddenly, seething. "Your newest postulant is unfit. She's a heretic."

Beatrice smiled a tight smile. "You have no idea what she is. You think you do, but all you know is your Church's idea of her."

Volmar drew himself up, indignant. "Our God's ideas are all

there is." He gestured at the queen and Hildegard and me. "All of us, the ground we walk on, these gardens, this earth. Even the demon that lives in that *thing*"—he pointed at the figurine—"was created by God to test the faithful. If you deny that fact, then you shall find your place in hell."

Hildegard made a comment in the language of priests, her expression stern. The queen snorted. "*Qui beffe!*"

Before anyone could stop me, I took the figurine back.

Hildegard turned to me, her lips pressed tightly shut. "Heed Brother Volmar's words, Haelewise," she said. "There is truth in them."

Her eyes flitted briefly to mine, then fluttered shut. Volmar's bearing changed entirely as he watched Hildegard, his expression panicked. A split second later, she let out a soft moan and crumpled. He reached out awkwardly to steady her, his eyes flitting around for something to stabilize himself. Small though Hildegard was, Volmar was too frail to hold her upright for long. After a moment, Hildegard recovered, straightening in his arms. She shaded her eyes from the torchlight. She squinted at me, her voice hoarse. "The Living Light commands me to take you in." She glanced at Volmar, the figurine in my hand. "Repent, and you can come back with me to the abbey. Smash that demonic thing, confess, and the Lord your God will forgive."

The queen watched me, raising an eyebrow, the pale golden hairs that had come loose from her braids framing her face.

Hildegard waited to see what I would do. I knew she was trying to save me from being branded a heretic, but smashing the figurine was not an option. I held it tight. "Mother. I can't. My late mother gave it to me."

Hildegard glanced at Volmar, who looked scandalized. She shook her head. "It's the only way, Haelewise. You're being tested."

I stiffened, angry that she would say such a thing. "This is no test, Mother. The voice that speaks to me is no demon. You know as well as I do, there are other gods beside yours—"

Volmar gasped.

"A shadow as well as a light—"

Hildegard opened her mouth, as if my words were a battering ram that had slammed into her throat. Her eyes flitted from Volmar to the corners of the chamber, where shadows fell.

My whole body bloomed with chills. The air went taut. The voice I heard was no whisper, a furious sound like the humming of a thousand bees. *The god is the goddess—*

The queen fell to her knees, her eyes wide. She had heard it.

I could tell by the look that crossed Hildegard's face that she had heard it, too—or at least that she'd sensed some change in the otherworldly weather.

"What?" the monk asked the abbess. "What did I miss?"

Beatrice looked up, shaking her head. "*Une mervoille*, monk. Your demon spoke."

Brother Volmar went pale. He crossed himself.

Hildegard glanced sharply at the queen, her expression poisonous. Then she pressed her lips together tight, drawing herself up with a great deep breath. I will never forget the way she looked at me then, her eyes cold. She knew I'd lied to her, and she was hurt.

"You cannot come back with us now," she said in a heavy voice. "You have shown yourself to be a heretic."

Brother Volmar stormed off toward the door.

Hildegard paused behind him, leaning toward me, her voice low enough that the monk couldn't hear. "You are making a mistake," she whispered, her voice urgent.

I didn't know what to say. I couldn't escape my guilt. "I'm sorry," was all I said finally.

She glanced over her shoulder to make sure Volmar wasn't looking, then clasped my hand and squeezed it. The look on her face was stricken, sorrowful. I felt great sadness, a diminishing sense of possibility, as she walked out.

Tears stung my eyes. Her disappointment weighed like a stone around my neck.

The door closed. I drew myself up, trying to master my emotions. I had to focus my attention on the queen.

Beatrice was watching me, her expression awed. There were tears in her eyes. "That was beautiful."

I opened my hand and stared down at the figurine, her breasts, her wings. "Who is she, really? Sometimes she brings comfort. Other times, she frightens me. I can't understand it."

Beatrice laughed. "Some call her the goddess of death or vengeance. Others link her with love or death. In stories old, she's the wife of the Sun Father, the Moon that chases him through the sky. The truth is she's all of these. She's misunderstood. The Church only allows some of her aspects to surface—in St. Mary, the Holy Spirit—but they allow the Father to be himself, a whole, of love and vengeance and anger."

Her words hung in the air. I felt a chill, remembering what the Mother asked me to do at the shrine. *Put me back together.* All of a sudden it made sense. I looked up at the queen, awed, determined. "I want to take the oath."

The queen raised her eyebrows. "Your grandmother—the one you said you were with in the forest—that was Kunegunde? The Gothel in your name is her tower?"

"Yes." I watched her carefully, trying to decide if I should say more. I needed to win her trust. "I was apprenticed to her this winter."

"I thought so. You're a midwife, then? You know the healing arts?"

"Yes," I said.

She nodded, deciding something. She cleared her throat. "I should apologize for my husband's decision to lock you up so unceremoniously. His judgment has been, how do you say, *impaired*, since Frederika's death. His temper has gotten the better of him."

"Has he found Ulrich yet?"

She shook her head angrily. "When the kingsguard got to his castle, Albrecht told them his son was hunting. They're searching for him in the forest, but he has the wolf-skin."

Anger filled me. "Rika's death can't go unpunished."

Beatrice nodded, her expression guarded. "I will do whatever I can to ensure otherwise, I promise you, but there are limitations."

I shook my head. My whole journey here, my visit to Frederick's court, might be in vain? Something about the queen's guarded expression made me think there was another meaning beneath her words. What was she going to do to see that he was punished? Was that part of what the circle did: right wrongs like this? "Miss—er—your majesty. What should I call you?"

"Beatrice."

"Beatrice." I looked her in the eye, my heart clamoring in my throat. "Admit me to the circle. I beg you. My gift is strong, and I have a fighting spirit. I would like to help right these wrongs, restore the Mother's place on earth."

She stared at me, her expression turning serious. "I do think there is something you can do to help. We should go somewhere more private."

She took my hand and pulled me from the room. The guards bowed as we passed.

She led me through the stone courtyard, which glowed in the bright light of the waxing moon. From there, we walked to the north wing of the palace, where another guard stood beside a locked door. He nodded as the queen pulled out her key ring to unlock it. Inside was a well-decorated hall with a series of doors. The last room had heavy drapes, thrown back so the sunlight could stream in through the shuttered windows. There was a four-post bed with a pale-blue canopy. On the table in the center of the room, a large white basin sat, covered with the same golden symbols that were engraved on the mirrors and birdbath. The queen ushered me to the table and shut the door, locking it behind us.

"The oath is a blood-vow," she said, her voice hushed. "You must make a sacrifice, prove your fealty. And then you must swear an oath of secrecy. Are you willing?"

Her words hung in the air. An uncomplicated relief poured through me, a certainty I could feel in my bones. This was it, my chance to redeem myself, to prove that my mother's gift had not been in vain. My first instinct was to jump at the chance. Then my anxieties rose up. This path had been taken from me before. Don't get your hopes up, a small voice inside me said. You will no doubt fail in this, like you've failed in everything else.

I squelched the thought, pushing it down, refusing for once to be controlled by my pessimism. "Whatever you want me to do, I'll do it."

She met my eyes. "Are you sure?"

"I have never been more sure of anything."

She was silent for a long moment, measuring me up. "Very well," she said finally. "The first thing you need to know is that figurine of yours is powerful. If you rub it, it pulls power from the next world into this. You can use it to improve the sensitivity of your gift."

I nodded, tears in my eyes. "Do you know how I can use it to summon my mother? I called her once with it, or at least I think I did."

"No," she said apologetically. "But someone in the circle will." She pointed at the basin. "Have you seen one of these before?"

"Kunegunde has one. The symbols. It's the old language?"

"Yes," she said. "They're runes. There was a time we all knew it. I wish we remembered more than we do. There is power in its words."

She gestured for me to close the drapes. When the room was dark, she lit a white candle next to the basin. She took a pitcher from the dresser and poured water into the bowl. Then she gestured for me to come close. As I did, she began to move her lips, muttering a strange incantation. The words were mesmerizing, repetitive, with a lilting rhythm like Kunegunde's chant. *"Roudos, roudos. Ursilda osmi und deiko me."*

As she spoke, the air went taut, and I felt the water tremble. It rippled, a shiver bubbling up from inside it. For a moment, it shimmered with mist, and colors swirled on its surface. I gasped as an image in the water became clear. Princess Ursilda, now hugely pregnant, lay wild-haired, surrounded by pillows in an extravagant bed. As we watched, a servant-woman gave her a plate of food. Ursilda moaned, pushing it away, cradling her belly. The queen pointed at her, her finger close enough to the water that Ursilda's image rippled. "Princess Ursilda is due to give birth any day now. I just found out today that that woman"—Beatrice pointed at the servant-woman standing near the bed—"is Ursilda's new midwife, secretly sent to her a week ago by my husband."

I raised my eyebrows, concerned at her ominous tone, peering at the innocent-looking servant with blond hair. On the plate was a pile of rumpled-looking leaves.

"The midwife has been poisoning Ursilda and her baby."

I stared at the leaves on the plate in horror. "What? Why?"

"Frederick has lost all reason. He's disconsolate. The midwife's mission"—she gestured at the servant in the basin—"is to kill Ursilda and the child, since he can't get to Ulrich." Her voice broke. "I confronted him earlier today when I found out. I tried to tell him Ursilda had nothing to do with the murder, but Frederick is mad with grief."

I stared at her, incredulous. Ursilda had been so kind to me that night in the hall. My heart went out to her. I could understand the rage a parent might feel over the death of a child, but killing an innocent woman and her *baby* as revenge against the woman's brother evidenced a level of cruelty that seemed incomprehensible. I shook my head, trying to clear it. There was something I didn't understand. "If you can summon images in the basin, why didn't you use it to find Frederika?"

"I did," she said. "But all I could see was that she was living in some sort of settlement on a mountain. And I worried for her safety if Frederick found out whom she was with."

Beatrice met my eyes, and I realized what she meant. She hadn't told him. The image in the basin faded, until all that was left was water rippling over runes.

"Ursilda is like a sister to me. We grew up together. I can't warn her with the water-*spiegel* unless she casts the spell on the other end. I need someone to go to her. I wish I could go myself, but Frederick would notice my absence and send men after me. Your presence here is a boon. As a midwife, you can attend the birth and heal Ursilda, after you get rid of the assassin."

Get rid of the assassin, I thought, drawing a deep breath. That sounded dangerous. But it explained why my audience with the king had gone so poorly. I was meant to be here when Beatrice found out about this threat.

"Do you know the general antidotes for poison?"

I nodded.

"Ursilda will need them."

I thought about what she was saying. Her husband was clearly a dangerous person to cross. "Won't the king expect me to be here?"

"Yes," she sighed. "But he might not call for you for weeks yet. By then, you'll be long gone."

I nodded, considering her plan. I wanted to join the circle—to fulfill the promise that lay dormant inside me—but her husband might well be the most dangerous man in the world. "How could the king betroth his daughter to someone like Ulrich in the first place?"

Her expression darkened. "I've tried to tell him, believe me. But Frederick thinks the wolf-skin is a wives' tale. Ulrich can be deceptively charming."

A laugh spasmed, pure and dark, in my chest.

Beatrice looked at me, puzzled.

I mastered myself. "*Charming* isn't the word I'd use. When we met, he tried to take my virtue." This time, I didn't have trouble saying the words. My voice was hard. The passing weeks had encased my memory of that night in a crystalline ball of rage. "I suppose you could say he was *forceful* with me. I barely escaped with my life."

Beatrice's face crumpled. Tears welled up in her eyes. "Must all men be so—?" Her breath hitched. She didn't finish the sentence. I looked into them and felt her desperation. "I am sorry, Haelewise. It's all a game to them. We are like pawns on a chessboard, which they move at whim."

A wave of sympathy passed through me. For Ursilda, for Rika, for all the women who had been caught up in this game. They had been misrepresented in gossip, in the stories folks spoke beside the fire. It wasn't their fault which men asked for their hands in marriage, which land belonged to their families, which houses their fathers or husbands antagonized. None of us deserved the way we were treated. We were all in danger of being cast aside, like the Mother was cast aside by the Church. "If I warn Ursilda, I'll be able to join the circle?"

Beatrice nodded. "That will be your test."

My head swam. My temple pounded. I tried to think of anything else I needed to ask before I said yes. And then it hit me, with such force that I hated myself for not mentioning it yet. "Do you know if the king apprehended the man who tried to clear my name?"

She nodded slowly. "Frederick locked him in the tower."

"*Matthäus*—" My voice shook. "Is he hurt?"

She paused. "He wasn't when he got here. How do you know his name?"

"I grew up with him." My heart beat in my throat. He had come here on my behalf. He was missing from his house because he came here to clear my name. "I will help Ursilda only on the condition that you set him free."

She nodded slowly, surprised that I had a condition. Just a minute before, I had been desperate. In all truth I was surprised myself. "That is within my power."

I nodded. "I'll do it."

"You'll need to sneak into the castle. The guards are no doubt only letting the royal family in and out. But I'll give you cloaks that will allow you to go unseen. *Tarnkappen*."

My heart filled with awe. "*Tarnkappen*. They exist?"

"There are only four in existence, but there are perks to being empress. I have all of them." She laughed that tinkling laugh again. "When you wear one, it pulls your shape into the next world. You become part of the mist. They'll be useful in the forest. If Ulrich is out there, hunting, you don't want to run into him."

The thought gave me a chill. She was right. "Kunegunde said the wolf-skin worked best at the full moon, which is soon. Will Ulrich be at his most powerful then?"

"Unfortunately. And the *tarnkappen* will be at their weakest." She went silent for a long moment, thinking. "I can give you a hand-mirror to help you watch over Ursilda until you get there. It works like this basin."

"A hand-mirror?" I fumbled in my sack for the one I found in my mother's trunk. "Like this one?"

A look of concern passed over her face when she saw how the glass was shattered. "Where did you get this?"

"It was my mother's."

"What happened to it?"

I thought about this. Not long after Kunegunde nursed my mother back to health, my father had told me she was dead. I could piece together what happened. "My father smashed it."

There was sadness in her eyes, understanding. "Would you like me to make it whole again?"

"Yes," I said, my heart filling with an unexpected gratitude. "Please."

"I assume you know the old language?"

I shook my head. "Only a phrase or two."

"But the Mother speaks to you. I can teach you. That is good luck. Very few have the gift."

CHAPTER THIRTY

B eatrice went to an ornate trunk on the west wall and pulled out
a locked book like Kunegunde's, where she'd set down all of
the spells she knew. On the front of it was a gilded circular sigil,
decorated with stylized birds and slithering snakes. She opened it
and turned to the page that bore the incantation for fixing something that was broken. Holding her hands over the shattered mirror, she recited the runes. *Wer zi wer*, she chanted, *bedehrben*. The
air went taut. Soon enough the mist and light within the glass
surfaced. The mirror shimmered, and the shards went liquid. I
watched in amazement as the mirror became whole.

"Thank you," I breathed, turning the now-perfect mirror this
way and that. There was no way to tell that it had been broken.

"We need to hurry," she said. "It's long past dark. The king
expects me soon."

She set about teaching me the incantation I would need to use
the mirror. I was a quick study, as I had been when Kunegunde
taught me to read. I understood as soon as she pronounced each
rune, the way each word should taste in my mouth. *Roudos, roudos*, the chant began. *Osmi und deiko me*, it ended. The word in the
middle varied: the person or place you wanted to see in the reflecting surface. The spell could be cast on a basin, a mirror, or a bowl
of water, as long as the reflective surface bore the runes.

The first thing I asked it to show me was my mother's garden.
The glass rippled, coalescing into a wild tangle of green. The alrūne
had gone wild—the old plants grown large, new plants covering
her grave, rooting and spreading their stalks—casting shadows. I

stared at them for a long time, reflecting on the woman who made them grow, thanking her for the life she had given me with her own. Her love for me had gone wild like those plants, choking out everything else inside her, even her own desire to live. Her love for me had gone wild, and I had eaten of it, I thought, a sob catching in my throat.

Watching my face, Beatrice waited until I looked up and the image in the mirror disappeared. Then she said we needed to hurry. Someone needed to get to Ursilda as soon as possible.

"Do you have something to protect yourself?" she asked. "What you are about to do will be dangerous."

I nodded. "I keep a knife in my boot."

She scoffed. "I'll find you something better."

She pulled the guard at the door aside—an old man with white hair and dim eyes—and spoke with him. In a moment, he nodded and walked off with purpose.

"Take me to Matthäus," I said.

She led me to another part of the palace with a great stone door. Inside, no windows let any light from outside in. The chamber was lit by a single guttering torch on the wall. Our footsteps echoed on the stones as Beatrice grabbed the torch and led me up narrow stairs, passing small cells with iron bars. The openings were small enough that it was difficult to see into them. Peering into one cell, I understood this was a place the king put people he meant to forget. A chill crept through me as Beatrice led me up the dark stairs. Rats darted, shrieking, as her torchlight lit the steps.

There were small holding cells along the stairs, barely large enough to call rooms. They were closer to the size of my cupboard at home but half as tall, as if they had been built for child-sized prisoners. Most of them were empty, but a few we passed were in use. About halfway up the tower, Beatrice stopped outside one and held up her torch so that we could see in. Inside, a figure sprawled on the floor, wrapped in a filthy cloak. As she bent over his cell, the torchlight lit the grime and dirt on his fingers, which were wrapped around a cup. His hand was outstretched toward the iron bars as if he had been begging for a drink when last awake.

"Matthäus?" I said.

He startled and looked up, blinking. Beatrice unlocked his cell.

As he scrambled out, a terrible guilt filled me that I had brought this imprisonment upon him. I searched his face, pained to see him like this, looking for the man I loved under the soot and grime. His eyes widened at the sight of me. He clasped my shoulders, pressed my face to his chest, and kissed the top of my tangled hair, breathing my name. "*Haelewise.*"

He smelled of sweat and blood and dirt and another scent that brought tears to my eyes, a salty scent that I recognized only as his. I held him tight, almost afraid he'd disappear if I let go. His shoulders had grown even broader in the six months we'd been apart. He had shot up in height, too, as men often do during their eighteenth or nineteenth year. When he turned my face up to look at him, his eyes glistened with tears.

"I thought I'd never see you again," I whispered.

"Your eyes. They're golden, like they were when I last saw you. I thought it was the moon."

I nodded. "I'm taking a curative for my spells. It does something to my eyes as well."

He raised his eyebrows.

Beatrice was watching him watch me, an amused expression on her face. She cleared her throat, lowering her voice. "Haelewise. There is very little time. You can talk in the carriage."

Matthäus looked at her, confused. "Am I being freed?"

She nodded. "Explain it to him. I'll be right back."

As she turned to go down the stairs, I took his hands. "Ulrich killed Frederika. The king is trying to avenge her death. He sent a killer to pose as a midwife for Princess Ursilda. I'm leaving to stop her tonight."

Matthäus blinked, as if he couldn't quite link what I was saying with his notion of me. "You negotiated my release?"

I nodded. "Will you come?"

He met my eyes. "I would go with you anywhere."

Beatrice returned with a bag, which she handed to him. "The things they took from you."

Matthäus took the bag as we followed her downstairs. Hurrying, holding his hand, I was filled with a wicked glee. I should've been concerned for his welfare—he had been *imprisoned*—but all I felt was a selfish delight that we were together again.

When we emerged from the tower, an earthly mist—glistening with the light of the swelling moon—had descended over the palace. A blessing, I thought, a good omen. In the hazy courtyard a black-cloaked driver sat atop a bright blue carriage, the same one Beatrice had ridden into my hometown. The driver was the old man she had spoken with earlier outside the door. Close up, I could see golden accents on the cart and wheels, pale-blue roses painted on its canopy.

Hitched to its front were Nëbel and three other horses dressed in gold and black. I gasped when I saw the great white mare shifting her weight from hoof to hoof, beneath a black caparison inscribed with golden runes. The moon shone down on the cloth, making the rune-threads glitter. Nëbel looked dignified and wild, like something out of a tale. I rushed toward the horse to kiss her forehead, then stopped, turning to Beatrice to ask if it was wise for me to take her.

"My husband ordered her destroyed. She reminds him of his daughter. He cannot stand the sight of her." Beatrice pulled the canopy at the back of the carriage aside so Matthäus could climb in. Inside the cart were two benches, one on each side. Everything was covered with a shining blue cloth—the benches, the canopy, the floor—silk, I thought, though I couldn't be sure. There wasn't a stain anywhere. Anxiety filled me. I thought of the beggar back home who haunted the steps of the minster. How hard my mother worked sewing poppets so we could buy a wheel of cheese.

"The driver will take you far enough down the river that you won't be recognized," she told us as we climbed in. "After that, he has to turn back so no one will notice my carriage is gone. Ride the horses hard after that, and you should be fine. You know how to find Ursilda's castle?" I nodded. "You have the mirror?"

"Aye." I patted my sack. "When will I see you again?"

"Use the mirror to scry on me when all this is over. When I sense you watching, I'll cast the spell on my end so we can talk. May the Mother bless you and keep you safe."

Matthäus and I climbed into the carriage and sat across from each other under its canopy. It bumped into motion, the wheels turning awkwardly over the stones. Out of the back of the carriage, we could see the palace courtyard falling away. We heard the gate open before us and watched it close behind. I breathed a sigh of relief as the palace grew smaller behind us. The carriage bumped. As my eyes adjusted to the moonlight that shone through the back of the carriage flap, I could see that Matthäus's face was darkened with grime and soot.

"How long were you in that cell?" I asked him, feeling terrible about using his wife's family name.

"A month or so? I'm not really sure."

"I'm so sorry I used your name. I didn't think—" My voice broke. "I was a fool."

"Haelewise," he interrupted. The way he looked at me then made my breath catch in my throat. His knees were touching mine. I could feel them pressing my own. "When Phoebe told me Ulrich's guards came looking for you, I set out to find you. I'm here of my own free will."

When he put his hand on mine, it was as if no time had passed at all from the last time we spoke. I remembered our kiss in the garden, how he hadn't wanted me to go.

"How old is the baby now?" I dared to ask.

"I don't know. He was only a week old when I left. One month? Two?"

I stared at him, unable to believe so little time had passed. I cleared my throat, feeling awkward to ask. "Will you and Phoebe have another?"

Matthäus shook his head. He looked as if he wanted to say more, giving me a tortured look. "The marriage is in name alone."

I remembered what I saw when I flew to his estate—two rooms upstairs, one with the cradle and one without.

When I met his eyes, I knew what he wanted to say—that he didn't want her because he wanted me. His unspoken thought was like an elixir, a balm for all my anxieties. It pulled me to him, the way the earth pulls autumn apples from trees. The girl I was before I left home might've given up because he was married to another. She had balked at the idea of becoming another man's mistress, worried about what everyone would think of her. But I had seen enough of the world now that I could fathom another option.

I met his eyes, leaning forward, searching for the right words to make him walk away from the world he knew. "I'm yours, if you'll have me."

The invitation surfaced something in the air between us, a power drawing us together. I could tell by the way his mouth fell open, the want in his eyes, that he felt it too.

"My father," he said, but he didn't sound certain, and he stopped in midsentence, his voice trailing off.

"To hell with your father, Matthäus," I said, laughing. "His opinion doesn't have anything to do with us."

Matthäus stared at me for a moment, wide-eyed, shocked. The carriage around us shifted with shadows. Then he burst into laughter. I could feel his shame and fear leaving him. "Who are you, and what have you done with my Haelewise?" he whispered softly, reaching for my hand.

I let him take it, though his question was a good one. I thought
for a moment about how to answer it, as the mist that was settling
over the path swirled outside the door-flap. He was right. I wasn't
the same girl who had kissed him in the garden. He needed to
know what I had become. When I finally spoke, my voice was soft.
"I should be honest with you, Matthäus. I am myself, but not. The
fisherman's daughter, but not. Since I last saw you, I've been cured
of my spells. I've learned incantations. I've been blessed and cursed.
The fisherman's daughter you knew might as well be buried in the
garden with my mother. I have become someone else."

He stared at me. A finger of mist curled through the door-flap,
glistening with light. I couldn't tell whether it was from this world
or the next. We heard the sound of the horses outside, their hooves
hitting the dirt. He smiled, leaning closer to me across the carriage,
his breath quickening. The shadow, the shimmering, between us
deepened. It felt a thousand years old.

"What I'm about to do will be dangerous. If you want, we can
part ways before we get to the castle." I bit my lip, trying to speak
without bitterness. "You can go back to Phoebe and your son."

He cringed. The carriage stopped, teetering to one side. We
could hear the driver jump off and start puttering with a wheel that
had fallen into a rut. The door-flap fell half open. Bright mist crept
into the carriage, swirling and glistening in the air around us. Matthäus shook his head, as if awakening from a strange dream, and
squeezed my hand. "I begged my father in Zürich," he said under
his breath. "I was desolate the night I brought you that cloak."

I met his eyes. My voice trembled. "Everything that is done can
be undone."

Matthäus looked troubled. "Even wedding vows?"

I took a deep breath. The air around us trembled.

"I can't abandon Phoebe, or her son. He isn't mine, but he is. Her
family would take care of them, no matter what. But my father—"
Matthäus trailed off.

I thought of his father, resolute, in his bedroom. His mother's eyes red from crying. The proud little tailor shop. His world was so small. The carriage tilted upright, rolling out of the rut, and the door-flap fell shut. Outside, we could hear the driver climbing back onto the front of the carriage. The wheels began to turn over the dirt.

"I've been miserable," Matthäus said finally.

I stared across the carriage at him, searching my mind, again, for the right words to say. My mother's advice swam back to me. *Their way isn't the only way. All you have to do is hold hands and speak vows. There is power in the words themselves.* I reached for his hands, clasping them tight, interlacing our fingers. Then I took a deep breath, drawing in the mist that swirled between us. "Run away with me into the forest."

He didn't answer at first. He only watched me from across the carriage. I squeezed his hands, seeing our life together spool out in my mind's eye. The life I'd always wanted. The life my mother wanted for me. A humble hut in the forest with two rooms, one of them the room with our bed. I saw us lying in it, tangled up naked in a blanket, glass beads glinting in the windows, fabric spread out over the table, a pincushion, a thousand needles. My midwifery bag, waiting for me, beside it. Outside, a garden, a water-*spiegel*. Our children darting in and out of the trees.

Matthäus leaned in close enough for me to see his expression. The life *he* was imagining for us written all over his face. The hairs on the back of my neck prickled. The mist and light inside me thrummed to life. My body hummed.

"God's teeth." I looked into his eyes. They were gray and glowing, lit from within. "Do you feel that? Matthäus. Doesn't this feel *right*?"

He nodded, his eyes wet with tears. He was struggling. He wanted all of the same things I did, but he didn't share my certainty that they were within reach. He searched my face, his desire so clear. When he finally spoke, he clasped my hands tighter. The words fell out of him like water through a sieve. "I want you. I always have. I have never wanted anyone else."

I smiled at him, overcome. He pulled me to him, his kiss so hard and desperate I could taste his desire. Salty and earthy and bitter, it coursed through me, pulling us together.

He undid the cloak from around my neck. It fell to the floor of the carriage, pooling at my feet. Moonlight filtered through the canopy, setting the blue silk aglow. Then he kissed me again and all the mist, all the possibility in the world around us, shimmered to life. It was dizzying. An indefinite amount of time passed, which I spent enchanted by his touch. When his hand found the space between my legs, my spirits grew quick within my flesh. I felt a pressure, an earthy pleasure, building up within me. He kept kissing me and touching me until all the possibility, all the moonlight and magic in the carriage exploded, opening me up.

When it was over, I climbed onto his lap, lifting my skirts so we could undo his pants. He unlaced my dress so that he could see my breasts. When he pulled away to look at them, the only sound I could shape was his name: "Matthäus." The word held such a sweet taste on my tongue that I wanted to say it again: "Matthäus." Hearing me say his name like that, twice, did something to him. He let out a shaky breath and guided me to the floor of the carriage. How gentle he was. How tender. How cool and soft the floor-covering was on my back. The wheels of the carriage rattled beneath us as he climbed on top of me, the moonlight and mist glowing in the air around his head. And then he was entering me, filling me up, with the most delicious wantonness.

CHAPTER THIRTY-ONE

When the carriage stopped, hours later, we were sleeping. I woke first, startled at the sight of Matthäus asleep next to me. As the events of the last few hours came flooding back, I smiled. Although we were on a dangerous mission, for a moment, all I could think about was the fact that we were together. A giddy delight filled me, delight mixed with disbelief. When Matthäus woke, he smiled back at me.

Together, we peeked through the door-flap. Moonlight fell over the path that led back to Bingen, lighting the rocks and pebbles that scattered the dirt road. Mist clung to the trees that grew, crooked and tangled, along the path. The driver jumped off the front of the carriage and addressed us. He smirked, and I realized he must've heard us earlier. I smirked back at him. Matthäus blushed.

"You're awake," the driver said kindly, forgoing the opportunity to shame us with a crude comment or wink. "This is as far as I can take you. The queen wants me back at the palace 'afore dawn."

I cleared my throat. "Two of the horses are for us?"

"Aye," the driver said.

He unhitched the white horses from the front of the carriage and saddled them with caparisons and reins. I went immediately to Nëbel, meeting her eyes, patting her forehead. Nëbel nuzzled my hand, prancing nervously, then let out a snort.

"Good girl," I murmured. "Sorry to be so long away."

The driver reached into the front of the carriage and tossed us two packs filled with food and supplies. Then he pulled out two lengths of deep rust-colored fabric. Ancient hooded cloaks, the cuffs of the hood and sleeves embroidered with golden runes, like something out of a story. Awe filled me, as he handed one to Matthäus and the other to me. "The *tarnkappen* the queen promised. The horses have them tied to their reins too. Wear them in the forest, near towns—anywhere you might see anyone—in case Ulrich or the king's men are looking for you. But don't wear them for too long at a time. They'll be at their weakest now, but the longer you wear them, the more undetectable you become. If you wear them too long, the shadow will swallow you up. Especially you." He met my eyes. "Even this time of the month. Beatrice said you have the gift."

I nodded, anxious to learn of this limitation. How would we manage this when we entered the forest around Ursilda's castle?

"Another gift from her majesty, for protection."

He held out a shining silver thing. In the dim light, I didn't recognize what it was. Taking it, I gasped at the familiar weight, the wolf emblem on its hilt. It was the dagger that Ulrich's man used to kill Frederika.

Cleaned and polished, it was ready for use.

Matthäus gaped at the blade, his eyes wide.

I made haste to fasten it to my belt.

The driver handed me a bag filled with rags and herbs and phials. With his other hand he offered a scroll, sealed with blue wax. The sigil with the birds and beasts. "Here is your birth bag and the letter for Princess Ursilda. Once you get inside the castle, find the westmost corridor. Show the letter to the guard named Balthazar at Ursilda's door. He's loyal only to her."

Finally, he pointed at the road that led east. "This road will take you east. From there, you can follow the trade route south. The castle is a three-day ride from here."

The driver turned the carriage around and left us. Matthäus stood beside his white mare, cloak in hand. "*Tarnkappen?*"

I grinned at him. "Like in the stories."

I pulled the heavy hood over my dress, shivering as it fell over my face. The cloth felt like ordinary fabric, a bit heavy, perhaps, but the way my hair stood on end—the pull I felt when I put it on—confirmed that they were *tarnkappen.*

"Haelewise? Where did you go?" Matthäus looked as if he had seen a ghost. "By thunder," he whispered, his voice full of awe.

In our sacks we found two wheels of cheese wrapped in cloth and wineskins. We ate and drank, hoods down so we could see each other, as we rode through the misty night.

Matthäus was fascinated with his cloak, turning it inside out to try to see how it worked. He asked me to tell him what I knew about the runes embroidered on the cuffs. As we rode, I told him about the fruit I'd eaten, the way my mother visited me in the garden, the wise woman to whom I'd apprenticed myself in the woods. I told him about the runes she'd inscribed in her book, the spell she cast to send her soul into a raven, the figurine my mother gave me, the voice that spoke to me when I carried it. I told him about the murder I witnessed, explaining that the dagger the queen gave us was the weapon Ulrich used to kill Frederika. When I told him what Ulrich tried to do to me, he flew into a rage.

"He what?!" It took an hour, after that, to calm him.

After I explained, I showed him my mother's mirror, carved with runes, and told him about the spell Beatrice had taught me to cast. He traced the runes on the mirror with his fingers, then looked at me sideways, as if he couldn't quite believe what I was saying.

I didn't blame him. Speaking the story aloud, I found it difficult to believe myself.

When we drew near a town, we put our food away and drew down our hoods. As soon as we did, Matthäus disappeared and I saw only a riderless white horse at my side. It was the strangest sensation to look down and see only the white of Nëbel's back where my body was. I pulled down her hood and she disappeared too, so that it seemed I was floating over the ground. Matthäus did the same. As we galloped past the city wall, orange lights flickered in the towers. I imagined guards hearing our invisible horses gallop through the pasture. I imagined the ghost story they would tell their wives, voices tinged with disbelief.

We galloped past, riding at a heightened pace far enough along the old trade route that the city was only a shadow at our backs. The mist was thick out there, glistening in the gloom before dawn. There was a rotting wood pole, leaning out at the roadside, which looked as if it was used for hangings. I was just about to ask him to take off his hood so I could see where he was, when we heard distant voices carrying from inside the forest. The sound of fighting. Drunken cheers. "We should keep going," Matthäus said, his voice low. "Men who are still up and drinking at this hour could be dangerous."

Peering into the trees, I fumbled in my pouch for the figurine and prayed for the Mother to protect us. After a while, the voices went quiet. Mist drifted over the path. The horizon was beginning to turn pink with the first fingers of sunrise. When neither of us had heard anything in some time, we removed our hoods and led our horses from the road to look for a place to rest.

After everything that had happened, I wasn't surprised to stumble upon the perfect resting place, a safe distance away from the path. An old wooden hut in an overgrown clearing scattered with saplings. Our journey seemed blessed, this resting place foredestined. A brook babbled through the edge of the clearing, a dozen feet or so from the hut. The hut itself was ancient, with not much more than vines left of the roof. The faint moon was setting on the horizon, only a night or two from full. I smiled at the ruined beauty of our campsite, but Matthäus seemed distant. As we tied our horses by the brook, I could tell something was bothering him.

When he lay down next to me inside the hut, turning on his side to look at me, his expression was serious. "Your father thought you were dead," he said, holding his head up with his hand. "He was shocked when I told him you'd intentionally left the city."

This revelation amused me. It hadn't even occurred to me that Father would notice I was gone. But of course he would've come for supper at some point, to give me news of Felisberta's pregnancy or shame me for not making him a proper dinner. I imagined him walking into our hut, calling my name, then wandering back home, wondering where I had gone. How many times had he come to look for me before he presumed me dead? "How long ago was this?"

"Last autumn. I came over several times to see if you'd returned. When you didn't come back by February, well, I started to fear your father was right. I was overjoyed when Phoebe said the guards came looking for a Haelewise." He turned away, suddenly, so I couldn't see his face.

I wondered again what they'd done to him when he came looking for me at the palace, but I didn't want to press.

After a moment, he shook off whatever was bothering him and turned back to me. He touched the runes on the *tarnkappe* we had pulled up over us to ward off the chill, his eyes gone wide and bright. "Haelewise. It feels like we're in one of your stories. Running an errand for a sorceress, wearing *tarnkappen* and carrying a magic mirror." He burst into uneven laughter, shaking his head. "Frederick's beard, all your stories about wise women and fairies, magic mirrors and wondrous plants. I thought you were making them up. But— Haelewise—" His eyes glowed bright gray, anxious, almost feverish. "They're true, every last one of your stories, aren't they?"

I shook my head. "No."

"Right. Right." He nodded, his hair falling into his eyes. He spoke quickly, his words tumbling each into the next. "I know. I know. They didn't happen word for word. But they speak of an earlier time, a time before this one. What used to be possible—"

"In stories old."

He stared at me, excited. "Yes."

I fumbled in my pouch. Now seemed as good a time as any to show him the figurine. I held her out for him to see. Her black stone glistened. "This is the figurine my mother gave me."

He took it from me, shuddering when he saw her naked breasts, her wings, her claws. His expression clouded. "I don't understand. It looks like a demon."

My heart sank. I needed him to see the figurine as I did.

I told him that my mother had worshipped the Mother in secret, that the voice that had been speaking to me for months belonged to her goddess. I told him what Beatrice said, that the Mother was the ancient wife of the Father, whom everyone had forgotten since the Father became so revered. When I told him about the tincture Hildegard had given me, his eyes widened with awe.

"You met Mother Hildegard?"

I nodded. "The Mother speaks to her too." I didn't mention her uneasiness about this.

He thought for a moment. "Are you talking about the Mother of God?"

I took a deep breath. "Maybe that's one of her names. But the stories the priests tell about her don't make sense. She's no Virgin."

Matthäus looked at the figurine in his hand again, examining her carefully, his expression fearful. "She's—not a saint."

I shook my head.

"And you're sure she's not a demon?" He handed it back, holding the figurine at arm's length.

I returned her to my pouch, which I put in the grass that was my pillow. "She's no demon. I can promise you that. She's a protector, a seeker of justice."

He nodded as if he understood, but he looked uncertain. He went silent for a long time before he gave voice to his thoughts. "How far are you willing to go?"

"What do you mean?"

"Beatrice gave you a dagger. For protection, she said. But the midwife is an assassin. How far are you willing to go to protect Princess Ursilda?"

I remembered how kind Ursilda had been to me at the settlement, how much pain she had already experienced. And the baby. The assassin was supposed to kill her baby too. My memory of holding the miller's son swam back to me. I remembered the innocence, the need in his eyes. Anger filled me that the king would hurt something that helpless, that pure. "As far as I have to, Matthäus. Two *lives* are in danger."

"I know. I know. It's just—" He trailed off, struggling to put his thoughts into words. "I'm a tailor. I never thought I would see someone killed. And—you—this goddess you serve. She's no Virgin. She's fierce—"

"Yes," I said. "And there's nothing wrong with that. A woman doesn't have to be pure to be good. Girls get angry. Mothers fight for their children."

He watched me steadily.

"Matthäus," I said, my voice catching with feeling. "This is my task. You don't have to come with me. I'll understand."

"No!" he said quickly. "I can't leave you. My God, your life will be in danger. I won't be able to live with myself if—" He shuddered, unable to say the words.

"All right. But I warn you. I will do anything I must to keep them safe."

He nodded as if he understood. But he was awake for a long time—restless, staring into the dark—before he went to sleep.

I woke at midday to the sound of twigs snapping. The place where Matthäus had lain beside me was empty. Looking up, I saw him headed into the trees. I crept after him, afraid that his uneasiness about the Mother was driving him away. He stopped a stone's throw from the clearing where the brook turned, forming a pool.

Hiding behind a bush, I watched from behind as he took off his breeches and shirt. There were long, thin cuts on his back, scabbed over with a crust of dried blood. I had to cover my mouth when I realized why he didn't want to talk about his imprisonment: The king's men had tortured him.

The guilt I felt then was overpowering. It brought tears to my eyes, and a terrible regret filled my heart. I averted my eyes from the cuts, watching him wade into the stream, the muscles of his legs and buttocks tight. The water made a rushing sound as it slid around his thighs. Birds chirped. The sun cast a thin veil of light over the pool. He ducked underwater, submerging himself. All was quiet until he emerged, smoothing his hair back, dark and wet. His expression was brooding, and there was a tightness in his shoulders that the water had failed to relax. I stayed behind my bush, heart-sick over what he'd endured in order to find me. I watched him splash water beneath his arms and wash his face.

When he turned toward the shore, I saw the cuts on his chest and arms and gasped. How many times had they whipped him? How had I failed to notice them the night before? I thought on our time together. He hadn't taken his shirt off. Feeling sick, I wondered if I'd hurt him when I pulled him to me, when I wrapped my hands tight around his arms.

Then he made his way out of the water, and I crouched behind my tree, praying he wouldn't see me. As he dressed, my eyes wandered to the creature that lived between his legs. It was pinker than I'd imagined, with large stones hanging beneath and a tangled nest of hair. Once he walked past, I circled the clearing to pretend I'd gone into the woods to relieve myself.

When I reached the hut, he was waiting for me. "How do you know the voice you hear isn't the Mother of God?" he asked, his expression solemn. "Or your own mother's ghost?"

"I thought it was my mother's ghost at first. But it isn't—or it's not only that." I tried to think of a way to explain it.

"What do you mean?" Matthäus's voice was quiet. "What has the Mother told you to do?"

"Seek Hildegard. Protect the princess. Protect myself."

He nodded slowly. "That doesn't sound like a demon."

"She wants to be restored to her rightful place beside the Father." I clasped his hands. "Does that help?"

He nodded again. "Actually, yes."

As we made ready to go, I reflected on the journey ahead of me. I had everything I needed to make the life I wanted: a path to join the circle, my love beside me. I reached for the figurine in my coin-purse. Thank you, I prayed, sending the gratitude up, up, up.

Matthäus rode in front of me as we followed the old trade route south. Watching his back, I found myself thinking of him instead of the mess we were riding toward. I remembered what we had done the night before and wished that we could stop and do it again. It was as if I had been enchanted, as if I was in his thrall.

We talked about various things as we rode. Our plan to get into the castle. Our fears about running into Ulrich in the wood. Our relief that we had the *tarnkappen* to keep us hidden. News from home. His mother was pregnant again. She thought this time it might be a girl. The terrain became mountainous as we rode south. Near dinnertime, my stomach began to growl. The sun fell in the sky, and we were surprised, turning a curve in a mountain path, to see a linden grove in the valley below. It reminded me of the linden grove we had practiced shooting in back home. The trees were ancient with tangled branches and deep shadows around each trunk. They were thick-trunked, heavy with leaves. As the last rays of sunlight disappeared, we looked at each other from atop our horses.

"We should stop here for the night," Matthäus said.

I nodded, as eager as he was to eat. We tied our horses in the middle of the grove and gave them their feed sacks. He gathered tinder and stones from the nearby trees and went to work building a fire ring. As he did, I sat down and spoke the spell over the mirror, to see if Ursilda was all right. The mirror showed her sitting up in bed, the midwife hovering. Matthäus watched me warily as I spoke the incantation. He stopped working to look at the mirror over my shoulder, his expression awed and horrified.

I thought he would speak, but he went back to building the fire in silence. Once he got it crackling, we sat down together at the base of a nearby tree to eat. It was too late in spring by then, even with the evening chill, to need the fire for anything more than light. Without discussing it, we settled into similar postures to the ones we had developed as children, sitting with our backs against the trunk but closer than before, our thighs touching, side by side. We devoured our cheese and bread and drank the wine Beatrice had given us. By then, the grove was dark except for the firelight and the moon. Mist began to gather at the edges of the firelight. We sat and ate in comfortable silence. The wine Beatrice had put in my flagon was flavorful and dark.

"That was good," Matthäus said, when we were finished, patting my thigh. It was a natural gesture, friendly. He had probably done it a hundred times when we were children. But just like that, the feeling that there was something between us, drawing us together, returned. He looked at his hand, then back up at me. The firelight was fading.

As his lips drew near mine, I abandoned myself to the kiss. I could feel the rest of the world falling away as the now-familiar enchantment encircled us.

When his lips finally pressed mine, my eyes closed. I was no longer myself. I was no one. I was anyone. I was every woman who has ever been kissed. I felt drowsy, suspended in our desire. Soon enough, we were unlacing our clothes, and I was sitting on his lap at the edge of the firelight. As I pushed into him, the rest of the world fell away, and everything went dark. There was only him and me and our interlocking bodies. There was only the myth of us.

Afterward, we sat together for a long time, intertwined. Then it happened again. We felt the pull. Three times, that night, something pulled us together. After the third time, Matthäus whispered softly that he could never leave me. Then he fell asleep on the grass beside me, a half smile on his face, his skin glistening with sweat. Our bed of grass beneath the linden tree was dark. I took a bite of my alrūne and tried to sleep.

Lying next to him, unclothed, I was filled with a preternatural unease. I put on my underpants and shift and tried to sleep, watching him breathe. But the night closed around me, making me anxious. When I finally fell into an uneasy sleep, the Mother sent me another dream. I was pressed against the wall of Princess Ursilda's chamber, watching a masked man climb through the window. Behind him, a waning half moon hung in the sky. The masked man wore black breeches and a black hood over his head. His blue eyes flashed above his mask. His movements were soundless and liquid as he snuffed the torch and drew a knife from a sheath engraved with the king's seal. Then he drew it across the throat of a sleeping figure on the bed and crept toward the cradle.

I jolted awake, the Mother's voice buzzing through the veil, hissing, furious: *Another assassin.*

As I sat up, the tension in the air collapsed. My heart pounded in my throat. How could I sleep, knowing there would be a second murder I was supposed to prevent after this? I clutched my figurine, stomach knotting, praying I would know what to do to stop both killings. The moon would not be waning like that for another week or so.

When the sky finally began to turn gray at the horizon, I woke Matthäus. He startled awake, a terrified look in his eyes, until he realized where he was. "Sorry," he said, embarrassed at his outburst. "They woke me at all hours in that cell to try to get information."

I waited for him to say more, but that was all he would offer. I reached out and squeezed his hand. "Don't apologize, Matthäus," I said, kissing his forehead. "Please. I'm the one who got you involved."

When he was calm, I told him about my dream and what I thought it meant. As soon as I was finished, we decided to ride the rest of the way as hard as we could.

CHAPTER THIRTY-TWO

We were like ghostly demons speeding down the trade route. My need to succeed at my task pulled me onward. Matthäus rode beside me, sharing in the urgency I felt. When we entered the northern tip of the ancient forest where Ulrich's castle stood, we pulled our hoods down, letting the shadow-world envelop us. There was no telling where Ulrich was hiding—he could be anywhere in that forest. Elder oaks and ash trees held hands over our path, as if they were keeping our passage secret. The only signs of our progress through the woods were sounds—the gentle stutter of our horses' hooves, the sound of our breathing.

We didn't dare speak.

Before that, we'd only pulled the hoods on for short periods at a time, when we approached villages or towns or heard sounds in the distance. By the time we'd ridden two hours without removing them, my fingers and toes were numb like they were after a fainting spell. I remembered the carriage driver's warning that I would need to be careful. How long was it safe for me to wear a *tarnkappe* when the moon was full? "Do you feel that?" I whispered. "The pins and needles?"

"No," Matthäus breathed.

"I think we've worn the *tarnkappen* too long."

I didn't want to stop. The longer we dallied, the greater the chance was that we would be too late. But the horses began acting strangely soon after that, and I realized that if the shadow-world swallowed us, we would *never* arrive. Reluctantly, I searched the wood beside the path for a hiding place where we could uncloak.

Before long, I spied a thorny circle of sweetbriar rosebushes. So tangled, so tall and wild, we could dismount our horses in the center without being seen. "This way," I said, turning off the path. I heard Matthäus follow me.

In the middle of the sweetbriar bushes, surrounded by tangled thorns and the fragrance of their buds, I pulled off my hood. Matthäus did the same, and we set to work uncloaking the horses. We all stood perfectly still, and I was relieved to feel the pins and needles in my limbs gradually fading, as if my soul was settling back into my flesh. It took about half an hour for the sensation to go away. When I felt it no more, I nodded grimly. "Let's go."

We pulled the hoods back on and returned to the path, the gravity of our task pressing down upon us. We stopped to uncloak every couple hours for the rest of the way through the forest, but the closer we got to Ulrich's castle, the harder it was to convince myself to stop. By the time we reached the part of the forest I recognized from my long walks with Kunegunde, my heart was thudding in my ears, and I wanted to push all the way through to the castle.

Just after sunset, as we crested a mountain, we saw the fortress across the valley below, gray walls rising from cliffs, the round moon hanging over it. We slowed slightly, gazing at it without speaking. The night was eerily still. The only sound was the crunch of our horses' hooves.

When my fingers and toes went numb, I was determined not to stop. We were too close. As we rode down into the valley, Nëbel began pulling on her reins and prancing wildly, picking up on some change in the otherworldly weather. Perhaps she could feel the numbness in her extremities too. I winced, knowing whatever sounds she made would carry.

There was no sign of Ulrich as we approached the castle. No howl, no movement in the trees. The forest was eerily quiet. Up the mountain we rode, into the trees cloaked with mist. By the time we grew close to the castle, I could feel the pins and needles creeping up my thighs and into my shoulders. I could no longer feel most of my body. It was as if I was becoming the shadow.

I whispered toward the sound of Matthäus's horse. "We should wait until the last possible moment to uncloak. I'm afraid Ulrich will find us so close to the castle."

"Whatever you think is best," he whispered back.

When we could see the castle gate up ahead in the distance, it was lit up with a hundred torches. The drawbridge was open, as if they were waiting for someone to ride in or out in a hurry, and there were bonfires on either side of the gate, burning bright. I wondered if they expected Ulrich that night, if he came back to the castle secretly from time to time.

I turned into the wood and dismounted, removing Nëbel's hood. I tied her loosely to a tree far enough from the path that no one would see her, and Matthäus did the same for his horse. Then I grabbed Matthäus's hand and led him back to the path.

The only sound we made as we approached the torchlit castle gate was the sound of our breathing. I squeezed Matthäus's hand as we approached, praying Ulrich wasn't around.

Several men were standing guard in leather jerkins, passing around a wineskin. The mist and darkness made it difficult to see how many guards were inside the gatehouse. We could hear them laughing and shouting, casting lots.

By then, the numbness had spread to my breast and my groin. As we approached the gate, I gritted my teeth, moving as silently as possible, hoping we had fallen deep enough into the shadow-world that the *tarnkappen* would swallow the sound of our footsteps too. We would have to pass within six feet of the men outside the gatehouse.

Only one of the men looked up as we passed into the gate, a question on his face. His expression was quizzical, and he scanned the place where we were standing. I held my breath, rubbing the figurine in my pocket, praying the Mother would keep us safe. Seeing nothing, he shook his head, drinking from his wineskin.

We crept through the courtyard to the western wing of the castle, where the driver had told us to go. At its western edge was a vast, torchlit hall with a floor of stone. The westernmost corridor. When we entered it, there was no one around, so I led Matthäus west down the middle of the corridor. We passed unseen through the flickering dark, until we heard a door creaking open at the end of the hall. As light spilled into the corridor, I saw three guards keeping watch at the door. A wild fear filled me that Ulrich would come out.

Two figures walked out, the bright light behind them making them unidentifiable silhouettes. Squeezing Matthäus's hand, I pulled him to the side of the hall so they could pass without bumping into us. We held our breath, pressing our backs against the wall. The closest man had a well-trimmed grizzled beard. "She's weak like her mother," he was saying. "Albrecht will be furious if she dies on our watch."

"The new midwife will take good care of her, surely."

"If she doesn't, this will be the last birth she ever attends."

The other man smirked. "Albrecht will make sure of it."

In a moment they were close enough for us to reach out and touch them—and then they were past. I waited until they had left the corridor to move. When I did, I could barely walk, my legs were so numb.

"Uncloak," I whispered to Matthäus, pulling off my hood. "Now, while the guards aren't looking."

The pins-and-needles feeling began to ebb immediately. The guards came to attention as we approached.

"Balthazar?" I asked, using the name the carriage driver had directed.

One of the guards stepped forward.

I showed him the seal on the scroll. "I am Haelewise, daughter-of-Hedda, and this is my escort. I am a midwife of considerable skill. I have come to assist with the birth."

He looked down at the seal, eyes widening. Then he nodded, fiddling with the key ring at his belt. Taking their cue from Balthazar, the other guards stood aside.

It took Balthazar a minute to find the right key on his ring.

Inside the door was a long hall lit with lanterns. A shadowy tunnel, flickering, with a bone-white floor. I became aware of my boots, the dirt they must be tracking in. I dusted off my cloak and smoothed my hair, wondering how tangled it was, how much like a seer or sorcerer I must look in this rune-hood.

"Irmgard!" Balthazar called.

A woman came out of the farthest door. The same woman I had seen with Ursilda on the mountain. Her freckled face was as drawn as before, her hair pulled up tight in a bun, but her clothes were rumpled. She looked like she hadn't slept in days. As she drew close, I held out the scroll, waiting for her to recognize me or mistake me for Frederika, but she only took the scroll from my hands, distracted, noting the seal.

We waited while she read it.

"I'm glad you've come," she said when she had finished. She met my eyes, her expression uneasy. There was no recognition in her gaze. "Ursilda is not well."

"How long has she been in her chamber?"

"Two days now. The pangs have started, but they are still very far apart."

"Has her water broken?"

"This morning. As soon as she got out of bed."

Irmgard pulled out a key ring and unlocked a door.

She turned to Matthäus. "You cannot come to Ursilda's chambers, of course."

Matthäus squared his shoulders as if he wanted to argue. Then he thought better of it. "Of course not," he said with a bow, but as soon as she turned her back, his expression was fierce. He wasn't going to let me go in alone. He gave me a pointed look, fingering the hood of his cloak.

I nodded to show him I understood, then followed Irmgard out. I felt righteous, as she led me across the square. I felt determined.

The door opened into a garden courtyard, like the one at the Kürenberg cottage, but ten times larger. In the thin moonlight, lilies and gilliflowers glowed. Cracked statuettes like the ones Kunegunde kept in her garden—grotesques with snouts and horns—sneered and danced. A birdbath similar to Kunegunde's stood in the corner, ancient, covered with the same gilded runes. At the center of the courtyard was an ancient linden tree, thick with bright-green leaves. It had to be a thousand years old. A good omen, I thought, for me and my shadow.

The round moon brightened the stones.

Irmgard led me up the stairwell, an interminable series of six-stepped flights. At the last landing we paused at another locked door.

As Irmgard unlocked it, I could feel Matthäus standing behind me, his hand on my shoulder. I hoped he would be all right, that the mist wouldn't swallow him, that the brief break from being cloaked would be enough to keep him in this world.

A looking glass hung on the wall just inside the doorway. I made a show of stopping to check my reflection so he would have time to slip past. My golden eyes glowed in the lantern-light. My face was covered in dust, my hair wild, unkempt. No wonder no one had recognized me here. My mission had transformed me. I didn't look like myself.

Irmgard opened the door into a hall with many adjoining rooms. Fine rugs covered the floor, masking Matthäus's footsteps. Candles glowed in eerie lanterns. Tapestries hung on the walls. They were covered with intricately embroidered images of winged women, forest scenes with owls and nymphs, bees and snakes and beasts edged with golden thread.

A scent assaulted my nostrils: acidic, spicy, peppermint. Several of the doors were dark as Irmgard led us past them. Dim light shone through the keyhole of the door at the end of the hall. As we approached it, the smell of peppermint grew stronger, and I knew we were approaching Ursilda's birthing room. I held my breath as Irmgard unlocked the door, preparing myself to see the room I had seen in the mirror.

Stepping inside, I saw the tapestries hung over the windows. Princess Ursilda lay on the bed in a deep-green robe, curled into herself, her huge belly red and glistening with peppermint oil. Her red hair was coiled in a thick braid around her head. She had grown even more thin and pale. Her face looked almost gaunt.

The blond-haired midwife from the water-*spiegel* stood behind her, massaging her back. She startled as we walked in.

Hatred rose in my throat. The room was surprisingly empty apart from the bed and the fire burning in the hearth. Where were all of Ursilda's relatives? Her mother? Her aunts? The air in the room was tense, the otherworldly weather confusing. It swung furiously with a quick-shifting balance to the next world and back. I couldn't make sense of the feeling at first. Then I realized what it meant.

The presence of strong magic. Matthäus, at the edge of the shadow-world in a *tarnkappe*. The possibility of birth and death.

Irmgard announced us with a curtsy. "Ursilda. Beatrice heard of your troubles. She sent you another midwife." She brought the letter around the bed so that Ursilda could see the seal.

Ursilda continued to moan, barely glancing up at it.

Massaging Ursilda's back, the midwife glanced back at us, her eyes full of what looked like concern. "Thank you for coming. We've been struggling to coax this child out."

Her performance was so convincing that for a moment I almost wondered if Beatrice was wrong about her. Then I noticed how tightly she gripped Ursilda's shoulders, how white the skin was under her fingers. "Careful," I said. "You'll hurt her."

The midwife looked down and loosened her grip. "It's been a long two days," she said, as if she were genuinely embarrassed.

My eye fell upon the water pitcher and plate of rumpled-looking leaves on the bedside table, which I'd assumed were poisonous when Beatrice showed me the room in the bowl. Even through the smell of peppermint oil, I could identify their shape and grassy scent as rapunzel. That plant wasn't poisonous—I would have to work harder to figure out what poison the midwife had used.

The midwife saw me looking at the plate. "She's been craving it."

Ursilda moaned one last time, then looked at me as the pang passed. Her eyes were red and watery, unfocused, her face blotchy and pale. Loose hairs stuck out from her braid. "Haelewise," she breathed, before she succumbed to a pang.

I waited for it to end, sitting down beside her.

"We were to speak in the morning, but you left—"

I folded her hand in mine. "Beatrice sent me here to help with the birth."

Ursilda's eyes went out of focus again. She looked like she was having trouble staying conscious. "Something is wrong," she said helplessly. "The child won't come. I feel terribly ill."

The midwife drew herself up, her eyes beady and treacherous. "Like I said, she's having troubles."

I wanted to stab her right then and there. She was the king's tool, I knew, but I couldn't understand how a woman could hurt another woman in her time of need. What price could possibly be enough to betray your kind?

I tried to help Ursilda from the bed. "You've got to walk during pangs," I told her as my mother had told dozens of women.

Tears streamed down Ursilda's face. Her sobs seemed to bring on a pang. She groaned, curling into herself. "I can't—"

"I've tried to get her to walk, but she's too weak," the midwife said.

"What have you given her?" It sounded more like an accusation than I meant.

The midwife stiffened, then forced herself to meet my eyes. Her voice seemed to tremble with concern. "Only the rapunzel she craves and pennyroyal. Should we try somethin' else?"

The pennyroyal might explain some of the paleness of her skin but not all of it. I cleared my throat and tried not to sound frustrated as I explained the first things my mother had taught me, basic facts that any midwife would know. "We should give her caudle, if you haven't already. It helps with the pain."

"She's right. It's been too long since we made her drink," Irmgard said, looking at the midwife. The midwife shook her head, tight-lipped. "I'll ask the cook."

As Irmgard slipped out, I turned to the midwife. "Irmgard said her pangs are still very far apart?"

The midwife nodded. "She has hours of labor left."

I helped Ursilda out of bed and tried to get her walking. The midwife looked on skeptically. Ursilda collapsed after a single step. "I can't—"

Her legs were too weak to support her. She was probably too weak even to use a birthing stool. I helped her back to the bed, wondering if she could support herself well enough to deliver on her hands and knees. I'd helped my mother deliver several babies in that position, when other labors went on too long. This would be easier if more of her family were here to support her. "The rest of her relatives," I asked the midwife. "Aunts. Her mother. Where are they?"

The midwife gave me a bitter look. "Everyone has left the castle. There is no one else here. His highness," the midwife said, crossing herself, "is accused of murdering Princess Frederika, if you haven't heard. He's gone into hiding. Ursilda's parents have gone into hiding too." The midwife was trying to pretend she was angry on Ursilda's behalf, but the hatred she felt for Ulrich was clear in the way she spat his name. "Ursilda won't tell me where they went, so we have no way of contacting them."

"I don't *know* where they are," Ursilda cried weakly.

The midwife narrowed her eyes at me, lowering her voice. "Ursilda's mother would want to be here for the birth. Perhaps you could get Ursilda to tell you where she is so we could send for her."

I blinked at the midwife, my voice hard. "That won't be necessary."

Irmgard hurried back into the room, followed by the cook, a thick, solicitous-looking woman with a pitcher and mug.

"Add tosh and primrose," I told the cook. The woman did so and brought the mug to Ursilda. The princess drank it quickly. "Give her more."

As the cook complied, I wondered what Matthäus was doing. Probably watching the midwife from a corner. I wondered how he felt, being here, what he thought of these forbidden proceedings. Was he anxious? Was he angry on Ursilda's behalf?

I had Ursilda drink the second mug and asked the midwife to help me make a nest of rags on the floor so she wouldn't hurt her knees.

"Now look here," the midwife said. "I'm the one in charge of this birth. You can't just come in here and take over."

"Oh, but she can," Irmgard said firmly. "I've a letter from the queen that says she will. Do what she says, or you will find yourself dismissed."

The midwife blinked up at her. "As you wish."

Ursilda seemed to come alive, a little, as we helped her get to her nest on the floor. The midwife's mood seemed to have darkened, as if she suspected her time with Ursilda was coming to a close.

"How long has it been since she's eaten?" I asked.

"Too long," the midwife said, turning to Ursilda. "Do you want some more rapunzel, dear? It could help to speed your labor."

Ursilda looked at Irmgard, who looked at me, and I nodded.

That much was true. Ursilda nodded, her expression weirdly ravenous.

I watched the midwife offer her the plate from the bedside table, eyeing the leaves. They all looked and smelled like rapunzel. Perfectly innocent. As Ursilda put a leaf in her mouth, I wondered how the midwife was poisoning her.

"Water," Ursilda said. "I need water."

Instead of using the water pitcher from the bedside table, the midwife went all the way to a table on the other side of the room, where another pitcher sat. She poured a cup of its contents and brought it to Ursilda. Then she rubbed her hands with peppermint oil and began to massage Ursilda's back.

Ursilda drank the water and coughed. Then she got back down on her hands and knees. She was barely able to support herself, her limbs were so weak and trembling. The water, I thought. What's in it?

I coughed myself, then moved toward the pitcher on the other side of the room. "Is there another cup?" I asked the cook. She nodded and brought me one. I poured myself a drink, watching the midwife's expression as I brought the water to my nose to smell it. The midwife watched me coldly. The liquid had no scent at all. I thought back on Ursilda's symptoms: her weakness, her red and watery eyes, how thin she had become. Was the midwife using arsenic?

I set down the glass without drinking from it. "Beatrice decreed that I examine Ursilda in private. I would do so now."

"I can't abandon her during her pangs," the midwife said.

"You can and you will," said Irmgard. "By the queen's decree."

The midwife glared at me, her expression dark. Her eyes darted from me to the princess. "I am here by the order of the king!" Her hand went to her belt. Looking closer I thought I saw an oblong shape there. A knife.

Ursilda looked up in surprise.

I felt the otherworldly weather shifting fast in the opposite direction.

A strong pull into the next world. The possibility of death swirled around—the air going taut—like a snake waiting to strike.

A cacophony of feeling rose up in me. Certainty, that I was supposed to be here. Outrage, at the midwife's intent.

The figurine buzzed in my coin-purse, humming, furious. I knew what I had to do. I threw my body between the midwife and Ursilda.

When the midwife drew her knife, the anger inside me burst.

I was not myself when I pulled the dagger from its hilt. I was my mother, lashing out to protect me. I was the Mother's impulse to protect her daughters on earth. I thought of Rika, how I had failed her. I thought of Ursilda, the child in her belly, as I slit the midwife's throat.

The cut was jagged and deep. Blood seeped from the wound onto her dress. She crumpled to the floor.

I heard a stifled cry behind me.

Blood began to pool, thick and red, beneath the body on the rug. My body sagged with relief. Ursilda was safe. I said a quick prayer for the midwife's soul as I watched it exit this world, a thin breeze that hissed on its way out. When it was gone, the tension in the air didn't collapse. The pull into the next world continued.

The disembodied sound of sobbing filled the room.

Matthäus materialized in front of us, removing his *tarnkappe*. The sobs were his. His expression was shocked; he stared at the midwife's corpse in horror. "God have mercy," he said.

Irmgard gasped: a man, in the birthing chamber. She eyed the spreading pool of blood.

"Princess Ursilda," I blurted. "Forgive us for bringing a man into your chamber. The queen warned us you had been beset by an assassin."

Matthäus nodded, averting his eyes. "I couldn't let her face this alone."

I met his eyes, trying to gauge how he felt about what I'd done.

There was relief in his eyes, but also fear. Despite our conversation on the way here, he wasn't sure what to think. We would have to discuss this later.

I turned to Ursilda. "The midwife was sent here by the king to find out where Ulrich was, or kill you. To punish your family."

"Why?"

I met her eyes, uncertain whether I should upset her further. "Your brother ordered Frederika's murder."

Ursilda's mouth fell open, her face crumpling into a sob. "No." She began to hyperventilate. "My brother?"

I nodded, gritting my teeth. "I'm so sorry."

"Why would he kill Frederika?"

"He found out she was handfasted to someone else. A peasant."

Her face crumpled in horror. "No." She burst into tears. "No—"

Irmgard reached for her hand, trying to comfort her.

Ursilda pushed her away. "Frederika." Her voice shook. She kept shaking her head in denial. "He—*I can't*—"

"I'm sorry, Ursilda. I saw his man do it with my own eyes. He berated her for running away from him."

She stared at me, horrified, a darkness creeping into her green eyes. They narrowed, and I saw an anger there that I knew must've simmered for a very long time.

"Beatrice sent us to warn you. The king—he wants revenge. Since he can't get to your brother, he wants you dead. The midwife has been poisoning you, I suspect, with arsenic."

Ursilda's mouth fell open. "That's why I've felt so weak?"

I turned to the cook. "Is there sysemera, betony, and rue in the garden?" She nodded. "What about hydromel? Garden spurge?"

The cook nodded again, rushing out for the ingredients.

I helped Ursilda away from the blood that was seeping into the rags. She listened as I described the murder I'd witnessed, what happened when I testified against Ulrich at court. When I finished the story, a pang overwhelmed her.

I closed my eyes, taking stock of the otherworldly weather. There was no trembling, no soul at the threshold. The pull into the next world was still strong.

"Breathe," I told her, panicking. "Rock your hips. You've got to stay calm."

She arched her back, moaning with pain. All of the color drained from her face. Her eyes rolled back in her head.

I feared that her soul was about to leave her body. She didn't have the strength to push. When the pang passed, she began to pant with shallow breaths, so quickly I worried she might faint. "Breathe deep," I reminded her.

As we waited for the cook to bring back the ingredients for the antidote, Matthäus asked in a small voice, "Should I wait outside?"

"Yes," I said, meeting his eyes. "Thank you for coming with me."

He searched my eyes, his expression wary, full of fear.

Irmgard looked at him. "There's a sitting room across the hall."

As Matthäus slipped out, I pushed my concerns and fears about him down; I made myself focus on the birth. I instructed Irmgard to massage Ursilda's back. Ursilda wailed, her body going rigid, as the cook hurried in with the herbs.

"Another pang!" Irmgard cried.

I nodded as I began to work on expressing the juice from the plants. "They're coming faster now. It's all the excitement." I turned to Ursilda. "Can you push?"

Ursilda screamed at the top of her lungs, arching her back. Her eyes rolled back in her head, then fluttered shut. She crumpled to her belly in the rags.

I left the nearly finished preparation to lay her on her side, putting my palm to her belly, feeling the contraction roll beneath her skin. The baby was still moving. Alive. I could feel it. Moving my hand over her belly, I could feel the baby's head, deep down in the pelvis. Ursilda's breathing was growing more ragged, more shallow.

I felt for her pulse. It was weak.

The contraction stopped.

"Is she going to live?" Irmgard asked, her voice quavering.

I didn't know how to answer the question. There was no way to know whether the preparation would work. I finished making it, quickly, mixing the juice of sysemera, betony, and rue, with garden spurge. I poured it into a cup. "We have to get her to take this."

Irmgard went to Ursilda and shook her. "Your highness—"

"Be gentle," I warned her.

"Wake up!"

Ursilda would not stir.

Taking a deep breath, I went to the princess, cupping the bottom of her jaw to open her lips, as I had once done for my mother. I poured the mixture into her mouth, pressing her lips tightly shut so the liquid wouldn't leak out. "Give me the hydromel," I told the cook. The woman complied.

Ursilda's belly contracted again. She stirred, moaning softly without opening her eyes. It was worrisome that her pangs weren't waking her up. I waited for the contraction to pass, checking her birth canal to see how far along she was. It was nearly time, but I could still feel no soul at the threshold. The pull still went in the other direction. Ursilda had to wake up soon, or both she and the child would be lost.

When the contraction passed, I opened her mouth again to give her hydromel. She gagged involuntarily on the foam it brought up in her throat, but otherwise she did not stir.

Mother, I prayed, clasping her limp hand in my own. Help me save them. I cannot bear another death on my watch.

Ursilda lay still on her side on the rags on the floor. My heart thudded in my throat.

And then, after a blessed moment, Ursilda began to sputter and cough, as foam leaked from her mouth. I sat her upright so she wouldn't choke. I told the cook to bring the chamber pot.

As the cook held it in front of her, Ursilda's eyes flew open. She threw up a foamy substance, her eyes animal-wild and panicked.

When she was finished, I asked Irmgard to pour her a mug of the caudle. Ursilda drank it down between pangs, as if she suffered from great thirst. I checked between her legs and saw that the birth tunnel had opened enough for her to push. "Do you feel any stronger?"

She shook her head.

"Do you think you could try the birthing stool?"

She stared at it skeptically, shaking her head again.

"She needs more caudle," I said.

The cook hurried to pour her another mug. I held it to her lips.

"Now could you try? Sometimes it helps to change positions."

She hung her head, and I knew that she would, though I worried she simply didn't have the strength to argue. I helped her over to the birthing stool and told her to gather her strength for the next pang. She could barely hold herself up. Her legs trembled violently. Her hands shook. I took her wrist, checking for her pulse. Her heartbeat was weak, irregular. The antidote could only do so much. I motioned for Irmgard and the cook to come over and help hold her up. They did so, murmuring soft words of encouragement. "You can do this. You must."

When the next pang came, Ursilda finally began to push, half growling, half screaming a terrible animal cry.

I could still sense no soul, no trembling at the threshold. I crouched on the floor before her. The babe crowned, a little pink circle emerging from the birth canal, sticky with blood and mucus. Was it going to be born dead?

The pull into the next world was so strong, I felt dizzy. As the veil between worlds opened, Ursilda looked at me, her expression woozy—eyes crossed—and let go of my hand. She slumped on her stool.

"Ursilda?" Irmgard said, her voice trembling.

I felt for her pulse again. For a moment there was nothing. Then I thought I felt a faint, single beat. I moved my fingers to see if I was missing a more regular pulse. The princess slumped on the birthing stool in Irmgard's arms, completely unresponsive. A long moment passed during which I avoided Irmgard's gaze. I was afraid we were too late, that in an instant, I would see a dewy soul lift from her mouth. The poison had been too long in her blood.

I reached for the figurine in my pocket, rubbing it, praying for the otherworldly balance to shift. I heard a shadowy voice from the next world. *Move her*, the Mother hissed.

Suddenly I understood. This position wasn't going to work. Panicking, with all my strength, I began to pull her to her hands and knees. "Help me," I told Irmgard.

Another pang contracted Ursilda's stomach as we moved her. She moaned, her eyes flying open.

And then I felt it: the trembling in the air. The child's soul. "Push," I said, crouching beside her. "Ursilda. It's time. Push!"

The princess started sobbing. She summoned up all the strength she had and pushed, letting out a terrible animal growl.

And then the child was out, an angry pink baby girl with a full head of bright-red hair. She was small for a newborn, but not unhealthily so. A squirming weight in my arms, silent.

The princess craned her neck to see the child, her eyes full of exhaustion. Tears streamed down her face. I wiped my hand on my cloak and reached into the baby's throat to clear it of debris. As I finished, I felt goose bumps. A whisper-wind slipped past me. Her soul, flying to enter her.

Her mewling cries awakened a longing so deep, my breath caught in my throat. Her softness, her weight in my arms. Everything about holding her felt *right*. When she looked up at me, I saw her eyes, full of need—and completely black. I gasped, awestruck. This baby was like me. She would have the gift.

I held her tight, looking into those eyes, cooing, the strongest mother-greed I've ever felt choking my heart. When Ursilda reached out to touch her—may I be forgiven—I winced. Ursilda tried to stand from her stool, her legs wobbling, falling backward.

"Let's get you cleaned up first and in bed," I said, smiling, using her weakness as an excuse. My eyes fell on the corpse on the floor, the blood pooling around it. It was a dark thing, to see a body as a nuisance. But that's how I felt, staring down at what was left of the midwife: I cursed the trouble she had made for us. "Could you take care of that?" I asked the cook.

"Aye," the cook said. "I'll go get help."

As the cook left to go find the guards, Irmgard used a rag to wipe Ursilda's legs. I bathed the child, swaddled her bottom, and put her in a pretty white embroidered gown. I rocked her and rocked her, my heart full of a greed so pure, so perfect, I couldn't stand it.

Irmgard helped Ursilda over to the bed. She was so weak, she nearly fell three times before she collapsed on the pillows. I watched Irmgard prop her up, straightening her robe, noticing how pale she still was. The midwife must have been poisoning her for a week. Who knows how much arsenic she had been given and when? I hoped her body had protected the child from the poison. Kunegunde would say the best cure for that was mother's milk, but would Ursilda even be able to nurse?

The child had gone silent in my arms. Her black eyes watching me watch her. When Ursilda was settled, I made myself give her the baby, propping her up with a nest of pillows, a choking sensation in my throat. Mine mine mine, a terrible voice inside me whispered. I cursed that voice when I first heard it, I did.

At first.

Irmgard opened Ursilda's robe, and the child began squirming, healthy, hungry, searching out her first meal. As the baby rooted, I breathed deep, trying to push the horrible voice away. Thank you, Mother, I prayed, for everything you've done so far. I have done everything you commanded. Is there anything more I can do to help?

The child latched onto Ursilda and began to suckle.

By the time the guards came back with the cook to take care of the body, we had covered the pair in blankets. Ursilda's eyes fluttered closed, as the baby tried to coax milk from her breast.

After a moment, the child began to squirm. "Try the other breast."

Irmgard helped her move the child. Ursilda looked worried. Her face was drawn. The shadows beneath her eyes were deep.

She straightened suddenly in bed, her expression panicked, as if something had just occurred to her. "What's to stop the king from sending someone else?" The child squirmed in her arms.

I looked up at her, remembering my dream.

Seeing my expression, Ursilda clutched the baby tighter, rattled. "Tell me what you know."

"The Mother speaks to me," I said quietly. "I have the gift."

The child began to mewl, impatient for milk that wasn't flowing. "We need goat's milk," I told the cook. "Get it yourself. Don't let anyone do it for you."

The cook nodded, understanding, then hurried out.

Ursilda shivered as she looked at Irmgard. The bedroom was still and quiet. Irmgard turned to me. "Tell us everything."

"You can speak freely in front of Irmgard," Ursilda said.

We all stared at one another for a long moment. I drew a deep breath. "As you wish. I am Haelewise, daughter-of-Hedda, a supplicant to the circle of daughters who worship the Mother. Sometimes the Mother sends me dreams. Visions that will come to pass unless I do something about them. I foresaw Princess Frederika's murder but failed to stop it. Last night, the Mother told me in a dream that the king would send another assassin after this attempt failed. A masked man who will creep through that window at the waning half moon to kill both of you." Anger made my voice choke. "I saw the knife he brought to the cradle. It bore the symbol of the king."

Ursilda struggled to control her emotions. She looked down at the baby, tears streaming down her cheeks. "To kill her?"

"I'm afraid so." I sighed, uncomfortable. "It's not safe here for you, for the child, until the king captures Ulrich and forgives the rest of your family. If he ever does—"

Ursilda started to sob quietly. Her breath hitched. "I can't go anywhere while I'm this weak."

She was right. She was too sick to walk. She couldn't even nurse. Her arms were shaking. She was struggling to hold even the smallest newborn in bed. The baby wailed.

The cook interrupted our stalemate, just then, with a bottle of goat's milk and a feeding horn. Irmgard bustled around, warming the milk and filling the horn. Ursilda and I fell silent, watching her work. When she handed Ursilda the horn, the princess offered the child the teat. The child wouldn't latch on.

I took the baby, who quieted at my touch. I showed Ursilda how to hold the horn so she could get a good suck. The baby drank noisily.

The look on Ursilda's face was heartbreaking. "I'm not doing her any good," she breathed. "She doesn't need me."

"Don't be silly," I said, but as soon as the child left my arms, she started crying again.

Beside the bed, Irmgard shook her head in protest. Ursilda looked at me. I could tell what she was thinking. It wasn't safe here, but she didn't have the strength to leave. She didn't even have the strength to hold a horn of milk.

The temptation was too great. It felt *right* to say what I said next. The words were out of my mouth before I had time to think twice.

"We could take her to Gothel."

I knew, as soon as I said the words, that Ursilda would say yes. She was weak, filled with motherly insecurity. I knew I was taking advantage of her. But my suggestion was a good one—the tower was safe—and I didn't want to give this baby up.

"She would be safe at Gothel from the king's assassins. When you recover your strength, you could join us."

Ursilda's eyes shone with hope as she nodded, eager. "Kunegunde is a daughter-of-the-Mother. We've been estranged for almost a decade, but she's still bound by oath to help."

The thought of seeing Kunegunde again filled me with dread—on second thought, I didn't even know if she would let us into the tower—but I wanted that baby so badly, any excuse to take her sounded good. And where else would Matthäus and I go?

"I will remind her of her oath. You can use the water-*spiegel* to keep an eye on her until you recover."

Ursilda nodded. "Thank you."

I held the child up. "Do you want to hold her again?"

"I don't have the strength," Ursilda said, kissing the child's forehead wanly. The baby stared up at her, wide-eyed, having already emptied the goat's horn of milk. "Keep her safe until I join you. But what do I tell my father? Where do I say the baby went?"

I stared at her for a long moment, a story forming in my mind. "Tell him the truth. But tell it like this. The new midwife was a witch. She took the baby from your arms when you were too weak to stop her, then flew away with your child into the night."

CHAPTER THIRTY-THREE

We rode to Gothel, cloaked, the child sleeping in her sling at my breast. So soundly, it was as if the Mother had enchanted her. We didn't talk as we rode, afraid Ulrich would find us, the only sound the echo of our invisible horses' hooves on the mountain path. The mist dressed the trees in ghostly lace. I thought about how I would convince Kunegunde to let a man stay at the tower. If only I had something to offer her to make it worth her while. I could only hope her oath to the circle would have weight.

I cradled the babe in my sling as we rode. Until her mother came to get her, I would be the one to hold her, to nurse her, to come to her when she cried in her sleep. I clutched her tightly. As I held her, my sense of self blurred into a thousand shadows. She was me, and I was my mother and every mother who had ever lived before her.

Gothel wasn't a long ride from the castle. As we drew close to the mountain where the tower stood, I could feel an unsettling presence, an ominous disturbance in the otherworldly weather. It was coming closer. I pulled on my reins. "Wait," I whispered. Matthäus stopped beside me.

I reached into my coin-purse with shadowy fingers, but the bird-mother figurine was cold. I rubbed her and closed my eyes, praying for the Mother to improve the sensitivity of my gift. After a moment, the figurine grew warm, and I could sense the shadow-world with greater precision than ever before. I was already half in it. Though I couldn't see Matthäus or Nëbel, I could sense their *tarnkappen*, two otherworldly rivers flowing, nearby, into the next world. And in the distance, where I felt the presence, I could feel a river flowing in the opposite direction, into the forest from the shadow-world.

Then I heard it. The distant sound of a howl.

Nëbel spooked, dancing nervously, her muscles tensing beneath me. A chill passed through me as I remembered what Albrecht told the king's men when they arrived at the castle—that Ulrich had gone hunting. God's teeth, I thought. That presence pulling shadow into this world. It's Ulrich, wearing the wolf-skin.

Nëbel snorted, nervous. I closed my eyes, trying to pinpoint Ulrich's location. He was headed this way. My first thought was for the child's safety, then Matthäus's. I clutched Nëbel's reins tight, resolute. The horse danced, and I could tell she was rolling her eyes with fear.

"What was that?" Matthäus asked, his voice small, as if he knew the answer to his question already.

"Ulrich," I said. "He's coming for me."

I patted Nëbel, trying to calm her. He'd been lying in wait for me in the woods around the tower of Gothel. How did he know I would return? I hadn't planned to. My thoughts raced. Maybe he didn't. One of the villagers could've told him that we harbored Rika at Gothel, or one of his guards could've found my name in the register in the porterhouse. There were so many ways he could've known to look for me here, in fact, that I felt foolish for not expecting that he would. The realization brought tears to my eyes. I was so naïve. How was I going to face such a conniving monster?

Nëbel snorted, sensing my anxiety, panicking, beginning to neigh and prance. I closed my eyes again, reaching out to see where Ulrich was now. I almost gasped, he'd closed so much distance so quickly. He was heading straight for us, as if he knew where we were. Maybe I hadn't been hooded long enough. Did the full moon make the wolf-skin stronger than the cloak? Maybe he was tracking my scent. He had a wolf's sense of smell. The *tarnkappen* were at their weakest now.

The child. Matthäus. Who knew what he'd do to them when he found us?

"I'm going to face him," I told Matthäus, working through it as I spoke, "so you and the baby can get away."

"No," he whispered fiercely.

"The child's safety comes first," I said, dismounting, my voice hard. There could be no argument about this. If Ulrich was coming after me, the baby needed to be far away. I fumbled for the place where I could feel Matthäus's *tarnkappe* working, finding his horse's stirrup. "Where are you? Here. Let me give her to you."

"Haelewise—" Matthäus touched my arm. His voice was tender, breaking. "I don't want to leave you."

"He's looking for *me*. I don't want you or the child to be around when I confront him." I found his hand and squeezed it.

He dismounted, arguing. "I won't—" But his protest was interrupted by my lips, fumbling for where I thought his mouth would be. They found his cheek, but he moved, fumbling to press his mouth against mine. It was a strange sensation to kiss when we were half in the shadow-world. My mouth was numb, full of pins and needles. The sensation made me dizzy.

Unwrapping the sling from around my breast, I fitted it around his shoulders, tucking the child into the fabric, pressing her to his chest, making sure she was fitted in tight. When she was settled, I kissed her forehead. She whimpered, a tiny squall.

"Keep your hood on. Ride away. I'm going to loose Nëbel. She's panicking. She'll give away my location."

"What are you going to do?"

"I don't know. I can't think while the child is unsafe."

"Where do I go?"

"It doesn't matter where you go. Just hide. I'll be able to find you as long as you're wearing the cloak."

He made a strangled sound, a final noise of complaint. Then he pulled himself together. "All right. If you see no other way. Godspeed, Haelewise. Be safe. I'll see you soon."

There was a pause. Then I heard the sound of hooves thudding the ground—he was fleeing. I uncloaked Nëbel and slapped her side. She took off after them.

Once they were gone, I found I could concentrate on the situation at hand. I turned it over in my mind, racking my brain for some weakness of Ulrich's that I could exploit. My thoughts were tangled, uncertain. Last time, I'd exploited his lust. Last time—

I reached for the figurine in my coin-purse, rubbing her, praying. Please, I breathed. Mother, please, guide me—

The veil slipped open, and the otherworldly balance tilted briefly toward this world. A buzzing filled my ears, like bees rising up to protect the hive. *Steal the wolf-skin*, a feminine voice buzzed from the next world—outraged—before the balance tilted back.

Certainty coursed through me. I blinked, grateful that I knew what to do. If I took the wolf-skin from Ulrich, it would steal his power. What was more, Kunegunde would be so happy with me, she might not turn Matthäus away. But how could I steal it?

He can't see me, I thought. I'm thinking of this wrong. I don't have to be the hunted. I can be the *huntress*.

I surveyed the woods around me. A nearby juniper tree with a tangled trunk looked like it would be easy enough to climb. I clambered up it, hurrying, finding a place to crouch about halfway up—far enough that I would be out of his reach, but not so far that I couldn't jump. Pulling my hood down, tying my *tarnkappe* as tight about me as I could, I drew my bow.

I could feel him moving closer, monstrous, malignant. As I lay in wait, I thought of the dagger he commanded his assassin to put in Rika's heart, the hand he slipped under my shift, the sickly sweet taste of his vile mouth on mine. Let him come, I thought, nocking an arrow.

And then there he was. The largest wolf I'd ever seen, loping out of the shadows. A terrible thing, *wrong*, with none of the beauty of the natural beast. He was grotesque. His shoulders malformed, bones sticking out, his chest barrel-shaped and huge. His fur rippled like smoke. He moved slowly, lifting his snout to sniff the air, as if he was trying to find my scent.

I smiled. He didn't know where I was. Pulling the cloak tighter about me had helped to obscure my location from him.

He loped closer, snout raised, sniffing the air without stopping to linger on my particular tree. He snarled something, a single sound, a guttural sound, more gnarl than speech. He growled, frustrated, tried again. This time, it was close enough to words that I could make out what he meant. *"Haeeel. I kno' yo' herrrre."*

I stiffened, afraid. Perhaps my leg moved slightly against the trunk. He looked up, snarled, ears flattening, hackles rising, sniffing the air around my tree. When I saw his face, my stomach turned with revulsion, with hate. Eyes like holes, gaping wide. I would only get one shot at him.

He growled, showing his teeth.

I aimed my arrow at his heart. If my shot killed him, problem solved. But if it didn't—he was so large—better that it lodge someplace difficult to get out. Saying a quick prayer that my aim would be true, I let the arrow fly. It soared down at him, striking him in his barreled chest before he could even flinch, and he let out a canine howl of pain.

"Haelllll!" He whined, pawing at the arrow. It had struck deep enough that it would not easily come out. When his paw struck its shaft, he whined in pain. Then his body was shaking, changing, the smoke of his fur beginning to ripple. Tendrils of shadow dissolved into mist where his shoulders had been. His fur disappearing, becoming nothing, leaving a man crumpled on the forest floor in its place, bloodied, moaning, inspecting the arrow in his chest.

As I had expected, he had taken the wolf-skin off so he could use his hands to remove the arrow. He moved to check the wound, squinting. It was so close to his heart, he was afraid to pull it out. The wolf-skin lay beside him, forgotten, a malignant thing. I could feel it pulling shadow from the next world—a cloud dark and stinking, hellish—even without him in it.

I returned my bow to its place on my back, pulled my cloak tight, and dropped from my tree. Everything was going according to my plan. He still couldn't see me.

He flinched at the sound of my feet hitting the ground. "Haelewise!" he screamed, furious, my name a moan of pain, his eyes wild, searching for me.

"I'm here," I whispered, taking great joy in imagining how the words would seem to him. My voice singsong like a child's, echoing from the shadow as if I were some sort of demon. I moved quickly as soon as I said the words, dancing as it occurred to me what to say next: the words he'd said to me in the hall on the mountain. "Are you afraid of me?"

Ulrich closed his eyes, shuddering, revulsion on his face. I couldn't tell if it was a reaction to pain, or what I'd said, or both.

His body went rigid, and I could see fear warring with anger on his face. The anger was to be expected, it was part of who he was, but the fear surprised me. I took a perverse pleasure in that fear, I confess. I never claimed to be a holy woman.

I laughed inwardly, imagining the world from his perspective, crumpled on the forest floor, arrowshot by the girl he tried to rape and kill.

Ulrich pushed himself up to his hands and knees, then stood, breaking off the part of the arrow that was not sunk in his chest. "No," he said, quietly furious. "I'm not afraid. You're just a girl. A girl who's very confused about the way the world works. You harbored my wife at Gothel. You accused me of murder, when all I did was deliver a punishment that was well within my rights. Frederika was a whore, a faithless wife."

His voice had gone very calm while he spoke, as if he was honestly trying to explain these things to me. He searched the forest around him, trying to ascertain my location. Without the wolf-skin, he had no idea where I was.

By then I was standing behind him, where the wolf-skin lay crumpled, forgotten on the ground. When I crept up to retrieve it as I had been planning, the otherworldly weather went berserk. Power zapped from this world to the next and back, ricocheting, drawn to my invisible hand. It was like being stung by a thousand wasps. I screamed, leaping away, realizing the *tarnkappe* and the wolf-skin couldn't be carried by the same person at once; the mist didn't know which direction to go.

Ulrich turned toward the sound. "There you are," he said, clearly taking pleasure in the sound of my pain, though I could tell he was also trying to decipher the reason for my scream. After a moment, he looked down and saw the wolf-skin.

He smiled and bent down to pick it up.

My heart sank. Dread filled my stomach.

He pulled one of its sleeves over his arm, speaking conversationally, his voice maddeningly calm.

"I'm going to punish you. You've done worse to me than Rika. I'll have to be in hiding forever. My family will live in shame. Did you really think you would be safe at Gothel? When I have *this*?"

He pulled the other sleeve on.

Terrible tongues of shadow began to lick the air around him, covering his body in grotesque sinew. His shoulders grew broader, his figure became bulkier, and shadows sprouted from his skin. His nose sank into his mouth, elongating into a snout. His eyes fell in on themselves. The process was so grotesque, I shuddered. Everything about it was wrong.

He sniffed the air, scenting me out. After a moment, his sunken eyes fixed on the air where I couldn't be seen. He lunged straight for me, snarling, raking a claw across my breast.

I fell beneath him. He pawed at me, pushing my hood to the forest floor. Unhooded, he could meet my eyes. He snarled, leering. His breath was foul. *"I'm goin' to ennnjoyy this."*

He pushed me down, the weight of his claws painful on my chest. They stung, tearing through the fabric of my cloak, my dress. I braced myself, waiting for it to happen. He opened his mouth, his teeth flashing white in the moonlight.

Then the smoke of his fur began to ripple. The sinews of his shoulders began to dissolve into mist. His fur disappearing, he whirled around, clawing at what appeared to be thin air.

I heard a yelp.

"Matthäus!" I screamed, pulling the dagger from my belt. It flashed, silver, as I plunged it into the great wolf's back.

The beast fell. The shadows shriveled and shrank.

Matthäus uncloaked beside the crumpled form of Ulrich, holding the wolf-skin in his hand, grinning a roguish grin. His sleeve had been torn, but it was only slightly bloodied. He followed my eyes. "Don't worry. It isn't bad. Are you all right?"

I looked down at the wounds on my breast. I couldn't feel a thing. My heart was pounding so hard, I had forgotten about them. "The baby," I said. "Where did you put the baby?"

He dropped the wolf-skin and hurried away.

I pushed myself up on my hand to look at Ulrich. He lay on his side, curled up like a child in bed, moaning. The dagger had gone deep into his back, and he was bleeding badly. His eyes were wild, as he looked at me. He knew death was coming.

I gazed at him without speaking, waiting for him to leave this world. I knew we would all be the better for it when he was gone. I felt no pity for him. The balance tilted, and I felt the next world pull.

In a moment, it happened. His soul left his mouth—a stinking thing, clouded. The veil hissed as it swallowed it up.

A few tendrils of shadow slipped out through the fissure toward the wolf-skin. I looked over at the miserable thing. I was revulsed by the way it clawed at the air, the malignant shadow it drew around it. As soon as I showed it to Kunegunde, I decided, we would destroy it. She would need to see it for herself.

Matthäus came back with the child.

"Where did you put her?"

"Forgive me," he said. "I made her a cradle from the sling and hung it from a tree. I needed to be sure you were all right."

Ignoring the pain returning to the wounds in my chest, I took the baby from his arms, wrapping her in the sling, looking into her eyes. She was so perfect, so pure, so unaware of anything that had just happened. For a split second, everything seemed right with the world. I held her tight.

CHAPTER THIRTY-FOUR

W e called our horses back and mounted them, debating whether
to wear our cloaks the rest of the way. We figured we should
in case the king's men should stumble upon us. But if we tried to
carry the wolf-skin cloaked, the otherworldly weather went wild.
In the end, we decided Matthäus and his horse would wear *tarnkappen*, but my horse and I would go uncloaked so we could carry the
wolf-skin in a sack. The tower wasn't far. It was only a little ways
into the forest before we were approaching the circle. Two ravens
dove from the sky to circle us. I heard Matthäus suck in his breath.
I could feel his anxiety beside me, though I couldn't see his face.
When the ravens began diving at him, despite being cloaked, I
squeezed Nëbel's flanks. She stopped, whinnying.

"What is it?" he whispered, his voice filled with dread.

"Animals can sense magic."

As we drew near enough to the tower to see the boulders that
spiked up like teeth, I reminded him about the protective spell that
kept this place hidden from the eyes of men. He nodded, remembering, his expression full of foreboding. I hadn't thought about
what it would be like for him to stay at Gothel. Without his sight,
he would be dependent on me until he learned his way around.

We dismounted our horses and took off their hoods to lead them
through the stone circle. They were spooked—neighing, wild-eyed—
with the ravens flying about and the mist. We wrapped their leads
three times around our arms. The ravens flew back to the tower,
calling out. Their croaks echoed. The baby cried out. I held her tight
and rocked her, swaying my hips. "Hush," I told her, "hush—"

Then I turned to Matthäus. "Remove your hood."

Matthäus shrugged his hood off and reached out, letting me lead him toward the stone circle. The horses pulled on their leads behind us, whinnying, reluctant. The spell snapped through the air between the boulders, eager for the chance to make something happen. The hair on my arms and legs stood on end. The baby went quiet too, as if she could sense the magic. And then, blinking with the insight, I realized that she probably could. She had the gift.

As I bent down to kiss her forehead, everything seemed to fall into place. It felt right to be hurrying toward the tower with the child and Matthäus.

We stepped through the stone circle, clutching each other's hands. Our feet landed in unison. The air around us was thinner than ever.

Up ahead, we could hear the sound of water burbling into the pool where I had once bathed. Through the trees, I could see the water glittering. A family of gray geese and their half-grown yellow goslings were floating on it, fast asleep, beaks tucked under their wings. As we drew close, most of the gray geese flew away in a burst of feathers, but the mother goose stayed behind with her goslings to hiss at us.

Matthäus let out a nervous laugh as we circled the pool, a safe distance away from her. "She's so angry."

The bird Kunegunde called Zweite dove down at Matthäus, until I shooed him away. Matthäus's voice was frightened. "Haelewise. The spell. I can't see."

"I can. Hold my hand," I told him. "Don't let go."

I led him through the trees, the horses following behind us. The baby watched me, wide-eyed, from her sling, more aware than I had ever seen a newborn be. An amber-eyed raven flew back toward us and dove at Matthäus's face. *Kraek*, the bird screamed, as Matthäus threw up his hands. It dove at him again and again, pecking his cheeks, his forehead.

"Go home," I screamed, immediately regretting it. The effort of screaming made the wounds on my breast sting, and the baby started crying. "Give me a chance to explain," I continued more quietly, as I tried to soothe the infant.

The bird dove at Matthäus one more time—a warning—then flew away. Behind me, he cleared his throat, his hands still protecting his face. "Is it gone? Did that bird just *listen* to you?"

"Yes," I said, knowing he wouldn't believe me if I tried to explain it. "Are you hurt? Let me see your face."

He opened his hands, and I saw that his cheeks were covered in pockmarks. They looked just like the ones my father had after he found someone to write a letter to the bishop. He came *here*, I realized. Kunegunde wrote that letter for him.

My mind reeled. "Do they hurt?" I asked after a moment.

"I'll be all right."

Cautiously, we resumed our walk. Soon the tower rose up before us, hazy with thin moonlight, the vine-covered walls of the garden behind it, the stable shadowy and peaceful. The sight of the place made me draw in my breath with a strange mixture of relief and anxiety. On the one hand, with Ulrich dead, we were safer here than we had been fleeing the castle. On the other, there was the matter of Kunegunde and the fact that I had brought a man with me.

I put the horses in the stable, then took off our hoods and led Matthäus slowly toward the tower. Behind me, with his free hand, he fumbled for the paternoster beads in his coin-purse, saying the prayer under his breath.

Kunegunde opened the heavy door when we were a stone's throw away. "Haelewise," she called out in a warning tone, her black and white hair tumbling down over her shoulders in wild tangles. Her golden eyes flashed with warning. "Men are not welcome here."

The baby made a mewling sound at my breast. I clutched Matthäus's hand tighter than ever. He squeezed mine in response, his face stricken with fear. I was glad he couldn't see the look on my grandmother's face. "We had nowhere else to go."

"What have you got in that sling?"

"A child with the gift. The mother, Princess Ursilda, was nearly killed by King Frederick's assassin."

Kunegunde shook her head slowly. "King Frederick—"

"Ursilda says you're still a daughter-of-the-Mother. That you're bound by oath to help us."

"The daughters are enlisting the help of men now?" She looked at Matthäus, sizing him up. "He is of the enemy. Do you not see the beads in his hand? The prayer he invokes?"

"It's the Mother who has been speaking to me all this time. I know you know that. She wants to be restored to her throne, to reunite with the Father on earth—"

"You're going to get yourself killed," Kunegunde said bitterly. She shook her head, then closed her eyes and drew a deep breath.

I met her eyes. "Not if you let us in. Kunegunde, please. This child's life hangs in the balance."

Kunegunde glanced at the baby in my arms. All she could see was the back of its head. "Boy or girl?" she asked, her voice hesitant.

"Girl," I said. "Let us in. This man helped me kill Ulrich!"

"He what?"

"Ulrich is dead. Matthäus took the wolf-skin from his back."

Her eyes widened. "Did he *really*?"

I showed it to her. She took the malignant thing from my hands, her nose crinkling at its stench. Then she gave me a giddy smile. "Oh, Haelewise, thank you. What a gift. We'll burn it tonight!"

"Now please," I said. "We're wounded. Let us inside."

She shook her head, meeting my eyes. "No. This doesn't change anything. You and the baby may stay, but he cannot."

Matthäus straightened, uneasy. The paternoster beads rattled in his hands. "I won't tell a soul what happens here," Matthäus spoke up, his voice pleading. "I swear it. I'd never do anything that would harm Haelewise."

My thoughts raced. How could I convince Kunegunde to let Matthäus stay? I couldn't bear to lose him again. Not after all we'd been through. "Gothel is safe now, Kunegunde. We're handfasted. Matthäus is to me what your lord was to you. I would trust him with my life."

Kunegunde closed her eyes, breathing softly, as if she had grown tired of arguing with us. When she spoke, there was a finality in her tone, a frustration that she needed to explain herself again. "I pity you, Haelewise. In truth, I do. But this is not my law. It's the law of this place. Nothing you say now can change the choice before you. You can protect this baby here, or go with him. If he tries to stay, I'll drive him out."

My stomach dropped. All my plans, the life I'd imagined with Matthäus, the task I was completing for the Mother, began to waver. I loved him with my whole heart, but where would we go if not here? Gothel was the safest place for the child, now that we had the wolf-skin. We couldn't run from the king's assassins indefinitely.

I imagined what it would be like for the three of us to flee the king. We would be like the Holy Family fleeing Herod, crossing rivers and deserts in search of some distant hiding place. A mountain village in Moravia. A cave in Egypt. Everywhere, looking over our shoulders. All because I couldn't bear to be parted from Matthäus.

I looked at Matthäus, saw the shame on his face. He didn't want me to have to make this choice any more than I did.

The baby made a cooing sound, looking up, her black eyes—wide and innocent—watching, waiting.

It wouldn't be fair. I couldn't put her life in danger.

I searched Matthäus's face. Grief ripped through me. I wanted to pull my grandmother limb from limb.

"I'm sorry," I told him quietly. "This is the only safe place."

Kunegunde chuckled. "Finally, you understand—"

"I can't endanger the child for our sake."

Matthäus bowed his head. It took him a moment to answer. "I understand."

"Would you wait for me until Ursilda takes the child back? You could go back to your wife—" I winced. "You could work in your father's shop."

He nodded, quickly, trying to master the hurt that showed clearly on his face.

"I don't know how long it will be, I'll be honest."

"I would wait for you forever."

"What a *sweet* little arrangement you've made," Kunegunde said, a shadow passing over her face, quickly enough that I didn't recognize what it meant. She smiled, as if she were moved by the love we had just shown each other. I thought at first that it was genuine. Then her voice turned monstrous and cold. "You've figured everything out, haven't you, little one. But I'm afraid it isn't enough."

I thought back to what had happened after Albrecht left the tower, the lies he told the king, the writ that had been issued for her death. She wasn't going to let Matthäus leave. "Kunegunde," I said. "Wait—"

Her posture straightened and her eyes snapped up from her feet. She drew up her shoulders and opened her mouth, a sorrowful expression on her face.

"*Xär dhorns,*" she sang, her voice shaking with regret. The words drew the air taut. Something zipped through the air, a power, and my skin prickled with a horripilation of dread. She fumbled in her pouch and uncorked a phial. With a flick of her wrist, a cloud of powder hit Matthäus. His face crumpled. "My eyes!"

The babe began to cry in her sling.

"Kunegunde?" I screamed, my voice rising with desperation. "What are you doing? Please, I'm begging you. Stop!"

When Kunegunde spoke the words she spoke next—words I only heard once but found in her spellbook after she died—the world collapsed in on itself. "*Kord agnator vividvant-svas!*"

All the power her words summoned seemed to hang for a moment in the air around Matthäus. I was sure it was going to kill him, terrified I was going to watch him die. Then it entered him, like a blast of mist against his chest. He stumbled backward, and when he looked up next, his face was blank. Not blank as it had been before due to blindness, but blank due to forgetfulness.

"Matthäus?" I whispered.

He turned toward the sound of my voice. "Who are you? Where am I?" he said, letting go of my hand. "Why can't I see?"

The baby cried louder in her sling. I rocked her, staring in horror at him. "It's me. Haelewise."

"Haelewise?" he said, as if he were repeating the name of a song he hadn't heard.

Kunegunde met my eyes, smiling sadly. "I'm sorry."

"Why doesn't he know who I am?"

"He can't leave here with his memory of you intact. He'll keep coming back, over and over. He'll lead men to us. The place will be crawling with them."

I sobbed. "Kunegunde. What have you done?"

"Everything that is done can be undone."

It took me a moment to understand what she meant. I turned to Matthäus, panicked. "My name is Haelewise," I said, my voice choked. "Your childhood friend, your—"

"Don't listen to her, dear," Kunegunde interrupted. "She'll just confuse you. This will all be over soon. Don't worry. I'll lead you out of this mist and home to your wife."

His eyes widened, searching the mist for the source of her voice. He nodded, slowly, as if remembering. "Phoebe," he said, looking relieved to be sure of something. He turned toward the sound of Kunegunde's voice. "Yes. Please. Take me to her."

I forgot to breathe. The world went white. I went numb with disbelief. It was too much to see his love for me so completely unmade.

I couldn't watch as Kunegunde led him from the tower. My breath hitched, and my shoulders shook. I wanted to run after them, stop Matthäus from going to Phoebe, find a way to break the spell and run away with him and the child into the desert. But I had made my choice.

The child began to wail in my arms. After a while, her cries became more insistent, and I knew she needed to be fed. I found Kunegunde's birth bag and the goat's horn with the cloth teat. Then I walked to the barn and milked a she-goat in her sleep. When the horn was full, I found my way back to the chair where Kunegunde often sat. The baby calmed immediately when I offered her the goat's horn. As she suckled, I cradled her in her sling, rocking her, nursing the ache in my heart.

Tears wet my cheeks.

I don't know how long I sat there, crying. Long after the babe had fallen asleep. The sobs that poured out of me were wretched. The next thing I knew, the shadows in the room had changed, and the baby was crying again in her sling. Had I fallen asleep? How much time had passed? Was she hungry again? Was she wet?

I changed her swaddling. Then back to the barn I went to milk the she-goat. As I sat in the chair with her, the child sucked noisily on the goat's horn, making soft little gasping noises. I rocked her back and forth.

She looked up at me, her eyes hungry and full of gratitude.

For a while, I found myself numb even to the pleasure of nursing her. But when the horn was empty and she threw her head back into the crook of my arm, milk-drunk, the mother in me reawakened. The heft of her, her softness, the smoothness of her skin. She was alive. I had saved her like I was supposed to do. She was a boon, a gift. The only thing that I'd ever done right.

I took solace in the comfort I felt, rocking her as she slept in my arms. I felt my mother's presence inside me, as I sang the lullaby she sang to me and my brothers. *Sleep until morning, my dear one. Eostre leaves honey and sweet eggs—*

With these words, I conjured her, and I understood what all mothers must. The babe looking up at me was a person, a living breathing person, and it was a blessing to be responsible for her.

She needed a name. I needed something to call her.

I thought back to the herb her mother asked for all those times from the midwife. The baby had craved it when she was inside her mother. She was a tough little thing. She had already survived so much.

I held her close and whispered the word in her ear: *Rapunzel.*

CHAPTER THIRTY-FIVE

Y ou have no doubt heard the story Princess Ursilda told her father. It spread like wildfire, took on a life of its own. A witch stole the baby from the castle, locked the girl in a tower, and kept the girl out of greed. The witch let the vines of her garden go wild, snaking their way up the tower, choking the window where the girl looked out, singing. The truth is the girl was there with her mother's permission. After Ulrich's body was found, the grieving Albrecht went mad. Blaming the king for all of it—his son's death, the baby's kidnapping—Albrecht withdrew from court and locked his family in the inner chambers of his castle. He wouldn't come out until thirty years later when King Frederick died.

When Kunegunde returned from escorting Matthäus home, she treated the wounds I'd sustained in the battle with Ulrich. The next day, she burned the wolf-skin in the garden. She tried to make a ritual of it. The fire stank. She offered me spiced wine, but I had no stomach for it. I left the cup untouched, watching the bonfire with Rapunzel in my arms. I wanted more than anything to leave Gothel, but before my wounds had even healed, a pregnant woman brought news that the king had issued a writ for my death. Nowhere else was safe.

I had no choice but to serve as my grandmother's apprentice, isolated from the circle at her insistence. I looked everywhere for the lockbox full of alrūne she'd once kept beneath the stone in the cellar floor, but I never found it. During that first month, we fought every day. I tried to convince her to let me eat the alrūne; when she refused, I railed at her, but there was nothing I could do. I needed to keep Rapunzel safe.

Sometimes, as I was feeding Rapunzel a bottle, the air would shimmer, and I would know Ursilda was watching. In those moments, I was near overcome by the sadness I sensed from the other side of the shimmering. Without alrūne, my attempts to cast the spell to speak with her were hopeless.

I thought of Matthäus every day. Sometimes, when Kunegunde caught me sobbing, wretched, she offered to erase my memory. "Let me make you forget him," she said. I told her no, of course—I treasured my memories—but I never tried to leave the tower to see him. Any attempt to correct his forgetfulness would cause me too much pain.

As the months passed, I resigned myself to a life without him. Even when I grew ill in the mornings. Even when my belly began to swell. For you see, what the stories do not tell is that Rapunzel grew up with a sister. A girl with black eyes and dark curls. I named her after her father: Matthea.

She lived without knowing him for five years.

Then one October, Kunegunde died of a fever. As soon as I buried her, I poured out the gift-taking powder she had been making me take in the wood. I went to gather alrūne fruit from my mother's garden, and soon, I felt the Mother enveloping me, filling me with love and purpose.

I pulled the locked spellbook down from the top shelf where Kunegunde kept it in the kitchen, unlocked it, and started working my way through my grandmother's spells. I stared for a long time at the last spell in the book, a working that was supposed to bless a daughter with great power. When cast on a girl who already had the gift, it dedicated her to the Mother completely. In return, the Mother would grant her love, good health, and a long, full existence. There were only two ingredients to the spell: a dozen alrūne plants, eaten whole, and a human life.

In those first weeks of quiet study, at night, while my daughters slept, I used Kunegunde's books and the water-*spiegel* to reach out to Beatrice and the other daughters-of-the-Mother. I joined the circle and took the oath. Of what came of that, I can say very little. I am bound by blood-magic not to speak or write of it. I can say, however, that we worked to put the Mother back together. Beatrice introduced me to a woman who knew my mother when she was part of the circle. Hedda had been a promising apprentice of startling power, not easily forgotten by anyone who met her, before she married my father. This woman taught me the secret of the figurine. It only worked to conjure a ghost on the first full moon after the autumn equinox and the nights surrounding it.

On the full moon, I used the figurine to conjure my mother's ghost. I still remember the joy I felt when she embraced me again. We talked for hours that night. The spell worked better at Gothel and on the night of the full moon proper so she could stay in this world for longer. She told me why the Mother sent me on the quest that led me back to Gothel. I was needed to keep the tower, to be there for other women who needed the Mother's sanctuary.

She also told me Matthäus might remember me now that Kunegunde was gone. The next night, after I put the girls to bed, I sent my soul into Zweite and flew to Matthäus's cottage, telling myself I was only going to look in on him. But when I got there, I couldn't help myself.

I guided the raven to land on his windowsill and croaked to get his attention. He looked up from his sewing, five years older, a man's beard at his jaw, his eyes tired. There were calluses on his hands. When I flew in to land beside his needle, he mouthed my name, a question on his face. I croaked at him, nervous, dancing this way and that through his sewing room. He grabbed his things, hurried outside, and followed me into the wood, speaking excitedly as he walked. He said his memory had returned to him like the memory of a dream. It had come back over the last few weeks in flashes: our childhood friendship, his imprisonment at the palace, the nights we spent together on our journey, the choice I had made to keep the baby safe. He wanted to find me and ask me about it, but he couldn't find the tower. "Did it all really happen?" he kept asking with an expression of complicated disbelief. "The *tarnkappen*, the mirror, the wolf, the spell that made me forget?"

Kraek was all I could say until we reached the tower and my soul could reenter my flesh. "It was real," I said, running to the edge of the stone circle to meet him. "All of it."

His face crumpled, and he tried to walk into the stone circle to embrace me, but he couldn't see anything but mist inside. That spell hadn't faded when Kunegunde died. I led him back out, and we talked for a long time just outside the stone circle, the spell zapping behind us. He cried when I told him that I had borne him a child.

After a while, I knew he would follow me back to the tower. It wasn't something we discussed. It was just the way he looked at me, the tension in the air. As we stood together in the woods, talking, I got goose bumps. The feeling that there was something between us, drawing us together, returned. I reached for his hand. He was silent, his palm warm against mine, as I led him through the stone circle, toward the tower, upstairs. After five years apart, the thing between us had grown strong enough to speak for both of us. In the chamber that had once been Kunegunde's, we reached for each other. Blind, he ran his hands over the curves of my body, seeing me the only way he could on the bed covered in furs. We cried together that night, holding each other tight, mourning all the time together we'd missed. We didn't sleep at all. He told me about the children Phoebe had borne him. The softness she'd developed toward him. In the morning, after he met the girls, we said goodbye until Yule, when he promised to return. We both understood. I had my life and he had his.

Those first few years, I spent most of my time raising the girls, seeing clients—woodwives with troubled pregnancies, young women in times of great need—saving lives, telling stories, doing the work I was called to do. Ten years after I returned to Gothel, I received a letter from Mother Hildegard, delivered by a trusted nun who had transferred to a nearby monastery. The letter was written in the *lingua ignota*. The nun had to translate it for me.

Mother Hildegard had met a nun from Zwiefalten whose dearest sister I'd brought back from death's door. This nun reported that when I laid hands on her sister, I spoke an ancient prayer in a language like none she'd ever heard. Hildegard wondered if this was the same language she'd found engraved on the stones from the shrine. At the bottom of the letter were several columns of runes. She asked me to let the nun teach me the *lingua ignota* so I could write her back and teach her to translate them. It was thus that we struck up our long correspondence.

Between letters and clients, I gathered herbs. I raised my daughters. I wrote in this book. Once a season, Matthäus came to us. Once a season, we were a family. He came four nights a year, without fail, meeting me at the edge of the circle on the night of the solstice or equinox. Holding hands, we walked back to the tower together, the shadow between us drawing us together, as always. After the girls went to sleep, he spent the night with me in perfect darkness, running his hands over my body, seeing me the only way he could.

He didn't stop coming to see me, even when Rapunzel left the tower. He didn't stop coming, even when Matthea married a woodcutter and he could visit her on his own. He didn't stop coming, even when he grew stooped and old. When the solstice passed one winter and he didn't come, I knew he would come no more. I found his grave behind his cottage and worked no magic for a year. The girls grieved him with me. They have children of their own now, whom they've taught the old ways. We're all part of the circle. After Matthäus died, my children and grandchildren began coming to the tower to celebrate solstices and equinoxes with me.

That was ten years ago. I no longer know what to do with myself when I am alone in the tower. I'm lost when there are no visitors to care for, no potions to make. Casting spells no longer fills me with excitement. My mind wanders. My hands shake. I have become an old woman, getting ready to leave behind the world of things. One day soon, the air will grow taut, and my soul will leave my body for the last time. I will find out what the next world is like, the world beyond the veil.

I suspect only my obsession with finishing this manuscript—with writing this story—has kept me here as long as I have stayed. This is the last task the Mother has set before me, to gather her fragments, record these events for a world that has forgotten her. Now that I have reached my story's end, I am hesitant to turn the page. If I call this book finished, what have I to look forward to, except the last journey I will make?

EPILOGUE

I blinked, eyes burning, when I finished the last page of the codex. The parchment sprang under my touch, still flexible after all these years. Closing my eyes, I felt my heart ache for Haelewise and Matthäus and Ursilda. I saw Rapunzel and Matthea dancing in that legendary garden. I saw a saint—unlike any saint ever described by holy scribes—carefully copying down a list of pagan runes. I saw Alemannic words and phrases on the backs of my eyelids, the doodles in the margins of wild men and women, wortcunner's tools, misshapen roots and bright green herbs. In all my years studying Middle High German literature, I had seen nothing like this codex. A translation of it could make my career.

Rubbing my temples, I reached into my purse for the bottle of sumatriptan, which had been my stalwart companion throughout the reading experience, wondering how I would classify the manuscript in my preface. As literature? As visionary text? Or something else?

The cellar spun. My head ached. I had taken three doses of sumatriptan already, one more dose than my physician advised. Every few hours, that bizarre static electric charge would return to the air, and the lightbulb hanging from the ceiling would start to seem too bright, flickering faintly, as if the cellar had electrical problems. About halfway through the manuscript, that static electricity had come on and stayed on, so palpable that it seemed less a symptom than the *cause* of my migraine. I tried to tell myself it was just a shift in the air pressure, a symptom of the rainstorm that was battering the mountain, but after so many hours immersed in the manuscript,

my thoughts kept circling another explanation entirely, like an air-
craft whose pilot was desperate to put off a landing.

When I read the passage where Haelewise pulled the lockbox
from the uneven stone in the floor, I'd looked up at the stone in
front of me and seen her do it as clear as day. Haelewise, daughter-
of-Hedda, introduced herself as a storyteller. Of course there would
be exaggerations, the sort of details that bring a fireside yarn to
life, but I couldn't discount the manuscript altogether as a fiction.
There was the declaration of truth, and it'd been found in a place
mentioned in the manuscript. It had to have some autobiographical
elements, didn't it? The cellar where I sat was the inspiration for
the actual cellar of the tower in the manuscript. It *had* to be. The
architecture was a fit; the buttresses and curved archways were pre-
Romanesque, old enough to be built centuries before the signature
date.

I closed the book, careful not to put undue pressure on the cover.
I stared at the sigil for a long time, giving in, finally, to the urge to
trace it with my finger, wondering if Frau Vogel had any idea of
the historical significance of this cellar. I put the codex back in the
lockbox and headed upstairs, wondering if she would allow me to
digitize the manuscript right away. I could write both German and
English editions. Two books! The thought filled me with a giddy
relief. If I signed a contract before I applied, the promotion and tenure committee would have no choice but to accept my application.

Opening the cellar door, I had no idea what time it was. The
kitchen was dark. The only sounds were the ticking of a clock, the
planks of the ancient wood floor creaking beneath my feet. I called
for Frau Vogel, but she didn't answer. Through the large window
I could see the moon hanging low in the sky, round and full. I
caught myself thinking about what that meant for the otherworldly
weather, then chided myself, though even the reluctant pilot in my
mind had to admit it would explain the static electricity in the air.

My migraine was about to put me out of commission altogether, despite the sumatriptan, and—if my thoughts on the moon phase were any indication—my sanity was evaporating. I tried to drag my thoughts out of the manuscript and back into the modern world, where I was an academic who *studied* medieval literature instead of *living* it, but the modern world I thought I knew was slipping out of reach.

I felt warm; my face was flushed. Frau Vogel was nowhere to be seen. Since I arrived, I'd only emerged from the cellar a handful of times to use the bathroom or eat the meals she prepared for me, but she had always been waiting for me in the kitchen. When I tried to talk to her about the manuscript, she refused, telling me she would prefer to wait until I had read the whole thing.

The cuckoo clock on the wall said it was half past three. Looking out the window at the tangled yard, I was struck by the sudden desire to see this place anew, now that I understood what it had once been. I set the lockbox on the coffee table and crept outside.

My rental car glowed cherry red in the moonlight. It seemed like a relic of someone else's life entirely.

From the end of the drive, I turned to take in the rambling cottage that had been built over the cellar. It was a typical Black Forest cottage with one of those giant thatched roofs that swept almost all the way down to the ground. The ash trees that shaded it glistened with raindrops, bright and wet. I squinted, trying to imagine the ancient tower that had once stretched up from the cellar, the garden wall that would've enclosed the yard behind it. For a moment, I saw it in my mind's eye, and then it vanished.

"*Frau Professorin?*" Frau Vogel was standing at the door in a long white nightgown. Her hair was loose, falling all the way down her back, glistening an unearthly white. "*Sie sind fertig.*"

I nodded. "I'm done."

She motioned for me to come inside, and I followed her into the living room, where she turned on several lamps. She took the codex from the lockbox and placed it in her lap. She sat in a chair, and I sat beside her. "*Und?*" she asked.

"It's astonishing."

I launched into a description of the contents of the first half of the manuscript: the declaration of truth, Haelewise's early life, her desire to be a mother and midwife, her journey to the wise woman's tower. Frau Vogel listened closely, especially when I talked about the tower's cellar, which so closely resembled the one beneath this cottage. I explained that I thought the tower had once been a real structure. That centuries after this manuscript was written, it could've crumbled, and her cottage built where it stood. That Haelewise, daughter-of-Hedda, could've put that manuscript in that lockbox herself. That the story held some fragments of truth.

She searched my face, her expression solemn. "Do you really think so?"

"I do."

A complicated smile spread over her face. Her eyes watered. She smoothed her nightgown over her lap and nodded for me to go on.

I smiled back at her, tears burning my own eyes. "It would be tempting to classify the manuscript as fiction—a late example of the Middle High German 'flowering time.' Or we might categorize it as mystical literature, notable not least because of its heresy. The wise woman teaches Haelewise to cast incantations, and she claims to witness a murder through the eyes of a bird. But the story also involves real historical characters, details that match up with history."

As I talked, Frau Vogel turned to the illuminations that illustrated the events I referenced. She found them surprisingly quickly, as if she had memorized their locations. As if she had been reading the manuscript for years.

"Frau Vogel," I blurted, professional courtesy be damned. "How long has it been since you found the manuscript?"

She smiled. "My mother showed it to me when I was little. She couldn't read it, but she showed me the pictures, passing down the story her mother told her, and *her* mother before her."

My mouth dropped. "You—"

She waited for me to piece it together.

"You—you're Haelewise's descendant?"

Frau Vogel nodded gently.

I met her eyes, but she didn't elaborate. My head spun. The tick of the cuckoo clock seemed suddenly too loud. Questions buzzed in my brain like a swarm of bees, purposeful, insistent. Why did she pretend she didn't know what the manuscript was? I remembered her question about my religion in email, how long she let me talk about the manuscript just now before she opened up. She had been testing me all this time. But what did she want me to *do* with this information? What did this mean for the manuscript's veracity, for the static electricity I could still feel in the air? The energy buzzed, insistent, demanding that I reckon with it. I cast around in my brain for something coherent to say, trying to decide which question to ask first.

"What do you want from me?" I said finally.

"A translation, of course. Publication. I want you to teach it."

"Why go public with it after all this time?"

Her expression was so pained, my breath caught in my throat.

"I don't have anyone to share it with," she said. "I am childless. I tried to interest my sister and her children, but they're very *orthodox*. They don't want anything to do with it." Her face crumpled, and she turned so that I couldn't see her expression. I could tell she was working hard to keep her composure.

"*Entschuldigung*," she said finally, her voice choked. She got up and stepped into the next room. I heard her moving about the kitchen, opening a cabinet, as if she was looking for something. When she returned, she was holding something, though I couldn't see what it was.

"I want you to teach the codex. Write about it. Spread this story far and wide. I think it's time."

I met her eyes, baffled that she had chosen to approach me, an

American, when there were so many more acclaimed Middle High German scholars here in Germany. "Why me?"

"That talk you gave years ago at the Bücherschiff in Konstanz, about how illuminated manuscripts could reveal forgotten medieval women's lives. I wanted to show it to you then."

I thought back to the talk I gave at the Bücherschiff. It was one of my first lectures after I graduated. An older woman with salt-and-pepper hair had approached me after the talk. Frau Vogel, I realized now, a decade or so younger. Eyes shining, she'd squeezed my hand and whispered that my conclusions were more right than I knew.

We *had* met. The static electricity zapped through the air, suddenly twice as insistent, impossible to ignore. My head pulsed. I blinked, disoriented. Could Frau Vogel feel it too? She was watching me. I thought of Hildegard, the headaches she suffered, which historians now speculate were migraines. The visions that accompanied them. I could feel cracks forming in my carefully cultivated academic skepticism.

The pilot had finally decided to land.

Frau Vogel extended her arm, fingers closed tight around whatever she'd retrieved from the kitchen. She met my eyes, as if she were asking my permission. At first I had no idea what she was holding. And then, suddenly, I did. When I nodded, she opened her fist, and my heart soared with decades of suppressed ecstasy at the sight of it.

It was black soapstone. It had wings.

ACKNOWLEDGMENTS

I am grateful to so many people without whom this book would not exist.

I want to begin by thanking my late mother, who told the most incredible folktales at bedtime with great enthusiasm, and my late father, who filled the bookshelves of our childhood home with books. I want to thank my daughter, whose reactions to the folktales I told at bedtime inspired me to write this novel. And finally, I'm deeply grateful to my husband, David S. Bennett, the love of my life, whose support of my writing career has never wavered, not once. Thank you, thank you, thank you—for giving me the child who inspired this book, for the late-night brainstorming sessions, support, and encouragement when I needed it most. I love you.

In the publishing world, I want to start by thanking Sam Farkas, my wonderful agent, whose brilliant feedback, unwavering belief in this book, and nurturing presence have made the professional side of my writing life an utter joy. Thank you for your friendship and for being such a supportive force. I'm also grateful to the rest of the fantastic team at Jill Grinberg Literary Management; it's a wonder to be represented by such a talented, collaborative agency.

I am deeply indebted to Brit Hvide, my brilliant editor at Orbit/Redhook, whose excellent feedback, advocacy, and enthusiasm for Haelewise and her story have been a dream come true. Thank you for believing in Hael, for your advice on the prologue and epilogue, and for your tip that I wasn't quite done with Ulrich. I am incredibly lucky to get to work with you. I also want to thank Angeline Rodriguez, Bryn A. McDonald, Lisa Marie Pompilio, and the rest of the fantastic team at Orbit, as well as Emily Byron and Nadia Saward at Orbit UK, and Amy J. Schneider. It's been an honor to work with all of you.

I have been incredibly blessed with writing friends, whose support over the years has been invaluable. To Ronlyn Domingue, my writer soulmate—thank you for the decades of emails, phone calls, and manuscript reads. I'm so glad that we ended up in that workshop together, all those years ago, writing our weird speculative stories and dreaming of France. To Carolyn Turgeon and Jeanine Cummins, thank you from the bottom of my heart for your excellent advice, multiple reads of this manuscript, and many years of friendship. To Sally Rosen Kindred, thank you for reading and offering gentle guidance and support when I needed it most. To Sayward Byrd Stuart, thank you for decades of friendship, blue Lycra couches, and excellent advice on the Latinate phrasing of sexist peer reviewers. To Fox Henry Frazier, thank you for reading a late version of the manuscript and providing feedback, laughing with me and live-texting terrible TV during the pandemic, and serving as a contemporary real-life model of a witchy single mother in a tower.

I'm grateful to my teachers: Mara Malone, Jim Bennett, Moira Crone, David Madden, Andrei Codrescu, Rick Blackwood, Chuck Wachtel, and E. L. Doctorow; my colleagues and friends: Chad and Julie Brooks Barbour, Donna Fiebelkorn, and Barb Light; and my students, from whom I've learned so much.

I want to thank the many scholars of history, religion, language, and folklore whose research inspired me during the writing of this book, including the historian David Sheffler at the University of North Florida, who generously offered advice on twelfth-century Germany and Middle High German, and the translator and medieval German–literature scholar Peter Sean Woltemade, who offered expertise on German dialogue and Middle High German literature. All mistakes are my own. The following books were especially instrumental: *Daily Life in the Middle Ages* by Paul B. Newman (McFarland & Company, 2001); *Medieval Germany 1056–1273* by Alfred Haverkamp, translated by Helga Braun and Richard Mortimer (Oxford University Press, 1988); *Practicing Piety in Medieval Ashkenaz: Men, Women, and Everyday Religious Observance* by Elisheva Baumgarten (University of Pennsylvania Press, 2014); *At the Bottom of the Garden: A Dark History of Fairies, Hobgoblins, Nymphs, and Other Troublesome Things* by Diane Purkiss (New York University Press, 2000); *Witchcraft in Europe, 400–1700: A Documentary History* edited by Alan Charles Kors and Edward Peters (University of Pennsylvania Press, 2001); *Hildegard of Bingen: The Woman of Her Age* by Fiona Maddocks (Doubleday, 2001); *Hildegard of Bingen: A Visionary Life* by Sabina Flanagan (Routledge, 1998); *Hildegard of Bingen: Scivias* translated by Mother Columbia Hart and Jane Bishop (Paulist Press, 1990); *Hildegard von Bingen's Physica: The Complete English Translation of Her Classic Work on Health and Healing* translated by Priscilla Throop (Healing Arts Press, 1998); *The Personal Correspondence of Hildegard of Bingen* translated by Joseph L. Baird (Oxford University Press, 2006); *Hildegard of Bingen: On Natural Philosophy and Medicine: Selections from Cause Et Cure* translated by Margret Berger (D. S. Brewer, 1999); *The Chalice and the Blade: Our History, Our Future* by Riane Eisler (HarperCollins, 1988); *The Classic Fairy Tales* edited by Maria Tatar (W. W. Norton & Company, 1999); *The Annotated Brothers Grimm* edited by Maria Tatar (W. W. Norton & Company, 2004); *Breaking the Magic Spell: Radical Theories of Folk and Fairy Tales* by Jack Zipes (University Press of Kentucky, 2002); *Yiddish Folktales* edited by Beatrice Silverman Weinreich, translated by Leonard Wolf (Pantheon, 1988); and *A Middle High German Primer* by Joseph Wright (Oxford University Press, 1944).

Finally, I would like to thank the Sustainable Arts Foundation for the award that enabled me to travel to Germany to research this novel and walk in Haelewise's footsteps, as well as the National Endowment for the Arts and Vermont Studio Center for the parent-artist scholarship that paid for my residency at Vermont Studio Center, providing much-needed time to work on this book.

MEET THE AUTHOR

David S. Bennett

MARY MCMYNE has widely published stories and poems in venues like *Redivider, Gulf Coast, Strange Horizons,* and *Apex Magazine,* and her debut fairy-tale poetry chapbook, *Wolf Skin* (Dancing Girl Press, 2014), won the Elgin Chapbook Award. She is a graduate of the New York University MFA Program.

READING GROUP GUIDE

1. *The Book of Gothel* tells the origin story of the "Rapunzel" fairy tale but also imagines how other tales were influenced by historical events, including "Little Red Riding Hood" and "Snow White." Why is reexamining these tales important? Why do people keep retelling them? And what do you think the author is trying to say about the origins of folk and fairy tales?

2. In the three best-known classic versions of the "Rapunzel" story, Rapunzel's kidnapper is portrayed as a cruel ogress who entraps the maiden with magic (Basile's "Petrosinella"), a more sympathetic fairy who forgives Rapunzel at the end (De La Force's "Persinette"), and an evil witch (Grimm's "Rapunzel"). De La Force is one of the few female fairy tale authors whose stories are still popularly discussed. Given this information, what do you think these differences may say about the writers' own biases? What does *The Book of Gothel* say about Mary McMyne's views?

3. What fairy-tale characters do you feel deserve a second look and why? How would you explain their motives and actions?

4. Haelewise is discriminated against in her village because of her black eyes and fainting spells, and she is blamed for a sickness that falls over the village. During the late Middle Ages and beyond, huge numbers of women were persecuted as witches in Europe—for their physical and neurological differences, for perceived slights against others who were more powerful, or

for the threat they were thought to pose to society because they lived alone. Anyone who wasn't Christian was subject to extreme persecution too. How do you think the way we describe and talk about villainous figures in stories and real life has changed or stayed the same? What kinds of people do we villainize today?

5. Motherhood is a major theme in this novel; both Haelewise and a character in the frame story wish to be mothers. Why do you think Haelewise desires this so deeply? What do you think the novel has to say about why some women become mothers and the relationship between mothers and daughters?

6. Mary McMyne blends real historical figures into this otherwise fantastical tale—Hildegard of Bingen in particular plays a significant role. In history, Saint Hildegard was an abbess, writer, composer, philosopher, mystic, visionary, healer, and natural historian, despite church limitations set on women at the time. What does this portrayal of Hildegard say about her goals and beliefs? How is she able to maneuver within male-dominated spaces? What challenges does she face?

7. The mystical Tower of Gothel is a place where women in difficult and dangerous circumstances can seek refuge. Kunegunde offers women a safe haven and healing, including access to abortion. Why might women of the time require this service? How did you feel about this portrayal?

Dive deeper into *The Book of Gothel* with our reading group guide:

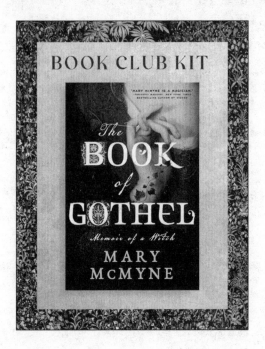

Scan the code or visit:

https://bit.ly/3BlWDfP

if you enjoyed
THE BOOK OF GOTHEL
keep reading for a sneak peek of
MARY MCMYNE'S NEXT NOVEL

My name has only been whispered heretofore....

Rose Rushe's passion for life runs deep—as a musician, an astrologist, and a sensualist. She laughs with her friend Cecely at warnings to guard their reputations. When Rose's father dies and a noble accuses them of witchcraft, they flee to London and to the only refuge available to women like them: marriage.

But while their reputations are safe, Rose can't hide who she truly is or the growing feelings she has for Cecely. When Rose's husband disappears abroad, the women return to their roots as occultists to keep themselves afloat, secretly selling love charms and astrological advice. Their thriving underground business leads them to young noble Henry and playwright Will Shakespeare, and so begins a brief, tempestuous, and powerful romance—one filled with secret longings and deep betrayals.

When Shakespeare's incendiary sonnets begin to circulate, Rose's world is turned upside down, and she must finally choose between the security of marriage and the magic, hardship, and love of a life with Cecely.

My name has only been whispered heretofore, so that is where I'll start. *Rose*, my mother christened me, like the thorny blooms in her garden. *Rose Rushe*. Her name for me was prescient. I grew into a woman much like those flowers: petaled, prickly, blood dark. Delightful to look at from a distance, but like to make you bleed if touched.

Let no man fault the barbs in my disposition. I came of age during the latter years of Queen Elizabeth in southeast England, a time and place where women like me were especially scorned. I was the daughter of an ill-starred musician and a witch who refused to hide her Catholicism. A flower that grows in such a garden needs thorns.

Though my identity be hidden, much has been written of my character. It is true I broke my bed-vow; I loved my friend too much, my husband too little. It is true I am a wanton woman—no virgin, no goddess. I stand accused of using my wiles, or worse, some hellish power, to plague a certain poet with lust.

The truth is, that poet—a pox on it, I'll say his name—Will Shakespeare pursued me freely, of his own choosing. And the sonnets he wrote of our encounters, the bitter spew of a jealous lover, nearly ruined me.

No doubt it was a fault in my stars that made me what I am—a lusty and shrewish wench. Venus was enjoying Aries while my mother laboured to bring me forth, and the moon and Jupiter were conjunct in Aquarius. I have always been bold, contrary. Not the sort of girl who dreamed a man would woo her, wed her, and carry her off to a farmhouse to raise his children. Given the choice, in truth, I would have chosen a case of dropsy over a husband.

I do not shun all womanly pursuits. I can embroider a fine handkerchief, make an excellent mead, mix a potent potion. I love to wear a fine gown; I have mastered the art of being alluring. But I am also a lover of astronomy and poetry, of music and merriment. The sort of girl whose grandmother had to lock the cellar where she kept the mead, who kissed five different youths before she turned fifteen, who convinced boys to take her to plays at the inn yard.

Mother scolded me harshly, claiming my fame would make me unmarriageable, but that was suitable to me. I did not wish to marry any of the youths with whom she caught me "venturing." I saw them as they saw me: sport and little more. What else was there to do in sleepy Allhallows?

From a young age, I dreamed of escape. I wanted to wander the bustling streets of London, watch plays at the Shoreditch Theatre. I wanted to see Whitehall Palace, the famous houses of ill repute. I wanted to hear performances by great musicians, attend masques and decadent feasts.

To live in London, I thought I might have to find my mother's family, Italian immigrants of whom she refused to speak. Or that

I might have to take a position as a servant in a great house. But the escape plan that appealed to me most of all, my dream, was to become a court musician. Performing soothed my choleric disposition even more than fine clothes, adventure, food, and drink, and a position at Whitehall would mean a surfeit of all those things. There were no women in my father's company, but women sang in the streets and performed in masques at Allhallows Place. I didn't see why the queen's court need be different.

If there were no female musicians at court already, I wanted to be the first. I was blessed with a singular talent. When I sang hymns in church, other women stopped singing to stare. Father's musician friends said my voice was like a siren's.

As I approached marrying age, my parents encouraged me to practise my music because they thought it might boost my chances of attracting a husband. Mother warned me to be chaste and modest in my playing, so I didn't do further damage to my name. Their matchmaking attempts were going nowhere. No one wanted a woman like me for a wife, no matter how beautifully I bedecked my hair or brightened my cheeks. Garlands and ribbons cannot repair a reputation.

I listened when Father, a spinet player, advised me on my music. I practised during every spare moment. By eighteen, I was uncommon skilled with the virginal—my favourite instrument—and well adept with psaltery, viol, and lute. Father said the songs I wrote evoked the music of the spheres. I knew I was good enough to play at court; the question was how to get there.

One summer evening, when some of his company were visiting our cottage, they heard me singing my little brother to sleep and called me down. I put on one of my mother's cast-off dresses, a rose-coloured gown of damask and silk. I checked my appearance in my mirror, coiled my hair into a net, and carried the psaltery into the garden, slipping a rose behind my ear.

It was almost twilight. Mother's garden glowed with a reddish golden hue. The bees whose wax she used for candles buzzed as they returned to their hives. The air was heavy with the scent of blooms. Roses, of course, whose petals my mother used in love charms. Lavender to soothe jealousy. Dianthus, rosemary, rue.

Beautiful, but they reminded me of what I wasn't. I had tried to learn charms and candle-magic from my mother when I was little, but I was terrible at both. I didn't have her sight either. I only seemed to have access to the world of the senses.

Father's friends gathered around me in the garden, dressed in faded summer attire, sipping mead from cheap pewter goblets. The jug sat unattended beside a rose bush. We had no servants to pour for us. I pretended I was playing for an audience of much greater rank that night, a visiting duchess or count. The strings tinkled at my touch. A haunting tune filled the garden, a fairy song I wrote for my dear friend Cecely at Midsummer. I met the men's eyes as I sang, enjoying the attention.

When I finished, our guests applauded, wildly appreciative of my performance. Mother stood at the back door in a threadbare silk gown, looking on with undisguised disapproval. She didn't like me to play for strangers.

Father ignored her, rewarding me with a goblet of mead. I savoured the honeyed taste; it was like drinking sunlight. His friends said my song was original, inventive, that they'd never heard anything like it. The elderly lutist announced that a boy as skilled as I could play at court. "Though boy she clearly is *not*," he said, raising a lecherous eyebrow, drawing a laugh from everyone but my father.

I raised my own brow, pressing the psaltery to my chest, smiling prettily. "I'll be sure to tell your wife you noticed."

Master Rutherford paled. Father and the others howled with laughter. Pleased with myself, I drained my goblet, bade them goodnight, and went upstairs to bed.

I lay awake for hours that night, plotting, too excited to sleep. I had been waiting for the right moment to tell Father about my musical ambitions, and this was the perfect opportunity. I took a deep breath as I headed downstairs, preparing myself to deliver the speech I'd planned, my heart tripping like a child playing hop-egg at Easter. I wanted this so much. Usually, I am blunt of speech— perhaps too blunt—but the stakes were too high to be careless about this subject.

When the last of my father's guests were gone, I wrapped my robe tight around my nightgown, a frayed rose-and-cream silk castoff from my mother. I found my father in the kitchen, draining the last drops of mead from the jug. He seemed to be in good spirits, his dark eyes merry behind his spectacles. "You're still awake?"

"I had difficulty sleeping. All the excitement."

"You distinguished yourself in both music and wit tonight." He laughed, shaking his head. He had always been proud of my skill with rhetoric. "Rutherford deserved that barb."

I righted a goblet that lay sideways on the table. "Mother says your recent matchmaking attempts have proved difficult?"

Father set down the mead jug, puzzled at the change of subject. His eyes crossed slightly as they always did when he was in his cups. "You haven't made things easy, Rose," he laughed, as though he disapproved of my behaviour. He doted on me.

I met his eyes, launching into the speech I'd practised in my head. "Perhaps marriage isn't as foregone a conclusion for women as it once was. A new era is dawning. There's an unmarried woman on the throne. Richard says women perform in acting troupes in France. The queen even employed a female painter."

"What are you getting at?"

I smiled at him hopefully, summoning all the earnest feeling I could muster. I made my voice pleading. I needed him to agree. "Do you think Underhill would ask the Master of Revels to audition me as a court musician, if you offered him a wager?"

Father blinked at me—once, twice—looking both shocked and impressed by my proposal. Our old friend Lord Underhill, an alchemist with connections to Whitehall, had visited last week with his son, Richard. When he bragged about how close he'd become to the Master of Revels, Sir Tylney, I had seen an opportunity. Underhill, whom my father knew from their time at Eton College, had a terrible weakness for gambling.

Father didn't laugh. I'll give him that. Suddenly he looked completely sober. He drew a deep breath, closing his eyes. The moment stretched out so long I thought he might say no. "Where would you live?" he asked finally.

I had already thought of this. "I could use my salary to rent a room from Underhill."

Father opened his mouth, but I continued.

"This is highly irregular, I know. There are a dozen problems to solve if it works. But I'm good enough to play at court, Father. You know it. Get me the audition, and I'll prove myself."

Father's gaze was steady, his expression sympathetic. He let out a deep sigh. "Offering him a wager is a brilliant idea," he admitted. "The next time Underhill visits, I'll ask, but I doubt anything will come of it."

Lord Underhill visited with his son, Richard, the next week on their way to Prague. To my father's surprise, his friend was quite entertained by my father's wager. If Tylney hired me, our friend would rent me a room. If he didn't, my father would give Underhill his astrolabe, which Underhill admired each time he visited.

That night, while Father and Underhill played Mad Queen chess, I asked Richard to describe what it was like to live in London. He told me about the upcoming Queen's Day festivities: the jousts that would be held in Her Majesty's honour, the massive horned effigy of the pope they would burn, the elaborate musical performances that would echo through the tiltyards. He told me what it was like to live at Swan House. Although the Underhills visited our house regularly, I had never been to theirs. Their home was three stories, he said, finely arrayed with rich furnishings, an expansive library with shelves that stretched from floor to ceiling. They had a maid to clean and a cook to prepare meals.

I couldn't believe that might soon be my life. I *ached* to live in a place like that, where the chairs didn't have wobbly legs and the tapestries weren't tattered hand-me-downs a hundred years out of fashion. I also found the idea of sleeping under the same roof as Richard quite agreeable. He was charming and handsome, tall and dark. Although the Underhills had visited dozens of times, we had never "ventured" together—though I'd often thought of it.

Unfortunately, by the time Underhill wrote back with good news and a November date, my father had fallen ill. We thought it was the ague, at first—he contracted it habitually each summer—but my mother's healing spell didn't work, and the smelling herbs the physician prescribed didn't improve his condition either. The week before the audition, Mother purchased an elixir from my friend Cecely's parents, mountebanks who had just returned from one of their medicine-selling tours. Their remedies were supposed to be of dubious quality, but that didn't stop us from buying them if we were desperate.

When Mother brought home the red elixir, Father made a jest about whether she was trying to kill him or cure him. But instead of laughing, Mother reminded him of the brevity of the lifeline on his right palm. "Secundus," she said, her expression mirthless. "This illness could be what kills you."

I thought she was just trying to get him to take the medicine until Father called me to his room the next night. It was late. The sun had long since set. The moon was quarter waxing, casting a silvery glow through his window, which lit the faded scenes from Ovid on his bedcurtains. His black sheepdog, Hughe, lay at the foot of the bed like a shadow. Outside, the stars hummed in the night sky—Saturn in Aries, Mercury opposing in Scorpio. I checked the almanac daily to learn their influence.

Approaching my father's bed, the floor creaking beneath my feet, I considered the stars' arrangement. Saturn in Aries caused a conflict between caution and impulsivity. Mercury opposing in Scorpio bred suspicion and secrets, unlucky changes in circumstances.

Something pressed my ribcage. Fear, perhaps, or dread, a reluctance to tease out the implications of these influences. Behind the bedcurtain, Father's breathing was laboured.

He won't survive this illness, I thought, with a certainty that surprised me. My bodice felt, suddenly, as if it had been laced too tight. The walls of the bedroom seemed close.

All my life, I'd been envious of my mother's sight. For the first time, I hoped I didn't have it.

"Rose?" he said in a gravelly voice. "Is that you?"

I drew the bedcurtain. His brown eyes wandered up to meet mine, enlarged by his spectacles. My prediction caused me to look at him with fresh eyes. He was only forty, but his hair, once as red as the queen's, had gone white. He'd lost two or three stone in as many months.

"I'll be plain," he said. "I'm afraid your mother was right about my illness."

Nausea turned my stomach. The stars never lied, but my interpretations of them weren't always correct. "You can't be certain."

"I have no appetite. I can't stop coughing. The physician told me to review my will."

"Mother's sight isn't infallible."

He sighed, meeting my eyes. The room fell silent except for the branch of the alder tree outside that kept scraping the window. "My death will leave your mother and brother vulnerable. We must reconsider our plans for your future."

My stomach dropped. "Reconsider?"

"My plan was to leave this farm to your mother, but your uncle Primus will fight it. If you marry, I can arrange for your husband to take in your mother and brother."

I blinked at him, setting aside my shock to consider what he was saying. The phrase *your husband* called up a sorry image of me in a ragged nightgown, black hair wild, a babe nursing at my breast. A much older man in bed behind me, moustached, a widower who wouldn't be bothered by my reputation. The vision fought with the future self I'd envisioned in London—dressed in finery, hair carefully arranged, surrounded by music and singing. When I spoke, my voice was tight. "Why wouldn't he let Mother stay here like Aunt Margery stayed in Uncle Tertius's house after he died? They're still there, all these years later!"

Father sighed, a rattling sound. He turned the skull ring on his right hand, one of a set his father had bequeathed to his living sons upon his death. "Your uncle plays favourites."

"He wouldn't be so cruel. We're family."

Father scoffed. "I wish that were so. Perhaps your husband will let you sing with the choir here."

"*Perhaps.*" I glowered at him. How could he think I would be happy with that? He should know better. "With my reputation, I'll be lucky if my husband lets me out of his sight."

Father laughed at my boldness, but it quickly devolved into coughing. "I cannot change the past, Rose. Or set the future." He removed the skull ring from his ring finger—an easy feat, it had grown loose—and held it out. "Keep this safe. Don't let your mother sell it, no matter how hard things get. I want Edmund to have something to remember me by when he's older."

I glared at the ring. Here he was destroying my future, and all he cared about was getting a trinket to my brother.

He met my eyes. "Go on. Take it."

Enough, I thought, *enough*. The ring was heavier than it looked: a thick gold hoop with a flat face, emblazoned with a rough enamel skull and the inscription MEMENTO MORI. It glinted in the candlelight. It was fine, perhaps the finest thing my family owned. The only possessions my mother passed down were women's things: gaudy bodices embroidered with silver thread, old-fashioned damask gowns, worn silk robes from before she married my father. Fine enough to hint that Mother's family *could* afford to help us, but not gold. "Couldn't Mother take Edmund to live with her family?"

"Your mother's people are in no position to aid anyone," Father said. He opened his mouth as if he were going to say more, then shook his head. "I'll speak to my brother tomorrow."

"Why must he be involved?"

"Don't be obtuse, Rose. Where else would we get the dowry?" He sighed. "Go to the Queen's Day festivities tomorrow. Bless the Protestant martyrs. This will be easier if you make it clear where your loyalties lie."

He waited for me to signal agreement. *Yes, father. With all my heart. Even so.* But he was so sure of himself, and I was so sure he was wrong. The best I could do was nod.

I wanted to throw the ring at him.

The next day, I went to the Queen's Day festivities with no intent to bless the martyrs, certain my father was wrong about my uncle. I thought Father might be overwhelmed by the suspicious influence of Mercury, or that his illness had made him delusional. I stopped at Cecely's house to ask her to come with me, thinking she might've heard something to help me prove him wrong. Her grandmother was quite the gossip.

Mother forbade me from associating with Cecely because of her family's reputation, but I disobeyed her all the time. We had become close a few years before when her parents stopped taking her on their medicine-selling tours and started leaving her with her grandmother. Both Cecely and her grandmother were deeply superstitious about fairies and ghosts. I loved the way she saw the world. Sometimes when I was with her, I saw it as she did—a magical place full of spirits and secrets, instead of a fever-ridden marsh.

Her grandmother lived in a lonely cottage on the edge of town with three trees in the yard. A hawthorn, whose berries made a syrup that went into her father's nostrums. A blackthorn, whose berries were too sour, but which her grandmother wouldn't cut down for fear of bad luck. And a service tree, which they'd planted beside the door to protect its inhabitants.

The hawthorn was skeletal, having been picked clean of its red haws a few weeks before. The blackthorn berries glowed bright blue, covered in a thin layer of frost. The service tree shivered as I approached, as if it were trying to decide whether I was a threat. I tipped my hat in greeting like Cecely did, though I felt silly repeating the custom alone.

When the shivering stopped, I was delighted.

Cecely agreed to accompany me, but said she needed to go back upstairs to freshen up. When she came back down, she was wearing the powder-blue brocade bodice with the broad lace collar I had given her a few weeks before, a slightly scandalous style that showed a bit of her shoulders. She had brightened her cheeks with fucus, coloured her lips, and pulled her hair back in a golden net. She was breaking the sumptuary laws in at least three ways for her family's income, but she was grievous beautiful.

"You look *splendid*," I breathed, instantly wishing I hadn't. I complimented her too much. Her beauty was a theme to which my thoughts returned too often.

"I try," she said with a coy smile. She tugged on her bodice, straightening the way it sat on her hips, then smoothed its fabric over her chest. Holding up her hands, she turned in a circle. "It suits me, doesn't it?"

"Indeed," I said, smiling at her immodesty.

Cecely had become an expert on costuming herself from performing in her father's street show. Her mother played the fiddle, and she danced. I had been envious of their freedom to perform in public until Cecely told me how difficult their travels were. The reason she had to stop touring with her parents was that they lost their travel license when they were run out of Southwark.

As we passed the hawthorn, Cecely eyed the circle of stones around it, checking to see it was unbroken. She said the circle guarded the entrance to our world from the world of the dead, keeping fairies out. Finding the circle undisturbed, she caught up with me.

"Have you heard anything about the Rushes?" I asked.

"What do you mean?"

"My father thinks they want to take the farm back. I fear his illness has made him delusional."

Cecely's eyes widened, and she shook her head. "I'll ask my grandmother if she's heard anything."

Approaching the square, we saw the small straw simulacrum of the pope that the Basketweavers Guild was preparing to burn. At the sight of the tiny quartet setting up on the small stage, I wondered how many musicians the Queen's Day performance would have in London. I ached to live the life I'd planned, far away from my parents' watchful eyes, seeing plays in the famous theatres, entertaining myself however—and with whomever—I pleased.

Perhaps Father would recover, or my uncle would make it clear that he would let my mother stay in our cottage like Aunt Margery.

When the musicians began their warm-ups, Cecely and I exchanged a pained glance. The fiddler hadn't fully tuned his instrument; every time he slid the bow over the bottom string, the note was slightly false. As we neared the platform, he noticed the out-of-tune string and fixed it.

"*Finally*," Cecely mouthed.

I stopped beside her, watching her with faint anticipation. Sometimes when we stumbled across street musicians, Cecely moved her body without realizing it—closing her eyes and doing a subtle version of the brawle—as if she were remembering her part in her parents' show. I loved watching her. The noise on the platform stilled, and the musicians looked at one another, ready to start. The fiddler counted, and the four of them leapt into motion at once. As they conjured their first song of the day, a bright and dizzy tune, Cecely swayed her hips slightly. The bodice truly did suit her, cinching her waist, the skirt shivering around her hips. She nodded her head in time to the music, scanning the crowd.

"Who are you looking for?"

"I can't say," she said with a mysterious smirk.

She was seeing someone, and she hadn't told me? We usually told each other everything.

She studied me. "Is your father still so sick?"

Her question reminded me of the dilemma I'd forgotten, watching her dance. I nodded, drawing a deep breath. My eyes burned.

"What is it?"

I worked to master myself. "Father changed his mind about my audition. He wants me to marry."

Her eyes widened. "What?"

"Hot codlings!" a passing peddler called.

"Ripe chestnuts, ripe!" shouted another.

"Hip, hip," someone cheered. "God bless the queen!"

Then we heard it, in the distance. My little brother's voice above the din. "*Rose!*" he was shouting. "*Rose!*" He was snaking his way through the square toward me, his little brown flat cap bobbing up and down as the crowd parted to let him pass.

I felt a rush of affection at the unexpected sight of him. His small, freckled face. That merry little brown cap. Then I saw his expression, and a nauseous music stirred in me. I bent and held out my arms, knowing what he would say before he spoke.

"*It's Father—*" he cried, pressing his face against my chest. "He's dead."